The Fear

Also by Mark Cunnington

Volume 1 of The Syndicate Series – a set of humorous fictional
novels based on the world of extreme angling

Details at www.carpbooks.com
Available at www.carpbooks.co.uk

The Fear

Mark Cunnington

Trio Publishing

First published 2014

Published by Trio Publishing

www.triopublishing.co.uk

ISBN 978 0 9537951 7 8

Published in electronic edition by Trio Publishing 2014

Printed in Great Britain by Clays Ltd, St Ives plc

Thanks to Karen and Paula

PART I

LEST WE FORGET

My fifteen-year-old son, who has never knowingly turned off an electrical appliance in his life, is continuing to use energy in his usual unconcerned manner. Supposedly, the younger generation are the most aware of green issues, but I suspect, given a direct choice between saving Planet Earth and being denied their gadgets, our globe could be in trouble. I can recall one occasion when he left a room devoid of artificial lighting, but only by inadvertently bumping into his bedroom light switch after tripping over a pile of discarded clothing.

Mentally cocooned from reality by a swathe of electrical devices, he sits on the settee watching a DVD on the HD TV while conducting his social life with dextrous fingerwork on the keyboard of his laptop. He only pauses from this seemingly full-time task to occasionally look up and laugh at the film and to answer the constant stream of text messages on his charging mobile phone. I notice the laptop has a lead running from it and is charging. My son has also charged himself. Discarded chocolate biscuit wrappers, a crisp packet and the remnants of a bowl of cereal lie at his feet like flotsam being washed against pier struts.

Another message arrives on his phone as I secretly watch from the living room doorway, a voyeur in my own home, and Jack replies by texting on his mobile in a blur of nifty double thumb work. Fingers for laptops, thumbs for phones – a complete aerobic workout for both hands! I briefly ponder whether he'll be a surgeon or a concert pianist when he grows up. The smart money is on him being neither. Maybe he'll be completely unemployable. I admit to worrying about what he'll 'do' when he reaches the end of Year 11 if his dream of becoming a professional football apprentice doesn't come to fruition.

Underneath Jack's hoodie, which is pulled up and covering his head in the traditional manner of shock-horror-endemic-social-breakdown-feral-youths-are-everywhere newspaper articles, I know there lurks the two telltale white threads that connect iPod to eardrum. If it weren't for the heavy bass rumble emanating from the surround sound system I would probably be able to hear their hissing sibilant signature – the modern digital music equivalent to an irritating mosquito.

I can't begin to quantify why he's got the sound up on the TV and has iPod headphones stuffed in his auditory canals.

This snapshot of the modern male youth, to a man in his fifties, isn't an attractive sight and I feel, once again, compelled to launch into Monologue 3. I resist, bite my tongue and say nothing. Monologue 3 consists of a series of vaguely connected issues (my issues) concerning the nature, content, pixel resolution, colour – or lack of it – and number of television channels available during my teenage years. It also covers the physical contact required with a TV in accessing all three of them. Music comes within M3's remit – proper music, not today's fifteen-minutes-of-fame karaoke 'stars' – and, specifically, the art of listening to an album all the way through. It covers the inherent difficulties involved in attempting, should you have a hideous attention deficit, to track jump, or in today's parlance, to 'shuffle'. Once in my stride, this invariably leads me to pontificate on the art of lifting a stylus without scratching prized vinyl before moving on – rather hypocritically – to the sensations felt during the monotonous fast forwarding/rewinding through pre-recorded cassettes in order to find the start of a certain track on a battery-drained Sony Walkman. I usually finish this section with a short diatribe concerning the labour intensive delights of recording a personally compiled, all-killer-no-filler C90 from a mono Dansette record player, via a microphone, to a cheap

Bush cassette recorder where you can, if you listen carefully enough, actually hear the washing machine start its spin cycle halfway through Highway Star by Deep Purple. M3 then concludes with a passing observation on how talking face to face with another human being was once the most popular form of communication. It was, after all, how I met Jack's mother. I asked her out, face to face, at her best friend's 25th birthday party when both of us were in the same room at the same time.

M3 is usually given a seven out of ten on the eyeball rolling scale of derision from my son and daughter. If I'm brutally honest I'd probably give it at least a five myself. Who in their right mind would ever want to listen to a music cassette again, even with the advent of gap search? Not with it likely to haemorrhage its shit-brown skinny ribbon of ferric oxide music muffler at any moment, saddling the would-be listener with the task of having to re-embowel it via the surgical application and twisting of the blunt end of an HB pencil.

In truth, I'm no Luddite. I'll take my dose of digital when it suits. I sneak a glance at my revolving glass CD stand, rammed with a selection of duplicated music mimicking the bulky vinyl I squirreled away in the loft years ago. Not all progress is bad. Besides, the way I've been feeling lately I think I might need to get a bit more with it. Unfortunately, I suspect the use of the phrase 'with it' immediately ensures I have no chance whatsoever of becoming it. And thinking the CD is a modern method of listening to music is as dated as it is laughable.

In my defence I'm not completely mired in the past and don't view life through the rose-tinted spectacles of nostalgia. Far from it. I have a smartphone, a laptop, am reasonably computer literate, I surf the net (what an over-glamorised phrase for such a mundane activity), use email and we own an HD TV, a DVD player and a Sky+HD box. If gadget-wise we're fairly fashionable then the same can't be said about our family modes of transport. Clare runs a bland estate car and I have a white van for work. Needless to say there is no smart sports convertible parked on our drive and nor is there a motorbike to up my cool status. Tantalisingly, what I have got is a full bike licence and somewhere scattered about the house there are pictures of me riding various motorbikes in my youth. The one of me astride my last bike, a red Honda CX500, is in a frame sitting on the mantelpiece.

"I'm off to do Nan and Pop-Pop's shopping and take it round to them," I hear myself say.

(There was a phone call after midnight last night from my father's neighbour saying he had knocked on her door in a state of confusion. The neighbour had to take him back home and put him indoors to make sure he was safe. I hope it's not the start of another worry thread.)

Jack doesn't hear thanks to the headphones, so I send him a text instead. The last one I sent him read, 'Dinner's ready!' – I was in the kitchen, he was in his bedroom. A disheartening glimpse of modern family life tempered only by the fact we all ate together, at a proper table, off plates using cutlery. I sent that text with a capital letter, apostrophe 's' and an exclamation mark. I shake my head at the recollection, conceding my grammatical insistence both dates and ages me. If I don't buy a motorbike soon it may well be too late. Too late for what, as ever, remains indefinable.

By the time I've shut the front door Jack's already sent me a text back. 'Gd luck hope pp ok', it reads. Ruefully I admit to needing it.

The first dozen or so times I did my parents' shopping made for a peculiar experience. Without my wife or two children in tow I became acutely aware of how it felt to be a single man of a certain age groping his way around a soulless superstore. If pushing the trolley solo wasn't bad enough, then filling it with goods for a man and a woman in their eighties massively compounded the unease. Plucking out Steradent tablets, denture fixative creams and talcum powder from my trolley and placing them on the conveyor belt of

10

ridicule, for all and sundry to see, including the checkout girl thirty years my junior, was nothing short of horrific. It wasn't only the occasional purchase of those squeamishly embarrassing products that made me cringe, it was the everyday humdrum items as well. It was the fourteen readymade meals. It was the endless tins of soups, baked beans (some with sausages, some without), spaghetti hoops and ravioli. It was the sixteen bottles of supermarket brand isotonic drink, the cream cakes, the coldwater prawns, the biscuits, the packets of Werther's Originals, the chocolate bars, the one box of cat food and the hideous 2 litre bottles of milk with their beacon of a blue cap. The blue cap of cholesterol. I was buying full fat milk. Throwback milk! What single person below the age of sixty-five, disregarding those with a death wish, drinks full fat milk nowadays? And to top it all, in a similar vein (one hideously furred up), I was buying white sugar, white bread, salted butter, and to further boost the sodium chloride scene, individual plastic cellars of salt.

My uncomfortable self-consciousness wasn't caused only by what I was buying. By definition it was ramped up a few notches by what I wasn't buying. I wasn't buying any fresh vegetables. I wasn't buying any fresh fruit. I wasn't buying any fresh meat. I wasn't buying any fresh fish. I wasn't buying any fresh poultry. I wasn't buying anything fresh apart from the milk, the cream cakes and the coldwater prawns – the last two items being my mother and father's respective favourite delicacies. I wasn't buying any single individual component of any one meal. Everything in my trolley said, 'Heat me up in a microwave and eat me within ten minutes flat.' And because I wasn't buying anything specific for children or for a woman I felt as if everyone thought I was eating my 7½ minutes-in-a-800-watt-microwave culinary delight in a one bedroom flat, on my settee, plate on my lap, watching porn, with only a flea-ridden cat for company.

I wondered if I should be made to wear a disposable boiler suit for the duration of my shop with 'Pending Coronary' written across the back in orange letters. However, to have worn such a garment would have been a falsehood. The crux of the matter, the unknown detail to any casual observer, was the food in my trolley was not for me. My parents both have dementia and the food is for them. Without me to buy it they would starve because they are now incapable of buying or cooking food for themselves.

The last thing to add, in response to any food fascism, is I buy what they like to eat and what makes life easy for the carers who prepare their food. The carers are allotted a solitary hour to prepare an evening meal for my mother and father and get them ready for bed. I'd like to see any health-conscious celebrity cook deal with such a ridiculous timetable. Besides, eating a high fat/high salt diet is the very least of their worries.

The first time I did their shopping, when the checkout girl asked if I needed help with packing, I was so self-conscious and confused I genuinely considered it a judgement on my helplessness. Such was my state of mind I completely failed to appreciate the question was standard issue.

My reply tried to set the record straight. "No. I can manage, thanks... I'm actually doing this shop for my parents. They still live at home, but they've both got dementia."

It sounded, to my ears, more of a lie than an assertive statement of fact. My refutation popped out into the open like a wilful jack-in-the-box at the first opportunity. It was a desperate denial, one stating my shopping was in no way a marker for my life. I immediately felt I'd mouthed the adult verbal equivalent of a school sick note for being excused from cross-country – one bearing a forged parent's signature. I remember becoming extremely flustered by my conflicting assessment of the situation and wondered if over-egging the pudding wasn't self-defeating. By association had I partly become what I was trying to deny? A stronger personality wouldn't care what anyone thought. Perhaps the checkout girl hadn't thought anything of the kind. After all, she was a checkout girl dealing with hundreds of people a week, from all walks of life, passing her till like endless ships in the night. More likely, the uppermost thought in her mind wasn't one concerning insightful customer lifestyle judgement, but how much longer to go until her shift ended. On the other hand, when her shift did end and she met up with her fellow checkout operatives, the conversation may well have turned to the 'loser of the day' award.

With conflicting thoughts careening across my head I opted to repeat my emphatic denial. Accordingly, when I paid, I made an elaborate point of putting the store loyalty points on my supermarket bank credit card and paying with another. I paid with a debit card wielded by myself but funded by my parents – my Lasting Power of Attorney debit card.

Faced with this ongoing embarrassing prospect, and shopping at a similar time every week, I soon found myself recognising members of the checkout staff to who I had previously enlightened my parents' plight. Yes, sad or not, I stuck to the verbal denial and my, 'This isn't my shopping...' mantra every time. Consequently, over the weeks I gravitated to being checked out by one particularly friendly, tiny bird-like Thai lady. From the outset she seemed to accept my sick note without questioning the iffy signature and I found myself going to her checkout even when there were others with a shorter queue. She seemed safe, she seemed to accept me and it saved me the embarrassment of repeating the mantra to an inordinate number of checkout operatives who might well cross-reference at the end of the day. I used to picture a huddle of them standing alongside their lockers with one saying, 'The man doth protest too much, methinks.'

On one solitary occasion, Jack came with me – under protest, obviously – and on seeing her perched on her chair, like a sparrow on a fence, I suddenly felt a deep justification to prove to her I wasn't a fraud and to show off my son. I wanted to show her my wonderful eldest child and demonstrate my life wasn't as reflected in my trolley. I made some lame excuse to Jack about how quick and efficient she was and we installed ourselves behind a couple buying enough food to keep a family of eight going for a month. Jack, who is always on a tight time budget when it comes to anything not directly linked to his benefit, grimaced and moaned constantly during our wait. When eventually it came to our turn and she started to run my parents' food across the scanner, she asked me a question in her accented English.

"This your son?" I nodded expansively. She looked fondly at Jack and then coolly at me. "He don't look like you."

I've avoided her like the plague ever since. Now she probably thinks I'm a sad lonely paedophile.

Here's the thing, Jack doesn't look like me and from my point of view, for all the wrong reasons. From his point of view it's for all for the right reasons. Physique-wise, we're not too far removed; what has set us apart is time. Lack of exercise and the dreaded middle-age spread has robbed me of my once reasonable body whereas Jack is nearly as tall as me and has a bona fide body fat percentage of nine – as opposed to my estimated twenty and rising. A county standard sprinter and currently signed to a professional football club's U16 team he has a lithe muscular torso, powerful legs and a cardio-vascular fitness level I can only dream of. I reckon I could still take him in a fight – if I could catch him. It's facially we're worlds apart. Jack has jet-black hair as thick as a lion's mane, dark eyes and implausibly perfect and blemish-free skin – all of which he inherited from his mother. My hair, what's left of it, is light brown where once it was blond and my sagging skin has the faint pock-mark remnants of teenage acne. I wasn't bad looking when I was young, but Jack is a here and now Adonis. The trouble is, strangers don't readily take me for Cinyras. I can understand it, but it doesn't mean I like it!

Walking alongside Jack underlines my invisibility to any female under the age of thirty-five and the bulk of older women. I watch with muted pride as women double-take him, despite his tender years, and then with a tinge of disappointment as they studiously ignore me. At the athletics club, where he works on his sprinting during the summer football break, his posse of young girls wait their turn to talk to him during rest periods and the same admiring eyes turn whenever they can to watch him storm down the track. Football's no different. If he's playing for his school there's always a gaggle of giggling girls watching him until a teacher shushes them off to class. If the match is taking place after school they invariably stay on and watch. He takes the attention with easy charm, as if it is the most natural thing in the world to have every female within sight clamouring for his company or a glimpse of his body.

I once asked him if he realised how good-looking he was only to be smacked down with a blistering riposte.

"Oh, my, God! How much up my own arse do you think I am?"

"I didn't mean it like that…" I started to protest.

"You're a freak!" he told me, walking away.

'Freak' is one of Jack's buzzwords – mainly as an adjective for describing me and Chloe, his younger sister, or anyone else not upholding his viewpoint. In fairness he might not be too far off the mark using it to describe me.

Jack's school-based female adulation is a sore point as far as Chloe is concerned and she constantly rails against the intolerable burden of attending the same school as her 'hot' elder brother. Being two years younger her friends are not on Jack's radar, but this fundamental mixed-school rule doesn't appear to diminish their enthusiasm for using Chloe as a conduit for their fantasy to get to Jack. I can appreciate it must be a bit wearing, fielding constant enquiries as to his whereabouts, what he's got in the pipeline, his current social status and whether Chloe has heard Jack ever mention their name or, better still, say he fancies them. When she moans about it I often tease her and tell her to hang on in there

15

and consider a time in the future when Jack is a professional foot-baller and the opportunities this might afford her in becoming a WAG. She normally gets physical when I mention this, either hitting me or throwing the nearest object to hand at my head.

"Shut up! God! You make me so cross when you say that!"

As I see it, the situation is this; Jack is stepping through the sunlit front door to embrace Alpha manhood as I slink out the back at night into the rain trying to…? What? Hold on to Beta manhood? Gamma manhood? Have one last desperate stab at reclaiming Alpha manhood, even if it's only an A-? Jack, my parents, and me stuck in the middle. More than what I once was in youth, what I might become in old age and what I am now.

It's the middle bit that's the sobering thought because it's the 'now', the present, the immediate, the reality I may be able to do something about. I certainly don't want to end up like my parents, although I realise I may have no control over it, and if my son has a better youth than me, then good for him. I'm his father and I love him and my daughter far beyond any notion of envy. Like any parent I deeply want them to be happy and have the best of every-thing. The fact of the matter is, and I know it's a dreadful cliché, lately I have felt pressure to make what I am now different. Differ-ent and somehow, in a way I cannot as yet define, better. And to do it quickly, before my time runs out and I no longer have the means, the mental capacity or the energy to make it happen. The trouble with all this hyperbole is the past has started to get in the way.

Like most men faced with a mid-life blip, to put a tag on it, I'm not too sure what it is I want or how to obtain it. The idea mid-life redemption can be found waiting around the corner has destroyed many a man because most men see the corner as a route demand-ing to be circumnavigated via a reckless manoeuvre. A reckless manoeuvre sure to destroy loved ones and many cherished ideals. In the grand scheme of things, so what? All logic tells me to deal with it, stop being so stupid and grow up. And grow up gracefully.

Deny all the marketing, the glossy lifestyle magazines, stop worshipping at the altar of celebrity culture and age as nature intended. Quite. If nature had intended me to take up skateboarding she'd have made my knees more flexible. (Is there a form of plastic surgery to obtain flexible knees? I expect so, the knife seems to be the in vogue panacea to counteract ageing.)

The truth is, this is all nothing. In my case, skulking alongside this timeless hackneyed male crisis, there sits a much older, unique dilemma. It hovers outside my mental peripheral vision and rarely affects me on a day-to-day basis. Occasionally, it catches my mind's eye, when memory nudges it into play, but overall I have learnt to live with it remarkably well. Recently, since my parents have become ill, my memory has started to nudge it into play more than I would like and I find myself recalling this older dilemma more than I have for decades. The past appears to be reaching out and trying to impinge on my present. It's all very disconcerting.

The reason I have dealt with this older predicament so easily over time is my undiminished belief in The Pact I made years ago when, aged thirteen, I lay terrified on my bed crying uncontrollably in a state of numb disbelief. That odious night, the one indelibly etched on my memory – I would say 'until I die', but I've got parents with dementia and have seen what can happen – I made a pact only a thirteen-year-old boy could make. In my head, my young naïve immature head, I dealt with my chilling situation in the only manner possible. I told myself the reason why it had happened again was so it wouldn't happen to me. In my mind I made myself the chosen one and rationalised that the reason yet another had been taken was so I might have the right of safe passage.

That was The Pact. Others had been taken so I could live. I still believe that today, completely, utterly and wholeheartedly without question. I also believe the cover of safe passage now extends to include my wife and my two children. I have to believe it. To do otherwise would have left me in a state of pervading anxiety exactly like my mother's before her dementia struck. Even at the tender age of thirteen I was sufficiently aware I didn't want to live the rest of my life the way she was living hers. If I hadn't squared it in my head it would have destroyed me like it did her. My mother suffered from what I coined 'extrovert paranoia'. She wasn't frightened everyone was out to get her, she was frightened The Fear was out to get everyone she loved.

On the night I made The Pact I encountered, first-hand, in the stunning Technicolor, Dolby 5.1 surround sound we call reality, what I believed was the second manifestation of The Fear. The first manifestation (which I later discovered wasn't the first, but was, in fact, the second), was only a childhood story and not an experience. A sad story told to me by my mother, often supplemented with faded monochrome photos, always with endless tears. In those early years of growing up, if I ever asked my mother why she forbade me from doing anything I wanted to do if it involved me being out of her sight for more than ten minutes, she would answer, 'You know why, John. You know the story. I *can't* let you go. The worry would kill me.' Fortunately, others were around who would let me do things, but not until I was a little older. Not until I started primary school did they begin to gently unwrap the smothering blanket in which my mother tried to swaddle me.

My mother met her first-hand version of The Fear many years ago and, apparently unable to make her own pact, had been mentally crippled by it. It happened when she was a young woman of seventeen and had recently met my father. Undoubtedly in the full embrace of teenage love, her family – she, her sister, her younger brother and her parents – were hit by a giant wrecking ball of tragedy. What I didn't know, until eighteen months ago, when I found and read the ancient newspaper cutting, was her father suffered an even earlier first-hand version of The Fear. I now had proof it had struck my mother's family three times and not twice, as I had always believed. My father's family had only been hit once, as if once wasn't bad enough, making a grand total of four attacks of The Fear in all.

Finding the newspaper cutting was nothing short of a revelation and, if I'm honest with myself, it was the start of The Fear revisiting my mind. The newly highlighted event happened a very long time ago and although I didn't feel threatened by it I did feel the start of the past's influence touching my present. In a way, the newspaper cutting underlined the strength of The Pact – another had been taken and I hadn't even known about it – and was a retrospective affirmation of The Pact's integrity, albeit an affirmation hidden for decades, eventually revealing itself to me purely by chance. The problem was finding the newspaper cutting made me feel as if I was slowly being drawn into a time I would rather not have to consider. The awful events from that era were long ago dismissed thanks to The Pact and my life has been unaffected by them for nearly forty years. Yet, with this new discovery and my parents' regression, due to their dementia, I felt the beginnings of an unease I hadn't experienced since my teens. In my heart I felt the vague hint of a warning, while my head dismissed it all with two words. The Pact. It had never failed me, so why start to doubt it now?

Having negotiated the shopping run and while travelling to my parents' home I play a game. It's an old game I developed in my late teens, one I thought was unique until, somewhat amusingly, I read a newspaper article detailing the finer points of what I had always considered to be my invention. The game goes like this; I scrutinise the oncoming female drivers and have to pick one out of the next ten I would most like to have sex with. The edge to the game is in achieving the most desirable woman possible and not getting left with the unattractive number ten having spurned an 'okay' number three, or picking the 'okay' number four only to lose a positively gorgeous number nine. It passes the time and still mildly amuses me. Underneath this piece of nonsense is a slightly more serious theme. If it came to the crunch and my game became real, would I really want to be a contestant and pick any of the women, carry it through and bed the 'winner'? Is extra marital sex part of the answer to my mid-life blip? I really can't compute the impact of an affirmative to those questions, so I usually turn my thoughts to what kind of motorbike I might like to buy and whether I would bike-to-leathers colour co-ordinate.

I pull up on my parents' drive and view the familiar frontage minutes after picking a lovely number six who was evidently the best of the ten. This is the home I shared with my parents until I left it to live with, Clare, my wife. There were just the three of us as I was an only child. It is festooned with memories; mine, my mother's and my father's, though I am fast becoming the sole reliable source for tales from the past.

Lifting the shopping from the back of my car I ask myself the questions I have recently started to consider. My answers, over hours of introspection, have become succinct, yet still not definitive.

Had my mother been able to deal with The Fear in a more balanced manner before my birth? *Yes*.

Was my birth the vital catalyst for her downfall? *Yes*.

Had I made The Fear a vivid and palpable threat to her via my potential loss? *Yes*.

Did she focus all her dread on me because I was her only child, like some form of high intensity laser beam? *Yes*.

Did ten years of a childless marriage, a struggle to conceive and a traumatic birth putting my mother's life at risk and slamming the door shut on future pregnancies compound her anxiety? *Yes*.

If she could have had more children would this have somehow dispersed the beam, weakened it and made life more tolerable for her, for me and for my siblings? *Possibly, but somehow I doubt it. She would have loved us all with equal intensity.*

And how come my father never seemed to be touched by my mother's crippling anxiety or The Fear itself? *His personality.*

Did he have his own secret pact, one similar to mine? *Maybe, he never mentioned it.*

Was that why I could make one? *Possibly.*

Was it because I had my father's genetic mental disposition enabling me to negotiate my way around the devil I called The Fear? *Possibly.*

But if that was the case then how come my mother's parents, my Nan and Pop-Pop as I called them, were such marvellous babysitters providing a riot of fun laughter and unimaginable joy every time they looked after me? *See next question.*

How had they dealt with it? *See next question.*

Had they mastered the dark art of compartmentalisation, an art beyond the wit of my mother? *They must have done.*

Was the bitter truth that my mother was the only one in the family incapable of being able to move on sufficiently in order to live life with something approaching normality? *Yes.*

And was she the embodiment of how everyone else close to The Fear truly felt, deep down, underneath the veneer of a brave smile and the concept of 'soldiering on'? *I have no doubt whatsoever that's exactly what she was.*

I ask these questions and answer them as a relative layman. I, thanks to The Pact, have never lost a child or a spouse and by circumstance will never lose a sibling. What I have lost is one great uncle I've only read about, one uncle I've only heard about – although his photo was a constant in my youth – one uncle who caused me to make The Pact and one cousin whose death I briefly thought I might have caused.

Whatever the answers are it doesn't matter in the slightest now. My grandparents are long gone and both my mother's deference to The Fear and my father's apparent non-compliance to it have disappeared. All recollection of it has been silently eroded into oblivion by two failing brains. All their memories, both good and bad, have either disappeared or are slowly disappearing into the ether.

Despite this collective lack of memory, when I found the revelatory newspaper cutting, I couldn't help but ask them both, many times over, if they could remember anything at all about this titanic event. I tried on different days for weeks, even after turning up a long succession of garbled blanks, hoping beyond hope I might catch them on a day when the fog of dementia had rolled back sufficiently for them to remember some scintilla of information. It was important for me to know because the event I was questioning them over was nothing less than the beginning of my family's awful history. It was the original manifestation of The Fear and thus constituted a significant aspect of my life, despite the paradox of me only learning of it in middle age. Many times I asked my mother and father if they could remember being told of it by my mother's parents, or remember reading of it in the newspaper cutting. I implored them to think hard to see if they could recall any one single detail however small. All I got back was a hail of confusion – except on one occasion, when I wasn't too sure what I had got back.

The accepted view on dementia states long-term memory is the last to fail. Although this is true of my father, my mother's most distant memories are getting thin on the ground. At the time of my unearthing the newspaper cutting, eighteen months ago, my mother's long-term memory was better than it is today. Despite this, she was still unreliable when answering any questions regarding her early life. So much so I couldn't accredit any worth to them whatsoever. Sometimes she would tell me things I knew were true and at other times I knew her answers were muddled and incorrect. With my father, though, I always had higher hopes. It was to him who I predominantly turned in my quest for information.

One time I quizzed him on the subject with real hope. He'd been much more alert than usual all morning, his general speech and cognitive functionality were better than of late and I felt as if now was as good a time as any to, once again, broach the subject of the newspaper cutting. Having hurriedly stored away the food I had bought them I made them both a cup of tea and went and sat in the living room. I can remember my heart beating much faster than was customary. (I've always had a slow heartbeat, going right back as far as I can remember. I still take my own pulse in bed and revel in the knowledge a resting rate of forty-five beats per minute means I must be fitter than I think I am.) It was caused by a gut feeling convincing me I was in with a decent chance of digging up family treasure.

"Do you remember anything about Mum's uncle? Frederick, he was called," I casually asked him.

"Who?"

"You know Mum's dad, Cyril? Well, his younger brother, Frederick?"

"Is he still with us?" my father, Owen, asked.

"No, he died a long time ago. Rather tragically really."

"Did he?" my father answered, sipping his tea. "Can't say I remember."

"You don't recall anybody talking about him or you reading about him?" I pressed.

"No... Except one thing."

"Go on," I nudged.

"They're in the same grave. We went and saw it last week didn't we, Mary? They'd moved it and we didn't know where it was."

I was unsure whether the fog of dementia had rolled back for an instant or swept in off the sea, engulfing everyone, myself included, in a dense cloud of befuddlement.

"That's right," my mother said. "It had gone."

"What do you mean the same grave? Who's in the same grave?"

23

I asked. "What do you mean it's gone or been moved?"

"I've got to go and shoot those doors in for Lawson later," my father informed me, dunking a biscuit with a shaking hand. "Fire doors. Bloody heavy."

And that was it. He was gone. I'd lost him to his past vocation and Mr Lawson, the owner of a small building firm my father had sub-contracted to for many years. Despite asking again and again he never once mentioned anything more to do with graves and as his mental abilities slowly unravelled I gave up. Gave up asking and gave up hope of ever knowing more.

In spite of getting nowhere with my parents I still can't bring myself to overlook the matter of the newspaper cutting. However I dress it up it still boils down to one fundamental question; Why hadn't anyone within my family ever told me about Frederick's death? My memory is fine and I know nobody did. The only rational explanation I can come up with to date is the most obvious and simplistic. The original manifestation of The Fear became lost in respect of passing it on to me due to it happening a long time ago. It occurred when both my parents were very young and somehow the details of it seems to have escaped them. My father's comment about the grave seems unlikely to be genuine so I am left with the bare facts I know to be true; that of the details set out in the newspaper cutting. An item only resurrected into living memory by my need to rummage in my parents' affairs because of their dementia.

If Frederick's demise was the start of my family's chilling history then it was by no means the end. His death happened before WWII and there was to be a break of a decade before the second tragedy. This attack was the event that smashed my mother's family asunder when she was seventeen years old. Nearly thirty years after that event comes the night when I cried uncontrollably in a state of numb shock, one forcing me to concoct The Pact. Only months later The Fear struck again and I felt, with balanced ferocity, the emotions of empowerment and guilt The Pact afforded me.

These awful events have started to significantly enter my thoughts recently and I find myself picking over their old bones like a famished buzzard in the hope of making sense of them, especially in regards to their effect on my mother. I cannot know of her feelings concerning the original manifestation of The Fear or its ramifications, if indeed there were any. All I can do is make an educated guess and surmise, from bedtime tales she told me from a time predating the second instalment of The Fear, that she remained unaffected by the first one. Having recently deliberated, for more hours than I care to admit, on the subject I'm now absolutely convinced it was the second hit from The Fear that truly changed her forever. The one caveat to this statement being the full impact on her life never took place until my mother gave birth. Only then could she potentially mirror the circumstances of her mother's loss.

When the third blow came (the night I made The Pact), my mother was crushed completely. If the cumulative effect of three blows from The Fear was devastating for my mother, then logically her elder sister must surely have suffered more. Yet remarkably, to my eyes at least, Olive appeared to manage her greater loss more ably than my mother. It seems my mother was the only one of her family whose reaction to loss was to hold on tighter – even at the risk of causing suffocation by smothering.

The fourth blow had little discernible impact on my mother. Still at rock bottom from the night eight months earlier, my father's side of the family's one contribution was a strangely disconnected affair, one unable to move her one way or the other. (I think by then my mother was brim-full of despair and grief, a vessel simply unable to take on board any more pain. When you've hit the seabed there's nowhere further to sink.) Never close to my father's side of the family, the death of my father's nephew seemed to rage around

25

my parents rather than through them. It raged through me, though, until I could once again square things in my head and conveniently exonerate myself. It raged through me because of the choice I made only hours earlier, a choice I never – have never – told to another living soul. I was left cocooned in my mind that evening wondering if by my actions I had caused Graham's death. In the end I blamed The Fear, thanked The Pact, and moved on.

I start to lug the plastic bags laden with shopping up the side of my parents' house. It's a three bedroom detached property and was built by my father over fifty years ago. A carpenter by trade, Owen was way ahead of the game when he bought the half-acre plot set in a quiet leafy road a couple of miles outside the seaside town of Hastings in which he and Mary had always lived. Her Catholic family originated from what is called the Old Town of Hastings. Nestling in a valley between the East Hill and the West Hill – both of which have funicular railways – and with Europe's largest fleet of beach-launched fishing boats moored on shingle alongside the tarred and weatherboarded net huts, the Old Town used to be, and still is to a lesser extent, a close-knit community dominated by a handful of extended families. In the years following WWII, the time when my mother and father started dating, it was very much an introspective and insular society. My father often told me how his relationship with my mother was frowned upon by the locals because he was an outsider and not an Old Towner. I used to laugh to myself at the concept of him, 'The Outsider', riding into town on a horse (actually a BSA motorbike) and stealing away in the dead of the night with an Old Town woman when he only lived a mile up the road. A mile was more than enough – a mile took you out of the Old Town.

Around the same time as Owen started to court Mary, Mary's sister, Olive, began dating the man she would eventually marry. Harold was from Old Town stock and bore a surname synonymous with that part of Hastings. Harold belonged to one of the dominant families with aunts and uncles and nephews and nieces and cousins found at every bar in every one of the myriad of public houses dotted all over the Old Town. He was a quiet understated man who followed a long line of male ancestors to become a fisherman, one who eventually owned his own boat.

Although placid in nature, Harold was as hard as iron and could fight like a demon when required. I remember my father telling me how he was roughed up by a couple of men in the toilets of a pub a month or so after starting to go out with Mary. They had gone to the pub with Olive and Harold and when my father reappeared out of the toilet looking dishevelled and distressed he told Harold what happened. Harold immediately confronted the two culprits, offered them a chance to step outside to resolve the matter – one they foolishly accepted – and he knocked them both out. It was no wonder my father took an instant shine to him.

In the fullness of time, my father eventually became accepted into Old Town circles as one of their own, or at least as near as damn it. In a society monopolized by pub life, his tactic of buying endless rounds of drinks for would-be antagonists, coupled with Harold's friendship and fighting prowess, proved to be an irresistibly compelling combination. With Mary deeply in love with him my father finally became one of the clan via wedlock. Twelve years after the newspaper cutting and two years after the wrecking ball hit my mother's family there was a reason for celebration rather than mourning. The two local blonde-haired Old Town girls, Mary and Olive, aged just eighteen and twenty respectively, were married to Owen and Harold on the same day. A double wedding where my grandfather put in an extended shift giving away two daughters instead of the usual one. The double wedding took place at St Mary's Star of the Sea Catholic Church with the reception and wedding breakfast at The Rising Star public house. Sadly, there was no honeymoon. 'We both went to work on the following Monday morning because money was so tight!' my mother once told me.

The plot of land my father bought to build his house belonged to an old coach house and was originally the grazing field for the horses. After buying the land, my father then spent every waking hour he wasn't working to earn his wages building the house. It took him nearly two years of grafting evenings and weekends to complete it. He didn't do everything himself; specialist tradesmen did the brickwork, the plastering, the electrics and the plumbing, but virtually everything else was his handiwork. Initially, he cut all the grass down in the field with a wooden handled scythe and next, in a deed that had 'masochism' stamped all over it, proceeded to dig the footings and concrete them by hand. He laid the drains, he mated the bricklayer and once the brickwork was completed to plate height, the floor joists fitted and the roof pitched he then tiled it single-handedly. Next he fitted all the windows and glazed them to get the shell of the house watertight as cheaply and quickly as possible. Once this was achieved the small matter of all the internal work could commence. It was a huge effort, especially so when considering all tools were hand tools in those days and there wasn't a single lithium powered battery drill to be had anywhere.

The notion you could borrow money, or get a mortgage to purchase a piece of land in 1959 was laughable. Only once my father owned the asset could he obtain a mortgage to finance the house building. Amazingly, by spring 1961 it was finished – not as if by magic, more by endless grinding physical toil – just in time for my mother to move in with her newborn baby. The newborn baby being myself.

"I'm surprised you didn't deliver me," I once told him. "You were doing pretty much everything else!"

My father smiled ruefully. "It was the only way a working man could get somewhere in those days. I wasn't self-employed at that time. I was working on the cards and the money was poor. Your mother and I lived in a poky flat in the Old Town. It was no place to start a family."

"How did you afford the land?"

My father winked conspiratorially and tapped his nose. "Justers!" he exclaimed, smiling.

'Justers', I discovered, were cash jobs done on the side as in 'just do this for me'. They were the grease making the wheels of financial viability go round for many tradesmen in those hard days.

When I visit my parents I often think of all the effort my father put into their house. It has stood them in good stead living there all this time and has been the physical bedrock of their marriage. Unfortunately, because my father worked so hard and because he did the right thing for my mother and for me, I know there is a chance the house could be lost. If they deteriorate further and have to go into a nursing home I may well have to sell it to finance their nursing care fees. I shouldn't be bitter, but when I think about it I become so. If my father hadn't bothered and had sat on his arse for fifty years, never working and never paying a penny in income tax or National Insurance, the government would pay the nursing fees. How fair is that?

I'm determined to fight this travesty of justice if it comes to it. Romantically, I tell myself I will fight it as hard as my father worked on the house. Realistically, I know that is clearly a nonsense, but I will give it my best shot. Not so much because I stand to benefit financially as the sole inheritor, but because my parents wanted it to be mine or one of my children's one day. They wanted the house, or at least the value of the house, to stay within our family and be used to help Clare and I and eventually our children on their way in life.

I say 'they wanted' in the past tense because of the nature of their illness. Sometimes both of them aren't really sure what house they are living in. I'm incredulous. How can my father not recognise the house he built with his very own hands? It's unbelievable. When I've said to him, on many an occasion when he's lost track, that this is the house he built, he's disagreed.

"No, this isn't my house. This house is a copy. We're in Gillingham."

I have monologues for my children. I now have them for my parents.

Monologue 2 for my parents consists of me painstakingly recalling second-hand memories of building the house – memories they once told me – and regurgitating them. I remind my father the plot of land once belonged to the old coach house and it was the field in which the horses grazed. Sometimes, if I'm feeling energetic, I will take him outside where we can view, through a sparse hedge, the barely visible coach house. I will tell him how he did justers to raise the cash for the land purchase, how he worked on the house weekends and evenings only to keep on earning from the day job to finance the mortgage. How he cut the grass, how he got the plans drawn up, how he dug the footings, how he concreted them, how he laid the drains, how he carried the bricks for the bricklayer, how he fitted the ground floor and first floor ceiling joists, how he cut and pitched the roof, how he felt and battened and tiled the roof, how he fitted the windows, soffits and fascias, how he first fixed the door linings, window boards and the studding for the cupboards, how he made and fitted the staircase, how he put down the floorboards, how he plasterboarded the ceilings and some of the internal walls, how he fitted the external doors, how he mixed the plaster for the plasterer, how he fitted the internal doors, skirting boards and architraves, how he fitted the kitchen units and cupboards, how he decorated the house, how he landscaped the garden and how he finished all of it just in time for my mother to walk through the solid oak front door with me in her arms wrapped up in a blanket.

"I know all about that!" he snaps. "This isn't my house. It's a copy."

It makes no difference. If he's in Gillingham in his head I can't shift him. I've learnt this harsh lesson many a time. My conversations with my parents are like they're recorded on a looped cassette, although there is no sign of an all-killer-no-thriller C90 to be had anywhere. They say the same things repeatedly to me and then I say the same things repeatedly to them. Almost exclusively nowadays I'm constantly telling them what they are saying isn't true. At first I thought I might be able to stave off their altered version of reality by continually arguing with them and reminding them of the truth. This was their Monologue 1.

"You have to listen to me when you get muddled up." I urged. "I will *always* tell you the truth. I know what you think in your heads must seem real to you, but I can assure you it isn't. You're all muddled up!"

It doesn't appear to work very well. I still do it, out of habit as much as anything, and out of fear of losing them completely. I can't seem to accept it won't accomplish anything.

About two years ago I was advised by my parents' consultant to obtain a Lasting Power of Attorney - Property and Affairs for both of them. This advice came to light when I sat in on both the memory tests they undertook after I voiced concerns to their GP about their worsening mental state. At that time both of them had started to become a little confused, my father insisting he had to go to work and my mother enquiring as to why her dead parents hadn't been to see her. Alarm bells started to ring when these topics became constant themes of conversation rather than occasional one-offs. Having gone through the due process of seeing their GP, a test was arranged for both of them at the local centre for mental health.

The memory test itself is a series of generalised questions asking the patient details such as the date, year and season together with other fundamental personal information like age, date of birth, vocation and family relationships. It also involves writing a sentence, copying a drawing and the repetition of three spoken words. The subject is then marked and the score indicates a rough diagnosis on the state of their memory.

During the tests the consultant looked to me for confirmation of the answer he received when he had no way of knowing whether it was right or wrong. For instance, in asking how many brothers or sisters my mother and father had and how many were alive. Rather grimly I found myself shaking my head more than I was nodding.

"Have you got Power of Attorney for your mother and father?" the consultant asked me quietly after the tests finished. Once again I shook my head. "I would get it straightaway. Your parents both have definite early stage indications of dementia. It's impossible to predict how quickly they will deteriorate so a Lasting Power of Attorney, made now, while they are still capable of signing and understanding the document, will make your life much easier. If you wait until they are beyond a state of comprehension the whole process is far more arduous." The diagnosis was a double-whammy; unusual, but in these times of a burgeoning ageing population, not unheard of. The consultant warned me things wouldn't improve. "It's a degenerative disease," he informed me. "We may be able to slow it down with drugs, but I'm sorry to tell you they'll get progressively worse. On a practical level the LPA is the first recommendation I give to relatives."

I nodded. "I'll get the wheels in motion."

"Talking of which, do they both drive?" he asked. I confirmed they still did. "I'm afraid they'll have to hand in their driving licences. They can't drive any more. If I were you I'd get rid of any cars to avoid the temptation. People with dementia forget they're banned from driving and will simply get in a car and go."

"I guess that rules out Dad riding his motorbike." The consultant looked at me, his brow furrowing. "I'm not being facetious," I said, laughing at the accusation on his face. "He's got one in the garage and rode it all last summer. He loves his motorbike."

The consultant's face cracked into a rueful grin. "I'm sorry, Mr

Dennett. No cars and definitely no motorbikes."

As I left the building, oblivious to the true nature and implications of the diagnosis, my mind tried to assimilate what had happened. There was the situation, spelled out in black and white with my worst fears confirmed. Both of my parents had dementia, it would only get worse and I, as the only son, now had a raft of extra admin and responsibility to look forward to. I remember thinking how we are all fundamentally linked to each other and on the day of diagnosis I certainly felt the seesaw of life roles tip alarmingly. We were going full circle on the roundabout. They looked after me in my infancy and now, as they regressed to a more childlike state, it was my turn to be the adult.

It was awful news and because of it my unique dilemma reared its ugly head for the first time in years. Despite this I knew a fifth instalment of The Fear had not come to pass. The Fear had certain characteristics, none of which were present in this case. The Fear was brutal, horrific, sudden and chilling, otherworldly almost, in its macabre grizzly detail. Two old people, both octogenarians, being diagnosed with dementia was not its style at all. My parents' news, though sad, was humdrum, commonplace and unspectacular. The Fear, on the other hand, always made the headlines.

With a Lasting Power of Attorney in place I was able to start getting to grips with my parents' financial affairs. Firstly, I applied for the Attendance Allowance for which they now qualified and then turned to the more personal aspects of starting to run their lives. I knew my mother and father kept all their main documents in a large folder on top of their bedroom wardrobe. When I climbed on a chair I was relieved to see it still there covered in dust. The very first piece of paper I pulled out happened to be the original invoice for the land purchase. The invoice was a charming paper window looking back on to alien financial times. The princely sum for the half-acre building plot in 1959? A paltry £450. Less than a monkey, as those prone to the odd flutter would deem it, for a half-acre plot in one of the most desirable roads in Hastings. Today I guess it would cost at least 150K, maybe even more. You'd have to do a lot of justers to raise that sort of money. So many you'd attract the attention of HMRC tax evasion officers.

The land purchase invoice was tucked alongside all my parents' important documents; copies of their wills, their passports, various solicitors' letters appertaining to the purchase of the plot, copies of the Land Certificate from the Portsmouth District Land Registry, the original architect's plans and my father's private pension certificates. Each document was a little piece of family history. What I hadn't appreciated was how much more there was to come.

All the very important documents were put safely in the one folder in a time BD (before dementia) and had stayed there. Others that needed to be used more regularly AD (after dementia) were subjected to the trait of bizarre filing. And when I say filing I mean filing in the very loosest sense of the word. Once I began looking for everything I needed to effectively take over the running of their household, I quickly realised how much my mother and father were starting to struggle with the nuts and bolts of life. They were always fiercely independent and I envisaged a resistance to what I thought they might perceive as my meddling in their affairs. I couldn't have been more wrong. Both my mother and father gratefully accepted my offer of help and the more I dug the more I could see why.

Utility bills, bank statements, pension statements, shopping receipts, the car's logbook and insurance policy, my father's motorbike logbook and its insurance policy, other household insurance policies, cheque books, paying in books, premium bonds and their TV and driving licences and no small amount of cash in notes and coins were strewn throughout the house at random. I found important papers and money in a drawer in the kitchen, in drawers in the bedrooms, under the stairs, stuffed in a Tesco plastic shopping bag in a wardrobe, in coat pockets, in trouser pockets, under the kitchen sink, under pillows, under mattresses and the really tricky one, in amongst endless piles of old motorbike magazines. It took me a whole weekend to find everything I needed among the reams of other disposable material. Yet amid this apparent rubbish lay the newspaper cutting and many more family gems.

The disposable material in question comprised an overwhelming amount of tat and some arbitrary nuggets of gold. I discovered endless pamphlets, flyers and promotional crap for all manner of objects, stores and services, none of which I had ever seen my parents use at any time since I was born. There were reams of birthday/Christmas/Easter/anniversary cards from a host of friends going back over tens of years. Touchingly, there must have been virtually every card/drawing/painting/school project my two children ever made and gave to my parents and many I made for them in my childhood. There were all the cards, or it appeared there were judging by the numbers, Clare and I gave them since we married. There were even around twenty rather odd looking cards congratulating my mother and father on the birth of their newborn baby, many full of twee verse such as, 'A welcome to the baby, So lately come to bless, A pair of splendid parents, With new found happiness' – and – 'I know there's great rejoicing now, In your dear home today; For a darling little stranger, Has just arrived to stay; So Best Congratulations, dear, These kindly wishes tell; And I am very pleased to know, That 'both are doing well.'

In even greater quantity was a mass of loose photos, seemingly distributed throughout the house by a horde of inebriated gremlins. Oddly, I found four brand new unused photo albums with not so much as a Polaroid, holiday snap or picture postcard between their pages. Many of the loose photos were modern colour ones of Jack, Chloe, Clare and I in so many differing permutations it might have interested a professor of mathematical probability to start to work out which combinations, if any, were missing. Alongside these family portraits were the official professional stage-managed, and therefore cringeworthy, prints of our wedding day. Mixed in with them were endless hideous holiday snaps of my parents from countries as diverse as Spain, España, Spanien and Espagne. (My parents only ever holidayed in Spain and my father has the sun-damaged skin to prove it.)

There were pictures, if an individual had sufficient time and energy to organise them in chronological order, fully documenting, virtually on a monthly basis, the physical appearance of my two children from birth until the day they started primary school. And there were pictures, in a similar manner, tracking the growth of my parents' current cat and the three they owned before it – although these tended to be heavily kitten-era weighted. All four of the cats were black and white – 'Why waste the colour film, Dad?' I remember asking, thinking it was a great joke – and all were called, Jamie. I'm proud of the traditional cat naming policy in our family because I started it. I called the cat I begged my mother and father to buy for me, Jamie, when I was about eight. Why I called it Jamie I have no idea whatsoever – and I'm the one without dementia.

Apart from the photos of my children, most of the others did little for me apart from make me wonder why the hell I had ever chosen that suit to get married in. It was only the ones reaching further back in time that grabbed me. Coming across long forgotten photos of yourself when young can really make you sit up. I wasn't overly moved by seeing pictures of me when I was a baby or a child. Somehow, those types of photos are too far removed from what you are now to have much impact. What did make me pause and take stock were the ones taken when I was on the edge of manhood, the ones showing me to be of a similar age to Jack. One showed me sitting on the beach by the pier – long before it was sadly set on fire by a couple of arsonists – with my first ever girl-friend. She was a foreign language student and her name, Annika, leaps out of my memory without a moment's hesitation.

In the photo I'm young, tanned, pretty good-looking and my

full head of long hair, by today's standards, is bleached surfer blond. My arm is draped over her shoulder and the long tresses of her equally blonde hair lay across part of my forearm. She is smiling, showing off her perfect white teeth, and looks incredibly attractive sitting on the bum-numbing shingle in her tiny bikini. She came from Sweden and was one of the thousands of foreign language students who made possible Hastings' metamorphosis from the cold dour chrysalis of winter into the beautiful butterfly of summer. That summer I was in a cosmopolitan heaven and deeply in teenage love – until she went back home three weeks later and depression set in as I lapsed into provincial hell. (My angst wasn't all due to her going home. As I recall it coincided with the first week of September, the end of summer holidays and the prospect of having to go back to school and start my O levels.)

The very next photo – the gremlins must have sobered up for a while – saw myself outside a disco with my first motorbike, a derestricted purple 50cc Yamaha FS1-E. I was gobsmacked to see myself wearing a blue open faced helmet, blond curls sneaking out from the sides, sitting astride what was the fastest moped of its day. My first girlfriend and my first bike. The memories associated with these two photos, ones I hadn't seen for well over thirty years, released an overwhelming flood of emotion within me and I was moved to tears. Embarrassed, I felt them run down the side of my nose before I could drag my eyes off the photos and wipe them away. I don't know why it hit me like it did. Was it the loss of my youth and with it halcyon days that cannot be relived? Or was it because the circumstances in which I found them reminded me how our memories are a treasure trove and how they define all we are and what we've become – even if they sometimes need a visual stimulus to kick start them.

What the picture of me on the fastest – 50mph flat out, chin on the tank, on level tarmac in favourable wind conditions – 50cc two-stroke moped around also reminded me of was my father's utter dismissal of The Fear. As soon as I was sixteen I wanted a motor-bike because he had one, always had one, even if the latter ones were toys rather than primary modes of transport. And as soon as I was sixteen he let me, despite my mother's fervent protests. You see, if my father had one single seed of doubt, one atom's worth of concern over how The Fear might reach out and strike me down as it had reached out and struck down the others, he wouldn't have let me get a moped. He wouldn't have dared let me take the first step on the ridiculously short path to owning a two-wheeled, road-eating missile.

In those days, a proper bike was only a year away from sweet sixteen. At seventeen, a pimply youth could buy a 250cc machine capable of reaching over a ton and ride it forever on a provisional licence with L plates. Provided you didn't kill yourself on it. Many did. If you did survive, you could take your bike test, and if timed precisely, you could then ride the most powerful bike available at the tender age of seventeen years and a few weeks old – and have a go at killing yourself on that. Many did. No compulsory basic training, no DL196, no theory test, no practical test, no bewildering power output/age constraint categories and no experience apart from a year on the road riding a moped burning up buses and old lady drivers. (Subject to favourable road/weather conditions.)

I took my motorbike test when I was seventeen. The test, laugh-able by today's standards, involved driving your bike around a couple of blocks while the test inspector walked the course and observed you at various significant points. He would watch you make the manoeuvre for the right-hand turn across traffic, watch how you pulled out of a junction and assess your speed and road positioning nous on the straight sections. After completing this part of the test he would ask you to drive very slowly alongside the kerb, as he walked with you, to check out your slow speed riding/balancing skills. Then came the most dangerous part – the emergency stop. My moustachioed inspector told me at some point during the next circuit he would step out in front of me, raise his hand so – he demonstrated a Naziesque salute – and I would be required to perform an emergency stop with my bike remaining under complete control.

It was hard to keep a straight face and I don't think I managed it. Luckily, I was wearing a full faced helmet so he couldn't see my grin – a grin caused by a story I'd heard only a week earlier. The urban myth running around at the time was of a rider taking his test who wore a black leather jacket, black jeans and a black helmet. When told it was time for his emergency stop procedure he duly drove off around the block and out of his inspector's sight. The inspector then walked off to where he wanted the emergency stop to take place and waited for his rider to reappear. On seeing the rider dressed all in black approaching he stepped out off the kerb as promised, raised his hand in the prescribed manner and was promptly run over. It was the wrong rider, albeit one clothed in similar garb driving the same ubiquitous Japanese motorbike!

Thankfully, no such incident occurred on my test. I drove my bike, now a Yamaha RD250, petrol tank the shape of a coffin, around the block at a snail's pace 25mph and pulled up softly yards before my inspector, saving both of us the embarrassment of creating a large dollop of 1970s' roadkill. He was so grateful for me not smearing him into the tarmac, he passed me. I was now the proud owner of a full bike licence – the one for a car would come later and at the second attempt – and bigger, faster more powerful bikes were only a cripplingly expensive hire purchase agreement away.

But not for me.

My father would often lend me the money to buy a new bike at a much cheaper rate than any HP agreement. As long as I covered the savings interest rate he was more than happy – and so was I. As well as this generous offer, without exception, he'd magnanimously slip me a couple of hundred quid or more 'to put towards your new bike'. At the opportune moment of my heightened enthusiasm for my latest prospective bike, an additional wad of money would find its way inside the small brown envelope constituting my weekly wage packet.

I had left my grammar school by then to become my father's indentured apprentice, where he taught me to be a chippy four days a week at work with the local college taking up the baton/batten for theory via a day release course. My mother wholeheartedly approved of this move into manual labour – I presume she felt I would be much safer at work if Owen was there to guard me – whereas my schoolmasters rather snootily told me I was wasting myself by not taking my A levels and going on to university. Doubly so, seeing as I had opted for a lowly vocation where 'one got one's hands dirty' as my career guidance master told me.

All I cared, or knew, was justers do more than buy land and soon I'd be skilled enough to start doing them for myself. The plan was for me to go self-employed as soon as I completed my Advanced Craft City and Guilds Certificate in four years' time. Being on a full wage at twenty sounded much better to me than being two years into a university course earning nothing. I wanted to do justers. They helped buy freedom, thrills, huge adrenaline rushes and the unimaginable ecstasy, the shear unadulterated disbelief in whizzing uphill without having to do anything more energetic than twist a throttle. For all the mad episodes I had on a motorbike during my youth, the one overriding memory is of the initial amazement I felt at not having to bust a gut and pedal uphill. How fantastic to have an engine between your legs, one capable of whisking you up the steepest incline – and there were plenty of them in Hastings – without recourse to physical effort.

And now I don't even own a bike, let alone ride one.

My father was proud of me passing my bike test at the first attempt because he'd done exactly the same. A motorbike fanatic all his life, I like to think Owen's belated move into modern Japanese machinery from the past glories of the British made BSA and

Triumph bikes was due to my interest. His lack of deference to The Fear allowed me to have my motorbikes and as my interest blossomed so his fire for two-wheeled transport was rekindled in middle age. We bought bikes together, rode them off to nowhere in particular together and then swapped over and rode each other's back. Yamahas, Hondas, Suzukis and Kawasakis all lived in the garage attached to the house that Owen built. My final bike, the one I sold before I married Clare, was a red Honda CX500. Unkindly named, The Plastic Maggot, it was a shaft driven, water-cooled V-twin.

As I drifted out of the motorbike scene and into married life, my father's most recent choice of machine turned full circle. As the iconic Triumph brand revitalised itself, Owen revisited one of the bikes he'd owned in his youth. It's a modern Triumph Bonneville T100 still standing in his garage because although I took his consultant's advice and sold his car, I couldn't bring myself to sell his bike. Surreptitiously, and feeling like a thief, I took away its keys and placed them in a drawer at my home so he could never use it again.

Several times he asked me where the keys were and I lied to him saying they were lost.

"Still, you can always go and look at it, Dad. Whenever you want. It'll be there for you to polish and sit on, but you can't ride it anymore. It's too dangerous at your age. The doctors say it's too dangerous."

I felt terrible telling him. He never once answered me back and somehow his mute acceptance made the situation worse. God knows what he thought of me taking away the last of his two life passions (the other being football). Sometimes of late, when the emotion gets high and they've had a bad day and therefore I have too, I imagine the pair of them jumping on to his Bonneville and riding away on it. My mother on pillion – she endured a trip to Spain on the back of the first Bonneville, suffering exhaust burns to the leg and oil up her new coat – clinging like a limpet to my father as the pair of them tear off down the road in one final glorious hurrah. In my mind, my father rides the bike over a cliff, manic grin on his face, killing the pair of them and their predicament in a spectacular 'Fuck you!' V sign to old age and deterioration.

There's a reason why I make them die this way and it's all to do with The Fear and one of my uncles.

When all's said and done and my mind settles back to reality, it's not hard to fathom out what has happened. I'm not fooling myself – finding the two photos has also undoubtedly helped contribute to my mid-life blip. And although I can eulogise on mine and my father's past motorbike escapades there is no way their ownership is going to spread into a third generation. The simple fact is I'm not letting Jack have one, even if I get one myself. And that's not The Fear talking, it's me, John Alfred Dennett, hypocrite and concerned parent. In any case, Jack couldn't risk getting injured on a motorbike, not if he wants to get a professional football apprenticeship. End of, as I'm told by my children it's cool to say.

The other photos which grabbed my attention were the really old ones. Somewhat fittingly, the random manner of my finding them seemed perfectly in synch with their sizes. They were a complete jumble and hotchpotch of differing indeterminate dimensions. All of these odd sized photos were black and white apart from one of my mother where her clothes, skin and lips seemed to have been 'coloured in' by a process outside the realms of photography. She looked most odd with her overpoweringly red lips, doll-like pink cheeks and red striped blouse superimposed over what looked like an ordinary monochrome photo. In the bottom right-hand corner, written in ink pen, were the words, 'Yours always, Mary xxx'. The message was clear. This was a photo exclusively for the eyes of a sweetheart.

This dog-eared collection also contained prints of my parents in their teen years – loads of Owen on various classic motorbikes – my mother's parents, Mabel and Cyril, her sister, Olive, and her younger brother, Alfred. There were pictures of me as a toddler with my grandparents, a more recent picture of Mabel winning third prize at a Glamorous Grandma competition at Butlin's circa 1960 and even more bizarrely, a picture of a wedding cake flanked by a pageboy in a top hat and a young bridesmaid where the cake was bigger than the two humans. Admittedly, the two humans in question were children, but even so it was one hell of a cake. Ten minutes later, I found a picture of the same cake on the roof of a baker's delivery van in full marriage regalia complete with ribbons from roof to bonnet. I couldn't fathom how this massive cake had been fixed to the van's roof – there were no visible signs of bungee straps for a start– or how they'd managed to get it from the bakery on to the roof, drive it across town, get it down from the roof and into the wedding reception without it disintegrating. However, the photos were irrefutable proof they had. Transportation in the 1920s was clearly more adroit than I'd first imagined and I now consider the whole mystery of what was my grandparents' wedding cake to be something akin to the mystery of building the ancient pyramids – they did it, but nobody's quite sure how.

In the next batch of papers I found my grandparents' old National Registration Identity Cards. These slim pieces of blue folded card were stamped in 1943 for Mabel at an address in Blaydon-on-Tyne and then back in Hastings a year later. I knew my mother was evacuated to Newcastle with Olive and Alfred during World War II, but hadn't realised Mabel went too. Cyril, a fitter and turner by trade, received a secondment to work in the Vickers Armstrong factory making aeroplane engines. His card was stamped in 1951 at the same address as Mabel's. Despite this later date I do know they both returned home much earlier than 1951 to be 'Back beside the seaside! Beside the sea!'

If the NRICs looked amateurish then Cyril's miniscule plum coloured driving licence, looking like it had been made with a John

Bull printing set by a competent teenager with aspirations to counterfeit money, was even worse. Incredibly, it had an additional, new information, green stick-in sheet dated as late as 1971.

I found my County Borough of Hastings Maternity and Child Welfare Service weigh card where, according to the last entry I pushed the scales down to 21lb 3ozs. I discovered some of my milk teeth in an envelope (a bit creepy) and my alternative order of ministration of Publick Baptism of Infants where I was named John Alfred Dennett when, with a bit of cross-referencing, I weighed approximately 11lb. I then came across several quaint postcards with birthday wishes alongside 'colour' pictures on their front. They had the same look about them as the coloured in photo of my mother. There were quite a few of them and they were all hand delivered birthday postcards bar one. This one had been through the post and was stamped 'Hastings 3.30pm 12 Mar 1928' with two green halfpenny George V stamps attached. On the front of this postcard was an inset picture of a river surrounded by a garland of pink and yellow roses and the words, 'To my dear Son on his Birthday.' in a large font. Underneath a verse read, 'This greeting take with Mother's love, For years but make you dearer still; And Oh I pray that Heaven above, Shall now for you my wish fulfil, And grant you all your life requires;- The good to which your heart aspires.' On the other side it was addressed to Mr C Roberts and underneath the message read, 'Best Birthday wishes & love from all at home.'

Next up were a bundle of letters transpiring to be my father's love letters to my mother. I felt like a cryptologist trying to fathom out my father's faded handwriting on the fragile pieces of faintly lined writing paper. As I opened each leaf I saw chunks of it were missing, the frequent folding and unfolding over the years causing the paper to wear away. In the end, after much time spent decoding my father's hieroglyphics, although interesting, the notes weren't especially revealing. He sent them while working away on a large construction site in Gillingham (now I understood why he was always in Gillingham when he was at home) during the mid-fifties and were a succession of, 'My darling, Mary, I miss you so very much...' outpourings. No doubt brought about by the fact he was living in digs and was away from her for weeks at a time. As I read them I was secretly hoping for a shocking taste of fifties' sexuality, one where my father would graphically describe what he intended to do to my mother when they were reunited. There was nothing of the kind, only a gushing Mills and Boon style of prose littered with prim declarations of undying love. What they did tell me was my mother must have been well enough to cope with being separated from my father. This gave further credence to my theory that my birth was the catalyst for her falling completely under the shadow of The Fear.

The next item I found was a single page of writing in my mother's hand. It read, 'If I had to choose the one day to live my whole life through, it would surely be that Sunday, the day that I met you. Newborn whippoorwills were calling from the hill – summer was coming at last. Lots of daffodils were showing off their skills, nodding altogether, you could almost hear them whisper, go on, kiss her, go on and kiss her. If I had to choose one day to live my whole life through it would surely be that Sunday, recalling how it started darling it would be, when you smiled at me that way, that day, that Sunday.' I immediately sensed here was something odd. It was too good, and I don't mean any disrespect to my mother by saying that, but I knew there was no way she could have composed it herself. The issue was later resolved thanks to Mr Google. What my mother wrote, almost perfectly and probably off by heart, were the lyrics to That Sunday, That Summer by Nat King Cole. Perhaps they had adapted it as their song, a musical memory of how they met.

Behind my father's substitute red and white certificate of birth I noticed a pencil written note from him to my mother. It said,

'Welcome home my darling Mary (MUM) and little John Alfred. Owen xxx'. Here was the note my father wrote after completing the house just in time for her to come home from the local maternity hospital with me. It was written on the back of a torn-in-half bill-head my father used for writing out his invoices.

Finally, saving the best until last, I found the revelation – the newspaper cutting detailing the first manifestation of The Fear. The frail cutting was lying sandwiched between the birth certificate and another of the old postcards. Intrigued, I picked it up and read the headline, 'YOUTH'S TRAGIC DEATH' and a smaller one underneath reading, 'AMBITION TO JOIN THE ARMY'. My heart started to speed up and I read the article with its rather odd style of language and punctuation to a quickening beat. 'Desiring to go abroad and see the world, a youth of 18 left home and joined the Army. Five weeks later his family learnt of his death. He was Frederick Roberts, son of Mr Charles Roberts. During his schooldays he played football for both Hollington Day School and Tower-road School and later he often played for Hollington Utd 11. He was also an excellent swimmer. Mr Roberts had been employed by Messrs Sainsbury's as a counter hand, but always wanted to travel abroad. He joined the Royal Engineers and was stationed at Chatham. According to Army regulations he was vaccinated and almost immediately was taken to hospital, where he remained until his death. The funeral took place at the Borough Cemetery on Thursday, the Rev C. E. Evans officiating.'

The next part of the article was a list of chief mourners where I spotted the name, 'Mr Cyril Roberts (brother)', my grandfather. The boy who had died was my great uncle, my grandfather's younger brother. Before the question had a chance to pop into my head I noticed another newspaper cutting less than an inch wide. It was the in memoriam piece from the local paper and it told me all I wanted to know. 'Roberts – On April 18th 1936 at the Royal Naval Hospital, Chatham. Frederick, the dearly-loved son of the late Mrs

Roberts and of Mr Roberts, passed peacefully away, aged 18.' For some reason I turned over this thunderbolt from the blue and read, '£550 FREEHOLD West Hill – six rooms, scullery; possession – Taylor. Hastings.' On the next line, '£575 FREEHOLD – Lady's labour saving BUNGALOW electric light, power, telephone; sunny position...' the rest was gone, snipped out in an act dictated by the size of the more important details overleaf.

I was rocked. The three previously known incidents of The Fear within my family starting with the wrecking ball of tragedy smashing my mother's family asunder, now needed to be renumbered and collectively moved down the list to make four. This was how it all started. This was where and how it all begun. The question as ever was; Where was it all going to end? I turn to The Pact with confidence on this and tell myself it already has. It ended, categorically and unequivocally, with my father's side of the family's sole contribution.

The shopping, after several shuttle runs, is now parked in the front porch. When I walked up and down the side of the house, in the process of moving the shopping from my van to the front door, I noticed the overflow pipe from the main water tank in the roof was constantly dripping and made a mental note to check the ball valve later. I might be a carpenter, but thirty plus years of self-employment have made me quite adept at other trades

To get into the property I need to access the relatively new Yale lock key (which is my handiwork) via the key inside the keysafe fixed to the brickwork. I punch in the four-digit code, remove the front section and take out the key. It's a piece of cake. However, in the early days AD it wasn't always so simple and the situation was entirely my fault. Originally, going right back to the time Owen fitted the external doors, both the front and back doors were locked with mortice style locks. BD I would ring the doorbell and one of my parents would unlock the door with the relevant key and let me in. AD, however, it became a different matter. I would ring the doorbell and wait, listening to the soundtrack of my parents hunting for the key.

"Where's the front door key, Mary?"

"Don't know. I thought you had it."

"No. You had it last."

Sometimes they couldn't find the key for the front door. I might circumnavigate this problem by going around to the back door, where quite often its key would be lodged safely in the lock. I would call out to them, relaying this information, and they would let me in. As time passed and my parents' condition worsened I was often unable to enter by either the front or back door because both keys had gone AWOL. In this scenario I used my set – if I remembered to bring them. A few enforced trips back to my house to get them pretty soon hammered the point home and I started leaving a spare set in my van and in Clare's car. This solved the problem for a while until the issue became more complex once carers became involved. Due to the carers suffering a total lock out on a number of occasions, meaning I was dragged from work to provide entry, the management of the care company alerted me to the merits of a keysafe. I immediately bought one from a local security shop and fixed it to the porch wall's brickwork with rawlplugs and screws using a 24 volt rotary drill and a 14.4 volt driver just like the ones Owen didn't have when he built the house.

Job done, one might think. Not so. The trauma of keys hadn't been completely eradicated. They still formed one thread of worry in the multi-stranded hawser of dementia. The keysafe cured the problem of people accessing my parents and getting in the house. What it didn't help was the problem of what would happen if my parents had to get out of the house quickly – because of a fire for instance – and had lost their keys. Eventually, in a Eureka! moment, which was a ridiculously long time in coming, it occurred to me the best solution was to fit an additional Yale lock to both doors. A Yale lock works effectively enough by the simple act of closing a door and can be opened by the twist of a knob from the inside without a key. Once fitted, the pair of Yale locks rendered the old mortice locks redundant and their keys were happily binned. It solved the problem of locking my parents in and allowing them to get out in one stroke.

Looking back, I realise I was on a steep learning curve dealing with my parents and their dementia and I couldn't see the wood for the trees. I'm still riding the learning curve, but with hindsight – particularly early on – I never really envisaged the long-term problems. Foolishly, I felt I could slow down their dementia through my own endeavours and was far too easily convinced they were getting a bit forgetful rather than accepting their complete mental erosion was happening before my eyes.

Enough people constantly misplace and lose keys, even when gifted with full mental cognitive function, for the matter to be deemed normal. So normal the whole process has proven to be a veritable, if clichéd, comedic gold mine. Car manufacturers are muscling in on the act, advertising their keyless ignition vehicles after revealing to viewers a raft of humorous 'lost keys' situations. These minor lapses of memory are frustrating for the time it takes to recover the missing set, yet ultimately constitute nothing more than mild inconvenience.

For dementia suffers it most definitely does constitute something more than mild inconvenience because it's not restricted solely to keys. It's everything. Can you imagine what it must be like to have no recollection, whatsoever, of what you've just done in the last five minutes, the last hour, the last couple of days? Both my parents have looked at me nonplussed when I informed them Clare popped in to see them earlier during the same day. I have asked my mother, while reading the answer from the carers' notes, what food she'd eaten for breakfast/dinner/tea only for her to reply she'd eaten nothing all day. I have asked my parents if they remembered me phoning them earlier only to be met by blank expressions and their cat became the feline equivalent to a non-person because it was 'dead' due to them having no recollection of the latest living replacement, Jamie IV.

I've lost track of the number of times this sort of thing has happened. It's become so commonplace I treat it as the norm. What has also happened, to compound the issue, is they now constantly tell me things they do remember doing, which they patently haven't.

"We've been for a swim in the sea this morning," my father would tell me in the depths of winter. "The water was lovely wasn't it, Mary?"

"Oh yes," my mother would say, seamlessly entering into his world. "It was like a mill pond. And warm, too."

What I came to recognise very quickly was these random off-kilter claims were clearly genuine memories. However, they were memories from another time, their chronological order so jumbled it made them hopelessly askew and inaccurate. This was particularly evident when it came to the status of their dead parents, where a memory of meeting them or seeing them years ago instantly made them alive.

The idea I ran with in my mind, when confronting their predicament, was to represent a lifetime of memories as a huge deck of thousands of playing cards. In a normal brain, the top cards in the deck equate to memories of the most recent actions and are the most accessible, the first card flipped over being the action from minutes earlier. Going further down the deck means travelling back in time until the bottom card represents the earliest fuzzy recollections. Of course, not all the cards within a deck are the same value. Mundane cards, the twos, threes and fours and so on aren't so important and these cards represent the memory and status of actions such as putting down a set of keys and what food was eaten on a given day. In my memory deck, unlike a proper deck of cards, these lower value cards hugely outnumber the higher value cards reflecting the everyday nature of our lives. By definition, the higher value, less numerous cards relate to less frequent, more important special memories. Some memories are aces high. These high cards always stand out, no matter how far down the pack they sit and would constitute life's major events, both good and bad. For example; the name of a first girlfriend, the recollection of a first motorbike, a first sexual encounter, the birth of a child, winning a rollover lottery, falling off a motorbike, being kidnapped by Somali pirates and so on. With my parents, and other dementia sufferers, I imagine their memory cards to be in reverse so old memories become relatively more reliable at the top and new memories are virtually lost at the bottom. To account for memory loss whole swathes of cards, both high and low are set aside and destroyed. Finally, the remaining cards are given a random shuffle to distort the already reversed chronology. One ends up with an erratic, incomplete, chronologically unsound, older memory orientated recollection of a lifetime of memories.

Over time I have developed a strategy to try to deal with my parents' erratic memories. Morally, I have no problem with keeping a few secrets from them or telling them a few lies, such as the whereabouts of the motorbike's keys, if it helps keep them safe from themselves. I've lost count of the times I've done this and no longer feel any guilt as I've gradually begun to understand the nature of their disease and how best to address it. There are certainly no definitive answers to dementia – all is a compromise, a constant juggling act of balancing one undesirable possibility against another.

One time, very early AD, provided a perfect example of this. I turned up at the house that Owen built and once inside was hit by the smell of gas. My mother had tried to fry some bacon and left the gas knob on without it being alight. (The hob was an older design model and had no flame failure device. This detects the heat of the flame and in its absence automatically shuts off the gas.) When I checked, all the knobs were off, but she'd clearly experienced difficulty with lighting the hob or perhaps thought it was alight for some time when it wasn't. Irrespective of the reasons, I quickly opened up all the windows and allowed the gas to dissipate. A brief scan under the worktop revealed a gas isolation cock, an old style brass quarter turn one needing an adjustable spanner to shut it off. I nipped back to my van, found a spanner and returned to do so. I managed to complete this task without my parents seeing and once the hob was safely isolated told them it was broken and wouldn't work.

For a couple of months the issue of the broken hob frequently cropped up, with both my mother and father complaining about it. I fobbed them off with varying excuses, telling my mother it would be much easier to use the electric oven or the microwave to cook the readymade meals I was now buying – something she was capable of doing at the time. The diversionary tactic worked and like most things the hob issue eventually faded away as they simply forgot it.

The gas escape was a bit worrying to say the least, but it didn't faze me or make me question what I was doing. The essence of what I was trying to achieve, as remains the case now, can be summed up in one simple statement of intent: I want my mother and father to live in their house for as long as possible. The idea of them going into a nursing home is simply too horrid to contemplate. I feel very strongly the best place for them is at home and if that means there are a few bumps and scrapes along the way then so be it. Only when it is perfectly clear they are in too bad a state to stay at home will I accept defeat.

The mortice lock keys going missing became a template for many other things as my parents' dementia took hold. Clothing and shoes I hadn't come across before suddenly appeared on their bed, the settee or draped over kitchen work surfaces. Missing slippers returned from alien abduction in mixed pairs, individually and, more rarely, as a matching pair. The microwave plate disappeared so I bought a complete new microwave, only for the plate to reappear in the washing up bowl five days later. I was stunned and couldn't believe it. I scoured the house for that plate. Who knows where it was hiding.

Unbelievably, the toaster disappeared almost immediately after the plate turned up. Loath to do a repeat microwave performance my parents suffered a toasterless week before that too was back in place on the kitchen worktop, plugged in and working perfectly. For a short time the TV and Sky controllers appeared to have developed a rotational ploy of tag teaming me so only one of them appeared in the living room at any one particular time. Eventually, they bored of the game and the pair turned up – until the next time when one of them went walkabout and I was left pulling my hair out with frustration at the aggravation involved in changing a channel on the television set.

Asking my parents where they put things was a waste of time. Initially, I listened to my parents' explanations, some plausible, some absurd, but eventually I gave in. When you've handled more red herrings than a Scottish kipper factory it's time to stop asking. In hindsight, I suspect Owen was shifting stuff down into the super massive black hole I call his garage and then returning with it days later. Returning any matter from a black hole is no mean feat. Even more so when the black hole in question has sucked in fifty years' worth of paraphernalia collected by a self-employed man in the construction industry with an interest in motorbikes, gardening and home decorating. Within its festooned grotto-like walls there's a pretty fair chance you could name any item associated with carpentry, motorbikes, gardening or decorating and find it there.

I refuse to venture anywhere near the black hole – hunting for stuff in the house is bad enough – as I'm scared of spaghettification if I cross its event horizon. I'm scared of seeing all the tools; the hammers, both claw, club, ballpane roofing and toffee; the hand saws, tenon, pad, coping, floorboard and crosscut; the mitre saws, circular saws, jigsaws, table saws and reciprocating saws; the masses of wood chisels, some as sharp as a razor, others as blunt as a brick; the planes both electric and hand; the braces and their many bits; the L-shaped squares and the smaller triangular speed squares; the spirit levels, from weenie wooden boat levels to implausible 72" aluminium super levels; the myriad of tape measures, many disembowelled, their steel banded innards strewn everywhere like a trip hazard attack; the drill bits, metal and masonry; the speed bits; the screwdrivers and screwdriver bits in slotted, Pozidrive, Phillips, square, hex and torx; the Allen keys in metric and imperial; the spanner sets in metric and imperial; the ratchet spanner sets in metric and imperial; the socket sets in metric and imperial; the box spanner sets in metric and imperial; the long-nose pliers, the diagonal pliers, the linesman pliers, the slip-joint pliers and the groove-joint pliers; the adjustable spanners and the square jawed adjustable spanners; the stilsons and the mole wrenches ready to bite and not let go; the array of oil filter wrenches and spark plug spanners; bolsters, cold chisels, crowbars, plumb bobs, slate rips, brick trowels, pointing trowels, corner trowels, finishing trowels – many of which I used in my apprenticeship and looked ancient then. Scared of seeing the mass of items kept magpie-style that 'might come in handy' but never did. Scared of the rows and rows of cluttered shelving, scared of the mass of bewildering items hanging from nails hammered into every available square inch of wall and roof joist. Scared of the lengths of wood, cane, pipe and plastic conduit lodged in batten formed racks fixed to the roof joists. Scared of the endless exhausts, tyres, dynamos, alternators, spark plugs, spare bulbs, nuts and bolts, fairings, broken mirrors, scuffed brake and clutch levers, fuel pumps, leaking front forks, bent gear levers, cracked indicator stems and greasy broken chains. Scared of the tins of paint; tins of knotting, primer, undercoat, gloss, eggshell, satinwood, silthane, polyurethane gloss, vinyl mat, vinyl silk, vinyl satin, woodstain, varnish, Hammerite and Sandtex, all in volumes ranging from sample tubs to 10ltr behemoths. Scared of the empty tins, stored like Russian dolls, one inside the other, where one becomes two, three, four or five. Scared of all the brushes from ½" sable to 6" emulsion, both new, cleaned, used and useless. Scared of the bottles of turpentine, of white spirit, of linseed oil, the boxes of rock hard filler, the tubs of rock hard putty, the tubes of decorators' caulk and silicone, the sheets of used sandpaper, new sandpaper, aluminium oxide paper, wet and dry paper, boxes of sugar soap, sponges, rags, dust sheets, short and long pile rollers with their attendant roller handles and trays. Scared of the scrapers, knives, shavehooks, wallpaper scissors, joint rollers, junior and senior hacksaw blades and a host of screwdriver stirrers, points dipped in a rainbow of colours. Scared of the spades, the shovels, the picks, the mattocks, the hoes, the brooms, the shears, the secateurs, the garden trowels, the bow saws and the myriad of empty plant pots, also stored like Russian dolls, but in tottering towers of tens and twenties. Scared of the host of nails and screws; the panel pins, the tacks, the cut nails, the lost heads, the annulars, the round wires, the oval wires, the masonry nails, the copper nails, the plasterboard nails, the felt nails and the screws, so many, many screws of so many differing lengths and so many differing gauges with so many differing head configurations that were either brass, steel, stainless steel, black japanned, chrome plated, zinc plated, zinc passivated and yellow passivated. Scared, above all else, of the knowledge that one day I will have to sort it all out. Finally, there's his motorbike, an item equally as meaningful in my father's life as all the other clutter. As with everything else, it simply waits for a day when a decision must be made on its outcome.

Whereas the photos and paperwork came under the banner of 'random placement' and the missing/reappearing objects under 'temporary displacement', there was another sub group to consider. Running parallel with the two others was the category of 'bizarre placement' where I found objects in places so completely out of context I could only laugh at them. Believe me, it was either that or cry because every incident spelt out a message of two old people gradually sliding down a slippery slope.

On one occasion, Clare and I went to clean the house. The time the carers were allotted to do my parents' domestic work was nowhere near adequate and we tried to pick up the remaining chores whenever we could. I went to put on some washing and on opening the machine's door found a half-eaten apple pie inside the drum. I called out to Clare to come and look and we both shared a brief moment of levity together. As Clare disposed of the pie I put all my parents' dirty clothes inside the drum, shut the door and, in an even better moment of shock value and humour, I opened the machine's soap powder drawer to find a block of salted Anchor butter wedged in it.

From my supermarket trolley of embarrassment to my parents' soap drawer of bizarre misplacement.

I found loose biscuits under the sink next to the bleach. I discovered dirty underwear in drawers mixed with clean clothes, on the floor, in the bed, on work surfaces and best of all – a real ten out of ten on the bizarre placement scale – a pair of my father's skid marked underpants stuffed inside the teapot. I retrieved false teeth from the cutlery tray, found soup in the kettle, salt in the sugar bowl, cat food in biscuit tins, the stinking remains of week-old coldwater prawns under the bed masquerading as a dead rat, kitchen rolls in the fridge, clothes in the rubbish bin, Werther's Originals with the capacity to act like neutrinos rendering them capable of ghosting through matter and, ultimately, lodging un-neutrino-like in every nook, cranny and pocket, and my father's missing Omega Speedmaster Moonwatch – his single quality time-piece – wrapped in a duster and tied up so tightly with a shoelace I had to use scissors to get it out, shoved into the soil of a plant pot.

Maybe Owen was trying to grow a couple more.

However, all these quirks paled into insignificance compared to the constant unremitting issues of my mother's handbag and its contents – her jewellery and her cash.

At first, I noticed how my mother seemed to have a newly cultivated umbilical-like need to be in permanent contact with her handbag. The small fake crocodile skin bag always hung round her wrist when she was eating, sitting watching TV and pottering around the house. She even took it to the toilet. If I ever popped in to see them on my way to work, early in the morning, I would often see it poking out from beneath her pillow. She had slept on it, to keep it safe, like a child might sleep on a milk tooth.

One time, peering out of the kitchen, I secretly watched her as she sat on the living room's settee. She took out her cash, counted it out over and over, at least four times, and then she folded it up and started to count out her rings. (My mother always wears some of her rings and keeps the others in the bag until she decides to 'ring the changes' and have a jewellery shuffle. Some days she wears what I considered to be an appropriate number of rings and on others she might wear all of them, her unbending ring and middle fingers ensconced in a 9cwt gold splint from knuckle to quick.) Once she finished with the rings, apparently to her satisfaction, she got the cash back out and started to count it. I watched in fascination at what I assumed was a dementia-inspired version of obsessive-compulsive behaviour. As my mother counted out loud she made an error, mistaking a couple of twenty-pound notes for tens, so instead of making one hundred pounds in total she only made eighty.

Her face turned to thunder.

"The bastards!" she said, spitting the words out. "They've pinched my bloody money!"

"What's up, Mum?" I asked as if I had walked into the room by chance.

"They've taken my money!" she told me.

"Who has?"

"Those people upstairs."

"Mum, there isn't anybody upstairs," I answered, feeling confused.

"You know who I mean."

"How much should you have?" I asked, trying to distract her from her newly acquired lodgers.

"A hundred pounds." (She remembered that all right!)

"Shall we count it together and check it?"

She handed me the small bundle of cash and we counted together like I was an adult and she was a child. "Twenty pounds, forty pounds, sixty pounds, eighty pounds, one hundred. There you go! It's all there, all nice and safe."

She snatched the cash from me and put it in her bag pulling a face, as she used to say when explaining her dirtiest of looks BD, 'like a summons'.

Two days later she phoned me on my mobile while I was at work. At the time she still had enough organisational skills to find my landline or mobile number in her telephone book and ring it. Some evenings I was fielding multiple phone calls at home, but a call on the mobile was much less common. The usual thread of worry for the landline calls concerned the TV, how to put it on and the corresponding Sky channel number for BBC One, BBC Two, etc. and the Sky Sports channel showing Premiership football. I often tried to talk my father through the process of putting on the TV and these conversations turned into some of the most excruciatingly frustrating moments of my life. Often it was quicker for me to get in my van, drive to the other side of town, and put it on myself.

Despite being impressed she had managed to make a call to my mobile I soon realised something else was going seriously wrong in her head.

"John! Is that you? My handbag's gone! Someone's stolen it and

I'm going to phone the police."

"Mum, no one's stolen your bag," I said with a dispirited air. "You've put it down somewhere and forgotten where it is."

"I'm not that stupid!" she snapped and there was a tone in her voice I had never heard before, not even when she was cross with me as a child. "I know what you're up to. I know you want to get my house. I know you want to take it away. You and your tribe."

"What are you on about?" I protested. "No one's taking your house away. It's yours. Yours and Dad's. You and Dad own it," I reiterated.

"What Cyril?"

"No, not Cyril! Not your dad. He's dead. *My* dad, Owen. Your husband."

"My dad's dead?"

"Mum, he died thirty-five years ago!"

"Well, nobody told me." I heard her turn her head away from the phone and shout out to my father. "Owen! Owen! John said Cyril's dead. I told him nobody's told me. Here. You come and speak to him."

"Mum, there's no need for me to talk to…"

"Hello, John."

"Hello, Dad. Mum's on about losing her handbag," I began to explain, "I was saying to her she hasn't lost it, she's put it down somewhere and forgotten where it is. Then she went off on one saying I was trying to take your house away and she got muddled up about Cyril still being alive…"

"He is alive," my father chipped in. "I saw him down the Old Town last week."

"No, you didn't, Dad," I argued. "Because he's dead. He died thirty-five years ago."

"No he's not. On my life I went down the Old Town last week and saw him sitting down by the Winkle Island."

"Dad, you might remember seeing him sitting down by the

Winkle Island, but that's an old memory. That happened forty odd years ago. I can remember talking to him, but that doesn't make him alive."

"Hello, John. What have you done with my handbag?" my mother's voice cruelly snapped.

Flummoxed and then agitated by yet another accusation I realised my father had passed the phone back to my mother while I was talking and I hadn't noticed.

"I haven't done anything with your bloody handbag. You've put it down somewhere and can't remember what you've done with it," I told her flatly.

"Well, if you won't help your mother, I'm phoning the police."

"You're *not* phoning the police because no one has taken the bloody thing. It's lying in the house somewhere. Look on the settee. Look on the chairs. Look on the bed, under the pillows."

"Just a minute."

I heard my mother wander off with the cordless digital phone down by her side. I was left hanging on, listening to her shuffling around the house in search of her 'stolen' handbag. I was already cross and losing my temper further by the second. "Hello!" I shouted after a couple of minutes. "Hello! Will you answer me?" Nothing. "Put the phone up to your ear will you!" I screamed at the top of my voice. Still nothing. Two more minutes of intense agitation passed until eventually my mother spoke.

"I've found it," she said grumpily. "No thanks to you."

"What do you mean by, 'No thanks to you'? I told you to go and look for it in the first place. I told you it wasn't stolen."

"Well, that's your job, isn't it?"

"What do you mean that's my job?"

"Well, you're a policeman aren't you?"

"I'm not a fucking policeman! I'm your son, John."

"Okay, thank you."

And she hung up on me. I was livid. Absolutely fuming. That

evening, she phoned me up at home on the landline to see how I was and spoke to me as if nothing had happened. She was, in terms of her personality, back to her old self.

"Do you remember me getting cross with you when we last spoke?" I asked guiltily. "When you thought I was a policeman?"

My mother laughed. "Thought you were a policeman? I don't remember that."

There was no recollection whatsoever. I had learnt another rule of the dementia sufferer – they can never hold a grudge.

My mother's handbag has caused me more grief than any other single inanimate object I have ever known, even more than their TV and that's saying something. Since her dementia took root I think she spends nearly all her time picking it up, carrying it around, putting it down, losing it, looking for it, finding it, picking it up, carrying it around, putting it down… ad infinitum. Her obsession with her cash and jewellery dominates to the exclusion of everything else. It's become the centre of her existence and her raison d'être. However, there is something worse than the aggravation caused by the infernal handbag and that is the character change she occasionally undergoes – the mobile phone call being its first outing.

My mother suffered many emotional problems due to The Fear and they were reflected in several ways; in her outlook, her character traits and her general demeanour. Dementia has changed her again, in a different way, and the temporary shifts where she becomes an obnoxious cantankerous old cow – not to put too fine a point on it – accusing me of terrible deeds and of treating her awfully, both enraged and hurt me at first. I felt so indignant. I was spending an awful lot of time and energy, which was costing me money in terms of time off work, to try and help her and all I was getting in return were false accusations and character assassinations. When my father joined her in this phase of dementia and they were both nasty to me it really pained on a personal level.

Luckily, my adaptable nature – the trait allowing The Pact – afforded me the pragmatism I needed to deal with this problem and I managed to control my own anger and rationalised how to cope with theirs. Although it was my mother and father, in a physical sense, abusing me, it wasn't them speaking in the true sense. Their brains were breaking down and it would have been as unreasonable of me to expect them to talk coherently as it would of a leg amputee to walk without a limp. I learnt to let their accusations wash over me and I ignored them, secure, if you like, in the honesty of my own intentions.

The people upstairs are a bizarre phenomenon. My mother and father remain utterly convinced of their existence. In their heads the people upstairs have become the true owners of the house. Wrapped into this version of reality is the continuing premise of the house not being the one that Owen built. These two misconceptions continually provoke them to come to the conclusion that the house isn't their house, it's one in Gillingham, and is owned by the people upstairs. My father has explained to me on many occasions that this state of affairs means, in some undefinable way, that they are forbidden to go about their daily business and are restricted in terms of access and use of the house. Often their final act, when stuck in this mental rut, was to pack up their belongings in preparation for a 'return' to Hastings.

I regularly popped in to find random items of clothes and shoes in five or six black plastic rubbish sacks placed in the hallway. Thankfully, they never migrated any further than that. My parents always seemed to be on the point of leaving without ever actually getting round to doing it. As well as the plastic bags there was always the same solitary filthy carpet toolbag sitting next to them, one containing my father's oldest hand tools. So old and wise were these tools they managed to defy the obscene pulling power of the super massive black hole of a garage. Mingled in with the tools were loose screws, loose nails, loose rawlplugs of different colours, loose washers, pre-decimal coinage, Spanish Pesetas in small denominations and a liberal helping of dirt, dust and wood shavings. In amongst this squalor often lurked old sets of false teeth, old razor blades, hankies, the occasional toothbrush, a chocolate bar or two and a smattering of ex-neutrino Werther's Originals in varying states of physical decay either crushed, broken, partially melted, partially unwrapped, fully unwrapped or eaten – their gold wrappers lying in amongst the debris like shed snake skins.

"What the hell are you doing?" I asked, surveying the latest occurrence with sagging shoulders.

"We've got to leave, John. Get back to Hastings," my father explained.

"You are in Hastings!" I shrieked. "Don't start all this nonsense again, please. You can't go anywhere. You've nowhere else to go. This is your house. You live here! This is it! There's nowhere else!"

"It's the people upstairs," my mother butted in. "They want us out. The bastards!"

"There's nobody upstairs. This is Hastings. This is your house. You live here. This is your own home."

"No," my mother argued. "It's not our home, not the one we bought."

"Yes it is, Mum. This is the house that Dad built."

"What, Cyril?"

"Not, Cyril. Not your dad! *My* dad, Owen. Your husband. This is your house."

"I shan't stay here."

"But you've got to stay here."

"Why's that?" my mother asked.

"Because it's where you live. There's nowhere else for you to go."

"How do you know there's nowhere else for us to go?"

"Because you've only got one house and this is it. You're standing in it now."

63

"You have your opinions and we'll have ours," my mother stated curtly.

"What I'm telling you is the truth," I implored.

"We like the way we are, so I can't say any more."

"Look, all I'm saying is this is your house and this is where you live."

"Why's that? If we sold it we could buy another one."

"I'm not saying anything about that. All I'm saying is this is your house and it's where you live and where you must stay."

"Number sixteen," my mother said, trotting out the number of the flat where they lived directly after marrying. "Christ, it's enough years since I've been here," she added.

"No, number fifty-four is where you are."

"Well, that wasn't far out, was it?" was her indignant response. "I got fifty-four, no you got fifty-four. I got... I can't remember."

"Why don't I get you a nice cup of tea and then maybe later when Clare comes up we can get you in the bath," I suggested, trying to change tack.

"Good God!" my mother exclaimed.

"And get Dad in the shower. I expect you could both do with a good wash by now."

"I think we're capable of washing ourselves."

"The trouble is, Mum, you keep forgetting to do it."

"Huh!" my mother spluttered with ripe indignation. "Bloody cheek!"

I pick up several bags of shopping and go in through the front door. The demented version of Schrodinger's cat, Jamie IV – alive on observation, dead on recollection – shoots past me in the opposite direction as I do. On entering the internal porch my olfactory senses are assaulted by a house smell different and less inviting than in the past. It tells me old people live here. The smell is musty and fuggy with the overriding waft of stale urine, not all of it

64

emanating from the cat's litter tray. The last time I came with shopping exactly a week ago, after being summoned to the bedroom, I was greeted by the sight of my father sitting upright in bed with my mother attentively holding a used cat's litter tray up to his mouth, like a bowl, for him to vomit in.

"He feels sick," she explained.

"I'm not surprised," I said, taking the tray from her grasp and putting it on the floor. "Are you feeling ill, Dad?"

"Not particularly," my father answered. "Just tired."

I put my arm around my mother. "Dad's all right. He's not going to be sick, he's just feeling a bit tired."

"Is Cyril here?" my mother asked me.

"No, not your dad. *My* dad, Owen. Your husband."

"Have you seen my mum and dad?" she asked.

"They're dead, Mum," I reminded her gently. "They passed away a long time ago."

Tears started to well up in my mother's eyes and I hugged her tight. "I don't remember that. Are you sure? I never even went to the funeral."

"I'm sure, Mum. And you did go to the funeral. You were there for both of them."

My mother wiped her eyes. "Where's my Johnny?"

"I'm your Johnny," I said, taken aback.

Her expression turned hard and cold in an instant as she looked me up and down. "Don't be ridiculous. He's thirteen years old. "

It was a funny feeling to come to terms with. I knew it was only a matter of time before it would happen and had tried to prepare myself for the event. Even so it did knock me back. The person I called Mum no longer thought of me as her son.

"Mum! Dad! It's me, John Alfred Dennett. I've got your shopping. I've got you your favourites. Prawns for you, Dad, and cream cakes for you, Mum."

I can thank the second instalment of The Fear for my middle

65

name. I was christened John Alfred Dennett and my middle name, Alfred, was given to me in memory of my mother's younger brother, the unfortunate recipient of the second attack of The Fear. The reason my mother was so frightened to let me out of her sight and made her say no to everything I wanted to do was due to her conviction I would be taken as brutally as Alfred. Left to my mother's devices I would have led a life so seriously curtailed as to make it, in effect, a prison sentence – albeit a prison sentence handed down with overbearing love. Luckily for me, my father was the perfect antidote. When I reached primary school age he gradually pried me from her tenacious grip, progressively loosening my shackles in a process lasting into my adult life and the end of my apprenticeship with him.

During the process of my release I was glad to be able to get away from her, even if seeing her anguish was difficult and hard to fully understand. I think I was around ten years old when I became sufficiently self-aware to recognise more fully what was going on. Before then I had been too young to comprehend her predicament and had thought her clinging protectionism was normal maternal behaviour. There were no clues to suggest otherwise. My mother and father never once argued in front of me over the things I could or couldn't do. Whether they did in private I don't know, I certainly never heard them.

Once I became more independent, the gulf between what I wanted and what she wanted widened considerably. We argued and my tactic for breaking the stalemate was to approach my father and ask him. Most times he would sign my release papers, usually with a modifying constraint to nominally appease my mother. Less frequently, he would back her completely and totally refuse a request. From my early teens these flat refusals were rare.

It has occurred to me my mother and father did all their arguing once he'd let me go and I was out of the house. I can't imagine my mother capitulating so easily and not fighting her corner, given the strength of her feelings, but maybe she did. The strange thing was there never seemed to be any animosity between them, even though it was a one-way street in terms of who gave way. Perhaps my mother knew my father was right, deep down in her heart of hearts, even if, left solely to her, she could never let her brain over-rule her broken heart. However much I analyse it I'm convinced if it had been left to her I would still be living at home now, a Howard Hughes-like recluse living a horrifyingly stilted existence.

Despite my mother's negativity I can't recall, pre-The Pact, ever once mulling over the possibility of history repeating itself or thinking I was in some kind of danger. Of course, I pretty soon changed my mind when the third episode of The Fear struck. For the long hours I was in Olive's house and then afterwards at home with only my mother for company – Owen had gone straight from work to football training – I was terrorised. Scared witless and utterly convinced I was next on the list. The way my mother was hugging me and kissing me, telling me to never ever leave her side again, I felt I'd be dead in minutes. Between us we raised our collective anxiety through the roof and when my father came home and we shared the awful news it got worse. I had never seen my father cry, let alone clamp his hands over both temples, as if trying to stop his head from exploding, while screaming and swearing at the ceiling.

"Why? Why? Why him? Why the fucking hell take him?" he screamed between his sobs.

I was petrified. Both my parents were distraught. Both were frightened. This was alien territory and my blood ran cold to the point I couldn't stop shivering.

That night I lay terrified on my bed, crying uncontrollably in a state of numb disbelief. That odious night, the one indelibly etched on my memory, I somehow did what was needed and devised The Pact. I set in motion my slow release from the chains of hyper-anxiety caused by The Fear's attack. My father, in his own way, did the same and when a few months passed he continued his long-term plans to release me from my mother. If only she could have managed so well.

If I was going out, having been given the go ahead by my father, I often tried to placate my mother by telling her not to worry about me because I would be all right.

"How can you be so sure, John?" my mother asked with incredulity. "Do you think Alfred ever imagined he was going out that day and wouldn't come back? Do you think Harold knew what was going to happen to him on his boat? And what about Graham? You must always be so very careful," she warned. "Always. If anything was to happen to you…" She walked over to a photo frame standing on my set of bedroom drawers, her words of apprehension hanging in the air like steam in a shower room, and picked it up. "Look. This is Alfred." She showed me an old black and white photo of a boy with side parted blond hair. "Don't you look like him?" she asked.

I nodded. "I know it's him, Mum. And I know I look like him. You've shown me and told me a hundred times before."

She kissed my forehead. "I know. I'm so sorry," she said, wiping away a tear. "I can't help it. I'll write a note and say you've got a cold so you don't have to go to swimming lessons at school tomorrow."

"Mum! I'll be all right! Nothing's going to happen to me."

My mother held my eye and I could see the doubt in hers. "You *don't* know! You can *never* know!" she screamed as her emotions surfaced.

My eyes dropped away from hers and I didn't answer, merely giving an almost imperceptible shake of the head. I couldn't tell her of The Pact because its central clause and hold on me, my part of the bargain if you like, was it had to stay a secret. Besides, I knew by its nature that The Pact condemned others to death and I certainly didn't want anyone else knowing. In my defence I asked who in their right mind would accept death on themselves rather than on another? I was fourteen at the time and couldn't think of a single soul. It was all so obvious and straightforward. Now I'm over fifty and a father of two children the answer seems so much less clear-cut.

The death of Alfred was a far more physical demise than the recent discovery of my great uncle Frederick dying from a massive anaphylactic shock. Aged only a gut-wrenching eleven years old, Alfred went out with friends to the East Hill cliffs and never came back. In 1946 my uncle fell to his death before his life had really begun. It's why I always imagine Owen and Mary's swansong to be them going full tilt over a cliff on his motorbike. They end their depleted lives in an act of gross defiance whereas Alfred's life of blossoming promise was callously ripped from him. In my imagination they are diametric opposites – the two ends of the spectrum. One death has a certain poetic satisfaction while the other is dire with no redeeming factors whatsoever.

The exact circumstances of the fall, the harrowing gritty mechanics of how and why, have never been satisfactorily explained to me. All I can glean from the stories I was told is one unambiguous fact; Alfred died because he was an avid egg gatherer and egg eater – part of a wider characteristic inherited from his father. In those austere times after the war, chicken eggs were in short supply and seagull eggs were a passable, if rather fishy, alternative. The taken eggs were eaten hardboiled and even today, in some of the more upmarket restaurants, seagull eggs are considered a delicacy, particularly those of the black-headed gull.

In Alfred's day, as is still the case, gulls, predominantly herring gulls, were abundant and nested on the East Hill's cliff ledges. Incredibly, by today's standards of cosseted children, Alfred and his friends used to scour the cliff edges – there was no fence and no warning signs – and lower each other down to the nest-bound eggs on lower ledges by rope. After collecting them, the egg poacher would be half hauled and would half scramble back to safety. Then, with no more thought to it than if they had just played a game of Kick the Can, the group of friends would move on to the next nest until a suitable number were raided. It's beyond my modern day comprehension how pre-teenagers could risk their necks for a few eggs, yet that's exactly what Alfred did.

What caused the catastrophic fall, whether a fatal misjudgement of accessibility, of the condition of the cliff edge, or if some other factor such as horseplay, a playful nudge or a sudden angry push, will never be known. Sadly, what is undeniable is the outcome. Alfred fell and tumbled to his death on to the rocks below and the little girl who was with the three other boys, a mite aged only eight, ran back to Alfred's house. The little girl knocked on my grandmother's door and when she answered blurted, 'Alfred's dead. He's fallen off the cliffs.'

I'm told my grandmother collapsed and fainted. I'm told my grandfather ran to the bottom of the cliff, scrambling over shingle, rock and sand to identify the broken body of his only son. How the hell do you ever deal with that? What must that feel like? As if by rote I pray to the God I don't believe in I will never have to find out – and then I turn to The Pact and know I won't.

I often wonder if my grandparent's fantastic babysitting was motivated by the joy of having me. I don't mean in any sense of arrogance about how wonderful I was, but in the sense of me being a kind of second chance. I was named after Alfred and I was their only grandson. Was I, in some very small way, a replacement for Alfred? Were those wonderful nights something more to them than just a babysitting session? Did it bring back memories of Alfred? Had they played the same games with him as they did with me? And as I reached his age and then got older did they secretly imagine this is how it would have been if he had lived? Did they try their best to make it special for me because it was special for them? Because I looked like him and their blood ran through my veins?

I don't know. I never asked. By the time I was old enough to think of such things they had long passed away. What I am certain of is their wonderful baby-sitting wasn't an act my mother could repeat with my children. Her perennial viewpoint of the glass being down to the dregs at the bottom, let alone half empty, stayed with her forever. She could never enjoy what she had, only fear losing it. When my children were born, before they were born, she worried to the point of sickness whether the scans would be okay, whether the birth would be okay, whether the baby would be okay, whether the mother would be okay, whether the baby would feed okay...and so on ad infinitum. To my mother every small step up the staircase of life became a towering slaughter stone – the possibility of The Fear's sharp knife ending it all only a heartbeat away. She could never enjoy looking after her grandchildren due to her overwrought fear of something happening to them. She was like a kid with a new bike, frightened to ever take it outside and use it in case it got scratched.

Even going on holiday became problematic as death by car crash, aeroplane/ferry boat/hovercraft/channel tunnel catastrophe, food poisoning, military coup, drowning, amusement park disaster – the list was as endless as it was laughable – made her beg me or my father not to book it. My mother would always cry when she went on holiday and she would always cry if she was the one staying at home when I went with Clare and the children. She was never motivated by self-preservation, only in the sense she never wanted to suffer the loss of anyone close to her ever again. Doing something different from the norm, in her eyes, made the prospect of a visit from The Fear more likely. An odd thought because none of the episodes of The Fear bore that hallmark. It would have suited my mother down to the ground if all of us had moved into the house that Owen built and lived together, until she died, never going out, never doing anything, with her keeping an eye on us all 24/7.

My mother's mental illness – OCD, separation anxiety, post traumatic stress disorder, thanatophobia – whatever tag I give it, is deep within us all, as is the desire to go back and check to see if the front door really is locked on departure for holiday. Many people, as was the case with my family, learn to control grief over time and adapt to a way of living with it and are able to go back to operating somewhere within the band of normality they inhabited before their loss. No one can ever fully recover, I can't imagine that's possible, but most will attempt to live their life to some semblance of fullness so as not to waste it. This was the quantum leap my mother could never make. Ironically, it was dementia that eventually deleted The Fear, but in doing so it robbed her of the ability of inhabiting her band of normality. A band in which she only truly lived for a small portion of her life and in the brief respites of my childhood bedtime stories, ones where she retold tales of her youth with me safely tucked up in bed.

My father and my grandfather were fantastic in extricating me from my mother's grip and I wish, as is often the case when the time has passed, I had tried to help extricate her from The Fear more than I did. I'm sure my father tried, clandestinely, in his own practical, no-nonsense, no mumbo jumbo way. He may even have taken her to get professional help, not that I was aware he ever did. Whatever the case, nothing helped. The Fear got into my mother's head never to let go and she couldn't, with or without the help she may or may not have received, ever force it out.

As well as memories of playing games there are other memories associated with my mother's parents and unfortunately they are directly linked to Alfred's death. My grandfather loved anything to do with the countryside – especially if he could kill and eat it, grow it and eat it or, even better still, just pick it up off the ground or off a tree and eat it. This foraging trait, I'm convinced, was passed on to his son and to a lesser extent to me.

In their middle years my grandparents lived outside the Old

Town. Cyril was a skilled fitter and turner and they were able to live in the council-owned property for very low rent as part of his job package. They wouldn't have considered moving out of the Old Town otherwise. Inside the tiny cottage, Cyril kept many guns in a glass case. They were mostly shotguns and .22 calibre rifles plus a couple of BSA air rifles. He gave one of the air rifles to me when I was about eight. I became quite a good shot with the break barrel, direct-to-barrel-loading .177 calibre weapon and spent many an hour shooting toys and cans in the garden of the house that Owen built. Even better than shooting the puny air rifle were the times when Cyril allowed me to take pot shots at tin cans and wood stumps with the .22 rifle in the yard close to his cottage. He'd then take the gun from me and knock off a couple of grey squirrels just for the fun of it.

Cyril also kept ferrets for his rabbit catching expeditions. These creatures were kept in a cage and I spent many a fascinating hour watching his business of smelly, excitable, clucking furry tubes of fun. Occasionally, I would get to gingerly stroke one of them when he was handling it out of the cage. One time I went to look at them and noticed the big white hob ferret was missing.

"Where's the big one gone, Pop-Pop?" I asked. "He's not in his cage with the others."

Cyril ruffled my hair. "You know what, John. I went to take him out the other day and he bit me. Hard, too. Right down to the bone," he said, showing me a heavily bandaged finger in a leather sheath. "So I went and got my .22 rifle, shot him in the head and the bullet came out his bum. He won't bite me anymore!"

"Did you eat him?" I asked with shocked pragmatism. My grandfather laughed and shook his head. "What about those squirrels you shot?" He laughed again.

"This is what I'm going to eat." He took me to his Belfast kitchen sink wherein there were five or six freshly caught plaice. So fresh they were still flapping. "From Harold's boat," he informed me. "Look in here," he beckoned, turning me with a guiding hand on my shoulder so I noticed the large aluminium saucepan dominating the gas cooker. "Take off the lid."

I lifted off the lid and peered inside at six huge crabs. "You eat *them*?" I asked doubtfully.

"I cook them first, smash the shells and claws, then pick out the meat and eat that."

"Is it nice?"

"Beautiful," he replied.

Once I remember him taking me out through the countryside in his car and a pheasant ran across the road. Cyril quickly hauled the steering wheel round, not to avoid the bird, but to run it over. We nearly ended up in a hedge, but the bird escaped.

"Damn!" Cyril exclaimed. "That would have been a nice dinner!"

Anything, even game, was fair game. Rabbits and birds were hunted, berries and mushrooms gathered, apples and pears scrumped and on his allotment a huge variety of vegetables were grown with an all-embracing enthusiasm. However, there was one last pursuit that held him in sway more than all others – and that was the catching and eating of anything living in fresh or salt water.

I couldn't follow my grandfather and bring myself to shoot anything and motion sickness prevented me from going sea fishing on a boat. What I could follow was his passion for catch and release coarse angling. Only in Cyril's case he wasn't too keen to release anything he caught – or anything I caught for that matter.

"Oh, that's a good one! You want to keep that one for your cat, Jamie," he urged when I reeled in a skimmer bream on my tiny split cane leger rod.

"Don't chuck any eels back, John," he warned as I showed off a deep-hooked bootlace wriggling four feet below my cork float. "Cut its head off with my knife, chuck it away and put the rest in the keepnet. I'll take them all back and make jellied eels."

"John! What are you doing?" he chastised, after I flukily caught an out of season game fish from a river. "You don't put trout back! They make fine eating."

In retrospect, maybe it all revolved around me being such a fussy eater. I felt things would be far better for all parties if the fish were put back alive and not end up dead on a plate where I was expected to eat them. I didn't eat the crab meat, didn't eat the trout and could hardly bear to look at the jellied eels. The cat took my side too. It made do with its Whiskas, flatly rejecting the skimmer bream in the adjacent bowl. I did eat the plaice, but couldn't stomach shrimps, cockles, whelks or coldwater prawns for that matter – particularly when left under my father's bed.

My grandfather also encouraged me to dig for and unearth an amazingly fortuitous string of barely hidden half crowns and florins every time I met him on the beach, usually right next to where he'd been sitting. Once he felt I had accrued enough of these coins he produced a fantastic new moneybox to store them, one skilfully fashioned from an old artillery shell or from the guts of a piece of heavy machinery. He also made me a beautiful aluminium catapult with a leather pouch and on my tenth birthday gave me a bow and a quiver with six arrows, metal tipped, with duck feather flights. Best of all, next birthday, he made me a wooden go-cart with string steering using four old pram wheels he'd managed to obtained from somewhere.

Fending off my mother's protests, and encouraged by my father, I spent hours and hours careening down the hills near to the house that Owen built over the coming years. It was my greatest ever toy and he made it for me. The man who lost his son made it for his grandson, even though, and this is a quandary, he must have known his daughter wouldn't approve and would stop me from using it if she could. Maybe Owen gave him the nod and told him he would sort matters out.

"How's your go-cart?" he asked me a week after I got it.

"Brilliant, Pop-Pop. Best thing ever!" I ran and hugged him tightly, eyeing my mother as I did. She said nothing. Perhaps it was because of the look on her father's face.

Looking back at all the things I was allowed to have and do – the catapult, the air rifle, the bow and arrow, shooting the .22, the go-cart and the motorbikes which allowed me to go fishing on my own, tackle strapped to me and the bike – I'm absolutely amazed. By today's standards of modern parenting it appears I lived a youth of fantastic risk. Amid the implements of my childhood and teenage years death and dismemberment lurked at every outing. I may have been given a sick note excusing me from every primary school swimming lesson due to my mother's utter conviction I'd end up dead at the bottom of the deep end, but I had a catapult, a bow and arrow, an air rifle, a go-cart and two-wheeled, ground-eating missiles.

The truth is, I was as safe as houses thanks to circumstance and The Pact. All the things I fired, I fired alone and in the safety of the garden of the house that Owen built, except when I was with my grandfather. As I played I soon learnt the art of risk assessment. I learnt not to fire steel ball bearings from a catapult at a brick wall from point blank range. I learnt not to look down the barrel of a loaded air rifle and pull the trigger at the same time. I learnt not to fire an arrow straight up in the air and then look up to see where it went. When I shot the .22 with my grandfather I learnt never to point the gun at him and say, 'Stick'em up!' When I fished with him I learnt how to deal with hooks and take them out of wriggling fish rather than wriggling fingers. I learnt how to cut the heads off eels rather than cut my wrists. I learnt not to fall in the river or lake and, if by chance I had, I wouldn't have drowned because I taught myself to swim, not very elegantly it's true, in the warmth of the Mediterranean when I went on holiday with my parents to Spain. Equally, the house that Owen built resided in a quiet private road and in those days hardly saw a single car in an hour. This situation afforded me and my go-cart a virtual clear run monopoly of its poorly maintained surface. Consequently, I learnt how to steer around big hard objects. I learnt how to stop by digging in my heels so I didn't hit big hard objects and the one time I did do something stupid, the day I thought I caused Graham's death, the day I have never mentioned to a living soul, I survived my narrow scrape thanks to The Pact.

After the go-cart's time I learnt to ride a motorbike. I learnt they were very dangerous and the only safe houses riding a motorbike equated to were ones due for demolition. I learnt it really hurts when you fall off. I learnt not to trust car drivers. I learnt summer rain after a dry period meant the roads were like ice rinks. I learnt that ice makes you fall off. I learnt that the twist of a throttle could zap you into an awful lot of trouble extremely quickly. Yet, incrementally, step by dangerous step, I learnt to become a better rider and a safer one. Thanks to The Pact and my progression I managed to survive motorbike riding and never broke a bone or ended up in hospital or stiff on a mortuary slab. What I didn't learn is how to raid seagull eggs from a nest on a cliff. Both my mother and father were adamant I should never set foot on the East Hill for as long as I lived – until I reached secondary school and played football against our local rivals on the awful pitches that were marked out on the top of the cliffs.

"Don't you *dare* go and get the ball if it goes near the edge!" my mother hissed, issuing yet another warning.

"You listen to your mother," my father said intently.

"Don't worry, I won't," I replied, unused to both of them laying it on thick.

I didn't go and get the ball. I let someone else go and get it. No one fell off the edge.

The world moves on, constantly becoming more risk adverse. As a parent living in the 21st century with its myriad of attendant child-rearing issues, how do I view it? There should never be another Alfred – that's clear. I don't want Jack to have a motorbike – that's hypocrisy tinged with a healthy dollop of realism. Should he have had a catapult, an air rifle, a bow and arrow or a go-cart? Let's just call that a cartoon lifestyle as outdated as The Beano. (I used to read The Beano. I kept a pile of them, one over three feet high in my wardrobe.) Laptops? Smartphones? Console games? Facebook? YouTube? Twitter? My mother would have embraced them all because they encourage a sedentary 'safe' lifestyle. Whether they promote a rounded outlook or are conducive to physical well-being I seriously doubt. One thing is for certain, it's not going back to how it used to be.

Since AD, with both my parents regressing back in time, I too have developed a tendency to go back with them and I find myself pondering on old times more and more. I've barely given the time of day to The Fear and The Pact over the last four decades, but now I question that period in my life, when it was important, far more deeply than I've ever done since. Mostly it's to do with the essence of my upbringing. I'm now convinced the two male leads in my life were in cohorts to overturn my mother's extrovert paranoia. Thanks to their efforts I was allowed to do more adventurous things in my childhood than would now be considered normal. I think the pair of them consciously made the decision to allow me to live my formative years to the full, in a glorious celebration of living, rather than in the repressive fear of death. As my poor mother sank deeper into despair and energy sapping, all-consuming worry, they consciously raised their game to redress the balance. What I'm less sure about is how my grandmother fitted into this? What was her relationship like with her daughter? Mabel had experienced the loss of a son, whereas her daughter was ruining her life as she became depressed at the thought of the possibility of losing one. Regrettably, I'll never know. My parents can't answer because they have forgotten and Olive, my mother's sister, who may well have been able to shed some light on her dead mother's feelings, passed away BD prior to my ruminating on such matters.

When the third episode of The Fear struck, my mother endured a massive spike in terror that in time became a plateau. On the evening in question my mother received a phone call from a family friend saying Harold had had an accident on his fishing boat. I was in the room with her when this took place and immediately picked up on the stress and urgency in her voice.

"Is it bad?" she asked. "Is he badly hurt?"

My eyes blazed into hers asking the obvious.

"Harold," she mouthed back silently to me as she listened intently.

I experienced the horrible, yet very human emotion, of relief it wasn't my father who was hurt combined with, a second later, concern over my uncle's welfare.

"... So you don't know? Is it a hand? ... Olive knows... She's at home now? Not at the hospital? Thank you... We'll go and see her."

I remember my mother's face as vividly now as if it happened ten minutes ago. All semblance of colour drained from her and her hand shook as she replaced the telephone handset, like she had advanced Parkinson's.

"We have to go down to Olive's," she told me, flustered and distressed. "Harold's had an accident on his boat. I *knew* something like this was going to happen. You'll have to come. You can't stay here on your own. Your father won't be home until late. He's gone straight to football training from work."

And with those words my life was altered. With her decision made – one forced upon her by my father's coincidental absence and not wanting to let me out of her sight – she set in place my only first-hand experience of The Fear.

I'll never know for certain how badly my mother thought Harold was hurt as we drove to Olive's house. Her pervading anxiety would surely have convinced her, as she intimated, that the worst was bound to have happened and without doubt it did cross her mind he was dead. Yet, looking back with hindsight, I don't really think she did believe in the worst-case scenario. There were two reasons for this. One was the phone call from the close family friend who evidently pitched the deliberately vague details in a clever enough manner to fool my mother into thinking the accident was serious – but not that serious. He knew the truth and I suspect a combination of reasons – whose mouth such awful tidings should rightfully come from, an understandable reluctance to be the bearer of such news and, to a lesser extent, the protection of my mother – stopped him from telling her. The second reason is the more powerful. Some five or six hours earlier, when I was still at school, my mother and her sister were in the Old Town enjoying a crisp winter's walk along the shingle beach where Harold's boat, and all the others in the fleet, were launched and landed. They saw Harold's boat, the Hannah Dawn, RX53 (Rye, Sussex), anchored about a half-mile off shore and waved to it in a girlish display of affection. This act of waving to Harold, seeing his boat relatively close to shore made the concept of him being dead hours later impossible to comprehend. Unbeknown to them the chances were the accident had already happened as they stood on the shore waving.

My grandfather opened the door to Olive's house.

"How is he?" my mother asked, rushing the words out with the same frenetic pace we had run from the car.

My grandfather looked like a ghost and started to cry. Big gulping tears of despair.

"Olive! Olive! What's happened?" my mother screamed as she pushed me past her father and down the narrow corridor leading into the tiny living room at the back of the house.

I felt like a tumbleweed being blown into that room, my mother's hand the driving wind as she shoved me forcefully forward by the small of my back. By the time I went through the door I was physically and mentally reeling. I remember losing my bearings, feeling dizzy and light-headed as I surveyed the scene before me, the room a whirl of familiar family faces morphing into other family faces. They were all sad faces with the same red eyes, the same gaunt expression, an identity parade of family sorrow interchanging before my eyes.

Olive.

I managed to focus on my auntie and my universe stopped spinning, changing at once to a static singularity. My peripheral sound and vision were suspended. I had tunnel vision and her face was the proverbial, and in this instance, wholly inappropriate light at the end of it. She was slumped motionless in a chair, a wooden marionette with every string severed. She had no energy, no will, seemed drained of essence, a pervading air of listless horror cling-ing to her like a vile shroud. Her words came out in slow motion. The speed and pace from seconds earlier stalled from quick to dead slow – from unknowing agitated panic to the lugubrious, damning slow motion of truth.

"He's dead, Mary. My Harold's dead," she groaned, looking past me at my mother.

I spun my head to see my mother crumple. She reminded me of the vacuum-pumped, crushed-by-atmospheric-pressure oilcan experiment my physics teacher had demonstrated to my class two days earlier. As she imploded the weight of tragedy started to crush me and I began to quake, shiver and cry. I didn't know what to say or what to do. I was a thirteen-year-old boy plunged into an adult world where even the grown-ups didn't know what to say or do.

We stayed for what seemed like forever although it was proba-bly no more than two hours. Throughout that period I couldn't stop thinking, 'This is it. This is Mum's fear. This is what it's all about. One minute you're here and the next you're gone. Taken.

Just like that. Just like a grisly magic trick. This is the fear. This is it, this is The Fear.'

I remember the initial part of that evening extremely well. The part after the bomb went off is more of a blur. All I can recall is my constant mental repetition, 'The Fear. This is The Fear.' It was so real, so palpable I could taste it, feel it invading my body, seeping into me through every orifice and every pore. The only other thing left in my memory bank from that night was the dread I felt of turning into my mother because she was patently right. She was right to be scared, right to be frightened of losing another. It had happened again.

Once we were home, once we prised ourselves away from Olive's house and its aura of death, we had what seemed an interminable wait for my father to return from his football training. (There was no instant mobile access in those days.) During that period I imagined his death on the return journey by every conceivable, and most likely every inconceivable, manner possible. When he did arrive safely it was his turn to experience the trauma of tragic loss. Gripped by the horror of it all the three of us huddled together on the settee, clinging to each other like shipwrecked sailors to a lifebelt.

"All his clean shirts were on a clothes horse drying by the fire," my mother told my father. "Olive had just washed them all," she explained, this small vignette of domestic trivia holding within it a tidal wave of poignancy.

That night I lay terrified on my bed, crying uncontrollably in a state of numb disbelief. That odious night, the one indelibly etched on my memory I somehow did what was needed and devised The Pact to offset The Fear and set in motion my slow release from its chains of worry and deep-seated anxiety.

Even today I shy away from thinking too deeply about Harold's death, how he died and how long it may have taken him to die, because it's too gruesome to contemplate. Anchoring a small trawler a half-mile off shore was a common occurrence, usually to facilitate the cleaning of gear, and it wasn't until Harold's boat failed to show any lights after nightfall that the other fishermen became concerned. Three of them sailed out to his boat and went aboard. They found him lying on his side with his head trapped against the deck winch. The three men cut the trawl to lessen the weight on the winch drum and fed the chains back through the winch in order to free Harold. In the pitch black they towed Harold's boat back to shore where the emergency crews took him from the beach to hospital. It was too late. Harold was already dead, killed by cerebral contusions and haemorrhage as a result of fracture of the skull.

The inquest recorded a verdict of accidental death and could only guess at what happened. The most likely scenario was that as he stood alongside the winch drum, as it hauled in the heavy net laden with its catch, the chain started to foul or over-ride the drum. Harold's finger was severed, indicating that he tried to free the chain, and in the process slipped and fell on to the winch drum and got dragged into it. The remorseless powerful winch drum simply never stopped. The inquest noted chains coming off the winch drum were an occupational hazard and two of Harold's relatives told how they had damaged their fingers in similar incidents. Whatever the fundamental reason, or series of reasons, Harold's death, as with the deaths of Alfred, Graham and Frederick, made the headlines. The Fear got its front-page slot through its sheer bloody-minded audacity.

One spring evening, some months after the accident, I was in the garden of the house that Owen built kicking a football around with him. During a drinks break we started to talk about Harold.

"Do you know what Harold always used to tell me, John?" my father asked as I downed a glass of milk. I wiped my white upper lip with the back of my muddy hand, shaking my head. "He used to confide in me and say he would never make old bones. 'I don't know what it will be, Owen,' he'd tell me, 'but it'll be something to do with my boat.' I wonder what made him say that. I wonder what gut feeling he had."

"You haven't had one, have you?" I asked alarmed.

My father smiled. "No. Not yet, son… You?" he enquired, a glimmer of something going on in his eyes and in his voice.

I knew he was testing me, probing to see if the shock of the accident or my mother's negativity was brainwashing me.

I scrunched the corners of my mouth downwards, shaking my head. "Nah. I'm all right, Dad." I had my pact in place, not that I could tell him, and was confident of my own safety.

A few months later I felt a spasm of guilt when The Pact delivered me safely, but took yet another in dreadful circumstances. The latest victim was my father's sixteen-year-old nephew.

The aftermath of Harold's death, the oldest recipient of The Fear by some margin, must have been terrible for Olive and her two daughters, Hannah and Dawn. From my viewpoint I saw my mother disintegrate further into a mire of depression, only for my father and grandfather to somehow drag themselves off rock-bottom and resume what appeared to be something approaching full functionality. Even Olive and her daughters managed, with a Herculean will, to move on against the most difficult and challenging of backdrops. In conclusion, it all returns to my mother. My poor mother and her wall of angst towering above her, plunging her very soul into constant shadow.

I poke my head into the living room because no one has answered my call. Both my parents are sitting on the settee watching the TV. My father has an upside down newspaper on his lap and is sitting wearing only a Marks and Spencer white vest on his top half. His bare arms have rodent ulcers on them and his vest has several marks where the sores on his torso have seeped through the white cotton material. This is the legacy of a lifetime of obsessive sunbathing. He looks even more unkempt due to the fact he is sporting a large white bushy beard and has had a late night. A month ago he stopped shaving and he won't let any of the care ladies near him to do anything about it. My mother, on the other hand, looks more presentable dressed in a blouse, knitted cardigan and a pair of elasticated waist trousers. She is cuddling her handbag. All her gold rings are on two fingers of her left hand.

"Hello!" I say perkily. "Prawns and cream cakes anyone?"

"Hello, John. That'd be lovely," answers my father.

My mother ignores me, looks at my father and then, facing me, rolls her eyes. "I shouldn't like him."

My mother's odd speech patterns are becoming more the norm of late. "What do you mean you shouldn't like him? I ask, knowing full well what she means.

"I just get the feeling," she replies.

"You have been married to him for sixty-two years," I gently point out.

This distancing herself from her husband, as if he is an unwelcome guest in her house, one with who she has only recently become acquainted, is a recent development and another worry thread. Unfortunately, my father reciprocated this thread on the telephone only a few days ago when he told me my mother was his sister. That's three new worry threads what with his night-time escapade, four if you include last week's shopping run revelation of my mother not accepting me as her son.

"No I haven't," she answers as if the concept of marriage is appalling.

"You have," I insist, thinking of a way of rewinding her brain to a point where I can set it back on the right track. "What was the name of the person you married?"

"Ben Williams," she states authoritatively.

I allow myself a chuckle. This was the name of my mother's only boyfriend before she started dating my father. His name was always a major taboo BD. In those times I would see my father's hackles rise, his lips thin and his face turn stony if he ever heard those two words emanate from her mouth. If caught out my mother would pull a face at me saying, 'That's narked your father!' Today he doesn't bat an eyelid.

"He was your boyfriend before you met Owen," I remind her. "Owen was the man you married. What's your name now?"

"Mary Mabel."

"Mary Mabel... what?" I say, nudging her memory.

"Roberts."

"Ah! No, that was your maiden name. What was your name after you got married? Can you remember? Mary Mabel..."

"Can't think of it," my mother admits.

"D... Den..." I encourage.

"Dennett," my mother finally decides.

"That's right. You married Owen Dennett."

She hooks a thumb at my father and coughs, rolling her eyes again and pulling a face of disgust.

I smile sadly at her brazen dismissal of the man I know she once loved so dearly.

"That's him," I tell her nodding my head energetically. "You've been married to him for sixty-two years."

"Get out of it! How can I have been sixty-two when I'm not sixty-two yet?" she asks.

I catch her drift although it hasn't come out right. "You're eighty-one," I tell her.

"Eighty-one!" she scoffs. "Don't be so silly."

"When were you born?"

"Don't know... Don't ask."

"Nineteen-thirty," I tell her. "You were born in nineteen-thirty."

"That's right," she says as the date clicks. "Nineteen-thirty."

"Do you know what year it is now?"

"No," she admits.

"Two thousand and twelve. So, that makes you eighty-one. Eighty-two this year."

"Owen's eighty-two."

"Eighty-three," I remind her. "He's two years older than you. You were two years younger when you got married, weren't you?"

"Yes, that's right," she agrees.

Pleased I seem to have reset her brain if only for small period, another rule of dementia, I change tack. "I see you've got all your rings on."

"Yes." She holds up her hand for my benefit. "I thought I better have them on in case some fucker pinches them," and she bursts out laughing as if she's cracked the funniest joke in the world.

I can't help but explode into laughter with her, wondering as I do if I'm seeing a glimpse of what she was like when she was young. When she was pre-The Fear. "Who's going to pinch them?" I ask, wiping away a tear of mirth.

"I don't know. They're worth a lot of money."

"They are," I agree. "But there's only you and Owen in the house."

"I see more than that. I see what goes on." Her voice has changed. It's accusatory, harsh.

"Do you?"

"Yes I do."

"What goes on, then?" I ask, genuinely mystified.

"Not interested really," she answers dismissively. "I just want to see my little family. Owen…"

"Yes, that's him sitting next to you." I let this, hopefully, sink in. "Who else is in your family?"

"My sister, Olive."

"She's already passed away, Mum."

"Nobody told me," she mutters indignantly. "Owen's in hospital."

She's off on a non-existent tangent. "No he isn't, Mum," I

contradict. "He's sitting next to you," I tell her.

"But he has been in hospital, hasn't he?"

"No. He has been over the road. Last night he was over the road. We got a phone call from Susan saying he'd been knocking on her door at midnight. She brought him back indoors while you were asleep."

"It wasn't me," my father chips in, suddenly taking part in the conversation.

"It was, Dad. She phoned me up and told me. She said she'd got you with her and she was going to take you back home. It was midnight. We were all asleep. You can't go knocking on another person's door in the middle of the night."

My father doesn't answer. My mother, who has been looking at him as I explained his nocturnal activities, waves a gold encrusted finger at his visage.

"Look at all this," she says, pointing to his beard, the disapproval evident in her voice.

"I know. He's looking more like Father Christmas every day," I admit, feeling upset at my father's dishevelled appearance.

"He's not so nice looking with all that on."

"I could get the worst off with some trimmers, but Dad's got to want to let me. He doesn't want anyone to shave him and I can't force him. No one can force him."

"Have you found out what's happened to my motorbike keys?" my father asks to my utmost surprise. Luckily, my mother drags all three of us out of the moment.

"He'd look much better with all this off." My mother points to the beard again, forgetting she's already mentioned it. "And he needs a haircut. Then he'll look like his old self," she adds, now seeming to accept Owen is her husband.

"Yes, my *old* self," my father repeats in a moment of rare insightful humour. "We've just been in that pub over in Sidley," he continues.

"When was that, Dad?" I ask, fascinated at yet another old memory masquerading as a contemporary one.

"Just a minute ago, before we came up here. Didn't we, Mary?"

"Yes," my mother agrees, falling into his fantasy at a stroke.

The notion she doesn't know who he is has suddenly gone. It could come back in a minute or in a few days. The best way I can explain these on/off new worry threads is to compare them to dodgy electrical wiring where the connection comes and goes, connects and disconnects, only to irreversibly breakdown with inevitable insidious atrophy. Given more time a worry thread can snap and disappear, or, like today with my father asking about the motorbike keys, magically self-heal and reappear from nowhere.

"It's just down the road from the football ground," my father states.

I know the ground he means. It belonged to the local senior football team who used to play there in the Sussex County League. I've watched my father play on that pitch, he's watched me play on it and I've watched Jack play on it for his league representative U11s team before he signed for his professional club. (U11s on a full-sized pitch with full-sized goals!)

"When you feel better you can take me for a ride on your bike," my mother suggests, popping a new old memory into the fantasy.

"I don't think I'd have the strength to hold the bloody thing up," my father admits. Once again I'm surprised at his self-realisation.

"I don't think you have been over to Sidley," I say, getting sucked into my usual role of chief reality enforcer. "It's an old memory making you think you've been there today."

"We have, John," my father states earnestly. "If I never move from this spot."

"You've been in here all the time," I assure him. "Except for last night when you went over the road at night and started banging on the door of Susan's house at number fifty-nine."

"Number fifty-nine?" Owen enquires.

"Yes. And this is fifty-four. Your house."

"This isn't ours, John."

Now we're back on very familiar ground. I have my arguments off pat here. This is my parental M2.

"Whose is it, then? How come all your stuff is here? All your clothes, your pictures, your knick-knacks, photos of me and Clare and the kids," I ask him.

"They brought all our stuff in I expect," my father answers.

"Why would 'they', whoever they are, bring all your stuff in if it wasn't your house?" I question, trying to argue logically with him as I have so many times in an attempt to unpick his version of reality. "If it isn't your house whose house is it? Whose house do you think it is?"

"We've had to get in through the football ground to get in here because of the people upstairs," he tells me.

"No. You would have come up the path to get in here." I try my old trick of pointing out a surrounding feature. "If you look out the window you can see Mr Smith's car."

"I wondered what it was doing out there."

This is a well-trodden response. My father can't absorb the visual evidence destroying his fantasy location, so, he twists it to an outlandish coincidence to keep what he sees in synch with what is in his head.

"It's there because you're in your house. No other reason. This is the house you built. You remember building it, don't you? All that hard work?"

"Yes."

"Well, you didn't give it away to anyone, so it's still yours."

"Look at those," my mother says, pointing at the sores on my father's arms. She hasn't been following the last bit of our conversation.

"I know. It's skin damage caused by too much sunbathing," I tell her.

"That isn't the sun," my father argues.

"Yes it is, Dad. It's all sun damage."

"No, it's not sun damage. It's where I hit myself with a hammer," he insists.

I don't want to argue with him anymore so I change the subject. "I'll just go and put the shopping away and I'll bring your cream cakes and prawns afterwards. Cup of tea to go with them?" They both nod.

"Lovely, John," answers my father.

"Yes please, dear," is all I get from my mother.

It's an innocuous phrase she uses and it's evidence of a connection still broken. My mother doesn't know who I am anymore. She knows I'm someone close, but she doesn't know I'm her only son. I hope her brain will reconnect and she'll know who I am again even if it's only for a short while.

I carry the bags I brought into the living room back into the kitchen, put them on the worktop, return to the porch and repeat the exercise with the remaining shopping. I close the front door, which shuts with a satisfying clunk on the Yale lock.

"How long did that take?" I ask myself under my breath.

As I start to empty the bags I hear the odd snippet of conversation coming from the TV. It's a pleasing sound. The carer who makes the first morning call to rouse them from bed and get their breakfast is the person responsible for switching it on. At one stage, before they were involved, this mundane task fell to me. The hours I spent trying to talk my father through the process of turning on the TV and then choosing a channel with the Sky remote were among the most frustrating I've ever suffered.

At one point, at the very zenith of TTOP (TV turning on problems) and with a hint of black humour, I considered keeping a timesheet so I could 'book' my hours out to the appropriate dementia worry thread. In the end I didn't because the resulting timesheet, where I could actually see in black and white the time I was wasting, would have been crippling. Thankfully, TTOP is a thread I can now virtually discount unless I get a carer who hasn't visited my parents before. Then I get a phone call from them asking me how to put the TV on.

As I take the shopping out of the plastic carrier bags, on autopilot, I meditate on my predicament. The combination of seeing both my parents start to mentally unravel, finding the newspaper cutting and photographs of me in my youth with my first girlfriend and my first bike, remembering the gun days and fishing trips with my grandfather, seeing Jack blossom into manhood plus the inordinate amount of time I'm spending looking after my parents have all contributed to my hackneyed mid-life navel gazing. On the debit side of the sheet I see no motorbike to ride, no time for fishing, feeling exhausted, with less energy for work and sex, plus lots of horrible things I don't like having to do having to be done. On the credit side are the children, Clare's wonderful selfless support and watching Jack play football at professional club level. My problem, as I see it, is that nothing I do is purely for myself. Seeing how my parents' lives are going to end, the awfulness of their decay, makes the now precious – and I'm frittering it away, pushing with all my might, trying to slow down the forces of dementia.

Sometimes at night, when I'm lying awake in bed feeling melodramatic and a bit sorry for myself, I sense the walls edging in and squeezing me into an ever-decreasing space. One where I don't want to be. I feel trapped. The easy opt out solution is to put my parents in a home, visit twice a week, then once a week, then once a fortnight, then once a month and then, eventually, not bother to visit at all. I can't go down this route; they're my parents after all and although I don't enjoy doing what I do for them I would feel guilty if I didn't. I'm obligated by love and respect and have already decided that the best place for them to be is at home. That notion cannot change until it is apparent they are in too much danger to continue living in the house that Owen built. Of course, there is a chance they might not realise where they are living, but irrespective of how muddled they are there's always a possibility they might. If they did realise I had put them in a home I know they would hate it and would wonder why I did such a thing to them. So, how can I take the chance? It's not as if I could move them back after taking the ultimate step. No, I'd lose them, I'd lose my self-respect and I'd probably lose the house in order to pay for the nursing home fees.

Taking things on further, the concept of an extra-marital affair where I bed the lovely number six in my game is both attractive and repulsive at the same time because I still love Clare and our children. Could I ever really work myself into a situation where I would be comfortable with having my cake and eating it? And if I did take the plunge, what time and energy would I have left after dealing with everything else to negotiate a double life? I suppose I could forget the sex angle and buy a motorbike, but when would I ever have time to ride it? Go fishing? Start playing golf? Ditto. Work less to give me more time? It's an appealing idea, one quashed because I want more money. It seems whichever way I turn I can't get out.

Once at this advanced stage of night-time machine-washing my mental thoughts I tell myself I really need to get to sleep. I have work the following day and as a self-employed carpenter if I don't work I don't get paid. With this in mind, my focus shifts and before I can stop it I start worrying about how much pitch time Jack will get on Sunday and how well he'll train on Tuesday and Thursday. His dream of ultimately becoming a professional footballer is my dream. I dreamt it from the moment I knew Clare was pregnant with a boy. Jack started to dream it some six years later when kicking a ball seemed to come so naturally. We've been synchronised ever since. He wants it. I want it. Who wants it the most? Sometimes I wonder if it's me and that's not necessarily a healthy situation.

My first task in the wider objective of putting the shopping away is to open the metal cabinet on the wall and take out the keys to unlock the double wall cupboard in the kitchen and the freezer. The metal cabinet is a glorified keysafe of larger dimensions. It has a four-digit entry code and holds the cupboard and freezer keys plus any communications from the carers like, 'Need more bleach', 'Run out of salt' and 'Haven't seen the cat for two days. Is it all right?' plus any remaining important post they've managed to get hold of before my parents spirit it away. (Incredibly, all medical correspondence is still directed to my parents' house.) The key to the freezer opens a simple hasp and staple lock I fitted with self-tapping screws through the thin metal sheeting of the side panel and door edge. The other key fits a larger hasp and staple lock fitted with wood screws across the front of the two doors belonging to the largest wall cupboard.

Inside the locked wall cupboard sits medication, all neatly packed away in blister packs, the carers' notes – they went AWOL when left in the kitchen – and food I would describe as treats; the crisps, the cakes, the chocolate bars, chocolate biscuits and the pre-neutrino Werther's Originals of this world. These have to be locked away; if they weren't they would all be devoured in a day or two. When they weren't under lock and key my parents would pig out on them like sugar-fixated schoolchildren. The freezer has to be locked because my mother kept getting readymade meals out of it, presumably with a barely remembered inclination to cook them – a task she is no longer capable of doing. Once I popped in to find them eating a meal oblivious to the fact it was still partially frozen. It was the final straw and I knew Clare and I needed outside help.

This period shortly before the carers became involved, when Clare and I stood alone fending off my parents increasing dementia, was the most difficult. Having carers in has taken a great weight off our shoulders, even if the initial decision to get strangers into the house that Owen built was a difficult one. During the period when we stood alone all sorts of problems surfaced, ones which eventually increased to the point that accepting outside care was imperative. Aside from the cooking of food and personal care, the constant need to reset the house was also a huge issue.

One of the resetting problems sprung from the isolation and unplugging of electrical appliances and systems. This happened so frequently I went round the entire house and Sellotaped all the power sockets to the on position. I also Sellotaped the microwave's power output knob to maximum after my mother complained it wasn't working properly. (I bought them a new, less complicated non-digital one with a rudimentary timer knob after the old microwave's plate went missing. It makes a satisfyingly nostalgic 'ting' at the end of its countdown.)

"It's brand new," I argued. "It can't have broken already."

"Well it has. The food's cold. It doesn't heat it up," my mother told me.

"Not as cold as when you were eating frozen fish and chips."

"Thank you," she said and walked out of the kitchen.

Ignoring her jibe I looked at the microwave and spotted the power output knob was set on defrost.

"Look at this bloody toaster. It's useless," my father moaned, pushing down a couple of slices of bread only to see them pop straight up. "And the kettle's had it."

"It needs to be switched on at the wall, Dad." I informed him, turning the socket on. "See. The toast stays down now. That's why I Sellotaped it on, but you and Mum keep picking it off. Leave the sockets switched on. That's why you had no central heating the other day, you'd turned the boiler off."

"I didn't touch them," he replied, denying all knowledge of the action.

"Okay. Let's have a look at the kettle," I said, wondering what audacious reason could have stopped it working.

On inspection I discovered the socket was on, it was plugged in, the 13A fuse was fitted – and not blown – there was water in it, yet there was still no sign of bubbling from the element.

"Mum hasn't been putting soup in it again, has she?" I asked.

My mother, who had just shuffled back into the kitchen, laughed as if it was the last thing in the world she would ever do.

"Where's my handbag? Have you seen my handbag?" she demanded before she shuffled off and left in search of it.

Once I took a closer look inside the kettle I saw distorted, partially melted plastic innards adjacent to the flat sheet element. Someone had turned the kettle on all right, but must have neglected to put any water in it. For some reason the element burnt out rather than the fuse.

The digital phone also became problematic. The tool so perfectly designed to have both my parents wander around the house with it in their hands, mostly still connected to me on the other end, had to go. Frequently, they both forgot they were talking to me at all and would abandon the phone leaving me to scream myself hoarse in a futile attempt to re-engage them. Worst of all they never hung up so my landline seemed to be in a state of permanent connection to theirs. A connection, when they had phoned me, I was unable to terminate.

"Any luck?" I said to Clare who held our digital phone to her ear.

"No. I can still hear them and the TV. They're watching EastEnders!"

"Don't knock it. At least it's on."

The upshot of all this activity, when coupled with a complete disregard for putting the phone back on its charging base, was dead batteries equating to a dead phone. At a time when they always answered the phone I often rushed round in a panic to check up on them when they failed to pick up, only to discover the digital phone was dead. With steam coming out my ears I made an on-the-spot decision after the sixth wasted journey and binned it. It was time for me to introduce a piece of retro telecommunication equipment into their house. It came in the form of a hard-wired BT Big Button 100, a lump of white plastic so archaic and anachronistic I half expected to encounter an operator asking what number I required on the few times I used it.

This new purchase solved the problem of dead phone batteries and stopped my parents being able to wander off with a phone in their hand. It also stopped the constant phoning to some extent due to the BT Big Button 100 being situated in the less frequented kitchen. Prior to this, during the zenith of my parents' phone activity, the record for them ringing me during a 24-hour period was a bewildering and teeth grinding twenty-three times. Now I wasn't obsessive compulsive about counting the calls, but when constantly phoned, often only minutes after the previous call has ended, day after day after day, it does tend to get under your skin. The subject matter of these phone calls was usually predictable and often inspired by one of my parents simply wanting to talk to me having already forgotten the four/nine/twelve/twenty-two earlier attempts. Other times they wanted to speak to me about the very thing they had just spoken to me about. Once stuck in this rut, one so deep they couldn't climb out, I often, in an attempt to preserve my sanity and break the continuity, didn't bother answering. Inevitably, when I did answer, one of the conversations would leave me connected to them for a time ranging from a few minutes to hours because they forget to hang up – the pair of them apparently impervious to the siren-like noise heralding their mistake. On seven occasions, yes I counted them, I drove to their house to hang up for them.

On the subject of multitudinous phone calls, at least, the worst is over. The number of calls has abated since the carers started visiting three times a day. Whether this is entirely due to their presence or to my parents' decreasing mental abilities I'm not sure. What I am sure of is how pleased I am to not have to field so many calls

97

and knowing my parents have a regular eye kept on them. Tempering the relief is my increasing awareness of how the sands of dementia shift. I fear my father's night-time escapade, the pair of them not recognising each other and my mother not knowing who I am are the next set of dunes I will need to scramble over.

Another thing is certain; the ordeal of unplugged household appliances has waned considerably thanks to the carers. They can constantly reset the house and its appliances and try to do likewise for my parents. The issues of their safety and the state of the house are also much improved. Nearly all the phone calls from my parents house now come from the care company, far less numerous, far less frustrating, yet always another problem or issue I have to deal with.

Very rarely of late I will get an oddly fascinating phone call from my father – it's always him – where he has a real bee in his bonnet over an issue needing immediate resolution. The last one of these calls happened only two days before the shopping run I am now completing. He phoned me to tell me he hadn't got a crash helmet.

"What do you mean you haven't got a crash helmet?" I asked.

"Well, exactly what I say. I haven't got a crash helmet to ride back with," my father answered. "I need to get back to Mum."

"When you say, 'Mum', do you mean your mum, Joyce?" I asked.

(This may seem an odd question to ask, but this conversational misunderstanding is a very common one I have with my parents. If I use the word 'mum' within a conversation involving my children where I might ask, 'Do you know where Mum is?' they instinctively know I don't mean their grandmother, but do mean their mother who is my wife. In this terminology, where titles are used rather than names, our brains pick up on the intended meaning rather than the literal meaning relating to the person who is speaking. AD both my parents have lost this ability to distinguish between the two interpretations and I'm never quite sure to who they are referring when they use titles.)

"Oh, no," my father replied. "I meant, Mary. Your mum."

"Right," I said, surprised he'd used the word 'mum' in the correct way. "She's in the house with you," I explained.

"No," he countered. "That's my sister."

"No, that's Mary." I told him, thinking another new worry thread had emerged. "Your sister Kathy's dead."

"Pardon."

"Your sister Kathy's dead, Dad."

"No she's not. She's here talking to me now," my father told me.

"No, that's, Mary. That's your wife, Mary," I insisted.

The phone went silent for ten seconds or so. In the background I heard it getting put down and someone else pick it up. My mother came on and after a few words of greeting I talked to her about the subject of who she was and who she wasn't and how she needed to remind my father of her name.

"I'm Mary Dennett," I heard her say away from the phone to my father, to my great relief. "Not Kathy... What a to do!" she said directly into the phone.

"I know," I answered. "He's getting a bit muddled up over who you are."

The phone went silent with more swapping of ownership taking place. Eventually, my father started speaking. "Hello, John."

"Hi, Dad... Do you see now that the woman who I just spoke to is Mary? Do you remember Kathy dying around a year ago?"

"Did she?" my father asked.

"Yeah, I'm afraid so. I did tell you, but you must have forgotten. She suffered a massive stroke over a year ago. Her son, Derek, was the one who phoned to tell me. He did invite you both to the funeral, only I decided you weren't well enough to go," I explained. "Anyway, the woman who's sitting next to you is definitely Mary," I pointed out.

"Blimey."

"I know, Dad. Don't worry about it, you're getting a bit confused, that's all."

"But I've got to get back to Mary," my father told me.

"That *is* Mary," I answered stridently. "You've got to stay indoors with her. Now do you understand what I'm saying to you? That woman is Mary. She's your wife. You've been married to her for sixty-two years and you have to stay with her in the house you're at now."

"Well…" my father paused for five or so seconds. "I don't know what to say now."

"I promise you I'm telling you the truth. It is Mary. She told you herself, didn't she?"

"Yes," my father admitted.

"Good. So the main thing to remember is you're in the right place and you don't need to go anywhere and you definitely don't need a crash helmet. Okay? It's bitterly cold out…"

"I know it's cold," he interjected. "But I need to get back home tonight."

"You *are* home, Dad," I reiterated, the familiar feeling of banging my head against a brick wall rising up in me. "Where you are now is your house. It's the one you built. You mustn't try and go anywhere because if you do it'll create a big problem and all I will do is go out, try and find you, and when I do I'll bring you back to exactly the same place you are now. So, you stay put and I'll be up in a day or two with the shopping and I'll bring you some prawns and cream cakes for Mum."

"Okay."

"Good. You do understand?

"Yes."

"I'll see you soon. Bye."

"Bye."

I allowed myself a self-congratulatory pat on the back.

Catastrophe avoided. As ever, the lingering thought was; for how much longer?

The biggest obstacle left unresolved, despite having the carers in three times a day, is the one of personal care. At this juncture in time my mother will let the carers undress her, strip wash her or pop her in the bath and put her in clean clothes. She might make a fuss about it, deny needing to have a wash, or say she will have one later, but with gentle cajoling and a bit of banter she'll eventually be compliant. My father, on the other hand, won't. He won't let the carers undress him, wash him, shave him, cut his hair, cut his nails or even change his clothes. His ability to dress himself is failing, so much so that recently he has stopped changing for bed and now sleeps in the clothes he wears during the day.

"We can't force personal care upon our clients," the manager of the care company told me. "It's considered a form of abuse to do so."

I agreed with her despite thinking the concept of wanting to make someone's personal predicament better, by washing and putting them in clean clothes, equated to some form of abuse was oxy-moronic. When I had time to mull this over I realised I was wrong. It's not as if you can overpower someone and drag their clothes off, force them into a shower or bath, hold them in or under the water and scrub them, especially if the person is old and frail. The only way is to try and convince them through the art of persuasion.

When it first became clear the pair of them were starting to forget to wash as regularly as they should, well before any carers were involved, Clare and I made the decision to ensure they both had a bath once a week – whether they needed it or not, as the old joke goes. If it was a necessary decision to take on their ablutionary needs then it was also a very difficult one. It was a very strange feeling for me and for Clare, in differing ways, to help undress my parents, see them naked, help wash them and then help get them dressed.

Clare was far better than I was at enticing them into a mood of cooperation and her constant presence and support helped alleviate my initial feelings of unease. Between us we could get them both bathed or showered, in clean clothes, have the dirty ones in the washing machine – having taken out any stray apple pies and blocks of butter – within an hour and a half. My father had an en suite shower room added within the confines of the original main bedroom some fifteen years ago. This chance upgrade helped us no end and permitted us the luxury of simultaneous bathing. Despite this, it was still a drain on our energies. I always felt mightily relieved the ordeal was over for another week when the pair of them were done and dusted and in clean clothes.

My father's sun damaged skin was an additional issue. The sight of his sores and their incessant weeping wasn't pleasant to behold. The first time I saw him naked I was appalled at how bad his skin had become and at how old he looked. This might sound a ridiculous thing to say about a man in his eighties, but up until the end of BD he had been remarkably fit. My father had been a good footballer and a very fit one, playing at a semi-professional level well into his late thirties. This, combined with his physical vocation, kept him in fine fettle throughout his working life. Even when past the age of retirement his natural energy and many interests kept him fit and active. Seeing him naked, his skin in such poor condition and his cognition failing, really caught me out. Obviously, I knew he was old and had dementia, but eyeing him in such a vulnerable state hammered the point home. It was as if his age had sneaked up on me and gone 'Boo!' behind my back, startling me into turning round and seeing the true reality of it.

It was a similar case of deterioration with my mother. Although never interested in sport and constantly in a state of angst, one putting her in varying degrees of depression, she had been an avid cleaner of the house that Owen built. One she forever mopped, vacuumed, scoured, scrubbed and sanitized with manic gusto in an apparent never-ending cycle mimicking the procedure for the painting of the Forth Bridge. I'm guessing the fever she devoted to cleaning the house was either OCD or a way of trying to give her life some small semblance of positive motivation. Perhaps she rationalised, for once, that houses never died or got taken away from you because of an injection, a fall, a slip or an error. With her dementia gaining a foothold the cleaning soon stopped and I'm sure the removal of this element from her life helped contribute to her physical demise.

Seeing my mother naked reminded me of a little bird – a totally different breed from the Thai checkout lady – one pitifully frail and shrunken, her sagging empty breasts a vision I desperately tried to avoid. Unsuccessfully, as it happened, because it was impossible not to notice when helping her in and out of the bath by her armpits.

Over time, as with doing the shopping, my initial repulsion to washing my parents was unceremoniously quashed by a practical need to get on and get it done. Clare and I held the fort until we could no longer cope with the mountain of other daily chores needing to be done. As my parents began to sink deeper they stopped washing, stopped changing their clothes, stopped washing their clothes, stopped being able to prepare their food, even when bought for them and stopped being able to look after the house. It was evident we needed outside help, we simply couldn't cope.

It was hard to turn my parents over to strangers, but it was a necessity – for them and for Clare and myself.

The shopping is correctly stored and the right items are locked away. I take two fresh cream horns, a bowl of coldwater prawns swimming in vinegar and two cups of tea into the living room. Both are enthusiastically received.

"How did Jack get on at football today?" my father asks as he tucks in.

"He didn't play today, it's a Wednesday. There's training tomorrow evening then an away game on Sunday morning."

"Are you still running his team?"

I smile. "No. That was a fair few years ago when he was little. He's signed for a professional club now. Been there for nearly five years."

"Has he?" my father exclaims. "That's good, isn't it?"

I nod. "Yeah, it is good. We're into the last season of his current two-year deal at the moment. It's early September so there's a fair bit of time left, but it will soon fly by. He only really has until the end of February to impress before it's crunch time. That's when the club will decide whether Jack's efforts merit the reward of a two-year apprenticeship. If they do, he'll get to train everyday and go to college under an FA education scheme until he's eighteen. After that, if he's good enough, he'll get offered a pro contract, probably to play in the U21 Development Squad."

My father smiles as if he's taken it all in. I tell him the same little statement every time he asks how Jack's got on at football. It's actually become an MM (mini monologue) and I employ it when other people ask about Jack's football.

For me, one of the most upsetting aspects about my father's dementia is his inability to follow the football career of his only grandson. Football was a massive part of my father's life. BD he used to watch Jack play every single match, come rain or shine, just as he had with me when I was a boy. At Jack's first match, when aged six, he scored a hat-trick for his team and in his bedroom is a trophy to commemorate it. On the plinth of the cheap plastic trophy, below the club badge and gold figure dribbling a football, are the words, 'Jack Dennett Congratulations on scoring a hat-trick in your first game Nan & Pop-Pop'.

As Jack got older and it became obvious to everyone watching he was a talented little player, my father lapped it up. Well-known in Hastings for his long service at the town's senior semi-professional club, many people in the local football community still recognised my father as the energetic midfield player from the sixties. The surname of Dennett on a team sheet resonated and the name that sprang to mind was Owen – and not, John, I hasten to add! When I started playing for the local County League side in the late seventies, as soon as I opened my mouth and said I was John Dennett I was invariably asked if I was Owen's son. On confirmation the person involved usually went on to relate a football anecdote involving my father. One where he scored the winner with the last kick of the game, or how he dictated midfield play with his tireless box-to-box energy and passing skills, or how, very occasionally, he blew a fuse and got sent off for a reckless tackle. Everyone in local football of a certain age either knew of, or had heard of, my father.

"He could have been a pro if he'd had the breaks. No one ever scouted down our neck of the woods in those days."

Christ! How many times did I have that thrown at me?

"What a good player your dad was. If you get as good as him, son, you'll have done well."

That was another favourite. And that was the crux of the problem. I didn't.

I played County League, still a decent standard, but not as good as my father. I was a good passer of the ball and had reasonable technique, but always lacked his energy and dynamism. I could never get fit enough to cover the ground like he had and ended my football 'career' as a holding midfielder, my job to cover defensively and get the ball off the back four and link it to the more attacking players. I never played any higher than County League standard and by the time I was in my mid-twenties I dropped down a notch to play well within my comfort zone in the East Sussex League, much to my father's annoyance.

I always felt, especially when I stood on the touchline as manager of Jack's team as yet another old player talked to my father, that Jack's football heritage was perceived as coming from his grandfather rather than from his father. No one remembered me like they did my father. Maybe it was for a good reason. After all, as it's been pointed out, Jack doesn't look like me, which is a good job as far as he's concerned and it's also been inferred he doesn't play like me. That's also a good job as far as he's concerned because there wasn't a hope in hell I would ever become a professional player, scouts down our neck of the woods or not.

Things changed when Jack was scouted at an U11 league representative game. Gullivers was the venue for the evening match – the ground my father convinced himself was a portal to his house. That night both my father and I watched with pride, intermingled with our own personal memories, as a third generation of Dennett males made their ground debut. I played on the pitch many times during my career and my father played there a handful of times, when he was very young, before he made the step up out of County League football to the semi-professional level of the Southern League. I'm not sure who was the most proud when Jack banged in the game's only two goals. What I do know is when the scout in the bulky black coat, the one with the professional club badge sewn on it, needed to find out about the goal scorer he spoke to me. Not my father.

The scout came from outside the local area, was only in his thirties, and didn't know my father from Adam. When I took Jack to the first training session of his six-week trial period none of the other fathers had heard of my father. Rather surprisingly, only slightly more than half of the fathers involved had ever played the game. I was, for once, the sole person responsible for my son's football talent and basked in the reflected glory of his skill and aspirations – like all the others, ex-players and non-players alike.

Invigorated by my new status I dropped news of Jack's trial within minutes of starting up a conversation at work or socially. I couldn't stop myself, despite being aware of my braggadocio. I loved him being involved with a professional club and the kudos that went with it. In response I saw a mixture of genuine enthusiasm and interest to the shifting unease of jealousy, in particular from some of the fathers of boys in Jack's youth team. (These dads I refer to as LFDs. The definition of a lesser football dad being the father whose son still plays at a local level. FDs, football dads, have a son playing at professional club level and are notoriously insufferable snobs.)

The culmination of Jack's six-week trial period ended with two consecutive substitute appearances, a week apart – I was more nervous than he was – where anyone could see he was better than at least half of the existing side. The coaching staff saw it as well. After enduring an agonising wait after the match, Jack was offered the chance to sign schoolboy forms for the rest of the season. I was ecstatic, more excited than Jack, and my head swirled with giddy images of him going through the youth ranks, playing in the lower echelons of the Football League, doing well and then being snapped up by a big Premier League club. And I was his father! Duly, I relinquished my now worthless managerial position at Jack's youth team to become a fully-fledged FD.

As it transpired, what I really became was a chauffeur.

The situation now remains the same as it was then; my importance to the club is the human equivalent to that of my parents' cat – i.e. I'm a non-person. No one on the coaching staff is interested in me in any aspect whatsoever other than my ability to deliver my son, on time, fed and watered, with all his kit, to training and to match day venues. That is the 'take it or leave it' deal – everyone takes it – and how it is for all of us. As parents we are spoken to with respect and perfect politeness, but at the end of the day, to use a football cliché, each of us is simply a means of transportation for our sons. No more and no less. The club are interested in our sons, not in us.

Once Jack was signed I soon got closer to some of the other FDs

I'd met during his initial six-week trial period and struck up new friendships. Believe me, there was plenty of time for us to get to know each other. The two evening training sessions lasted an hour and a half and we had to arrive forty-five minutes early. There was a similar time delay before leaving for home as we all waited for our offspring to emerge – unhurried – from the changing rooms afterwards. Training therefore accounted for three hours in their company twice a week. In addition to this there were the match days which lasted a tad longer. There was nothing to do but sit and chat before and after training and matches, and to stand and chat while watching our protégés train and play matches. For the last two seasons the second evening session has become even longer. The boys now have to do an extra hour weights session before the actual football training starts.

What we continue to do to pass the time, just as we did in the early days, is talk football. We talk about other people talking about football on TV and we talk about footballers who play football for a living. Most of all, we talk about our boys, our boys' team and the coaches associated with our boys. We talk about the coaches who might be associated with our boys, should they progress to the next year group, and we talk about the coaches who will ultimately make the big decision at the end of the U16 season when the apprenticeships are handed out. Over time we have inevitably divided into various like-minded cliques, although there is much fluidity here because many FDs and their sons are no longer with us. Cliques constantly evolve. Within our clique we talk about the other FDs who aren't in our clique – I don't doubt the other cliques talk about us – and when we occasionally pair up in one-to-one conversations we talk about the other FDs who are in our clique.

It's an odd little world to inhabit, one where I quickly became aware of the subtle nuances of angst and paranoia prevalent amongst all the FDs; ones running underneath the veneer of banter, bullshit and bravado. If any life experience has opened up a fleeting glimpse into my mother's world of The Fear, then Jack playing for a professional football club is it. I'm not worried about The Fear, thanks to The Pact. What I and all the other FDs are worried about is the dreaded R word. The R word that causes such fluidity amongst us and causes FDs and their sons to disappear.

The dreaded R word stands for 'released'. Released means professional club game over and a cataclysmically humiliating fall back into local football akin to an angel crash landing from heaven into a penalty box-sized cowpat – one witnessed by a crowd of baying intoxicated LFDs OD'ing on Schadenfreude. (Let's be fair, who could blame them.) As every season came to an end and the R word became ever more tangible and loomed large on the fast approaching horizon, the FDs whose sons were playing badly and who looked likely for the chop became either resigned or bitter. Those who were resigned simply shrugged their shoulders and readied themselves to pick up the pieces of a shattered dream. The bitter ones blamed the club and the coaches or a combination of obscure football detail, none of which was their son's fault. At this time of the season the boys who were most likely to suffer the R word became the topic of conversation superseding all others. The FD grapevine sprung into ADHD mode and the most insignificant of slights or approval, whether real or imagined, whether conveyed by words or by the body language of the coaches, became the subject of hysterical speculation, scrutiny, interpretation, and often, wild misinterpretation.

Picking the boys most likely to fall from grace, and to an equal extent the trialists to be signed, became the most important yard-stick by which an FD was judged. Within cliques forthright views abounded, tempered only by the taboo subject that no FD ever admitted to another FD, even when pushed, that the other's son was, in their opinion, going to suffer the R word. I soon became quite well respected as I picked those likely to get signed and those likely to be released with great accuracy. Over the years my opinion became sought, as if I were an oracle, on the R word situation. I spoke my mind and said exactly what I thought – in confidence, of course – unless it was to an FD whose son I considered was struggling. In this instance I prevaricated and lied, saying I thought they 'should be all right'. When it came to pass they weren't all right and were given the R word, my lukewarm support became a euphemism for the chop.

"You *knew*, didn't you?" one FD asked, once the released FD and son had gone.

I raised my eyebrows, smiled and said nothing, knowing my stock was ever upwards.

The only call I struggle with now is Jack's because high emotion shades my judgement. I knew, as has been proved so far, he was good enough to merit being kept on through the younger age groups, but as the crunch time approaches, because I want it so much for him, and for me, I have begun to doubt my ability to call his chances. This U16 season, his last with the club should he not receive an apprenticeship, is a massive test for all the boys in his team. It is, to put a biblical label on it, Judgement Day. The chosen players will inherit the kingdom prepared for them from the foundation of the club and the stiffs will crash and burn into the everlasting fire that is local football.

With no justification I am also worried his football career may be taken away from him, either through injury or a strategically important coach not rating him. When I postulate on the reasons why a coach might not rate Jack, they veer from a pragmatically perceived lack of ability to vague notions of partisan bias and unfathomable idiosyncrasy. I too find myself trying to analyse Jack's performance and get sucked into attempting to read hidden meaning into the most inconsequential of events – a trait I have mocked in others in the past.

Picking over the bones of conversations the coaches have with Jack is one way of trying to read the runes.

"You know when Ron stopped that passing routine when you had to drop off the cones...? What did he say to you?" I asked Jack on the hour-long journey home last week.

"Not much," Jack answered. He was barely awake and one hundred percent not interested.

"He must have said something!"

Jack pulled a face. "Oh, about receiving the ball on my back foot."

"That's all?"

"Yes!" he snapped.

"What did you think of the new trialist? Apparently, he plays wide midfield like you."

"He's all right."

"If you play against him in the match at the end of training you want to make life as hard as you can for him."

"I *know*. You've told me that, like, a hundred times before!"

Looking back over the years the main categories to edge up an FD's angst are, in no particular order; how much pitch time our sons receive (there's a big squad with a constant rotation of rolling substitutes during a game), what position our sons get to play (boys want to be recognised as good enough to play in their favoured positions), who they play with in terms of strength within the squad, who they train with when split into groups in terms of strength within the squad, the coaches attitude to our sons, how well our sons are playing (realistic appraisal only – not easy) and how well everyone else's son is playing in comparison. Lurking on the periphery of this list of concerns are the hordes of trialists who come in at an astonishing rate of at least one or two every six weeks, how good they are and what position they play in. If the FDs are nervy because of this constant pressure then so are the boys – and the older they get the worse it becomes. With increasing maturity comes increasing realisation of what is going on and what is at stake.

Aged eleven the boys just went out and played off the cuff. By the U16s, demands and expectations of a style of play, technique, fitness, positional play and tactical awareness are the considerations swirling around in their heads. The boys aren't kicking a ball around for fun anymore; it's more vocational and they're learning the trade. Now they're older, every match, every training session, every touch of the ball, every movement off it is performed in a goldfish bowl with many sets of eyes watching – and I'm not talking about the FDs. The coaches' eyes are always looking, appraising, criticising and judging – a bollocking delivered across the pitch, as if by loudhailer, only a heavy touch or a poor decision away.

Sometimes, especially if Jack was on the end of a bollocking, I used to wonder how any of them would improve or feel relaxed enough to do themselves justice when under such close scrutiny. How could a young player develop flair and technical excellence when under the constant pressure of being criticised for making a mistake? I also wondered if the whole process was some kind of ancient indigenous football ritual. An 'English Way' where the apparent madness of stern negativity was seen as the only method for sorting out the weak from the strong, from those who could play under pressure and those who folded and couldn't.

At this level of football the result and the team are secondary. This might sound counter-intuitive, but it's true. The whole reason for running a professional youth setup is to produce one or two players a year capable of moving into the reserve/development squad and eventually the first team. My football M1 for explaining this process is a fishing analogy. The club, any club, throws a big net into the sea and catches lots of fish. From these fish it picks out the best ones and puts them into a glass tank and feeds them. As they grow they are constantly monitored for progress and if it's felt the progress is slowing, or not as quick as it should be, they take out the failures and throw them back in the sea. Of course, the fishing never stops and new fish of all different sizes and ages are constantly put in the tank. As quickly as they're put in they're taken out because the tank can only hold so many. The one saviour to this being that once a fish is in the tank a new one has to be superior, not just equivalent, to replace it. When the fish are sixteen there is a massive cull and typically sixty-odd percent of that age group are thrown back. At eighteen it's an even higher percentage that get thrown back. You've got to be one hell of a fish to make it all the way to the end and get a professional contract.

In short, it's a brutal, ultra-competitive business. All the time you offer some prospects the club will keep you on. The minute they think you haven't got any you're gone with the R word. I soon realised my boasting about Jack having a trial was risible. Even signing schoolboy forms at eleven was nothing of any real consequence. From the squad of sixteen when Jack signed there are only five boys left today who are 'originals'. All the rest are back in the sea with their dreams shattered. If getting a pro contract, just one, even a solitary year-long one, is at the top of a ten rung ladder, then signing schoolboy forms equates to putting one hand on the ladder with both feet anchored on the ground. Get an apprenticeship and you're standing with one foot firmly on rung number one, with the other on rung number two, looking up in readiness to climb the next eight. That's the percentage deal. Taking it further, only a little over ten percent of football apprentices make a long-term living as a player.

It's so demanding for both of us. Taking him to football is like having another job and I already have another, another job looking after my parents. Not that all the hours of travelling and waiting around deters me one bit. I will support him to the hilt. If there's one thing I could give my son it would be a football apprenticeship. I know how hard he has tried, how desperately he wants it even if he does try to hide it underneath his couldn't-care-less-façade. I hope he wants it as much as me and I want it for him more than anything else in the world.

Although every self-help book states not to worry over elements of your life you cannot control and to only focus on what you can, this is so obviously complete and utter rubbish it's not worth the paper/digital file it's written on. None of the FDs have any control over their sons' chances of making the grade – although some delude themselves a little sycophancy goes a long way – other than their chauffeur duties and to keep their mouths firmly buttoned while standing behind the rope four yards from the touchline. (It was the one aspect I did find refreshing after putting up with bellowing idiots haranguing players/referees/linesmen/ other parents when I was the manager of Jack's youth team.) Yet, despite this complete lack of input, all the FDs now fret and get their jockstraps in a twist thanks to the excruciating importance of this football season.

There is, however, one FD who by rights shouldn't fret at all. This is because there is one boy in Jack's team who is, without doubt, a NO. A NO stands for 'nailed on', meaning definitely going to get an apprenticeship. The boy is Greg, our best-by-some-distance central midfielder, and his dad, Andy, is one of our clique. He's the FD who has no reason to fret – but try telling him that. I envy them both and wish Jack was as certain to get an apprentice-ship. The trouble is I can no longer read the tea leaves and have become no more insightful than the punter placing a red bet on a roulette wheel. As befitting my lowly status I can have no say in the matter. I can't buy an apprenticeship for Jack and I'm not allowed to give it to him because I am only the chauffeur and not the head of youth development. I dread the day he ever receives the R word with an understanding and a nod to my mother's dread of The Fear. I cannot state it any more powerfully than that.

My parents are still happily tucking into their respective treats. My mother has fresh cream all around her mouth and my father is holding his bowl up to his mouth, drinking the excess vinegar after devouring the prawns. I grimace. I hate coldwater prawns even more than crab meat, trout, jellied eels, shrimps, cockles and whelks. Without speaking I leave them to it and exit the living room, going out into the hallway and up the handmade staircase showcasing my father's joinery skills. Once on the first floor landing I take the metal hockey-shaped handle resting against the main bedroom doorway's architrave and use it to release the hinged trapdoor in the ceiling directly above. As the trapdoor opens downwards the aluminium loft ladder becomes accessible and I pull it down with the short end of the handle, extending and then engaging the bottom two sections until the foot of the ladder sits firmly on the carpeted floor. I climb up the ladder and into the roof, my arm groping for a light switch I soon locate and turn on. A fluorescent tube flickers into life revealing an area of the house that Owen built I haven't entered for decades.

As you might expect from a carpenter the whole area of the roof is immaculately boarded out. I acknowledge my father's thoroughness. My short journey to the main fifty-gallon cold water tank and its overflowing ball valve will not be a perilous totter along ceiling joists. Nor will it be an even more dangerous traipse over assorted lengths of unfixed floorboards, where a hidden trap might be ready to catch an errant foot and send it plunging through the plaster-boarded ceiling as once happened when I was a young apprentice.

I climb into the roof and stand in it, casting a professional eye over its timber construction, surveying the cuts to the rafters as they meet the ridge board and the hips. Impressed, I move over to rest a hand on one of the purlins and, as a test, try to dislodge it. There is no movement. Inquisitively, I squat down and run my eye down the length of it, like I did when looking down the barrel of my BSA air rifle, to see if the timber has deflected or warped. It's as straight as a die. My sight moves and I look upwards and focus on the still sound roofing felt visible between the rafters. On top are the battens which hold the roof tiles. I shuffle over to the centre of

115

the roof, directly underneath the ridge board and stand up straight, perusing my father's handiwork through a panoramic three hundred and sixty degree twirl and am suddenly moved to tears. The emotion of seeing all his hard work from a time of full mental cognition, combined with the future prospect of having to sell it to pay for his care, is too much for me. Tears trickle down my face and I feel no desire to wipe them away. They fall on to the chipboard flooring in delicate splashes.

The moment passes and, getting a grip on myself, I rub the mini puddles away with a twist of the sole of my shoe, like I was extinguishing cigarette butts. Wiping my cheeks with fingertips I make my way over to the puffy black bulk of the water tank's lagging set. Underneath the plastic coated fibreglass lagging is a fairly new round plastic tank. As I prise off the tight fitting lid I spot the original defunct rusted galvanised one parked up against the chimney-breast. With the lid off I can see the ball valve is letting by and water is slowly dripping through the defective valve, despite the water level being up to the overflow pipe. I push the ball valve's orange plastic float right down under the surface two or three times, letting water in at full bore to try and clear any muck that may have lodged between the rubber seating and the plastic insert. Then I bend the brass arm downwards, increasing its angle off straight into a slow curve dog-leg and let everything settle. Pleasingly, if a little surprisingly, the ball valve holds and lets no further water into the tank.

"I'd make a good plumber... cry!" I joke to myself as I refit the lid.

On my way back from plumbing duties I take in the other junk in the roof. There isn't a great deal and the roof is pretty clear apart from a smattering of cardboard boxes and six or so decrepit holiday cases. I immediately put this impressive clutter-free environment down to the super massive black hole's insatiable ability to suck in and store worthless crap.

116

Despite the meagre contents of the roof, curiosity compels me to have a quick poke around in the boxes. The first two are full of worthless tat, but in another I see the back of a portrait frame. I pull this box out into the brightest area of the roof, take out the framed photo and look at the face staring back at me. The photo is of my father's mother, Joyce, aged around sixty and was taken at some formal evening occasion. She's standing alongside a man in a suit who has his arm around her waist – the man isn't Owen's father, it's his stepfather. This photo, consigned to an old box in the roof space, speaks volumes of the relationship my parents and I have with Owen's side of the family.

While I am deeply familiar and very close to my mother's side of the family – they played a huge part in my childhood – this isn't the case with my father's relatives. When I was young, visits to see Joyce were few and far between, a handful at most, and my father was always reticent to talk about his childhood, his upbringing or anything whatsoever to do with his formative years. On the few times I did visit her, invariably with my father, never my mother, the atmosphere seemed reserved, cool and distant. There certainly wasn't any of the reciprocated love I felt for what I regarded as my true grandparents. In fact, it was always Nanny and Pop-Pop who babysat me. Joyce did not perform this most basic of grandparent duties on a single occasion, whether due to her not being invited or not wanting to I don't know. I cannot recall her ever being invited or visiting the house that Owen built once in all the time I lived there, let alone being left in her charge for several hours.

To compound the family vacuum I never met my grandfather on my father's side. Apparently, he was a civil servant, but by the time I was born he was long gone having left Joyce for another woman much earlier. Joyce brought up Owen and his elder sister, Kathy, on her own in a small terraced house in Ore. This is a district situated to the north east of the Old Town, just far enough away to make my father's courting of my mother more difficult than it should have been. I know virtually nothing of Joyce's background, her history, her relationship with my father or that of my father to his sister and her children. I can only recall ever meeting Kathy, her husband and her three boys once when I was about ten when they came and visited, seemingly out of the blue, one Boxing Day. Even now I have little contact with them.

If the closeness to my mother's side of the family seemed natural to me, so the lack of contact with my father's side seemed equally so. It was always thus and no one ever questioned the status quo. I'm sure there was no animosity between my father and his sister because on the odd occasion he did mention her BD he always spoke fondly of her. I'm not so sure this was the case with his mother. Perhaps it was when she remarried, when my father was a teenager, and a stepfather appeared on the scene things turned sour. Whatever the reasons it was how it was and everything I've discovered since taking over my parents' lives points to a hugely lopsided family bond. I've found all my mother's parents' paraphernalia – photos, documentation and life details – yet on my father's side I haven't been able to trace so much as a single death certificate, postcard, newspaper cutting or greetings card. The only thing I've found regarding my father's relatives is in my hand now, plucked from a grubby box abandoned in the roof space.

The single significant bearing my father's side of the family has had on my upbringing is, nevertheless, still an important one. Their sole suffering of The Fear is an event that hit me with a jolt commensurate to my unwitting first-hand experience of Harold's death, albeit in a totally different manner. The fourth episode of The Fear occurred only a mind-numbing eight months after Harold's tragedy on his boat. It seemed as if there was barely time for a solitary beat from a broken heart before The Fear rushed freakishly back into action. This era, undoubtedly, was The Fear's Blitzkrieg, its time of shock and awe – no decade-long break, no quarter-century plus sabbatical, just one sickening blow swiftly followed by another.

If I was in the trenches, right at the front line, for the third episode of The Fear, then I was a remote disengaged general drinking claret in staff HQ for the fourth. It was my father who received the phone call from his sister Kathy's husband telling him of an accident concerning their youngest son, Graham. Graham was sixteen at the time of the accident – I was barely fourteen – and his family lived on a farm near to Hythe, a fellow Cinque Port town to the east of Hastings. Kathy married into a farming family a few years after my father married and gave birth to twin boys several years into the marriage. An extended gap before Graham was born meant Kathy's third child had been alive and kicking for two years before my mother and father eventually managed to produce me. All the boys worked on the farm from an early age and as they grew into young men they were allowed to use some of the agricultural machinery. By sixteen, Graham routinely drove the tractor across the undulating fields of the farm with great proficiency. When he took it out one late summer evening no one could have envisaged the tragic consequences.

As with Harold, no one knows the exact split second where the decision Graham made caused a fork in his life path leading to his death. All that is known is that for some reason Graham stopped the tractor on a downward slope, pulled on the handbrake and went to do something. It might have been to move an object, an animal, or it might have been as mundane as to make a call of nature, no one can be sure. What is certain is as he moved in front of the tractor it rolled forwards and caught him with its bulk and crushed him to death. The inquest stated that if he had pulled on the handbrake by one more notch it would have held the tractor securely on the slope it was parked.

Theories on whether he applied the brake in haste or with an element of complacency, thus making the fatal error taking his young life, along with other questions, must have crucified his parents and brothers. How many times had he ridden it safely, parked it on a slope, jumped off it, got back on and drove away safely? Why, on this one flawed occasion, did he have to be in front of it? Why not to the side? Why not to the rear? Why not far enough in front to have noticed and got out of the way? Why hadn't he put the handbrake on fully? Why not by one notch more?

Once again, as a parent, I wonder how anyone can get over such a thing. How do you recover from your eighteen-year-old son dying from an inoculation designed to protect? How do you cope with your eleven-year-old son falling off a cliff? How do you deal with your sixteen-year-old son being crushed by a tractor? As a husband, I wonder how you cope with losing your partner in their mid-forties to the remorseless power of a tightening chain, the very thing that dragged home a family's livelihood. None of these things happened to me or to my mother, yet of all the people, including those more directly involved, she was the one who coped least well. The Fear swallowed her whole, condemning her to a life of hollow apprehension and a timorous forelock tugging deference to the outcome she dreaded happening – until she contracted dementia.

The shock wave of hearing of Graham's calamity from the side of the family with which we had so little contact is still palpable. After the phone call my father rushed over to see his sister in what must have been a futile attempt to console her. I knew, even though he was an adult, he wouldn't know what to do or say just as I hadn't known what to do or say as a thirteen-year-old boy. My mother and I didn't accompany him that day. We stayed at home alone, mimicking our wait for my father's return from football training the night Harold died. This time I don't think she spoke a single word to me and there was definitely no physical contact between us.

I can't remember saying anything to her. She'd already

imploded under the onslaught of The Fear to a state of speechlessness and, for my part, I had no mental capacity left to engage her due to my entire thought process laying elsewhere. Whereas the pair of us were thrust on to centre stage at Olive's house, here we both sat in the wings, a surreal ambience of one-step-removed horror making life appear before us as if through a filtering lens. The feeling of being so uninvolved, yet so involved, to be so unconnected, yet so desperately linked to the most hateful of human catastrophes was outlandish.

What was equally bizarre, if not more so, were the things going on in my head.

Standing in the roof space of the house that Owen built I can remember it all with alarming clarity. Earlier in the day of Graham's death I took my go-cart from my father's garage and pulled it by its rope to the very top of the road where we lived. From this glorious apex – you could see the sea from its peak – I sat in the go-cart, wrapped the steering rope in a single loop around both hands, and let it roll. As gravity did her stuff the go-cart picked up speed and started to accelerate. By three-quarters of the way down the hill I was approaching something like thirty miles an hour and was fast into my braking zone.

My so-called braking routines on the go-cart were usually achieved by running out of momentum via flat ground or an ascent. This way I gained maximum bang for my buck. (Bang = length of run. Buck = effort required to pull go-cart to top of hill.) Occasionally, a more proactive technique was required and the only method available was to push both my heels into the tarmac and allow friction to do the rest. The default method for my run on that day was a combination of both; to brake heavily with my heels for fifty or so yards and then turn left into the uphill cul-de-sac at the bottom of the run shortly before the set of crossroads. On the day in question, for the first time ever, I did neither.

Something, and I know what it was, allowed me to be overcome with exhilaration. Something in my brain failed, my logic and self-preservation circuits were by-passed by a desire for more thrills, and instead of braking and turning left I ran the gauntlet of shooting directly over the set of crossroads and down the hill on the other side. I never saw the car travelling at right angles to me until it was far too late. I'm sure I heard it first. The heavy screech of tyre as the astonished driver flung the steering wheel hard to his right to avoid the small wooden missile uncloaking itself directly in front of his bumper. As the car turned broadside and skidded, its rear quarters flashed past my left shoulder and I felt the draught of killer sheet metal waft warm summer air into my blond hair. How the car missed me I'll never know, but miss me it did. I never stopped, never looked back and rode my go-cart down to the bottom of the next hill, where, having run out of momentum, I got out. Dazed and shaken, on legs of jelly, with my heart beating faster than I had ever felt before, I pulled the go-cart home, put it in the garage and went indoors never to tell my mother or another living soul what happened.

With news of Graham's passing arriving within hours of my near death escape I became cocooned in my own mind. The Pact I made some eight months earlier had paid dividends in spades. Despite my own abject stupidity and utter contempt for my own life I was spared and another was taken instead. The whole glorious symmetry of perfect opposites, like an exquisitely balanced double planet where one protected orb teamed with life while the exposed world underwent global extinction, took over my brain. In my mind's eye I saw The Fear trying to strike me down. In response, The Pact rushed to my side, its impregnable shield deflecting its foe's snarling malice elsewhere. Running it over in my mind I felt strangely elated, powerful, blessed, immortal almost – but most of all, profoundly guilty.

For hours afterwards I asked myself constantly, over and over and over again, what would have happened if I had performed my usual default braking manoeuvre. Would Graham still be alive? Was it my fault for leaving the door ajar and giving The Fear an opportunity to barge in with its salivating, teeth-strewn maw of destruction intent on gobbling up another victim? Or was my sudden change of mind, my reckless compulsion for speed, a judgement swayed by The Fear itself? Had The Fear got inside my head and tried to kill me, only to be thwarted, literally, at the very death by The Pact, thus forcing it to look elsewhere.

Within a day I conveniently decided it was all The Fear's doing. I was the blameless party and, with one thought process, allowed myself the luxury of becoming guilt free. As time passed and The Fear receded I thought less and less about it. From the fourth episode of The Fear a year passed, ten years passed, twenty, thirty and nearly forty without any further incident. During those years I met Clare, married her, our children were born – both of them healthy – and my beautiful family lived happily, free from any true catastrophe. The Fear was consigned to the back burner. It took up residence hovering outside my mental peripheral vision and rarely affecting me on a day-to-day basis. It's where it's been for a long time – until my parents' demise.

My parents' dementia has altered the situation. Dealing with them has made the past come alive, as if its tendrils have reached out and touched me from a bygone age. I feel closer to The Fear now than I have done since I was a teenager. I also feel closer to The Pact. It's an odd, slightly disturbing feeling, this notion of my family's dark history reaching out and pawing at me from a time long past. It started getting in my head with the discovery of the old newspaper cutting – a double-edged sword of Damocles in terms of The Pact's status if ever there was one – and has continued as my parents have regressed and I've been sucked back with them. My memories of those dark times have been digitally remastered and made accessible through my involvement with my parents and the documents I found in their house. Prior to this, they sat fading and bleaching out on reels of incompatible unwatchable Super 8 cine film.

And it's not only The Fear and The Pact being rejuvenated. The photo I found of myself with my first teenage girlfriend and the one astride my first bike have also got under my skin. These two photos, along with the stress of dealing with my parents and seeing Jack on the cusp of adulthood, have helped form an uncertainty of desire and focus within me – one I have no idea how to deal with other than vague notions of buying a motorbike and having imaginary sex with women derived from youthful games of fancy.

I put the photo of Joyce back in the box and notice, lying in the bottom, a tiny A5-sized, landscape orientated 'Photo Snaps' album. I pick it up and start to leaf through the spiral bound pages adorned with monochrome photos. Needless to say it's an album I've never seen before. Above all the photos are pencil notes in my mother's hand. They are so faint it's hard for me to make them out, but I can decipher, 'Taken at the pier dance hall' above the first photo of my teenage parents sitting together, hand resting upon hand. I pass several more individual shots of my parents before coming to photos of the Old Town brewery where my mother once worked – a source of many entertaining bedtime tales. Excited, I move on, entranced by this rare, never-seen-before-footage of my parents' past. Five pages in I hit a photo that makes me a horror novel character cliché as the hairs on my neck stand up and a shiver runs down my spine. I stare in absolute disbelief. The photo is of a grave filled with flowers, its scrolled headstone fully visible and unhidden by flower or foliage. Above it, written in pencil are the words, 'Alfred's grave'. With shaking fingers I hold the photo up to the light. Tantalisingly, the carved words upon the stone are far too small for me to read. With reluctance I close the album and, keeping it tight in my grip, turn off the fluorescent light and descend the loft ladder. I need to get home to reading glasses, my magnifying glass and keen young eyes. The past has got to me again.

PART II

HERE AND NOW

"Can you read what it says?" I ask Chloe, who is looking at the photo of Alfred's grave through a large magnifying glass.

I haven't had a chance to look myself. As soon as I got home and told the family I'd found an old photo of my uncle's grave and needed to read what was written on the headstone, she begged me to let her have first go at trying. 'Wow! This is so cool!' she exclaimed, taking the album from me. 'It's like being in National Treasure!'

"Yes, I can," she answers. "There's a name at the top, 'Frederick Roberts', then underneath, it's harder to make out because the writing's smaller... I think it reads, 'died 18th April 1936 aged'... oh, that's hard to see... 'sixteen' maybe 'eighteen years'. It's got 'R.I.P.' written underneath that."

I wobble a bit at this and several thoughts rush into my brain at once. Frederick isn't Alfred and I wonder, for a split second, if my mother has made a fundamental mistake with her pencil headline. Almost instantaneously, barging my first thought out of the way, I recall my father's enigmatic statement, 'They're in the same grave.'

"Is there anything else on the stone?"

"Yeah. Underneath the 'R.I.P.' and on a new line there's an 'also', then underneath that, 'Cyril Charles Roberts'." Chloe looks up at me quizzically. "I thought you said it was Alfred's grave?"

"It is. Well I think it is," I say, flummoxed. "Alfred and Frederick's. Pop-Pop *was* right about it being a shared grave. He remembered that part correctly after all. He did know about Frederick's death. How bizarre! What's the date when Cyril Charles died?"

Chloe zooms the magnifying glass in and out. "I can't really read that bit very well. I can't make out the date. The month is definitely May. The year might be... I don't know... 1948? I'm not sure. It seems to go out of focus as you go down the headstone. There's something else written along the bottom, but that's much too small for me to read."

"Let me have a look." I take the album and magnifying glass from my daughter and study the photo. I can only make out the names and can't get anywhere with the dates. "You have a look, Jack," I say, handing him both items.

"Like he's going to see any better than me!" Chloe sneers.

"Shut up!" Jack retorts. He gives the photo a keen perusal through the magnifying glass. "No. I can't read the date for certain, Dad."

"Told you!"

"That's enough, thank you, Chloe," I tell her.

"So where's Alfred?" Clare queries, repeating the question in my head. "And who is Cyril Charles Roberts?"

We're all standing in a tight circle orbiting the photo album underneath the living room's brightest ceiling light. "I don't know where Alfred is, but Cyril Roberts was my grandfather. *My* Pop-Pop," I answer as an aside to Chloe and Jack. "And he was Frederick's elder brother. Charles was the name of Cyril and Frederick's father. It was all in the newspaper cutting I showed you. It can't be Cyril's grave as well, as in Cyril my grandfather, because he was alive at that time. Without knowing his age or the exact date of death of Cyril Charles Roberts I can't know who it is for sure. My mum always told me Alfred died in 1946 not 1948."

"I'm confused," Clare admits. "So, Frederick's the one who died from the inoculation and Alfred's the one who fell off the cliff? They were your great uncle and uncle respectively. Cyril was your grandfather and Charles was your great grandfather," she states in clarification of what is becoming a more complicated scenario by the second.

"Fell off a cliff?" Jack asks, butting in. "What the hell was he doing up a cliff?"

"Looking for seagull eggs," I tell him.

"That's a bit weird, isn't it?" Jack enquires, screwing up his face.

"Totally weird," Chloe agrees.

I can't begin to try and explain to my two 21st Century children how an eleven-year-old might be motivated enough to risk his life in the pursuit of collecting seagull eggs. Any explanation would need to encompass the harsh lifestyles suffered directly after WWII and a plethora of other outdated social conventions. Accordingly, I don't.

"What's weird is why my mum wrote, 'Alfred's grave' above a photo where his name isn't on the gravestone," I remark instead.

"Google it! Look it up on the internet," Chloe demands.

This is her standard response to virtually any problem.

"Yes, I suppose I could," I answer distractedly, still grappling with the conundrum in my mind.

"Search one of those genealogy sites," Clare agrees. "Try and find Alfred and Cyril Charles' death certificates." Her nose wrinkles. "I think if you know the date of death it would help resolve who exactly it is. I'm pretty sure someone who was researching their family tree told me all the older records are lumped together in three month batches," Clare adds as an afterthought.

I nod enthusiastically, but have thought of another line of investigation. "I guess I could find out from the grave itself about Cyril Charles. I've got two names and the date of one of the deaths. All I need to do is go to the cemetery's office, get them to go through their records and show me where to find the grave. Provided that's where this grave is, of course."

Chloe starts to jump up and down on the spot clapping her hands together. "Dad! *Promise* me the first time you go I can come with you. It's so cool! We'll be like detectives! Heir Hunters!"

I laugh. "Okay. I promise."

"Freak!" Jack states, turning away from his sister and looking at his phone, his attention span sated.

"When are you going to take Chloe to the cemetery?" Clare asks as she reappears in the living room. "She was full of it when I told her to put her light out."

I'm sitting on the settee alongside a reading lamp looking at the rest of the photos in the album through my magnifying glass. It'll soon be my bedtime let alone my daughter's. I'm feeling drained.

"As soon as possible. I'm really fascinated to find out." I shrug with resignation. "I can't go tomorrow. It's football training and I've got to leave work early to pick Jack up, so maybe on Friday. I could collect Chloe from school and drive along to the cemetery from there." Clare sits down on the settee and snuggles up to me. "Look at my mum and dad there," I say, showing her the picture of them at the pier dance hall. "Don't they look young?"

"Your mum was very pretty. How old do you think she is there?"

"Seventeen. That's why they look young. They *are*!" I flick over a couple of pages. "Look at this one of the brewery staff posing in the cobblestone yard. Even the horse and cart are in the picture."

"God! It looks archaic! That's your mum, isn't it?" Clare asks, pointing to a young girl with her hair covered by some form of headscarf.

I nod. "Here's one of all the girls pretending to drink the beer. You can see the wooden crates stacked up behind them."

Clare takes the album from my hands and flicks through it to the end. The last picture is one of my mother and father sitting on a shingle beach. His skin is a significantly darker shade of grey than my mother's.

"The sun worshipper," she remarks, passing back the photo album.

I look at the photo and I'm reminded of the one I found of me and Annika. All I need is to go on Facebook and find one of Jack with a girl on the beach and I've got the set.

"He used to lie with his arms up above his head so he got tanned under his armpits," I tell Clare.

She laughs, but it soon fades away. "It's sad how their lives are ending. All their memories and everything that made them 'them' fading away to nothing."

"It is horrible," I concur. "The only saving grace is that they're oblivious to it."

I'm convinced that last statement is true. At no time have my parents shown any form of self-awareness regarding their mental deterioration.

Clare kisses me on the cheek. "They'd be proud of everything you're doing for them if they could understand, despite what they say to you sometimes."

"You too. You've helped me no end. I don't think I could have coped without you," I tell her earnestly.

"Your family's so tragic it needs all the help it can get."

"I know," I admit.

Clare turns to me and looks me in the eyes, a question forming in hers. "Didn't it ever bother you when you were growing up? All those horrible deaths and your mum's constant worrying and permanent anxiety. Didn't it ever affect you? Don't you remember what she was like when I was pregnant? Especially with Jack." I signal my agreement, thinking of The Fear's apparent preference for snuffing out male lives. "She started to make *me* feel like it in the end," Clare expands. "She made me think he would be born with some monstrous defect or be stillborn. It gave me the creeps if I'm honest. I used to be glad to get away from her sometimes. Your dad was okay, he was always positive," she adds.

"She was all right when she baby-sat," I say a little defensively, surprised at Clare's candid confession. Clare and I were always at one concerning my mother and her doom-laden traits, but she has

129

never admitted that my mother 'gave her the creeps'. Now she no longer exists as she was I'm guessing Clare feels comfortable enough to tell me the truth.

"In a way she was, but when the kids used to play outside in their garden she was like a cat on a hot tin roof. Don't do this and don't do that! Be careful of this and be careful of that! No wonder they didn't want to go unless your dad was there." Clare pauses. "You're not like her. You're more like your dad, thank God. Which brings me back to my original question."

"What?"

"Didn't you ever get frightened and wonder whether you were next? Didn't you ever feel afraid for yourself or for our children, come to that? How come it never rubbed off on you? It must have bothered you, surely?" Clare asks.

I'm stunned. In over twenty years of marriage Clare has never asked me directly about The Fear and The Pact – not that she would ever describe it using those names. I have never used those names in her company, in anyone's company.

"Not really," I lie. "My mum could worry enough for all of us. It saved me the bother of having to do it," I add flippantly.

Underneath the façade I'm presenting to Clare it's a very different story. The growing feeling of the past flexing its muscles and reaching out to touch me has become even more tangible with this conversation. The past has entered the sanctity of my domestic world, which is far worse than it reaching the inside of my head. I feel uncomfortable being evasive and telling lies to her, keeping her in the dark about The Pact protecting her, our children and me. Slipping off at a tangent, I briefly wonder if this is what it would be like if I bedded the lovely number six from my game earlier in the day. An affair must be an arduous secret to keep, one worse than what I'm doing now, what with two sources capable of leaking the unpalatable truth. Am I the sort of man who could keep two major secrets from my wife? I doubt it.

"But you're not worried about it *now*, are you?" Clare persists.

"Why do you say that?" I ask, mindful of the inflection in her voice.

"I don't know. You seem a bit preoccupied at the moment, not your normal self."

"Do you think so?" My question is pitched with slow non-commitment. I'm trying to give myself time to cobble together some kind of explanation. "Maybe seeing my mum and dad go downhill is catching up with me," I admit. "It eats up a lot of time. What with work and taking Jack to football I don't have much time for myself. In fact, I don't really do anything for myself."

I hope I'm being clever – I'd rather hint at a mid-life blip than tell her about The Fear and The Pact. Evidently, I'm not so smart and Clare ignores my misdirection.

"You know, John, we've been married for over twenty years and I've never really thought too much about your family's history. Not until we started to look after your mum and dad and you found the newspaper cutting. When I read it, it all seemed to fall into place despite it being something your mum and dad never mentioned. I tried putting myself in her shoes and I could see why your mum was the way she was. The poor woman. What a horrid way to make a mother's instinctive protective love turn sour and ruin her. How terrible to have its power twisted from something so wonderful into something so nasty and debilitating." Clare looks at me as if she's measuring me up in some indefinable way. "And yet you've never really spoken about the reasons for it in all our years together."

My wife's eloquence is as touching as it is true. Throughout our marriage I've skimmed over my family's history, telling her the sketchiest of details and glossing over my mother's mental state with cursory explanations and glib patter. My mother was so ill for so long it's as if her condition was almost nullified by familiarity – something I can't look back on with pride. This mindset was also

131

reflected in my relationship with The Fear and The Pact at the time. The pair of them hovered outside my mental peripheral vision and rarely affected me on a day-to-day basis. Sitting on my settee with my recently discovered never-seen-before-footage of my parents this is no longer the case.

"If by that you mean that when I met you at Sandra's twenty-fifth birthday party I didn't say, 'Hello, my name's John Alfred Dennett. I'm called Alfred after my dead uncle who fell off the East Hill cliffs when he was just eleven,' as a chat up line then, guilty as charged."

Clare laughs, but also raises her eyebrows. "You know what I mean!" she gently chastises.

I blow air out through my mouth and realise levity won't work. "It's a horrible thing to say, but I guess it never really seemed important enough at the time. I was only a kid when I managed to move on, unlike Mum. And Mum was always Mum. Always. How much help she got to try and change things I'm not sure. I guess in the final reckoning only she could save herself."

"I think it might be different today. She'd get better professional help today."

"I'm sure you're right. It was different in those times."

"But weren't you worried when Jack was born?" Clare asks, going back to what really interests her. "What with your mum going into hyper-anxiety mode?"

"No," I answer, feeling rattled. "No more than any other father would agonise over the safe birth of his first child." And then I let it slip. "Deep down I always knew he'd be fine. And Chloe. And you. Us."

"But now you're not so sure?"

"No! It's not that at all," I bluster, lying again. "It's all this stuff!" I say, waggling the photo album. "The newspaper cutting. Photos of them. Photos of me when I was young. Memories of the past. They're losing their memories and I seem to be sucking them up and bringing them all back to the present. I seem to spend half my life telling them things they used to tell me. I'm constantly trying to reset their brains with *their* memories. I'm always telling them that things they think they've just done happened forty, fifty and sixty years ago. It's all the past. Everything's to do with the past." I look Clare in the eyes and my voice quietens. "And the past isn't good. I don't want to go back to being thirteen again. I don't want to go back to the night I witnessed the horror of Harold's death." I pause and rub my cheek. "I haven't told you this, but last week my mum asked me where her Johnny was. When I told her that I was her Johnny, do you know what she said back?" Clare shakes her head, her face a picture of sadness. "'Don't be ridiculous. He's thirteen years old.'"

Clare reaches across and kisses me on the cheek.

"Come on. Let's go to bed."

This night I lie concerned on my bed, fretting uncontrollably in a state of disbelief. I'm a man who's fifty plus; one who definitely doesn't want to go back to being thirteen again.

"Have a good one!" are my words to Jack as he gets out of my van.

He's distracted by seeing one of his team-mates walking to the changing rooms. "Yeah, sure," he mumbles. "Hey! George! All right?" he shouts to the big centre back who smiles and waits for him.

Jack hurriedly shuts the passenger door. He goes to the back of the van, opens its rear door, takes out his kit, slams the door shut and strides back past the passenger window to join George. He doesn't glance back at me. I don't mind. I know he's under pressure in this crucial year. This is the year he's been striving towards since he was eleven. At the end of it, if all goes to plan, is a crock of gold. At the alternative ending, the dreaded R word fork, sits a pile of shattered dreams – his and mine.

Once the two have disappeared into the changing rooms I puff out my cheeks and sigh, pulling my shoulders back in an attempt to relieve the tension in my neck muscles. My chauffeur duties are half done, the most important half. I've got Jack fed and watered with all his kit, on time, to the training ground. As usual it's been a frenetic rush. Knock off work early, collect Jack and Chloe from school, get home, have a quick bite to eat and then Jack and I are off to avoid the rush hour traffic and make the hour plus journey to the university based training ground. Mistime proceedings by ten minutes and punctuality becomes impossible thanks to the traffic-infested roads.

I glance around the car park to see who else is here. I recognise several cars so I make the decision to take off my chauffeur's uniform and don the garb of my alter ego – the FD. The outfit consists of a warm winter coat, a snood, a woolly hat, a pair of gloves, a change of footwear, an umbrella and a full magazine of banter – all the kit needed to while away the hours standing outside watching the boys train or play matches. As it's only early September I discard the snood, woolly hat and gloves from the coat's bulging pockets and leave them in my van. Hopefully, the banter is waiting to be fired within a suitably snappy response time, one capable of shooting down the last quip aimed at me. It's not raining so the umbrella and change of footwear can stay in the back with my tools, ready to be pulled off the subs' bench should the night turn inclement. I decide I'll need the coat.

I look at the time. It's gone half five. The part of training I'm here to watch doesn't start until seven thirty. This takes place on the floodlit AstroTurf training pitch situated alongside the car park. By then, Jack will have already done an hour in the gym working on his core muscles and developing his upper body strength. Until the external training starts the FDs who are sufficiently motivated to stay (virtually everyone) and have no unavoidable work commitments, will kill time by drinking, eating and chatting in the bar area adjacent to the changing rooms. The bar area is part of a section of the university campus, as is the entire training facility, one used by the club for their youth development. This is a typical arrangement for a lower league club which has insufficient funds to own a dedicated youth training ground. Tonight, Thursday night, will see the U13s and U14s train from six until half seven on the AstroTurf before the U15s and the U16s (Jack's team) come on to train and finish at nine.

At the moment the bar is at its busiest and housing a double shift. The U13 and U14 parents (almost exclusively FDs) have yet to move out from the bar to watch their boys begin training on the AstroTurf at six. The U15 and U16 parents (almost exclusively FDs) are arriving in dribs and drabs to help fill the bar area further. They are here early in order for their sons to be on time for the gym session. Within twenty minutes this brim-full situation will change and the bar area will thin out. Like a herd of wildebeest on the Serengeti, the younger age group parents will leave the older age group parents in the bar and go to the training pitch. An hour and half later comes the role reversal when, like a herd of wildebeest on the Serengeti, at precisely twenty-five past seven, the U15 and U16 parents will move out from the bar to go to the training pitch. They will take over viewing duties from the younger age group parents who will, like a herd of wildebeest on the Serengeti, saunter back into the bar to wait for their sons to get showered and changed. Sometimes a particularly harsh winter night will stop some of the less hardy and motivated wildebeest from migrating at all. At other times, out of interest, one or two of us more anally-fixated wilde-beest will ditch the herd and go out and watch the last fifteen minutes of the younger boys. This is an exercise in keeping tabs on who's coming through, and to compare them to how our boys were at the same age.

The last fifteen minutes of training on the AstroTurf invariably consists of an eleven-a-side game with rolling subs, the two sides a mixture of the two age groups concerned. Much can be gleaned from these short matches. Playing up against older boys is not only a physical challenge it is also a mental one. There is a simple natural hierarchy within the boys at football. Fundamentally, every older year tries to bully the one below by verbal means or by the tried-and-tested method of blatant physical intimidation. Watching these last-fifteen-minutes-of-training games is a throwback to past ideals where the rule of the jungle was the rule of the playground, long before childhood became less competitive and more PC. With the self-perpetuating philosophy of senior consultants wanting junior doctors to work horrendously long hours because they did, each year passes down its wrath to the next. Of course, what everyone is looking for is the younger boy who technically runs rings around his elders, batters them in a fifty-fifty tackle and when confronted shouts, 'Go fuck yourself!' Playing up a year, or in exceptional cases, two years, is gold dust. If your boy gets asked to play up in the next age group you know he's doing well.

Jack is at the top of the evening-session-training food chain as he is in the U16s. The youth team, the U18s, comprises a two-year age group of boys – the first and second year scholars as they are known – who are the paid apprentices. These boys train full time during weekdays apart from when they attend the FA regulated college course to study sports science. This is the goal Jack has been heading for since he was signed at eleven. Only once this has been achieved can he move on to any thoughts of making it as a professional. An apprenticeship, training full time to become a pro, is the thing both he and I want more than anything else in the world. It's the one thing I can't buy him, can't give him or can't help influence the decision in his favour.

Others are less convinced on this last point. This is a major taboo for our clique as we hate, in any form whatsoever, the bootlicking, grovelling, fawning, timeserving, toadying sycophancy of any parent trying to ingratiate themselves, and therefore their son, with the coaches. We're polite to the coaches, but we keep our distance and only speak when spoken to other than to say hello. To offer up any form of football opinion, unless requested, is out of the question. Secretly, I think the four of us are convinced this is the way forward because the alternative could be counter-productive. If it wasn't, and the opposite was true, would we all be so moral? I'd like to think so, but as a betting man I wouldn't put money on it. Football's a brutal business and any edge, ill-gotten or not, is still an edge.

I put on my coat, lock the van and walk over to the same entrance that Jack and George used. As I cross the car park I see, in the double doorway, 'The Man'. Ian Nash – Nashie (it's actually obligatory that his surname is 'footballised' in this manner) – is the club's director of youth football. As such, he is the main protagonist in deciding which of the U16s will get an apprenticeship. He is talking to Caroline, the mother of the goalkeeper in Jack's team. As ever, Caroline is flirting with him. She's an attractive classy well-dressed woman in her late thirties – and she knows it – and thinks by flirting with Nashie she's enhancing her son Billy's chances of getting an apprenticeship.

Caroline is unique because she is a genuine bona fide FM. She is not merely a woman who comes along with an FD, nor is she a woman who makes the first half chauffeur run because the real FD, who comes along later, can't dodge his vocational responsibilities. (Although if you're an FD who can't dodge his vocational responsibilities, you're not much of an FD in our clique's eyes.) Clare often accompanies me to the matches, but she is not an FM. Other wives/female partners accompany FDs, and they are not FMs. Caroline is, and she's universally accepted to be the only one we know. What we don't know is anything about her exact personal circumstances. All we know is what we see and what we see is her, and her alone, at all the training sessions and all the matches. There is never any sign of Billy's father, a male partner or even a porn-industry-inspired, stereotypically luscious and svelte female partner. Consequently, wild speculation on her personal life/sexual orientation/sexual preferences/sexual availability/sexual deviancy and current sexual partner – normally one of the coaching staff best suits our conspiracy theories – entertain all the FDs and stop them from worrying about the R word for short periods of detached reality. In truth, she keeps herself very much to herself with regards to us FDs and limits contact with us to brief greetings and inane pleasantries – unlike the coaching staff who get the full glorious blast of her rapt attention.

At training and at matches she always stands by herself, the latest smartphone clamped to her ear for much of the time. She is her own one-woman clique and this, combined with her attractiveness, expensive clothes, immaculate make-up and top-of-the-range BMW makes her at once remote, unapproachable, beguiling, tantalising, enigmatic, mysterious and desirable – and out of our league. To all of us FDs she's a top four Premier League FM. It's just a shame we're all players from the Ryman League.

Incidentally, in a fascinating insight into female competitiveness, I can unequivocally state that not one of the non-FMs seems to like Caroline or have a good word to say about her.

I near the pair of them, they're still engrossed in conversation, and mentally scoff. I'm always polite to Nashie, overly so if I'm honest, but as my father used to tell me, there's a difference between scratching your arse and tearing the skin off.

Nashie catches my eye as I walk past him.

"Good evening, Ian," I say, a blank expression on my face. I don't want to suggest in any shape or form I'm aware of what's going on here.

"Evening, Mr Dennett," Nashie replies, his eyes turning back to Caroline Briggs.

Caroline offers me a smile as well. She really is an attractive woman and I feel my plodding heart skip a bit faster, as if adrenaline has toed its accelerator. Let's hope Nashie is made of sterner stuff and can make a professional decision on her son, one untainted by lust.

I leave them to it and enter the bar area which is predictably heaving. I start to scan for my clique. Eventually, I spot them. Andy, Don and Ryan are sitting at a table in the far corner, the securing of this prized possession a badge of honour regards their FD commitment. Andy and Don are drinking pints of lager while Ryan tucks into a Twix, a poorly made cappuccino in a cardboard cup on the table in front of him. I walk over to them, greeting a few standing FDs from other cliques as I do.

"All right, guys?" I ask rhetorically. They greet me with non-verbal signs. "Anyone want a drink?" They all confirm they're sorted on the drinks front. I lean in close to them, my forearm resting on the table's smeared surface and lower my voice. "Caroline's outside chatting up Nashie," I tell them.

I'm greeted by groans of disapproval. It's a little less raucous than it should be because Caroline is a very attractive woman and her son is a goalkeeper. The goalkeeping position doesn't really affect any of our sons. There could be a hundred goalies on trial or signed and, to put it bluntly in the vernacular of the FD, we couldn't give a fuck. Billy is the only goalkeeper for the U16s at present and whether or not he gets his apprenticeship (personally I doubt he will) shouldn't make any difference to the number of outfield players.

The boys have been told, 'If you're good enough, you're good enough.' What this seemingly idiotic stating of the obvious means is that, taken to the extreme, if there were three left fullbacks all to the required standard they would all get an apprenticeship – even though there would then be three left fullbacks in the youth squad. Our clique takes this with a pinch of salt – one from a mechanical dredging machine – and we're reckoning on six outfield players taken from positions spread throughout the team, with a slight midfield to striker bias, getting an apprenticeship. This would emulate any conventional squad and means there's no chance half of this year's crop will be left fullbacks. What the expression also means is the apprenticeships won't be handed out willy-nilly. If only three are really good enough then only three will get it. We take this with a pinch of salt as well – only this time it's more a man with a shovel rather than a man armed with gigantic hydraulic machinery. There is a chance the figures may be swayed by the odd one or two, depending on the strength of the years above and below, but on the whole it's how our clique sees it. Six outfield apprenticeships plus the possibility of one goalkeeper, per year, is an average crop and is approximately the number of apprenticeship positions which are partially funded by money from outside the club. (The League Football Education manages The Apprenticeship in Sporting Excellence programme and is funded by the Skills Funding Agency. A fact I found surprising when I learnt of it.) A few years back, the club had such a strong U16s they took on ten boys as apprentices and paid for the extra ones themselves. No one within our clique is deluded enough to think that's going to happen this year. That year was exceptional, a year when the club experienced their 'golden generation' moment and seven of those boys eventually made it through to the first team.

"She ought to be giving him a blow job the way Billy played on Sunday!" Andy retorts, making us all laugh.

"You should be so lucky," I tell him. He considers this and pulls a face of anguished delight. With this image left in his head I ease myself up from the table to get a drink.

I go to the bar and after a five-minute wait get the chance to order a hot chocolate because the coffee's dire. I take it back and put it on the table next to Ryan's cappuccino, take off my coat, hang it on the back of the plastic chair and sit down.

"What's the news? Anything good?"

Today's Thursday and I haven't seen them since Tuesday.

Literally, anything could have happened.

"I was telling the others earlier," Ryan answers. "Sam reckons the youth team have got five out with injury. He heard Nashie say to Ron that a few of our boys might get to play up."

I'm as amazed at this snippet of vital information as were Andy and Don. It's always Ryan who gets this type of feedback from his son, Sam. The rest of us never get it from any of our boys. With Jack I always feel honoured if I get told the kick-off time, the venue and the opposition.

"That's going to be a bit of pointer. Dependent on who's out and their position, of course. Even if you go as a sub and don't get on..." I add, letting the sentence hang in the air.

"Shows they rate you," Don agrees.

"We're a bit light, too," Andy points out. "We had three out on Sunday. If a few of ours play up that might open the door for a couple of the under fifteens or one of the trialists."

There are two trialists at the moment. One is the lad who plays in the same position as Jack and the other is an out-and-out striker. Trialists are slightly less frequent now than when Jack played in the younger age groups. It appears the older you get the harder it is to bridge the gap between a local league club and a professional club.

"I'm not being funny, John, but the lad who plays wide midfield is decent," Don tells me after supping a mouthful of lager.

"That's the beer talking," I respond.

"No, straight up. He is. You *know* he is," Don counters, giving me a subtle compliment.

I pull a face. "Fair play to the lad, he's done okay in training. But a lot of them do okay in training. Let's see what he's like in a game before we get carried away."

Chelsea fan Ryan nods enthusiastically. "Man City were shite in the Champions League, weren't they?" he suddenly asks no one in particular.

"Nearly as shite as Chelsea were lucky!" I tell him.

"Fuck off!" he exclaims, laughing.

"Look at this," Andy says, offering me his mobile phone.

I take it and read it out aloud. "The FA announced Gary Glitter as the new England coach, but the deal collapsed because he wanted to put Seaman in the under sixteens. Bloody hell! Who writes all these jokes? The ghost of Jimmy Savile?" I ask, laughing and handing the phone back. "Talking of goalkeepers… Billy *did* have a shocker last game, didn't he?"

"My missus would've stopped the second goal," Don postulates.

"She would, you wouldn't!" Andy remarks and prods Don's ample stomach.

"Relaxed muscle, pal," he retorts, slapping his belly.

"Is that what they call a beer gut nowadays?" I ask.

"If you've got it, flaunt it. It cost me a lot of money!"

"If it gets any bigger you'll have to carry it around in a wheelbarrow," I warn him.

In response to this jibe he rubs his hand vigorously through his thick head of hair thus intimating I am follicly challenged. In comparison I am.

"Okay," I say, deadpan. "So you can afford a toupee. What happens when the wind gets up and the glue gets wet?"

"All my own, sunshine. All my very own!"

"Unlike his belly," Andy chips in. "That's his *and* his next door neighbour's put together. Works in a pie factory, doesn't he, Don?"

"I've actually lost a bit of weight," Don answers in all seriousness.

"What you've lost," I point out to him, "is the ability to see your own knob."

"Oh, well," he mumbles with a shrug of his shoulders. "You're only middle-aged once."

"You can say that again," I concur, ruminating on my unsolvable pathetic mid-life blip.

During the time I spend with my clique of FDs I rarely mention my parents although they are aware of their condition. I feel it's a subject matter utterly without place in the context of our group relationship. In fact, none of us talk at any length about our work, our home lives or any personal problems we may have. We all know each other's vocation, marital status and major life issues, but only on the most superficial of levels. We enjoy each other's company, enjoy the crack of our childish conversations, the play-ground taunting and the kudos of being involved with a profes-sional football club, albeit only as chauffeurs to our sons. True, we moan about the hours of our lives that are lost, the travelling and the fuel/time off work costs, the impotency of our condition and we constantly agonise over our sons' futures, forever fearful and para-noid of the dreaded R word. Even Andy, whose son Greg is NO for his apprenticeship, can't relax and take anything for granted. He thinks the minute he opens his mouth and admits Greg will get an apprenticeship fate will grind into action and conspire, as a direct consequence of his loose talk, to stop it. It's an attitude I can relate to, despite me poking fun at him for being that way.

Yet, for all this, we know we're lucky and we're the chosen few. The fact is, we love it. Even if all rational judgement, mathematical probability and honest pragmatism suggest it will end in tears one day. In an overwhelming endorsement of the, 'Tis better to have loved and lost. Than never to have loved at all' philosophy, we take it while we can. We grab with both hands and hold on tight, clutch-ing our dreams and our sons' dreams close to our chests. We hang on tight, with one eye always over our shoulders, fearfully await-ing the irresistible force coming to wrench them away.

The trouble is, Tennyson was writing poetry out of his backside and was wrong. Every study ever commissioned on the value of happiness, longevity, health and pretty much everything else, when equating 'love' to marriage as opposed to staying single, shows those who have never loved fare better than those who have and then had it taken away from them. Psychologists call it the 'loss hypothesis' and I suspect all FDs would suffer similarly, a gaping hole appearing in their lives should they and their sons ever get divorced from a professional club. At the moment all of us are still married, I won't go so far as to say 'happily', but long may it stay that way.

Anecdotally, boys R-worded from professional clubs suffer the most. Some give up the game they love altogether such is the impact of losing a lifelong dream. For those who stick with it, finding a new path within football is hard. Nothing ever quite matches up to what they have become accustomed to and they endlessly search for a niche with the unspoken hope of maybe, just maybe, finding a way back. The majority never do, but occasionally one or two will. Every now and then an R-worded boy has the strength of character to shrug off the shackles of disillusionment and, motivated by rejection, shove the negative words of his previous coaches back down their erroneous throats. Through sheer endeavour, hard work and self-belief he claws his way back and makes it somewhere else. He remarries, and if there's a strong enough bond, he may live happily ever after. If he makes it as a pro and scores against the club which R-worded him it's instant Nirvana. Job done! Kiss the new badge and celebrate wildly in front of their silent dugout!

Imagining myself as a spurned player I can only guess at how utterly fantastic that must feel.

There is much less banter to be had once we've migrated to the barrier surrounding the floodlit AstroTurf pitch. Our clique's mind is collectively focussed, thanks to Ryan's classified information of youth team spots being up for grabs. All four of us become more insular and retreat into our shells as we stand in the artificial light spilling out from the training pitch, our thoughts a whirlpool of football intrigue. We all recognise a good performance during training, and the match at the end of it, may tip the balance and give someone the nod to play up. For my part I have more pressing issues and I watch the new trialist, who plays in the same position as Jack, like a hawk. I watch him intensely as he partakes in the many differing drills designed to promote a good first touch and passing technique with either foot. As I do, I find myself hoping he will make mistakes when controlling or passing the ball. I want him to misunderstand a routine within a drill, bringing it to a grinding halt, and get a bollocking from Ron or one of the other coaches. I'm not shocked at my emotive thoughts because I've had them many times before. It's not nice to want this boy, any boy, to perform badly, but I love Jack. Unfortunately, he's a threat to Jack and his dream so my paternal instincts kick in accordingly. I can't change my feelings nor do I particularly want to. I say, give me some of that LFD Schadenfreude. I'm not proud. Bring it on!

The trialist doesn't make any mistakes throughout the drills and he doesn't get a single bollocking, not one, not even for step-ping on a rung of the rope ladder laid out on the ground during the 'fast feet' routine. He's wearing an England kit, the striker trialist is in a Manchester United kit, and the pair stand out from all the other boys wearing the same identical club kit. Technically, Jack's threat is very sound. Wearing the England kit emphasises this. It makes me feel irritable because if he were making a succession of howlers the England kit would emphasise that instead. I turn away, rub my face with both hands and hope Jack can make him look bad during the game. As I do, I look down the barrier of the pitch and catch Caroline's eye. She's looking at me, giving me a 500watt smile, and I have to tell myself to smile back as I'm completely caught on my heels by this unexpected event.

The game at the end of training throws me another curve ball. Ron has a quick word with Jack as he and the other coaches hand out the orange and yellow bibs to the two teams amalgamated from the U15s and U16s. When the game starts, Jack plays at right full-back with the trialist playing in front of him in the wide midfield position he would usually occupy. The FDs in my clique throw me furrowed brows. I catch them and chuck them back. Frantically, I try to evaluate what the hell is going on, rushing through a mass of calculations revolving around who's on whose team and who's playing where. In the end I give up. The tea leaves won't settle in the bottom of the cup and I discard the six different readings I've already made.

In the game the trialist does really well, benefiting – ironically – from some decent possession instigated by Jack who has got the ball off Billy and passed it to him. The last action of the game sees the trialist whip in a cross for the Manchester United kit-clad striker to score with a header.

"Well done, you! Good goal. Okay, boys. We'll stop it there... Greg! You take the cool down. Tom! The bibs. George! Balls and cones," Ron bellows across the pitch to signal time.

I turn and walk away from the pitch and pretend to make a mobile phone call. I don't want to talk to the other FDs because I don't know the answers to the questions they will undoubtedly ask. I mooch around in little circles some way from the pitch until all the boys have cooled down and are ready to make the short walk to the changing room. I 'hang up' and pocket the phone, my ridiculous charade over. Tradition now dictates I catch up with Jack as he walks past me, take his drinks bottles from him, and tell him not to take too long in the showers. His part in this ritual is to hand me his bag containing the drinks bottles and confirm he is willing to acquiesce to my request – only to subsequently ignore it. He is always one of the last ones out of the changing room.

"All right?" I ask Jack as cheerfully as I can, trying to contain my inner angst. Saying nothing, he grumpily thrusts me an old Nike boot bag with his two drinks bottles inside. "Not too long in the showers, eh?" I add, achieving the hint of a nod from Jack's head.

"Now, he *is* a handsome young man!" I hear Caroline remark. She's standing right behind me and I spin round to see her smile at me. "Like father, like son," she tacks on the end once I have made eye contact.

She flutters her eyelids at me – I've read of the phenomenon, but never experienced it – and I'm flabbergasted. A little coquettish smirk spreads across Caroline's perfectly lip-glossed mouth as she spots my mental flailing. She walks up to me and lays a black leather-gloved hand on my forearm. Like a moron I gawp at the gloved hand, thinking she's treating me with kid gloves. It's so evident I'm unused to this sort of attention she's actually treating me with kid gloves.

"Can I have a word, John?" she asks, sensuality oozing from her.

I can smell her expensive perfume, almost taste it, due to her close proximity.

"Sure," I answer, forcing out the single word. It's meant to come out relaxed, controlled and confident. It doesn't.

"In my car's best," she offers, tilting her head towards the white BMW fifty yards away.

As we walk towards it I feel as if we are walking down a red carpet at a movie premiere, the world's paparazzi and TV crews following our every step. My heart is pounding. I'm over fifty and my heart is pounding because another woman has asked to talk to me. Not any other woman, I quickly chastise myself, Caroline Briggs isn't any other woman. By the time we've got to her car I'm convinced she's hitting on me and wants to start a torrid affair. Once I've sat on the leather passenger seat – charmingly, I notice it does run smooth – soaked in the opulence of the BMW's Teutonic interior and she's opened her mouth again, I know different.

In essence, however much she tries to dress it up with a sprinkling of flirtatious flattery – her apparent default setting for football matters – Caroline is questioning me, as the cross-clique-approved-oracle, on what I believe to be the chances of her Billy getting an apprenticeship. Once I realise this my nervous inhibitions drop with a dull heavy thud and for the first time, when faced with this question, I'm less than circumspect. I defy the unwritten rule. In fact, I barely control myself sufficiently to fall short of brutal. I'm annoyed. Not so much at her, she only wants to have access to another opinion, but at myself. I was already agitated at not being able to work out Jack's predicament, misreading her attention so completely has now made me feel juvenile and unsophisticated.

"I hope I haven't upset you. That's truly what I think," I assure her, my anger waning fast by the second now I've told her my opinion.

"No, I appreciate your honesty," she answers with what appears to be genuine candour, her flirtatious manner gone. "Unfortunately, lots of men tell me what they think I might want to hear rather than tell me the truth. They think it might help get their hands inside my knickers," she remarks with unexpected crudity. "You certainly haven't done that!" she exclaims with raised eyebrows. She reaches to a compartment within the car and pulls out a business card. "If you're ever up this way during the week give me a call. Maybe we can have coffee together." She hands me the card. I note the gloves are off now. "Thanks, John." She smiles. "I guess I need to explore Billy's sixth form college options."

I take her appreciation and acceptance of Billy's football career prospects as a 'conversation over' euphemism and take the card, trying to stop my impulsive desire to read it and see what the hell she does for a very good living.

"No problem," I say, now wondering if somehow I've fluked it and overturned my initial hapless status into something completely different. I remain undecided and have far more confidence in my dire prediction for Billy's goalkeeping career.

Whatever my standing with Caroline I can't get out of the BMW and back to my van quickly enough. Once ensconced I sit and wait for Jack in glorious untroubled solitude. Unsurprisingly, it doesn't last. Within minutes my clique become iron filings, my van a giant electromagnet, and soon all three are stuck fast to the van's side panels. With both passenger and driver windows down they bombard me with questions. With frank openness I tell them what has happened, omitting only the last part where Caroline gave me her business card. I give them no inclination I am having second thoughts on my standing with her.

I'm spared further inquisition because, totally unexpectedly, Jack is fast approaching the van. He's the first one out and I know something must be wrong. The others, less in tune with my son's showering and changing routine, fall on him regardless – like the starving do on food. My escapade with Caroline is instantaneously rendered old news.

"What's the word, young Jack?" Andy asks. He's said it casually, but I know inside he's burning up.

"Um…" Jack starts distractedly, "Greg's playing up for the youth team, so are Scott and Mattie Smith. The two trialists are coming with us."

I catch the twinkle in Andy's eyes and wonder if now he'll admit to Greg being NO for his apprenticeship.

"We're still away?" Ryan asks.

"Yep," Jack answers, waving an A4 copy of directions plus a satnav postcode to the venue. "Still away."

"Well, we'll see you two on Sunday, then," I say to Ryan and Don, trying to wrap things up quickly. I desperately need to hear what's happened to make Jack want to get out of the changing room as soon as he did. "Good luck to Greg on Saturday." I give Andy a thumbs up. "Text me the result and how he plays."

The four of us say our goodbyes as Jack puts his gear in the back. Underneath the pleasantries I'm trying to make sense of what Jack has told us. Now the training game makes a bit more sense. If I'm honest, it's still not great news.

Jack gets in beside me and I start the van. We both wave and smile as we pull out of the car park. Once we're off down the narrow road leading out of it the smiles come off. Before I can open my mouth to comment, Jack explodes.

"It's fucking bollocks," he moans. "I'm playing fullback on Sunday and the trialist is playing in *my* position!"

"Did Ron say why? Because Greg and the others are playing up I presume?"

I'm answering my own question and trying to keep a lid on my concerns.

"That's what he came out with," Jack answers with disdain. "Ron said the trialist couldn't be expected to play out of position in his first game so I'*d* have to go and do a job because we've got so many injuries. Still shit, though."

These mitigating circumstances take the sting out of things to some extent and I try to explain this to Jack, putting as positive a spin on it as I can. He's having none of it.

"It's *so* crap!" he declares. "I didn't get picked to play up and they've put a trialist in my position. They've stuck *me* at fullback! Why didn't they put a defender like George or Jimmy there? Why did they put a trialist in my position over me? It's bollocks."

"For the reasons Ron explained to you," I say. I take my eye off the road to glance at my son and see, to my dismay, his eyes welling up with tears. Then, like a dam rupturing, it all bursts out of him.

"I don't think they rate me," he blurts. "They *can't* rate me if they put Connor in my position. They could have put *anyone* at full-back. They didn't, they stuck me there. Ron's such a fucking knob! If he really rated me he wouldn't move me from my position. Greg never has to play out of position. He always plays centre mid." Jack goes quiet and so do I. A few moments later he turns his head to me, his anger evaporated, disillusion in his voice. "What am I going to do if I don't get an apprenticeship, Dad? All that time I've spent training, it's, like, five years of my life gone. It'll all be a waste. A complete waste."

I don't tell him his first question is a variation of the very one I have asked myself many, many times.

"It's not a waste, Jack. No one can say chasing the dream of becoming a professional football apprentice is a waste of time. You do it, you give it your absolute all, and if you do come up short, you hold your hands up and walk away with no regrets. As I've told you before, the only thing you want to have stopped you is the single fact you weren't good enough."

This isn't gobbledygook. All it means is a young player doesn't throw away his chance by having a bad attitude or be robbed of it by injury.

"In someone's opinion. I don't think Ron likes me and Nashie never talks to me as much as he does Greg."

Jack has a point, a very good point. Our clique has often postulated on the importance of the right person liking you as a player. Football is a notoriously subjective sport, especially once universally respected top player genius is taken from the equation and you're left to deal with mere mortals. Especially, young developing mortals.

"There's always that," I agree. "But I think you're just reacting to what's happened tonight." I desperately hope I'm right, although I suspect Jack speaks with an element of truth. Greg is so NO for an apprenticeship, to the point of 'coaches' pet' status.

"Do *you* think I'll get one?" Jack demands. "What do you think? All the boys tell me their dads think you're best at picking out the ones to get released or signed."

Pleased as I am to have my oracle status confirmed twice in one evening I can't tell my son his father has a football blind spot, one caused by overwhelming paternal love.

I fudge it. "Jack, it doesn't matter what I think. It's what Ron, the other coaches and Nashie think. I reckon, as it stands, you're a fifty-fifty call. Step it up, get a run of improving performances under your belt up until Christmas and into the New Year and I

151

think you'll get one… And it has to start from this Sunday, even if you are playing fullback. *Because* you're playing fullback." I offer Jack a pair of lifted eyebrows. "If you don't push on and improve, it's a flip of the coin job. No one ever said this was going to be easy." I lean over and grab his arm with my left hand, squeezing it tight. "Don't give the bastards a reason to put the coin in the air."

Jack nods vigorously. His tears have gone and there's a more familiar look of determination on his face. I give myself a pat on the back, thinking I've pitched it somewhere about right.

By lunchtime the following day I've had enough of work. Under the thin premise of needing to go home to my empty house, to see if there's a cheque I've been promised for a job completed weeks ago, I get ready to leave. The real reason for my wanting to leave is different, although I do genuinely hope the cheque has arrived as I could do with the money. I've been distracted all morning and found it hard to concentrate, a combination of the previous evening's events and the prospect of solving the riddle of the double grave are to blame.

My time spent as an FD is normally a welcome distraction from my parents' plight and the recent notion of the past trying to reach out and grab me. Last night was no different until the incident with Caroline and Jack's outburst. I told Clare how training had panned out – I've always kept her updated on Jack's progress with post-training bulletins – but I carefully glossed over my chat with Caroline, completely omitting the part about obtaining her business card, much as I did with my clique of FDs. The card is sitting, safe from discovery, on the high level shelf above the driver's seat in my van. Like a poker novice, it comprises a hand I'm unsure whether to play or fold. Ridiculously, this one dilemma has eaten away at my mental energy levels all morning. Despite the other important things I have to concern myself with, and having previously questioned my ability to keep two secrets from Clare, I have already embarked down a road of deception. My innate reservation has stopped me from calling Caroline, but my pathetic mid-life blip won't let me throw the card away and with it the ability to ring her, should I want to. (If I do, to do what? Exchange platonic pleasantries over an American global corporation coffee or use the shady tryst as a stepping stone to something else.) I really have no concept of what might happen if I were to meet her for coffee and, as it stands, I really have no idea of what I might want to happen. Perhaps I'm secretly hoping the next time I meet her alone at football she will take the lead in these matters. That she will set out the agenda and I can simply follow it.

It's evident her card has given a long dormant section of my ego a significant boost and that, in my current state, is more than suffice to addle my brain. The card itself states Caroline Briggs is a 'Personal Financial Adviser' and I suspect she's a very good one – particularly in terms of what she gets out of it. I imagine the approach she takes to encourage some of her clientele to invest in her recommended portfolios is not too far removed from the treatment I initially experienced. Of course, I could be well wide of the mark. Maybe she's not like that at all and is the consummate talented financial professional, saving her flirtatious Jedi mind-tricks for social situations and for those she perceives as weak. Like me. Until my anger kicked in and I saved myself. Looking back, as I have all morning, I think we were both shocked in equal measures at how I resisted her siren call and told the truth in such a forceful manner. Maybe that was why she was impressed with me and gave me her card. Unfortunately, the way she credited this to me, via a crude sexual allusion, has got me thinking. Too much for my own good and I'm left in a state of heightened confusion.

Whatever the truth – I'm 'over analysed' out – it'll be interesting to see if Caroline pursues Nashie with as much zeal now I've given my opinion on her doomed son. Will she trust it and not try to flog the proverbial dead horse? Alternatively, will she disregard it, still believing she can influence the outcome? My temporary closure on the whole affair, to save my head from imploding, is to wait until the game on Sunday to see how she reacts to me. I'm already toying with tentative plans to dissuade Clare from coming, all in the name of getting a clearer indication of her feelings for me – if indeed she's got any. I've got my head in such a spin I even wondered why I used the word 'affair'? A Freudian slip, perhaps? Was its usage a sub-conscious revelation of what I really want to happen? Or simply the terminology that popped into my head? It is utterly ridiculous how I've got myself in such a state.

The photo I found in my parents' roof, the one entitled, 'Alfred's grave', has also given much food for thought. It too has claimed much of my internal CPU usage this morning. If all goes according to plan, Chloe and I will see the grave this afternoon. I'm not sure how I will react to viewing the physical embodiment of family tragedy from so long ago. The Fear and The Pact have become so tangible of late I'm wondering if the process will verge on being disturbing. In my head I can't get away from the thought that seeing the grave will somehow enhance the growing feeling I have of the past reaching out and pawing at me. At the same time, to counteract this off-putting thought, I still have absolute faith in The Pact. Nothing can shake that and I'm fascinated to see for certain who is buried in the grave.

Caroline and the grave have filled my mind to bursting point this morning, squeezing out my more usual FD thoughts. It's an unusual circumstance as there's normally one corner of it constantly contemplating and evaluating Jack's football career. The job in hand registers absolutely nowhere and eventually I can't be bothered with it any further. I decide to treat myself to an early weekend, pack up my kit, and head for home on a spurious mission to check for a cheque.

For once a builder has been as good as his word. The money I'm owed is lying on my doormat in amongst the junk mail. I open up the handwritten envelope and look at the cheque with a mixture of pleasure and relief. In my hand is the reward for a month's work plus materials. I can't afford to have too many invoices of this size go unpaid for too long. As I put the cheque down the phone rings, making me jump. I don't pick it up, I'm supposed to be at work after all, and instead I screen the call via the answerphone.

"Hi, you're through to John and Clare Dennett. I'm afraid no one is here to answer your call at the moment. Please leave a message after the tone…" I hear myself say. As ever I wonder if I sound as bad in real life.

An elderly female voice starts to emanate from the answerphone's speaker.

"Oh, hello, Mr Dennett. I've got your father with me at the moment. At least I think it's your father…"

I grab the phone. "Hello, John Dennett speaking."

"Ah, Mr Dennett, you *are* there. That's a relief… I was just saying I have your father, Owen, with me. He knocked on my door half an hour ago saying he lived here. I could tell he was confused, bless him, so I let him in and we've been sitting in my front room having a cup of tea. He's been telling me all about my house. He says he lived here when he was a boy."

I quickly confirm the woman's address and tell her it is the house my father grew up in. "How did you get my telephone number?" I ask, wondering if my father's memory was having a good day.

"Well, you see, I asked him his name and I looked it up in the phone book. Luckily, there were only two Dennetts. An O.B. Dennett and a J.A. Dennett. By a process of elimination I phoned you."

"That's brilliant," I remark, impressed at her logical thought process. "Thank you very much for looking after him. I'm sorry if he's been a nuisance. I can come and pick him up straightaway."

"No bother at all. I'll see you in, what… ten minutes?"

155

"Yes. I'll be leaving right away. I'm only local. Thank you."

By the time I've got into my van my mobile rings. The display shows it's the number of the care company manager.

"Don't worry, I'm on my way to pick him up," I answer immediately, laughing at what I envisage is the look of surprise on her face.

"Okay. That's good!" she answers, a surprised tone in her voice.

"He's been out on a little jaunt to his mother's old house," I explain. "The lady who lives there has just this second contacted me."

"Thank goodness he's safe," Diane states. "When Cheryl made the midday call your mum said your dad had gone out. She often says things like that, only this time Cheryl couldn't find him anywhere. She even looked in the garage!"

"Is she all right?" I ask with overstated concern. Diane has seen inside the super massive black hole on her original assessment visit to my parents' house.

Diane laughs. "She's fine. Mind you, she is worried about your dad. I'll phone her to let her know he's okay."

"If I'm not back before she has to go, tell her to make him a sandwich and leave it in the kitchen. I can give it to him and make him some soup when I get back."

"Will do, John."

As I drive, the humour rapidly falls away from the situation. Both my father and I have been lucky by coincidence – the woman was in and I was at home – and another worry thread, that of wandering, is now firmly on the agenda. I calculate my father has walked the best part of two miles, including a couple of steep hills, on pavements next to busy roads. What has given him the energy yearning and motivation to make such a journey is baffling. Lately, from a physical aspect, he looks barely capable of walking from one room to another and yet this has happened. I put it down to a case of mind – albeit a broken mind – over matter and the power of the human spirit to push the body onwards, even if the calling is a mere echo from a distant past.

The small terraced house holds no memories for me. Instead I'm once more reminded of the completely lopsided relationship I have with my father's side of the family. As I ring the doorbell I feel like I'm in the position of a young boy, but instead of asking for my ball back I'm going to ask if I can have my father back. I also find it a bit disconcerting that having found a photo of Joyce just two days ago, the first time I've laid eyes on a picture of her for decades, I'm now standing on the doorstep of the house she lived in for decades. This feeling of being sucked into a vortex, one turning the present into the past, is disarming. And I haven't even got to the cemetery yet.

Through the front door's frosted glass I see the distorted image of a body approaching. When the door opens I'm confronted by a smiling woman in her early sixties.

"Hello, John," she beams. "Come on in."

"Thank you... er?"

"Lucy," she answers.

"Thank you, Lucy."

I follow her into the small front room where my father is sitting on a well-worn sofa with a half drunk cup of tea in his hand. I'm guessing the tea is stone cold by now. I've noticed of late he needs constant cajoling to make him eat and drink anything bar his beloved coldwater prawns.

"Hello, Dad."

"Oh," he replies with tired surprise, turning his head slowly towards me. "Hello, John. What are you doing here?"

"I think I'm the one who should be asking that question," I say, smiling at Lucy.

Despite my genial facade, my heart is sinking. My father is still unshaven, his white beard full and bushy, and he looks decidedly unkempt in a dirty old zip-fronted fleece and grubby trousers. He's wearing his slippers, a pair of blue Marks and Spencer moccasins, that at least have some kind of sole. He looks drained, his face sallow and lifeless. Overall, he's an unedifying sight and I feel embarrassment, for him and for myself, that he's been out in public looking this way.

My father hasn't answered my question so I ask it again. "Why did you walk all the way up here, Dad?"

"To see, Mum," he replies, as if it's perfectly reasonable to walk two miles in a pair of slippers to visit someone who died decades ago.

"What, your mum, Joyce?" I enquire, making doubly sure.

"Yes. Joyce," he confirms.

"She's dead, Dad," I tell my father. "She doesn't live here anymore. She hasn't lived here for years and years. This lady, Lucy, lives here now. This is her house and her... husband's?" I look to Lucy for confirmation.

"Yes. Stanley's out at work at the moment." My father looks totally blank, as if he has no comprehension of what has been said. To kill this awkward moment of silence Lucy starts speaking to me. "Your father's been telling me what my house used to be like," she informs me in an upbeat voice. "There used to be an open fire there," she points to a modern electric decorative fire sitting on the tiled hearth. "The kitchen used to be much smaller, it's been extended out into the back garden, and there wasn't central heating with radiators when your dad was living here."

"Really," I reply, trying to match her enthusiasm. I just want to get Owen home as quickly as possible. "Well, Dad," I start, giving Lucy a frown and a head motion towards the road that I hope indicates a need for haste. "We ought to be getting home. Mary will be wondering where you've got to."

"Is she... all right?" Lucy asks delicately.

"About the same as Dad," I tell her. "They've both got dementia."

"Oh, how awful! And they're still at home?"

I suddenly feel defensive at this mild insinuation that they should be in a nursing home. Somewhere safer, more secure, where they don't allow people to wander off in the middle of the day even if it means they're kept under lock and key. Despite my defensive bent, it's a point well taken. I know if this kind of situation happens too often that's exactly where they'll end up – and sooner rather than later.

"Oh, yes," I say, trying to convey my lack of concern and faith in my judgement to keep them at home for as long as possible. "They have carers to cook for them and wash them. They've been fine. This is the first time Dad has done anything like this." I see Lucy eye my father and there's no denying he looks as if he hasn't been washed for weeks. "Dad can be a bit difficult," I whisper to her. "He's not too keen on being shaved or washed by another person." I make eye contact with her and distract her from looking at my father for any longer. "Do you mind if I give you my mobile number? Just in case this ever happens again. It was only by chance I was in."

She nods. "I'll get my phone book and a pen."

"Thanks."

Once she has it I remove myself and my father as quickly as possible from her sight.

"Was Pop-Pop all right?" Chloe asks me later, when I'm picking her and Jack up from school.

"He was well tired," I answer, not stopping myself from slipping into their teenage vernacular. "I don't think he'll be walking back there again too soon. I certainly hope he doesn't." I offer Chloe a reassuring smile and continue. "Once I took him back home, gave him sandwiches and soup and got him in his favourite chair in front of the TV, he was fine."

"That's weird," Jack decrees, screwing up his nose. "Walking back to see his mum who's been dead for, like, ages."

"Yeah, it's not good. Apparently, it's quite a common thing to happen to old people with dementia, this trait of wanting to wander off. I don't know why."

"What happens if he keeps doing it?"

"We'll cross that bridge when we come to it," I reply to my son, revealing the paucity of my strategy at a stroke.

I'm actually a little surprised Jack's in the van at all. His normal default for anything or anybody outside of his friends, his gadgets, his football, his running and his homework – I'm joking about the homework – is massive indifference. Yet, when he turned up with Chloe outside the school gates and I asked if he wanted to come, he nodded.

"I might as well be among the first to see it," he said, shrugging.

My first thought was he was only doing it to antagonise Chloe. To steal her thunder by negating her bragging rights. However, something about his attitude made me realise this wasn't the case. I couldn't put my finger on it until I realised he was genuinely interested. There was no doubting this nugget of family history had got under mine and Chloe's skin. Now it had permeated Jack's, the equivalent of a splinter penetrating a rhino's hide.

"Do you think the grave is going to be there?" Chloe asks me, thankfully moving the conversation on from my parental care strategy.

"I think so."

"You *think* so," Chloe mimics derisively.

"Well, I'm pretty sure. Put it this way, I'll be very surprised if it isn't. Where else would it be?"

"I don't know! That's why I'm asking you!"

"Dad doesn't know for sure. Just wait and see," Jack snaps. "Although to be fair I'll be pretty pissed off if it isn't there," he adds.

"You and me both," I tell him conclusively. "How about, as a suggestion, we put this pointless conversation on hold until we find out for sure."

They both nod and we drive on in silence. The pair of them seek refuge/entertainment on their mobile phones, the two devices appearing from nowhere in the blink of an eye. Once enraptured with their phones they withdraw from the world, like hermit crabs retreating into their shells. As they do I ponder on what it's costing me per month to have my two children enveloped in the alleged protective bubble of permanent contact – and then how many kids have been beaten up in order for some thug to steal it.

Turning from this paradox to the task in hand I ask myself if access to a mobile phone would have saved either Frederick, Alfred, Harold or Graham. Somehow I doubt it, although I'm sure modern medical standards would have saved Frederick via improved resuscitation techniques. Harold and Graham were killed too violently for a phone to help them and I can't see how one would have saved Alfred. Perhaps the parental thought process behind giving mobiles to children, the lack of interest amongst the young in obtaining seagulls' eggs should, in theory, stop any modern day Alfreds from going anywhere near a cliff. Yet, little boys will always be little boys and people of all ages will continue to suffer falls, have accidents at work and die from vehicle related traumas. However much mankind strives to create a zero-risk environment they will continue to happen. I heard with horror, on the radio the other day, of a woman who died from carbon monoxide poisoning when drying her washing indoors on a propane barbecue. The same bulletin told of another who died while decanting petrol in a kitchen with a gas hob alight.

I shackle my mental walkabout and reel in my mind. Will I find Alfred? Is Cyril Charles Roberts, Alfred? And if he isn't, who the hell is he? I feel the jittery sensation of butterflies beginning in my stomach.

Inside the cemetery grounds the main car park is near the administrative building. The three of us leave the parked van and enter an office-like environment. A middle-aged woman extracts herself from a black computer chair as we approach the front desk. I explain I want to find a grave within the cemetery and she asks if I have any details. I give her Frederick's name and date of death. She quickly reads the piece of paper, walks to an area hidden from my view and soon reappears with the largest tomes I've ever clapped eyes on outside of a Hollywood film. The books look ancient and, once opened, are shown to be handwritten in pen and ink in beautiful script. The woman cross-references the huge books, writing down the odd letter and digit as she does. She looks up at me.

"I've found him." With those words I feel my heart pound and I try to hold my body rigid to save myself the ridicule of giving an involuntary shudder. "I'll get you a map." She reaches under the counter for what transpires to be a photocopied layout of the entire cemetery. On this facsimile she writes 'MB B46' in the top left-hand corner, a note of the letters and numbers she has gleaned from the old books. She twists the map through one hundred and eighty degrees for my benefit. In a pink fluorescent marker pen she draws a line from a 'You Are Here' box up through the grid-like layout of the designated grave areas. It stops at a point almost halfway top to bottom and a smidgen left of centre. The designated areas are lettered AA, AB, AC, AD and so on until the BA, BB, BC areas start. I can see these aren't complete full sets and the first letters, only up to O for some reason, all have differing amounts of second letters attached to them. There appears to be no apparent rhyme or reason to the method. In the top right-hand corner of the map I spot an area designated, NEE, which only confuses me more. Nevertheless, despite the haphazard illogical system, on the cusp of a tiny slither of an area marked, GC, adjoining a larger sector, MB, the woman now draws a tiny cross in black biro. "The grave is here," she says, indicating the cross with her biro. "Right on the edge of these two areas, but actually in MB. You can walk to it or take your car, whatever you wish. This path marked in pink is in effect a narrow road."

She looks up at me and I nod my comprehension. "Just to let you know, the gates shut at four-thirty."

"That's great. Thank you very much." I take the sheet of paper from her. I spin on my heels and face my children. "Let's go. We have our man!"

My lame attempt at humour, for my own benefit as much as anything, is treated with derisive eye rolling from my son and daughter. I take it on the chin. I'm attempting to mask my nerves and my comment deserves their contempt. We walk quickly back to the van. Both Chloe and Jack remark on the size of the books and the immaculate handwriting within them. For once, digital representation on a screen has been well and truly usurped by traditional pen and paper – if only temporarily. Having bundled into the van, impatience and haste rife in the air, I drive off a tad too quickly down what, it turns out a few moments later, is the wrong road. My admission of this mistake gets short shrift.

"Oh, my, God! Come on, Dad. Get your act together!" Chloe admonishes.

I do as I'm told and take the next right down one of the cemetery's internal roads to get back on track and in synch with the pink marker pen. Within a minute I manage to successfully navigate our way to the area MB. We disembark en masse. I will soon know for certain if my mother's pencil heading was correct or not. We walk off the tarmac and across a border of long lush grass, my two children following me as I home in on what I perceive to be the shortest route to the black cross on the map. Before us lies a spread of dilapidated graves interspersed with the odd well-tended one hosting fresh flowers. Carefully, I pick a way through the graves in the slim area GC. Then I see it. By chance, we're approaching the grave from the same angle as the photo was taken. I recognise the scrolled headstone immediately.

"There it is!" I cry, pointing with an outstretched arm and index finger towards the grave.

We rush towards it and I see in reality what I have only ever seen before in a monochrome photo. As I read the epitaph I feel the hands of the past rest heavily on my shoulders. My feet feel as if they're being pushed into the grass and the soil below. This time I can't help but shudder.

"In loving memory of Frederick Roberts died 18th April 1936 aged eighteen years," I read, my voice wavering slightly. "R.I.P. also Cyril Charles Roberts died 18th May 1946 aged eleven years. The link in the chain is broken, love and memory remain."

"Well? Is it him?" Jack demands.

My eyes are blurred with tears and all I can do is nod. The physical embodiment of the original manifestation of The Fear, the one I unearthed by finding the newspaper cutting in my parents' house, is there at our feet. And so is the little boy. The little boy whose fate caused my mother so much mental anguish thanks to the dreaded prospect of me being ripped from her as he had from his mother.

I exhaust a wavering breath from my lungs. The chain has snapped asunder. Sadly, memory has all but failed. And how can I ever love those I never met or knew? Yet, deep inside, in this moment of revelation and high emotion I can almost convince myself I do love my ancestors. One forever lost until I discovered his story, the other a monochrome photographic doppelganger of myself whose image and death stalked my childhood.

"Are you crying, Dad?" Chloe asks, a look of shock on her face.

I wipe away my tears with no self-consciousness. Eighteen and eleven. Who deserves to die at eighteen and eleven?

"It's Alfred," I finally declare. "I don't know why it's engraved, Cyril Charles. Well, I do," I quickly contradict myself. "That was his name. Officially. He was named after his dad and his granddad and I'm guessing they called him, Alfred, in everyday life, to avoid confusion. To all intents and purposes, Alfred, *was* his proper name. It's why it's my middle name. It's why my mother wrote,

'Alfred's grave' above the photo. She gave me my middle name in honour of his memory." I breathe in deeply through my nose and look up at the darkening sky. "Now she can't even remember who I am."

I put a protective arm around my two children and walk them away from the presence of the past and back to the safety of my van. Over my shoulder I glance briefly at the scrolled headstone, thanking The Pact for keeping us all safe.

"Well, that's the end to quite a day," Clare remarks as she turns off her bedside lamp and slips under the duvet alongside me. In the darkness I nod my silent concurrence. "Which part felt the most surreal? Standing outside Joyce's old house to pick up your dad or seeing the grave in real life?"

"Both felt odd," I answer truthfully. "And I'm still really none the wiser as to why Frederick was never mentioned to me when I grew up. Both Mum and Dad must have known about it. Of course, they were only very young children when Frederick died so maybe that's why it didn't register deeply. I'm guessing the death of Alfred, when it happened, being that much closer to Mum and far more relevant to her, simply pushed what little there was of Frederick out of her head. I don't think my dad would have been a regular visitor to the grave and I know Mum wouldn't so perhaps that's another reason why he became 'lost'. I've always been convinced my birth was the catalyst for Mum going under and this sort of underlines it. Once I was born, that's when she really changed and suffered. She became frightened of losing me like her mother had Alfred." I turn my head towards Clare. "Seeing the grave of the little boy whose photo was always with me during my childhood was definitely the most surreal. And the most emotional."

"Yes. The kids said you were very upset. Not that you admitted to me you had been moved to tears. I don't know, you men..." Clare

165

lets this sentence hang in the air. I sense it's a pregnant pause and I'm not wrong. "They also told me something else you didn't tell me."

"Oh? What was that?"

"They told me you hurried them away from the grave as quickly as you could."

"Did they?" I ask with forced casualness. "I wouldn't have said I 'hurried them away', as such. We'd seen all we needed to see and answered the big question. What was the point in hanging around?"

"None, I suppose," Clare acknowledges. "You know, there's nothing to be embarrassed about by shedding a few tears over the death of a close family ancestor, don't you? It's not an offence against your heterosexual masculinity. You have to recognise that Alfred played a huge part in your life, especially when you were growing up," Clare informs me, snuggling up close, her head touching mine, a hand placed lovingly on my chest. There's a pause in her words and I can feel the warmth of her body next to mine and the even movements of her steady breathing. "Tell me what else is bothering you," she asks with quiet directness. "Tell me what you're afraid of."

Although she's well wide of the mark, thanks to my faith in The Pact, I have a compelling compulsion to tell her of The Fear and The Pact. I want to lay out all my secrets before her, to tell her how I dealt with my family's collective trauma and how I devised a way to live my life free from my mother's condition. I want to reveal how, via this process, I managed to ensure my own, my wife and my children's safety. Strong as this impulse is, it's easily counter-manded by the contract I made as a thirteen-year-old boy. Some vows are sacred, some can never be broken. On another level I want to tell her more fully of the feeling I have of the past imping-ing on the present. How this feeling is steadily increasing in magni-tude and is the reason why I moved my son and daughter away from the grave – despite my faith in The Pact. I want to tell her how my pathetic mid-life blip has grown, like an unsightly weed, out of my parents' battle with dementia and Jack's approach to manhood. I want to tell her how I feel stuck in the middle, powerless to escape the future of old age, powerless to repossess the zest of youth and powerless to manipulate the present into something tangible for myself. I want to tell her how this is causing me to feel trapped, confused and unable to work a way clear of my frustrated feelings. I want to tell her I'm debating whether something as simplistic as buying a motorbike will banish my discontent at the twist of a throttle. What I don't want to tell her is the other option I've considered, that of taking a lover, should I be able to interest one, and the intriguing possibilities engulfing the business card hidden in my van.

"I'm not afraid of anything," I reply as lightly as I can. "But, like I've said, it's the dredging up of the past I don't like. It takes me back to a time of horrid events. I've managed to move on from those events and believe me I *don't* want to be taken back." My resolve suddenly falters. " But..." I leave the conjunctive hanging out to dry.

"That's what's happening?"

"That's what's happening," I admit. "To a certain extent," I add, trying to put the cat back in the bag.

"You know, John, it's crossed my mind, too. Especially after today. Isn't it strange how you can find two photos in your parents' roof, from years ago, and within days they both feature in your life?"

"A bit," I concede. "More so with the photo of Joyce. That was peculiar. On the other hand, once I found the photo of the grave it was obvious I'd go and look at it at one stage or another. It just so happened I decided to go today and that coincided with my dad going on his little expedition."

"I guess so." Clare wriggles closer to me. "I'm glad you didn't stay by the grave any longer than necessary."

"Really?"

To my surprise, Clare rolls over away from me and sits up. I sense an air of desperation in her rapid movements.

"Oh God. I don't know. I think I'm turning into your mother!"

"Are you serious?" I ask as I turn towards her, propping myself up on an elbow.

"No. Of course not. Well... maybe a bit. Perhaps I'm coming back in time with you! Your mother's demons are finally becoming mine. After all these years. Who would have credited it. Now she's finally managed to lose hers *I've* started to pick them up."

"Everything's going to be fine," I reassure her. Underneath this bland statement I'm less than reassured. Clare is a solid person with a level temperament and I'm a little shocked at how she feels. Getting a grip of myself I try to lessen the growing aura of trepidation, one that has fed on our collective concerns. "You're only feeling this way because of what's happened today. By the morning everything will seem more settled. What my dad did really isn't so unusual. In fact, it's well-documented. I said so to the kids. And whatever you say or think, Alfred died in nineteen forty-six. Frederick in nineteen thirty-six, for God's sake!"

"How many years is it since your sixteen-year-old cousin died?"

"It's nearly forty years since the last episode of... those deaths," I answer, barely checking myself in time.

The Fear. If we're all safe, who else is there left to be taken? I'm so detached from all my family, both on my mother and father's side now, I genuinely have no idea.

"Good. Long may it continue!" She lies back down and pulls the duvet up over her shoulder.

"I'll second that." I reach over to kiss her on the cheek. Our pocket of paranoia seems to have passed. Normality is resumed. "Good night, darling,"

She kisses me back. "Love you, John."

My last thought as I drift into sleep after sifting through the day's events is that I forgot to ask Clare if she intended to go to Jack's match on Sunday.

I'm woken in the pitch black by a noise. An awful guttural groaning noise coming from outside my bedroom. My paternal instinct kicks in instantly and I know something is very wrong. I jump from the bed and dash towards it, following its sound to the adjacent bathroom. I pull on the light switch cord and see Jack, his boxer shorts around his ankles, convulsing on the toilet. Frantically, I pull up his shorts to maintain his dignity and haul him to his feet. I notice he's urinated in the bowl.

"Jack! Jack!" I shout, shaking him vigorously. I get no response. His handsome face has a frighteningly vacant stare upon it. His eyes are locked wide open in one position, without focus and set to a non-existent far distance. He continues to groan, a horrid noise emanating from deep inside him. It's a primeval noise, one that could come from any animal and whose meaning is blatant. It frightens me and rocks me to my core. With my arms around him to support his weight I grab a flannel from the basin, run it under the cold tap, and manage to squeeze it in his face.

"Jack! Jack! Are you all right?" I ask with increasing urgency as the cold water runs down his cheeks. My words have no effect, nor does the water, and I let the flannel fall to the floor. "Clare!" I call out. "Jack's having a fit! He's not responding to me at all!"

I literally drag my groaning son out of the bathroom and, after struggling with his not inconsiderable weight, manage to lay him gently on his back on the landing carpet. As I rest his head down he takes a solitary exaggerated deep-rasping breath and then stops breathing altogether. On the carpet, naked apart from his boxer shorts, Jack is completely motionless. His eyes are fixed at the ceiling and his chest no longer moves up and down. The groaning has stopped. I stagger back from this vision of hell so forcefully I smash my back against the wall.

"He's stopped breathing! Clare! He's not breathing anymore!" I cry out in panic.

Crouching by the wall I can feel my whole body shaking. I'm rendered powerless by events and I have no clue what to do. Through eyes glazed with tears I see my wife, haggard and drawn, phone clamped to her ear, coming out of our bedroom.

"... No, he's not asthmatic. He's not breathing at all now." Her eyes turn on Jack and I can see her fighting to keep a lid on her emotions and stay in some semblance of control. "No. He's just lying on the floor. Lying on the floor doing nothing," she manages to say into the phone, her voice oscillating in pitch and volume.

As she disappears down the stairs, an act I cannot even begin to comprehend, she glances at me, terror etched on her sleep-deprived face. She passes Chloe who is peering out on the carnage from her cracked bedroom door. I see her partially lit face immediately after Clare's and I'm transported back, in an instant, to the night my mother unwittingly allowed me to experience my first-hand experience of The Fear. Back to the night when I saw the sad faces, all with the same look, the same red eyes and the same gaunt expression. An identity parade of family sorrow interchanging before my eyes, exactly as I'm seeing now.

I collapse from a crouch down on to my hands and knees and crawl over the landing carpet to touch my son. His body is still warm, but I know it won't be for much longer. The Fear has got him. The Fear has won and gleefully snuffed out yet another young male life. All The Pact could do – my now so evidently impotent Pact, the one in which I have invested a lifetime's worth of faith – was wake me up so I could witness The Fear's triumph in all its ugly glory. I force an arm under Jack's back and scoop him up and hold him tight, pulling him close to my chest. I'm inconsolable. I don't even know what The Fear has done to kill him. My son is dead and the past has returned, like a berserker in the night, bringing with it all its inherent malice and myriad of cruel agonies.

Time passes, I haven't an inkling how much, and in amongst the chaos in my head I hear an ethereal voice. "They're on their way. The ambulance is on its way. They'll be here soon. I've unlocked the front door and put all the lights on."

The words permeate my brain, but I cannot devote any effort to understanding or reacting to them. My mind is so jangled, so incoherent, so enveloped in the machinations of The Fear it's devoid of any practical thought process. I'm lost inside my head and outside of it the only thing I can do is hang on to Jack and squeeze him tight. I have no other exterior response. I'm marooned in my own mind, caught in the Doldrums and becalmed on a sea of my own notions.

The Fear has taken him. For all my conviction and faith, The Fear has struck. This is how it feels when The Fear strikes. This is the bottomless pit of torture, the sheer overwhelming numbing sense of punishment horror and loss... This is my mother's neurosis. I'm experiencing what my mother always dreaded she might experience... It's the fifth time. Where was The Pact? Why did The Pact desert me? I kept my part of the bargain, I never told a soul... When I tell my parents their grandson is dead, will they have enough mental capacity to understand? Will they grieve for Jack? Or is he already a non-person, forever erased from their memories?... He won't be able to play on Sunday. Who will play in his place? I'll have to phone Ron and say my son can't play tomorrow because he's dead. Not because he's tweaked a groin or has a sickness bug, the reason he can't play is because he died in the night... Jack can't get an apprenticeship now, not now he's dead. 'The only thing you want to have stopped you is the fact you weren't good enough.' Not because you were killed before you had the chance to prove it.

"Excuse me, sir. *Excuse* me, sir."

"*John*! Get out of the way!"

I come out of my head and back into the real world. I look up

171

and see a paramedic in his deep green outfit, mumble my apologies, let go of Jack and stumble away from his inert body. Instinctively, I gravitate to Clare and we cling to each other like limpets to the hull of a boat.

"They're here now," she whispers to me in a fragile voice. Clare squeezes my hand far harder than I believe is possible. "They're going to save him," she tells me, her conviction rising. "They're going to make him better."

I look at my wife and through the refracting properties of water, hers and mine, I see her eyes burning bright – with terror, with foreboding and with hope. Hope. I have no hope. None whatsoever. I know nothing can stop The Fear once it's got this far and yet, in her eyes, I can see her defiance. In her body, as it stands touching mine, I sense her recalcitrance and resistance to Jack's death. In this instance, this brief moment in time, I recognise my wife as the true colossus she is. I floundered while she acted. As I pontificated and surrendered, my mind running wild, my body shackled by the chains of the past, she moved and took steps to fight back. She was proactive – I was reactive. All my love and respect for her is amplified in this instant and she is revealed to me afresh. The covers of complacency, the dust sheets of familiarity and the veils of presumption are whisked from her at a stroke. I see her for what she is, for what she has always been and I'm both smitten and humbled. I feel her resilience pass into me and I start to hope. For the first time since awakening I consider the possibility the ending in my head is not the inevitable conclusion in real life.

Paramedics surround Jack. One is pressing down rhythmically on Jack's chest, another is periodically squeezing air into his lungs via a face mask attached to a bag. Two more paramedics arrive and, after a brief conversation, one injects Jack's arm while the other makes ready a set of pads and places them on his chest. The pads are connected via two leads to a square box. In the surreal medical drama taking place on my first floor landing carpet I hear an oddly robotic voice. The box is speaking. Entwined with the rushing in my ears I pick out the words 'stand clear' and a second or two later Jack's whole body violently twitches as if it's been subjected to an electric shock. Dully, I realise that's exactly what has happened.

Nausea – a heavy deep-seated sickness in the pit of my stomach – and an emotional intensity surpassing everything I have previously experienced accompany my voyeuristic role. I'm beyond thinking. Images swim before my eyes, but the jarring impact of the event render me punch-drunk. I hang on to Clare, her defiance, her hope and the small kernel of it inside me. I have little else left. Jack's body convulses three more times in between the constant pushing on his chest. Again, over what time span, I have no idea. It jolts again for the fifth time.

"Anything?" I hear myself ask.

A grim paramedic looks up and shakes his head. "No pulse yet."

From somewhere, like I was standing on a touchline watching Jack play a game of football, comes an urge to encourage. I call out, imploring my son not to play better, but to fight for his life. "Come on, Jack!" I scream.

The paramedic who has been pushing on Jack's chest from the moment he's arrived moves clear. Jack's body contorts again and immediately afterwards he starts to groan. His chest begins to move up and down of its own accord.

"We've got him! There's a pulse!" one of the paramedics declares.

With these words it's like they can't get out of our house fast enough. The party of death has ended with the return of life and there's no reason to stay. With disciplined haste the four paramedics gather together their paraphernalia and disappear down the stairs. They take our son with them. Clare and I, caught in the whirlwind of their departure, follow to the front door.

"We have to get your son to hospital as quickly as possible. You

173

take your time. Get yourselves organised and come up to A & E. He'll be there. We've got a team waiting," the last paramedic tells us. "Now, don't panic," he warns. "We don't want to have to come back and clear you up off the road because you've crashed your car."

Clare is sufficiently with it to show our acquiescence to his request and, satisfied we have taken on board what we've been told, the last paramedic hurries to join his colleagues. Within moments the first ambulance is gone in a haze of flashing blue lights and sirens. The other leaves soon after.

We're alone without our son and I'm still reeling from the whole episode. I feel disorientated, as if I have vertigo, spinning without stability like a faulty gyroscope. I'm desperate for answers and I'm disjointed fractured and torn. The most significant event in my whole life has just taken place and I don't understand what's happened. I'm cut adrift, wallowing in a pool of questions to which I have no answers. My brain jumps and lurches, a video tape replaying what's happened in a chronologically non-linear montage of one catastrophic bombshell after another. I'm lost. Rudderless, with no hand on the tiller.

"John! *John*!" Clare shouts at me, taking my head firmly between the two palms of her hands and wrenching it around to face hers. I feel the quiver of her muscles in her touch. Her blotchy eyes lock on to mine. She has assumed command because she knows I can't. "You get dressed and go. Go to him. Be with Jack," Clare tells me, her voice still wavering as before. "I'll phone my mum and dad and get them to look after Chloe and I'll join you as soon as I can. Be careful in the car."

Dazed, I do as I'm told. I go upstairs and get dressed, do my best to reassure Chloe that everything is going to be all right, and drive off in the dark to the hospital. Tears roll down my face and I utter my son's name in anguish to myself like a mantra. I cannot take in what has happened. Everything has a dream-like quality to it, an aura of unreality I recognise, with huge despondency, as fake. This falsehood is my reaction to the trauma, a psychological and physiological reaction to the terror played out before me. What's happened has happened. It's real – all too real and there's no mistaking the calling card of The Fear. A very fit fifteen-year-old boy doesn't routinely drop down dead in the middle of the night. This bizarre manifestation bears the classic hallmark of The Fear – one more young victim felled by unusual circumstances. It's another headline grabber.

And yet, I remind myself, he's still alive at the moment.

The hospital is only five minutes from my house and thanks to the deserted streets I'm soon getting out of my car. My whole body is shaking as if I've been submerged in icy water and I desperately try to hang on to the hope instilled in me by Clare. It's the only thing keeping me going. I enter A & E's reception and once the member of staff behind the desk knows my circumstances I'm guided through a locked door into a restricted staff only area. Two of the paramedics who attended to Jack are waiting for me and they come over to speak. One of them reaches out and puts his hand on my shoulder.

"Are you okay?" he asks. I nod gamely, but it's only protocol moving my head. "Your son's with the specialist team. They're putting him into an induced coma at the moment to keep him safe."

Again I nod. Some of the questions floating in the pool in my head rise to the surface. I grab the biggest one and let it out. "What was wrong with him when you found him?" I ask.

"We found him with no pulse," the paramedic explains. "His heart had gone into a very dangerous life-threatening arrhythmia. He'd suffered a sudden cardiac arrest. Eventually, we managed to shock his heart into restarting."

I'm dumbfounded to hear these words. "But Jack's a good foot-baller," I tell them. "He's with a professional club. He's really athletic." I say it as a protest, as if what the paramedic has told me couldn't possibly be true. "I thought he was having a fit, an epileptic fit of some kind."

The paramedic slowly shakes his head. "It definitely wasn't a fit. What you saw was caused by his heart stopping."

I have another question on standby. My brain is crawling from the wreckage of its internal bedlam and is starting to function. Some small semblance of rationality is coming back. "Do you know for how long his heart stopped?"

"From the time your wife called to the time we got it started was seventeen minutes," he tells me. "We got to him in four." This last statement is said with the merest hint of professional pride.

Seventeen minutes. He could have said ten or fifty and I wouldn't have questioned either. And only four minutes to get to him. I caught the edge in his voice. The satisfaction in 'a job well done' and am appreciative of it. As a layman who knows nothing of response times even I realise four minutes is some going.

"Thank you so much for getting to us so quickly."

I feel a huge surge of emotion rise within me. I grip hold of both of them and hug them in turn, almost as tightly as I did Jack. I have no self-consciousness whatsoever and I cry openly as I show my utmost gratitude.

"You did your bit," the other paramedic tells me as I finally let him go. "You phoned us straightaway and you let us get on with our job. It must have been awful watching. Come on, we'll take you to the Sister in charge of intensive care."

The two paramedics locate the Sister and leave me alone with a dark-haired woman in her mid-thirties. She is calm, exudes authority, and offers me a drink. She might as well offer me a punch in the face, a favourable alternative given the biliousness in my stomach. I politely decline.

"Your son is stable in intensive care and we are doing everything necessary to look after him," she tells me. "For your part you must try to eat and drink, and eventually sleep, as best you can. We don't want you getting ill as well."

"I feel ill," I tell her truthfully.

"I know you do. Just try to look after yourself the best you can."

"I'll do my best. I just feel so sick." The Sister indicates her empathy. "Can I see him?"

"Of course you can. Follow me." I do as I'm requested. On the way she tells me more of the current situation. "Your son, Jack, is in an induced coma, which is the safest way for us to keep him in intensive care following what's happened to him. This means that when you see him he will have quite a lot of medical equipment surrounding him. That's completely normal and is done purely for his wellbeing. We're constantly monitoring all his vital signs and making sure he's safe. Hopefully, our paediatric cardiac consultant will see him sometime today, but ultimately any treatment won't take place here. We've arranged for Jack to be transferred to a London hospital. They're the experts in dealing with this type of incident."

I try to absorb what she's told me, but find it difficult. Nagging away is my utter incredulity that Jack could have a heart condition. "The paramedics told me Jack suffered a sudden cardiac arrest. He plays football for a professional club and he's super fit. He trains and plays four or five times a week. How can he have a heart problem if he can do all of that?"

"I think it's too early to say with any clarity what's caused Jack's problem," the Sister tells me. "Unfortunately, it's not unheard of for perfectly fit healthy individuals to suffer this type of event."

"Even in someone so young?" I ask.

"Yes."

I can only take her word for it and I let it go. "The paramedics also said his heart stopped for seventeen minutes. Are there likely to be any repercussions for it stopping that long?"

The Sister stops and considers what I've asked. "Oxygen deprivation is the main problem, but we don't know if..."

"Could Jack have suffered from oxygen deprivation?" I blurt.

A new horror has opened up inside my mind. One where Jack survives, where he lives, but where he is left disabled and damaged, a shadow of his old self. I feel my legs weaken and my whole being sag. Is there no end to this nightmare?

"I really can't answer that question at this point in time. I'm sorry."

She leads on once again and I struggle to follow, trying to suppress the feeling of panic welling in my gut. I feel as if I need to push hard on my temples with flat palms to stop my head exploding just like my father once did. The nausea is overpowering and I physically retch as we arrive at a door with the ICU sign above it. The Sister opens it, walks in and holds the door open for me to enter into the small ward with several beds. On the only bed that is occupied I see Jack lying on his back hooked up to all manner of medical equipment. He has an intravenous line in each arm, a tube running from his mouth to what I think is a ventilator and he's connected to a heart monitor that shows his pulse, his blood pressure and his oxygen saturation percentage. Below the bed I see a bag collecting his urine.

As I absorb the uninviting scene, a thought prompted by the urine bag flashes into my head. What if Jack hadn't woken up and gone to the toilet? He would surely have died in his sleep, fading silently in his slumber. It might be an ideal way to go if you're infirmed decrepit and in your eighties, but not when you're fit and fifteen. I would have gone into his bedroom in the morning, to chastise him for not getting up on time, and found him cold and stiff under the covers. I'm stupefied by this new observation. At the same time a morsel of optimism rises from it. The Pact! Is it possible? Has it played the only part it could in order to counteract The Fear's attack given the Machiavellian nature of its assault? What if it didn't wake me up, as I first assumed, to simply witness The Fear's triumph in all its ugly glory. What if it woke Jack up to go to the toilet? Realistically, what were the chances of him waking up of his own accord to go to the toilet seconds before a cardiac arrest? Did The Pact rouse him? By this action has The Pact ensured the commencement of a chain of events that might ultimately save him?

The Sister is talking again and I attempt to focus on her words. "We're hoping the retrieval team will be down from London some-time this afternoon. In the meantime we'll look after him. These two ladies will make sure of that," she says, nodding towards the two nurses on the ward. The Sister looks at me and must see my vacancy of mind. "I'll leave you alone with your son. If there's anything you want or need just ask myself or either of my nurses."

The pair smile encouragement at me as if to indicate every-thing's under control and they're on top of the situation. I return a weak smile and move over to Jack. I run my trembling fingers through his thick black hair and bend down to kiss him on the fore-head. Emotion engulfs me and I break down, crying loudly and freely. I turn away from my son and shuffle into a corner hiding my wracked face from the nurses. I feel impotent, mirroring and vastly magnifying how I felt at the birth of both my children. Standing in the corner, wiping my eyes, I feel alone and vulnerable. I want my wife to be with me. I want her strength and hope by my side.

Clare eventually joins me. She's delivered Chloe and the awful message to her parents and she looks as dishevelled drawn and anguished as I know I must. Her reaction to seeing Jack is much like mine. We hold each other tight in an embrace of agony, in an effort to quell the emotional overload. Once we've both had a chance to regain a little composure I relate everything I've been told, including the transfer of Jack to the London hospital. She takes it all in and, after steadying herself, tells me how she dealt with calming our distraught daughter and telling her parents the terrible news.

Her voice drops to a whisper. "I can't believe this is happening, John. I can't take it in," she confides in me. "It's like I'm going insane, like I'm losing my mind. The feeling I had last night, of turning into your mother... and then this happens. Your family's past has come back and it's got our son." Her words are said without malice or blame, but are laced with emotion. She starts to shake uncontrollably. I worry she's going to buckle and implode, to faint and collapse on the spot. From her core she somehow finds some inner strength and miraculously pulls herself back from the void. "He's going to make it, though, John," she tells me, straightening her back and lifting her head in defiance. "We *have* to keep believing he's going to make it and get better."

The intensity of her words drill into me and lodge in my gut. I desperately want to tell her about The Fear and The Pact and how I, in this room an hour ago, made a connection that may yet indicate she is right. Instead, I hold back. I mustn't yield to the notion, attractive as it may seem. My reinstating of The Pact in a positive light means I have to stay true to the original contract lest I bring it crashing down. I can't run the risk. I have to stick with what I know, despite the chance it still may have failed me.

"He'll make it," I say, as convincingly as I can muster. "He'll be all right. We're going to get our Jack back. He's going to be exactly the same as he was before this happened."

'But will he ever play football again?' is the question left hanging in my mind.

I try to ignore the unimportant, yet paradoxically, vitally important question of Jack's football career. In place of this I wonder if a grown man, one whose son's heart has stopped for seventeen minutes, has any right to adhere rigidly to a concept he devised as a thirteen-year-old boy. My ploy – for that is what any rational adult would call it – to deal with my family's history is tenuous at best. It's nothing more than a glorified version of crossing one's fingers. A logical individual would label my family's past as nothing other than a mathematical discrepancy, an anomaly of the laws of probability. In its simplest form my family's grotesque history is bad luck. A rational adult wouldn't describe this bad luck as an entity. Certainly not a snarling malevolent entity locked in an imaginary battle with a nemesis concocted by a thirteen-year-old-boy to preserve his own skin and sanity.

In spite of this acknowledgment, however much I can see the fallibility inherent in The Fear and The Pact, I can never backtrack. They're too engrained in my psyche. In this climax of terror, as I stand battered and bloodied, my son's life and its future quality – should there be one – hanging by a thread, they are as real and as tangible as anything else that's happening. I cannot now question their validity. They are. My only interest hinges not in their justification, or the theory behind their coming into being, but in which one is going to come out on top. I'm not so fanciful to imagine they're still fighting in another dimension, locked in battle over Jack's inert body, but I do subscribe to the viewpoint both have played their hand. Time will see who turns out the winner. Will The Fear take him or can The Pact deliver him back – intact and undamaged?

The morning ebbs on and Clare and I shuffle in silence, seemingly ever circumnavigating our supine son, first clockwise then anti-clockwise, pausing only to touch and kiss him or move out of the way of nurses as they go about their work. With the passage of time I feel myself start to slip into a darker mood. I look at my watch for the first time and see, to my astonishment, it's still only seven in the morning. This day will undoubtedly be the longest and most spiteful of my life. Time is crawling through treacle. All outcomes are rendered undetermined, the diagnosis indeterminate, as Jack's life is put on hold by modern medicine. There is nothing to do but wait and think. Think and wait. Think of all that has happened and speculate on how it will affect the outcome. Despite the presence of Clare and my undiluted feelings of how magnificent she has been and how she has coped, a new emotion festers within me. It's anger. Anger at The Fear. I feel bitter for it picking on my son. Why him? What has he ever done to deserve such an attack? All he's ever wanted to do is play football. He's never caused a fuss, never been horrible to anyone, he's just a decent young man who's applied himself to chasing his dream. Why would anything want to try and stop him from doing that?

Why him? Why her? Why me? I realise I'm hardly on a shortlist of individuals to have asked such questions when faced with adversity. Acrimoniously, I quote a truism for the world in my head, 'Misfortune stomps on the head of the righteous and the immoral with equal intensity.' Bitterly, I see there is no justice, no equality, no sense of fair play. Shit happens to the 'good' and the 'bad'. The well-intentioned don't get rewarded by default nor do the rogues receive their just comeuppance. What you sow you don't always reap and what goes around doesn't necessarily always come around. And what of God? How does He fit into it all? When I analyse it, is He really so different to The Pact? Is The Fear any different from Satan? Are both just different names for the classic confrontation of good versus evil? Cynically, I tell myself at least no one has died through persecution or war because they believed/disbelieved, fought for/fought against The Pact. The Pact never promised me heaven, but then nor did it threaten me with damnation in hell. It always offered to protect, never menace, which was far more decent. Of course, what it really did was allow me to live. And that's what I want it to do for Jack – in every sense of the meaning.

I'm acutely aware there are different versions of living, different qualities of life and that this is the crux of Jack's heinous dilemma. His life sits on a knife's edge, on two knives' edges, in fact. The first blade offers a simple yes or no outcome; the other a multitude of differing shades should the first knife answer in the affirmative.

Some shades of life are a death sentence in themselves and my mind cowers at the prospect because I've seen my parents suffer, at close hand, from one of the many odious versions there are.

My thoughts do me no good. Speculation at this juncture, however intense, holds no answers. My mental meanderings have got nowhere. Clare and I will have to wait to see if The Pact has won. When the time comes we will discover if to travel hopefully is a better thing than to arrive.

By midday both of us are drained emotionally and physically. It's obvious we'll have to heed the Sister's sage advice although it seems wrong – almost sacrilege – to leave Jack on his own while we eat. Encouraged by the nurses we do it anyway, guilt clinging to us like soaked clothing as we leave the intensive care ward.

The food I purchase from the hospital's cafeteria is virtually impossible to swallow thanks to my dry mouth and nausea. The cup of tea is only slightly more palatable. Clare picks at her food with equal distaste and her coffee is cold before it's half drunk. This reminds me of my father and a well of panic rises in me as I realise I still have my parents to deal with. I dismiss it as quickly as I can. There can only be one point of focus in my life and that's my son. Others will have to help deal with my parents while I am out of the equation.

Around us life goes on as normal. People come and go, laugh and frown and converse freely. They buy their food and drink and dispatch it to their stomachs with ease and relish. I feel an odd simmer of animosity at their apparently humdrum stress-free lives and their complete disregard for our predicament. My son's heart stopped for seventeen minutes and no one seems to care or notice. His young life may still be lost or, if he survives, he may end up in a wheelchair, a drooling vegetable in need of constant care. Why does no one give a damn? I begin to rage internally. Don't these people realise what's going on? Can't they see what Clare and I are going through as they flounce around without a care in the world?

I'm taken aback by my hostility and fight to rein in my inner tirade. I wonder, like Clare did, if I'm going mad as well.

In contrast to the scenes around us, proper conversation between me and Clare is sporadic and joyless. I am too pummelled and wounded, too irritated and caught in my thoughts for anything else. She, on the other hand, despite suffering equally, never stops giving me words of encouragement. She's working hard to keep me afloat as well as herself. Bonding ever more tightly I feel as if it's us against the world and all its evils. It seems a siege mentality is all I can muster to help pull us through.

By the time we arrive back at the ICU the paediatric cardiac consultant is there. As soon as I know who he is I can't stop myself diving in feet first and asking if Jack will suffer any permanent damage. I can see I've placed him in an impossible situation, but I don't care. He's the most expert person to fall into my sphere of influence and I want to know what he has to say. His words of reply are slow and considered, as if he's dictating a legal document to an unseen secretary.

"Seventeen minutes is a long time for Jack's heart to have stopped," he admits. "What is more positive news is that he was attended to by paramedics for a good deal of that time span."

"Do you think, looking at Jack now, he has any signs of brain damage? Of any other kind of damage?" I persist.

"I think what we all must do is pull for Jack and hope for a good outcome. Let's all do the utmost we can and see where it takes us from there."

I go to open my mouth, but see Clare out the corner of my eye. Despite it being subliminal, her message is clear. "Thank you," I mumble quietly.

"There is one thing I can tell you," the consultant adds. "I've heard that the retrieval team will be here within a couple of hours. Once they arrive they'll prepare Jack for the journey in their special ambulance."

The retrieval team comprises a man and a woman. The man is dressed in maroon scrubs and is clearly the senior partner. The woman, a specialist nurse, busies herself while the man comes over to talk to us. His manner is brief and to the point as he explains the procedure for the transfer. Jack has to be connected to their equipment so he can stay in the induced coma under a full monitoring system throughout the ambulance journey. Once they arrive in London they will move him into an ICU and continue to assess his progress. He tells us once they are ready to leave, in approximately two hours' time, we must go home, pack a suitcase for ourselves and pack another one for Jack. We should then drive to the hospital and leave our car in the main car park. The main car park is very expensive, but we are not to fret over this minor matter as we will be able to get a free parking pass due to the emergency nature of Jack's event. He reiterates, as others have, how important it is for us to drive carefully and to try and eat, drink and rest when necessary.

Having underlined this point with a solemn stare he continues with our instructions. With our car parked we should follow the relevant signs to the ICU where, by this time, Jack will have been admitted. He will be waiting for us and a decision on the next step of Jack's treatment will be taken. This could mean continuing to leave Jack in the induced coma or bring him out of it. On hearing this my stomach cartwheels at the prospect of knowing, finally, after the longest day of my life, how Jack has dealt with his seventeen minutes of death. Lastly, and quite matter-of-factly, he asks if we now wouldn't mind leaving Jack with him and his nurse so they can begin the preparation for transfer.

Clare and I do as we are asked and we leave the tiny ward to loiter aimlessly outside. As the two go to work I watch with anxiety through the glass windows of the ward. I see Maroon Scrubs pinching Jack's skin before lifting his eyelids and shining a torch directly into his eyes. He turns and speaks briefly to the nurse who nods in agreement. I've no doubt they have an inkling into Jack's state, but I know it would be futile to ask. Like with the paediatric consultant there is no chance Maroon Scrubs can commit to an opinion at this early stage. I divert my stare from the retrieval team. I can watch no longer. It's too painful and I haul Clare away from the scene to wait in trepidation elsewhere.

As we sit in silence I feel at the end of my tether. I'm exhausted and running on empty. The prospect of packing and then driving into central London seem as daunting as an assault on the north face of the Eiger. Part of me wants to curl up into a foetal ball, squeeze my eyes closed, put my fingers in my ears and shut myself off from everything. A bigger part knows I could never succeed. I look at my wife, think of Jack, and realise I will never be able to make what's happened go away – not unless one day I suffer from dementia. Somehow, for as long as I remain compos mentis, I will have to learn how to deal with The Fear's latest attack. With disgust I look back and sneer at my recent lamentable confusion and angst caused by my mid-life blip. What the hell was I thinking?

By five in the afternoon, Clare and I are outside A & E standing on the pavement watching Jack and his bed being lifted up on the special tailgate of the retrieval ambulance. Once level with the floor pan he's wheeled in and the rear doors are shut with the retrieval team in place alongside him. This is the final piece of the medical jigsaw to fall into place before they can leave for London. A minute or two later, for the second time in a day, we see our son being taken away in an ambulance. With Jack en route to London we gradually galvanize ourselves into movement. It feels odd to now have to do something rather than wait passively. Moreover, there is a sense of forward momentum – a motion towards a conclusion, however grim or positive it may be.

Going back home to the scene of Jack's cardiac arrest and into his bedroom, to collect some clothes for him, is agony. All his paraphernalia is there, strewn shambolically around the room in typical teenage style. My eyes fall on the large Scalextric box gathering dust on the top of his wardrobe. An eleventh birthday present from me and, if I'm honest, also for me – one where I could relive my childhood while playing with my son. My gaze lingers on his sprinting medals, football medals and his football boots, cleaned and ready for tomorrow; on his wardrobe full of T-shirts, jeans, hoodies, sweatshirts and football kit; on his iPod and dock and his phone; on his posters on the wall; on the pile of long unread old Beano annuals, my Christmas presents from decades ago; on the discarded socks and boxer shorts; on every item, no matter how small or insignificant, all of which scream out his name by association.

My heart feels as if it's being ripped in half. If Jack were to die, I ask myself as I close the door after Clare leaves with his clothes and phone, could I ever live again? Would Clare and I leave this room untouched forever, as if it were a shrine to his memory? Shocked by the lingering presence and massive potency of inanimate objects I get a genuine taste of how Charles, Cyril, Olive and Kathy must have felt all those years ago when The Fear took their loved ones and left only possessions behind. With a growing realisation and huge respect I speculate on how my grandfather managed to be so wonderful and entertaining around me. If anything happens to Jack it's a trick I'm not sure I could repeat with my own daughter. I'm left groping at the adage of time healing and play out images in my head of an older me 'finding' a five pound coin in amongst the shingle on Hastings' beach and handing it, with a surprised look on my face, to Chloe's young son who's the spitting image of Jack. It's an historical loop I want no part of if Jack's not alive.

Before we set out in our car I force myself to make the phone call I can put off no longer. An irrational part of me doesn't want to tell the club of Jack's cardiac arrest. As if keeping it secret might allow Jack, should he make a full recovery, to go back and play as if it never happened. I know it's ridiculous, but when a dream is at the point of ending so brutishly the brain looks to escape down any alleyway. When I tell Ron he is devastated. It's as if my elevated emotions have sped through the ether across our communicating mobiles, like high energy electrons speeding along the national grid, and charged him too. I'm left in no doubt that under his gruff football coach exterior lurks a compassionate father.

"Thanks for letting me know, John," he says, calling me by the name I never used. ('Hello, Ron. It's Jack Dennett's dad speaking. I've got some awful news...') "Ring me the moment you know how he is. Doesn't matter what time. You let me know." Ron starts to sound as if he's talking to himself. "I just can't believe it. He trained on Thursday night." He snaps out of it. "Good luck, John. I'm so sorry. All the club's best wishes are with Jack. We're all thinking of him."

"Thanks," I manage to utter before hanging up. It's another emotional focal point and I collapse on to the steering wheel sobbing in a state of complete desolation. "It's over, Clare. All those years of trying and it's over. Over like this."

The anguish drips from my last three words. It's the bit that truly cuts deep. I always knew one day there was a strong chance Jack's time at a professional club would end. But not like this. Never like this.

Clare slides her arm around me to console me, trying to be upbeat, always with the positive spin. "You don't know for sure, John. Miracles can happen. If not he can do something else. Coaching maybe. The important thing is he's well enough to do something else like coaching. Being a player isn't everything. He can still be involved in the game."

I turn and look up at her and know she's talking sense. In the scheme of things Jack's football dream is nothing. I can only rate Jack's chances of an apprenticeship as fifty-fifty due to my football blind spot caused by parental love. Most likely the real truth is only ten percentage points either way. In six months' time it might have ended irrespective of this trauma. The most important thing is Jack's life and its quality, a quality allowing him to do nearly everything he did before his cardiac arrest. If a stab at being a professional football apprentice has to go, so be it. In a trade for being able to do everything else we'd have to grab it with both hands.

"You're right," I admit, trying to control the uproar in my head. "I've got to try and put things into context. It's so tough to do, though. It's been his dream, Clare. My dream. Our dream. It's been my dream right from the moment the scan showed he was a boy." I break down again, memories of me holding a baby Jack filling my mind's eye.

"I know it was, John. And what a lovely dream. An exciting dream. Every little boy's dream." Tears are streaming down Clare's cheeks. She mops them up with her hanky. "Come on, we'd better go. Are you okay to drive?"

I nod. "It'll help keep my mind occupied."

The drive to London does occupy me, but only spasmodically. Intermittently, the intense levels of concentration required, especially towards the end of the journey when I'm on less familiar busy roads, cancels out The Fear's latest strike for a split second or two. Once these moments are past, it rushes in like a tsunami sweeping all else before it. A torrent of black cold water swamping my entire being. At other times, the majority of time, I drive on auto-pilot and find myself revisiting all that has happened. Occasionally, I glance over at Clare and can tell by her glazed stare she's doing exactly the same. We hardly speak, both of us transfixed in the horror of our longest day.

As well as the flashbacks of The Fear's attack I'm also drawn to my earlier feelings at the hospital. With rising condescension I look back on my former self and have even less empathy. How easy it was then to hold The Fear at bay with impunity. In reality, how easy was everything? The answer; everything was easy, relative to this. This is hell. Parental hell – a true Mum and Dad nightmare. Randomly, the opening line of Yesterday by The Beatles pops into my head and it seems so apt. I didn't know I was born. Troubles seeming so mighty then appear so insignificant and trifling now. Even my parents' sad plight seems less frightening in comparison. That's not to belittle the undignified ending to their lives, far from it, but the stark truth is The Fear doesn't bother to attack the very old. It's not newsworthy enough, not disturbing enough and not callous enough.

I ask myself how Jack, aged only fifteen, will deal with knowing his heart stopped for seventeen minutes, like a bolt from the blue with no warning, with no previous hint and without any prior indication. If he's compos mentis enough to ask the question. He might not be. He might end up in the same place as my parents. What a hideous irony. There was I, stuck in the middle and bellyaching, concerned at the prospect of ending up like my parents, and poor Jack might bypass me and go, mentally speaking, straight to the very end of his life. Not by virtue of a slow degenerative disease destroying an eighty-year-old brain, but by virtue of a short sharp shock of seventeen minutes' worth of oxygen deprivation killing off a fifteen-year-old one. My flesh crawls – a bland literary cliché until genuinely experienced – at the concept of Jack never being Jack again. When I consider it I genuinely fear for my own sanity. If Jack has lost his mind I think mine might go with it.

Driving, it dawns on me that I will never be the same person again. Much like my mother was radicalised by The Fear then so am I. I'm John Alfred Dennett 2.0 – contemptuous of the previous model, but hardly a superior upgrade. I'm still a work in progress. No one knows how I'll end up, least of all me. All I can figure at this point in time is my future is tied to Jack's. Unlike with Frederick and Alfred the link in the chain has not yet broken.

As we near the hospital tension increases inside the car. By the time Clare and I pull the two suitcases across the car park it's nearly dark and we're both stressed beyond belief. My whole body shakes and inside my head I pray to The Pact and beg it to make Jack safe. I don't do this once. I do it constantly, like a Buddhist monk repeating a mantra. Apparently, I do it with silent moving lips, like a child reading a book.

"What are you saying to yourself, John?" Clare asks as we walk down a bright hospital corridor.

"I'm praying for Jack to be all right," I answer truthfully.

She doesn't bat an eyelid at my newfound religion. Instead, she nods vigorously. "He will be, John. I know he will be." She hasn't weakened in her belief. Remarkably, her resolve is still as strong.

Clare is still my freshly revealed idol and it beggars belief I had considered not wanting her to be with me at Jack's match so I could gauge my 'relationship' with Caroline. Bitterly, I ask what I would now give for us all to be able to go to the game tomorrow and for Jack to be fit enough to play. I dislike what I used to be. Why has it taken something of this magnitude – a sense of perspective commissioned by The Fear's attack – to make me see sense? To allow me to see what I had was so special and the things I thought missing were merely phantoms of my ego's own making.

The ICU is surprisingly open plan and is softly lit for night time. The nurses on the ward seem too young for the responsibility, as if they'd be better suited to a nightclub than a children's intensive care unit. After the few words Clare and I share with them I'm convinced otherwise. They present themselves as composed artic-ulate and self-confident. Despite it being only a matter of minutes since we arrived on the ward I feel marginally buoyed by its ambi-ence and the staff's demeanour. Everything looks new and state of the art and I feel Jack will receive the best care possible. In an instant I know if Jack had to be anywhere given his circumstances I would want him to be here. I catch Clare's eye and she returns my look. I believe she feels the same.

One of the young nurses we spoke to earlier and Maroon Scrubs stand by Jack's bed. Jack looks as he did earlier; deeply asleep and peaceful, albeit surrounded by medical equipment. Clare and I have no way of knowing what damage Jack may have suffered. I ask myself what will happen next. Are we about to be given an answer?

"Glad you made it safely," Maroon Scrubs says, before moving to more important matters. "We've got to the point now where we can take Jack out of the induced coma. We're going to stop giving him the anaesthetic, observe him closely, and see what happens. It shouldn't take too long to wear off."

Both Clare and I nod, but no words come out. The answer will be with us soon. My stomach twists and dives like it's looping the loop. My normally slow heart rate rises and my mouth and throat feel as if they are filled with desert sand. Clare reaches out and firmly takes my hand, her chest rising and falling rapidly as she gulps in huge lungfuls of air in an attempt to steady her nerve. Her squeeze transmits more than a thousand words. We both know this is it. The question regarding Jack's life and quality of life are about to be answered.

Maroon Scrubs barely nods to the young nurse and on his command she alters some settings on the plethora of medical equipment connected to Jack. The anaesthetic ceases and I stare intently at our son, waiting and hoping for the first twitch to signify life. My whole universe becomes his face and time dissolves. As earlier, during The Fear's attack, my chronological gauges are shot. I could no more measure time than travel back in it.

"There! Jack moved!" I exclaim. "His head definitely moved!"

"Yes," Maroon Scrubs concurs. "I saw it too. He's starting to wake up. The anaesthetic is wearing off. Talk to him. Encourage him to wake up."

I move up closer to Jack's head. His whole body is starting to twitch and mobilise as if he's an actor in a science fiction film coming out of stasis. Clare goes to the opposite end of the bed and pulls up Jack's covers, rubbing both his legs vigorously. The pair of us start to call out Jack's name and ask him to wake up.

"Come on, Jack! Wake up!" I say, my face leaning in close to his, my hand waggling his shoulder. "Time to get up, Jack! Come on! Up you get!"

I look down at Clare and see she's now tickling Jack's feet, something he can't stand anybody doing. "Jack! Jack! Time to wake up!" she chimes.

One of Jack's arms moves quickly and paws at his face. I'm startled by the movement and don't like it. To me it looks unnatural uncontrolled and erratic. The worst case scenario shadows my mind and with it a fresh wave of sickness and dread claims my body.

"That's okay," Maroon Scrubs assures us. "That's an appropriate movement. He's trying to take the tube out of his mouth. Let me take it out. He's started breathing on his own now."

I make way for Maroon Scrubs and he pulls the tube clear from Jack's mouth. Moments later Jack groans. It's a different groan from the one that woke me up. Inspired, I try to rouse Jack with increased vigour.

"Come on, Jack! Time to wake up! Come on! Let's go!"

"Jack! Jack! Time to wake up, Jack!" Clare cajoles, still tickling his feet.

Jack's whole body lurches and he kicks out his leg so powerfully he knocks Clare's arm out the way. "Stop tickling my feet!"

His words are pronounced in perfect diction.

My son's tiny directive is like all the sunbeams in all the world shining down on me. Basking in their warmth I spin round to face Maroon Scrubs, punching both fists in the air like Jack has scored the greatest goal ever.

"Yes!" I cry. Quite literally. He's all right! My beautiful son is all right! Elation, gratitude and relief flood through me. The Pact has won.

Clare rushes to Jack's side as he pushes himself up in bed. "I feel sick. Get me a bowl. I'm going to be sick."

The young nurse is primed for the request and I watch as Jack is sick a couple of times before asking for some water. He drinks it and shuffles back down in his bed, closing his eyes and dozing off within seconds.

"Is that okay?" I ask dubiously, my doubt returning.

"He will be sleepy," the young nurse replies. "He's had a lot of drugs to keep him asleep. The important aspects are his vital signs are fine, his breathing is fine and his ECG looks good. He's in good shape considering."

I turn in euphoria to Maroon Scrubs and offer to shake his hand. He's beaming and accepts it, pumping it enthusiastically and slapping his other hand on my shoulder as if he's a lottery company employee who's just handed me a cheque for millions of pounds. In a way he has. It's like Jack's woken up with a sickness bug rather than having suffered a cardiac arrest. Everything about him seems to be Jack as he was.

"It's a wonderful result," Maroon Scrubs declares. "He's going to be fine." He puts his hand on my shoulder again, this time it stays put, and he guides me away from Jack's bed. "You know," he discloses quietly. "When I first got the message I had to pick up a young man who'd been down for seventeen minutes I wasn't expecting a good outcome. When I saw him, though, I was encouraged. It was evident his kidneys were still working, his skin looked okay and his eyes were responding. I thought he'd be fine." He pulls an apologetic face. "I couldn't tell you in case I was wrong.

I'm sorry for the time you had to endure not knowing. It must have been very difficult."

"I don't care," I admit dismissively. "He's all right now and that's all that matters. Thanks."

"You're welcome. I'm so pleased it turned out this way."

I leave Maroon Scrubs and run round to Clare and we embrace. I suddenly feel very, very drained.

"You did it," I tell her quietly. "You saved him. You acted when I was useless. You were fantastic."

Clare smiles and I can see her love for me in her face. I'm flattered and wonder if I deserve it. "You heard him, John," she admonishes. "You were the one who woke me up. You did your bit. Everyone did their bit."

Including The Pact, I don't say.

With Jack asleep, Clare selflessly elects to try to get some of her own in a chair alongside him while I move to one of the non-patient bedrooms close to the ICU. Lying in bed on my own the relief felt at Jack's recovery soon ebbs away from me. My bitterness and anger towards The Fear's assault on him returns. Concurrent with this, Jack worry threads seem to spontaneously generate in my head. I have one set for my parents and now one set for my son.

The newly perceived Jack worry threads cascade from my brain like a waterfall of consternation. How likely is he to suffer another cardiac arrest? The timing and location of this first one, coupled with The Pact waking him up to go to the toilet, have contrived to save his life and its quality. What if it happened elsewhere? What if it happened at a different time? What if paramedics couldn't get to him in four minutes? What went wrong with Jack's heart? Can the doctors fix it? What is involved in fixing it? What if it can't be fixed? And how is he going to deal with the knowledge he nearly died at fifteen? Long term, how are Clare and I going to deal with it? As usual, in my ignorance, I have precious few answers.

Faced with this cul-de-sac my mind turns towards my family's history, The Fear, The Pact and those who were taken and those who were left behind to pick up the pieces. The Fear's attack on Jack is like no other it has used in the past. All the others who were taken died because of something; an injection, a fall, a slip and a moment's distraction. As far as I can see Jack's cardiac arrest just happened. Nothing external or nothing he was doing could possibly have triggered it off. It was the ultimate bolt out of the blue. With a dark feeling I can only conclude The Fear has upped its game and this latest strike marks the beginning of a new strategy. The last time it tried to take me – my near miss on the go-cart – it failed and moved off to take another. This time I'm convinced it won't do so again and has aimed all its spite in one unwavering direction. This new attack, although initially thwarted by The Pact, has back up. It leaves a legacy, a permanent threat that stays and lingers.

As I'm lying in bed, eyes wide open in the pitch black, another new thought barges its way into my consciousness and makes my teeth chatter. It challenges everything The Pact was originally designed to combat and I'm suddenly scared, almost as scared as I was when Jack was attacked. The Pact was devised to afford me safe passage. In time, the cover of safe passage was extended to my wife and two children thus permitting me a life free from the anxiety and constant worry of loss. My son hasn't been taken – nor was I – yet to all intents and purposes I'm now in exactly the same situation as my mother was with me.

The Pact has given Jack back to me, but have I the strength to be like my father and grandfather and let him live? Will I turn into my mother? Will I fall into a pit of depression? Will I want to wrap him up in cotton wool and try to smother him in order to keep him 'safe', exactly as my mother wanted to do with me? It's clear my resolution will be tested as never before and if I cannot follow in the footsteps of my male ancestors I'll surely wreck what's left of my life and Jack's. A part of me marvels at the odious conspiracy and complexity of it all. I'm aged both thirteen and fifty plus and have a wall of old issues to climb. The Fear's latest attack is its most intricate and subtle yet. Gone are the days of gory brutality, it's moved on, its vile assault menaces on many fronts and I'm stunned at the historical connection to the past I shall need to overcome.

Shivering and damp from cold sweat I question whether I can ever hope to deal with all this. Am I mentally strong enough? Have I the strength to help my son in his most difficult hour? In answer I try to rally myself and push away my anxiety and the myriad of worry threads. I focus on Jack's miraculous recovery, trying to take strength and solace from it. I cling to Clare's part in saving Jack and how we as a team, along with The Pact, allowed others the chance to save him. Jack's imminent needs are medical and out of my hands. I quickly realise my main contribution will be to set the tone for the future. My mother or my father and grandfather? Who will I be? Whose lead will I follow? Mercifully, my longest day eventually takes its toll and reprieve from my returning ancient dilemma comes via fitful sleep.

I wake early on Sunday morning to a phone call from Clare. She tells me Jack is being moved out of the ICU to another ward, to the specialist cardiac section for children aged up to sixteen. She's going to take the opportunity during the move to have a shower and arranges to meet me on the new ward in half an hour.

"How is he?" I ask. "He must be doing okay if they've decided to move him out of the ICU."

"It's incredible, John. It's like nothing has happened to him. He's absolutely fine. The medical staff can't believe it, either. The nurses say the consultant on the ward will see him later on this morning and he'll decide the next move. They all speak very highly of him. Apparently, he's one of the best in his field."

"That's fantastic," I reply enthusiastically. "Have you talked to Jack?"

"Yes I have."

"What did he say?"

"He wanted to know what he was doing here. He can't remember anything."

That's not a bad thing, is my immediate thought.

"Not even getting up to go to the toilet?" I ask.

"No. Not a thing. I haven't told him what's happened to him in full, only that he was ill at home last night and he had to go into hospital. Luckily, he was tired and hasn't asked any more questions. I want you to be there when we tell him. Oh, the one thing he did ask for was his phone."

"I'll bring it to the ward," I say, smiling at my son's love of gadgets. "Do you think we should tell him the whole truth?"

"He's fifteen, John. He has to be told the truth." Clare pauses. "I do think we can gloss over the nasty details of what happened to him. The part we've been through. I can't see any point in telling him that at the moment."

Clare's thinking straight. In my mind, despite her having worried over it previously, I know she'll be too strong to ever turn into my mother. I'm the weak one. I'm the one who'll connect the circle of history.

"I think you're right," I concur. "I'll grab a shower as well and see you in a bit. Have you phoned your mum and dad yet?"

"Yes. I've told them he's okay and I've spoken to Chloe. She's very frightened. I tried to calm her as much as I could. It helped when Jack spoke to her for a short while. Are you going to phone yours?"

A memory of me trying to explain to my father how to turn on his TV flashes across my head. "No." I'm adamant. "I couldn't face the confusion of trying to spell it out to them."

"Have you told the care company?"

"No. Not yet. Once I know how long we're going to be here then I'll phone them. I guess they'll have to get the food in and do some extra hours if I'm not around."

"Of course they can. It's the least of our worries, John. Don't start fretting over that."

"No I won't." I feel relieved to have Clare spell it out.

"What about, Ron? Have you let him know?"

"Not yet. I will do. I think I'll wait until after the match is over."

"Okay."

"I'll get on now, love. I want to see Jack as soon as I can, but I really do need a shower. Bye now. Love you."

"Love you, too."

After directions from the ward's reception desk nurse I spot Jack sitting up in bed. He's ten or so beds from where I am and as I walk past them I see they're occupied by mainly very young children. I find this disturbing as I'd always associated heart problems with the old and obese, with smokers and the chronically unfit. Clare is already with Jack, sitting on a plastic chair next to his bed. She looks much better, refreshed after her shower and more her usual self despite the telltale dark rings under her eyes. Jack, on the other hand, looks like a million dollars and I greet my son with a prolonged hug and many kisses. It's an over-exuberant greeting. I can't help it. I cherish the touch of his body, his warmth and his smell. I constantly run my fingers through his black hair, fascinated by its thickness. Tears roll from my eyes and I never want to let him go. I want to hold him forever, cherish him always and never ever let him out of my sight. In a hot flush flashback a childhood sense of deep unease stabs into my brain and I let him go in undue haste. Stepping back in alarm I stare into the face of my son, not my middle-aged mother.

"Are you okay, Dad?" Jack asks, puzzlement on his face.

"Yeah," I answer, wiping my face. "Just pleased you're okay."

"I'm good," says Jack. "I feel tired. I've only just woken up, but apart from that I'm great." Jack looks around the ward. "Mum tells me we're in London."

"That's right, we are."

"Why?"

"Because you were ill. You were poorly very early yesterday morning and you had to go to hospital."

"But why London? Why not Hastings?"

"You were in Hastings for a while and then you had to be moved to London."

"I don't remember any of that," Jack confesses.

"No, you wouldn't. The doctors put you in a deep sleep because you were ill."

"How ill?" Jack demands, blatant and to the point.

I glance at Clare. There's no hiding. She's right, he has to know. "The truth is, Jack," I start slowly, "about as ill as you could get. It was touch and go. You nearly didn't make it. Your heart stopped for seventeen minutes."

"What?" Jack's handsome face is in shock. "I nearly *died*?"

"Nearly," I say. "But you pulled through."

"Do they know what's wrong with me?"

Jack looks bewildered and is panicking, his genial mood from earlier now completely evaporated. I can see he's shaken and frightened and my anger suddenly swells from nowhere in an act of stark protectionism. It hammers with ferocity on the inside of my skull. I want to swear out loud and ask in what fucking manner of justice, in what fucking sense of fairness should my fifteen-year-old son have to deal with this news?

"Not yet," I answer between clenched teeth, my white knuckles following suit. "Everything so far has been geared towards getting you better."

"What about football? Will I still be able to play? Don't tell me I won't be able to play."

Inside I'm raging. How typical of Jack to go straight to what matters to him. In truth, I expected nothing else. Football has been his life, he wants football to be his life. Irrationally, I start to hate everyone fit and healthy who fritters away their lives on a couch watching TV or playing video games. Why can't they have cardiac arrests instead of Jack? Why single him out?

I try to quell my frustration and hide my anger from him. "I don't know, Jack. It won't be my call, it'll be up to the doctors," I manage to utter, feeling inadequate. In response Jack's face becomes desolate. His dream is fading before his eyes in a manner no one could have ever predicted. I feel compelled to try and support him. "I'll promise you this, Jack. If it's down to me I won't ever stop you playing." I wonder if I'm saying this for my own benefit as much as for Jack's. Whatever the true reason, at least I've started out on the road I know I must try and follow. I must not be my mother even if it turns out I have given Jack the emptiest promise in the world.

My gesture makes no impact on Jack. I wonder if he's even heard it his state is so desperate.

"Can't we go home?" Jack begs, his voice distraught. "I don't want to be stuck in here. I want to get out."

Go home. Pretend it never happened and get on with life as if it were 'Yesterday'. This very human response of denial is in us all, whatever our age. If only we could act on it without repercussion.

I shake my head apologetically. "We can't, Jack. I'm so sorry, son. We have to find out why this has happened and try to prevent it ever happening again."

I've made out to reassure him, yet in retrospect may have inadvertently made things worse with my careless inexpert use of words. Jack buries himself under his bedclothes to hide his crying and it kills me to see his distress. In the wordless vacuum of this repulsive moment my perception unfolds. I look over to see Clare weeping and grasp that although we may have got Jack back to where we dreamed of being twenty-four hours ago, everything has moved on. The previous day was all about survival and the quality of survival, today it's the implications of the survival. I have no idea what tomorrow will bring apart from knowing it is linked to why Jack's heart stopped for seventeen minutes and if it is ever likely to do so again.

I realise the onion-like layers of our predicament are waiting to be peeled away as we discover them. Each one a new dilemma and certain to bring a new challenge. This latest battle with The Fear cannot be swatted away with disdain. I cannot shelter behind an all-embracing, all-powerful Pact as I once did when I was thirteen. I've grown up and have fathered precious children. I might now be a man in terms of my age, but if I am to successfully rise to meet each new challenge I know I will need to mature a whole lot more.

Jack's consultant is as impressed with his condition as the rest of the medical staff. He gets Jack to walk normally, walk heel to toe and then hop up and down the ward corridor. He fires questions at him, jokes with him and nods slowly as Jack tells him about his football career and how he is trying to earn an apprenticeship.

"He's in remarkable shape," the consultant tells me and Clare as we sit at a table away from Jack and his bed. "The paramedics certainly did their stuff."

"Was it definitely a cardiac arrest that caused this?" I ask, needing absolute verification for one last time. "I thought it was some kind of epileptic fit."

"Yes, it was a cardiac arrest. The ambulance crew's record from their defibrillator machine showed Jack was in VF, ventricular fibrillation. It's a very dangerous arrhythmia caused by the electrical signals in the heart going haywire. Instead of the ventricles pumping blood around the body they quiver. Nothing goes round. Without shock treatment death is inevitable."

"Is it rare for someone so young and fit to have a cardiac arrest?" Clare asks.

The consultant raises his eyebrows and shakes his head. "Not as rare as you might think. It quite often presents itself in young athletes. Many arrhythmias present themselves more readily when the heart is under pressure. In fact, some athletes suffer from a thickening of the heart's wall muscles and this can cause problems."

"So, what's the next step?" I enquire.

"First we'll do a series of tests on Jack to see if we can ascertain why this has happened. Having said that, whatever results these tests throw up, it would be virtually unheard of to alter the choice of action we always suggest once a patient has suffered a VF attack. Ventricular fibrillation is always life-threatening and my advice would be to give Jack an implantable cardioverter-defibrillator, an ICD, which will monitor his heart at all times. If it senses a dangerous arrhythmia it will administer an appropriate shock and revert his heart back to normal."

I had never heard of such a thing. "What are the consequences of having one fitted?" I ask. "Where does it go?"

"It goes in up here," the consultant replies, pointing to an area just under his left collar bone. "It's so big," he links his thumb and forefinger of each hand to make a shape some three inches long. "And this deep," he adds, indicating a depth of less than an inch. "The leads from it go into the main artery off the heart near to the collar bone and terminate within the heart itself. There's normally a two day stay in hospital after the procedure. For six weeks afterwards care must be taken not to move the arm on the side of the implantation above head height due to a risk of lead displacement." The consultant pauses and smiles. "At this point I'd like to advise you not to go on the internet and look this up. You may well get a rather frightening false impression of ICD problems," he points out, undoubtedly talking from previous experience. "On the whole, it's a relatively straightforward procedure and the devices themselves are safe and reliable."

"Are there any lifestyle issues? Are there any things you can't do if you have one?" Clare enquires.

"Ignoring the underlying cause for having an ICD there aren't actually that many caused by the device itself. It's true to say if a patient does receive a shock it's not pleasant, but we try to stop this from happening by the use of drugs. Other than that, you can work, travel, swim, play certain sports and go about your life with minimal extra consideration. Modern technology has made these devices very small and very reliable. Unfortunately, with an ICD, normally speaking, any contact sports, especially at a professional level at Jack's age, are out of the question."

My heart sinks on hearing these words. "So... that's the end of his football? Football was his life."

The consultant looks at me directly. "At least with the device fitted he has a good chance of having one. He was lucky this time. Survival rates vary, but as few as one in ten survive an out of hospital cardiac arrest."

"Is it our only course of action?" Clare asks.

"I can only say if it was my son it's what I would do. Talk it over amongst yourselves and with Jack and tell me your decision tomorrow. As things stand I could do the procedure a week next Friday. In the meantime, I'll organise the tests we need to run. There's one other thing. Have you got any other children?"

"We've a daughter, Chloe. She's thirteen," Clare replies as I'm still under a spell of depression regards Jack's football and the prospect of having to tell him.

"I'd like you to bring her here as well so all of you can be checked out thoroughly. See one of my staff, they'll help you sort out the details."

The consultant bids us goodbye and leaves. I'm left empty, tears begin to roll down my cheeks and my anger returns. By the sounds of it, Jack is going to have to live with his version of The Fear and The Pact. An arrhythmia waiting to strike and an ICD ready to stop it.

"It's not fair, Clare," I whisper, the bile in my voice not hidden by its lack of volume.

She takes hold of me tightly by way of response, arching her back to look at me as she speaks. "I know it's not. The world's not fair. Have you seen how many young children are in here? What have they ever done to deserve a serious heart condition at their age?" I let my gaze fall to the ground. I have no answer. "We have to concentrate on the positives. It's not what he can't do, it's what he still can do. When he was lying on our carpet, not breathing and his heart wasn't working, I'd have taken where we are now. Wouldn't you? Look at him!" she declares, smiling through her moist eyes. "He's still our Jack. Think how much worse it could have been. Think what it would have been like if we'd lost him or if he'd been brain-damaged."

She's right. She's so right. I nod my agreement, pulling in a deep breath as I do. "Shall we tell him now?"

"There's no other choice is there, John?"

"You know he won't like it and he won't want it, don't you?" I tell her.

"Then we have to explain to him the best we can and make the decision for him. If he was a lot older it would be different and would be more his choice. He's not. We have to do what's best for him."

I massage my temples with my fingers. "I'll tell him."

"I don't care. I don't want one! Not if it means I can't play football," Jack exclaims. It's the third time he's said this.

"Jack! Listen to your father. We can't take the chance. You can't take the chance. In any case, there's no guarantee the doctors would let you carry on playing even if you didn't have the device."

"I'll take the drugs."

"Drugs might not be enough."

"I'm all right, aren't I? Nothing happened to me, did it?"

"You are all right and you're perfect. You got away with it. You got away with it this time. The next time you mightn't be so..." I can't bring myself to say the word 'lucky'.

"*If* there's a next time," Jack counters before I have chance to think of an alternative.

I'm amazed by Jack's resilience and stubborn attitude. It's like we're arguing over something as mundane as him not doing his homework. He may be on the cusp of manhood, but he argues with the invincibility afforded by youth. His earlier moment of terror and distress has gone. Dismissed and apparently completely forgotten. For a brief second I wonder if he truly understands what has happened to him and the implications for his future. Whatever the truth I'm secretly pleased at the vigour of his argument for not wanting to have the procedure. It augurs well for a positive outlook. It's all very well me having to man up and be strong enough to let him live, Jack has to want to do it as well. The way he is acting now makes me hopeful this horrid event won't destroy him and he'll recover without too many mental scars. The chances of him wanting me to wrap him up in cotton wool seem slight.

I try a new tack, remembering what Clare said to me. "Being a player isn't everything, Jack. You could move into coaching. You've seen enough of it to know what works with young players and what doesn't. Take your badges and aim to become a highly quali-fied coach. You could still be involved in the game on a daily basis. It's not as if you won't be able to kick a ball again." For once the riposte isn't instant. I flick a surreptitious glance at Clare. "It's got to be the next best thing to playing."

"Suppose."

"And you'll be safe. You'll always be safe," Clare reiterates. "You won't have to worry."

"And I'll be able to do everything else that I do now?"

"That's what the consultant told me."

Jack wipes his nose with the back of his hand. "Okay, then. I'll have it done. I don't really want to die," he admits with a sheepish look on his face. Jack turns and looks at me with his dark eyes.

"One thing though, Dad."

"Name it," I say, proud of my son's inner strength.

"If there's any way it turns out I can play I want you to do everything you can to help and support me."

"I've already promised I won't stop you playing, haven't I?" Jack nods. "I won't go back on my word."

'No, you won't,' I tell myself. 'Your name's John, not Mary.'

PART III

DECISIONS, DECISIONS

I wait in my car outside the hospital, the text message already despatched. The car is primed, faces the exit and I stare intently at the glass entrance opposite anxious to spot the first glimpse of familiar faces. Within minutes I see three of them at once. My family – Clare, Jack and Chloe. They walk quickly to the car, Jack with his left forearm held unnaturally into his stomach as if it's in an invisible sling, Clare and Chloe pulling three suitcases between them. I lean over and open the door for Jack. He gets in, guarding his left arm with great care.

"All right?" I ask.

"Sore," he answers.

I pull out his seatbelt and buckle it for him, carefully passing the belt under his left arm so it sits underneath his armpit rather than over his shoulder and his new scar.

"If you sit in the back behind me the belt wouldn't be over your scar."

"No. I want to sit in the front," Jack answers.

"Okay. I'll drive carefully."

I check the rear-view mirror and see the reflections of Clare and Chloe. "Okay, girls?" They nod simultaneously. "Cases in the back?"

"Yep," Chloe answers.

"Right. Let's go."

I start the car and pull away. I have my precious cargo onboard and we're off. It's more than two weeks since Jack's cardiac arrest and we're finally going home. The procedure went as well as could be hoped and Jack's outlook is good. The one melodramatic turn –

the one no one foresaw – still doesn't register with me. It may not seem quite so meaningless when I have to confront the problem, but after all I had been through I actually let out a brief snort of ironic laughter when they told me. It was the final straw that didn't so much break the camel's back, but made me think I was the butt of some kind of practical joke – one I fleetingly saw the funny side of. The staff didn't think it was funny at all and wanted to admit me there and then. I politely refused, told them my priority was to get Jack sorted and would come back as an outpatient. They acquiesced, it wasn't an unreasonable request given my state of health, although I do suspect the minds of the adult cardiac team were made up on one matter. It was my fault. I was the link.

Jack's consultant also seemed mildly amused by what had happened. "We could do you a two for one deal," he quipped.

"I still can't believe it," I answered, shaking my head in wonderment. "I've never had a sign. Not a single symptom or indication," I replied. "I've led an active life and do a manual job. Carpentry's one of the most physical trades and when I was younger I was a local footballer who played County League." I started to reminisce. "I was never as good as my father, he always had much more energy than me. I couldn't get about the pitch like he could."

"Now you know the reason why," Jack's consultant answered. "You couldn't get your heart rate up high enough to sustain endurance fitness."

"Do you think it's the cause of Jack's arrest?" I asked. "Is it me? Is it my fault? Have I passed something on to Jack?"

"There's a chance, but I'm not convinced. Your heart's slow, Jack's went fast."

Any brief levity I experienced from the two-for-one joke has long gone. There's no amusement now we're finally driving back home. In its place are two main underlying feelings. One is that things couldn't be much better given the odious nature of Jack's attack and the other, counterbalancing the upbeat, is a feeling of

210

trepidation. There's a sobriety of mood, one understandable given we're totally on our own now we're detached from nurses, doctors, consultants and their monitoring machines, expertise and knowledge. We're escaping from the safe environment where death and disaster, although never fully conquered, are kept on a short leash and made to behave with some modicum of respect. True, we are escaping to where we want to go, but it's a mixed blessing on many fronts. For one, my mettle will now be fully tested. Out of the cloistered environment we've inhabited of late I will find out if I can emulate my father and my grandfather and not turn into my mother.

Another aspect of emerging from such a one-dimensional world, one centring wholly on Jack's well being, is the daunting prospect of still having to contend with everything else. My parents' dementia, earning a living and running my own business, paying bills and dealing with any number of other mundane irritating problems from car breakdowns to washing machine leaks. It's all very well having your perspective altered to a big picture viewpoint, but short of having a very fat wallet the nuts and bolts of life still have to be addressed. That said, I do feel some confidence in my abilities to pull it off even if I'm under no illusion as to how easy it will be. I have learnt lessons over the last sixteen days, the administering of CPR being the most literal example. Many facets of Jack's ordeal are clearer, although I still have to learn to dismiss the notion of guilt that Jack's arrest was my genetic fault. I've done it before with Graham's death and now I will have to do it again.

It's all so strange. I knew I was slow. I told them so before the test. I simply never thought anything of it, didn't put any emphasis on it at all. Why would I, having attributed my slowness to fitness? For the moment I'm left high and dry and will hopefully find out more in time. There is talk of genetic testing. Possibly there will be an answer. But only possibly. For all their tests, the doctors haven't found out anything to explain Jack's attack – I certainly didn't mention The Fear to anyone.

One day at a time. It's what Clare and I said when we were in hospital. One day at a time; through the endless days, the scary days, the days of relief, the days of worry, the one special day of joy and the day to look forward to. Today. Today's the day. A slightly scary day and a wonderful day all rolled into one.

Two hours later and we're safely home. I watch my son walk over the carpet where he once lay and feel an imaginary icy hand on my back. Jack enters his bedroom as if nothing untoward has ever taken place and I realise he's going to be better at dealing with all this than I am. I follow him to the bedroom, wanting to ask how he is, wanting to check up on him, wanting to make sure he's all right. I stop myself short of the door. 'Just the once,' I tell myself, 'then leave him alone. No hovering.'

"You okay, Jack?" I enquire, poking my head round the door to see him sitting on his bed texting.

He looks up from his phone. "Yeah, good thanks. I've been working it out, Dad. Six weeks takes us to mid-November," he informs me. "Then I can start doing some training on my own." I nod enthusiastically. "I reckon I could be back playing by December."

"I know," I say, fighting back tears of emotion. "Fantastic, isn't it?"

"It's cool," Jack agrees.

I may or may not have my father or grandfather's genes regards allowing Jack to live his life to the full, but he appears to have them in spades. Whether he's inherited a specific gene mutation from me remains to be seen.

Our time in hospital was an eye-opener. A window to a world where the eyes of the collectively healthy rarely feels the need to look. A parallel world where every family has a sad story; where babies, toddlers, young children and teenagers face personal ordeals which their parents suffer with them. A world, conversely, of uplifting moments – Jack's story – and ones, such as the three-year-old girl in the adjacent bed, that pull everyone into the abyss. A world of swapped experiences, where many sets of parents with sad stories congregate and draw strength from each other. None more so than the story of the parents of a fourteen-year-old boy whose whole life had been a constant struggle against illness. A never ending sequence of hospital visits, tests and operations, of recuperation periods, of coming home and then having to go back for more tests, more operations and more time in a hospital bed. A life seemingly incapable of breaking free from a hospital environment.

I met those parents the day after Jack's implant and, as is customary, I told them my story and they in turn told me theirs. Their son had never been so close to death as Jack, his ailments lacked the explosive, out of the blue, shock-horror – The Fear factor – of Jack's cardiac arrest, but his quality of life sounded dire. A hardship diagnosed soon after birth leading to a life, in my eyes, which had been endured rather than enjoyed.

As they stoically related his suffering with grace and no self-pity I experienced an epiphany. With it my anger died as I finally saw it as futile and wasteful. I, of all people, should have known and realised. The past cannot be changed, we may well be afflicted by it, but to rage at it is futile. As I stood half-listening, my mind distracted by the throes of revelation, I recalled an old song where the words, 'Anger is an energy' are repeated over and over again. It was the final piece to my puzzle. The blinkers were off and it's hardly melodramatic of me to say scales fell from my eyes. The solution became crystal clear. I had to employ the energy of my anger to shape what I could alter, what I could influence and, crucially, it had to be done in the name of positivity. I had to use this energy to try and mould the future. Not to waste it, not to burn it up and squander it against an immovable object like the past. How ridiculous was that?

It was a defining moment, yet, if I'm brutally honest with myself, one I may not have been capable of were it not for Jack's miraculous recovery. What if I was a parent of a fourteen-year-old boy with no apparent light at the end of the tunnel? How much harder would it be to not rile against such a constant loop of agony? When they were gone I wept silently at their dignity, their plight and their son's suffering. I thought how wonderful they were. I stood in the hallway of the charity house where Chloe and I were staying, tears running down my cheeks, my daughter looking on in discomposure and I hoped and wished with every fibre of my being their son would get better. Despite the obvious biblical links to what I had experienced I still couldn't bring myself to pray.

I collected Chloe from Clare's parents' house the day after Jack was taken out of the ICU. From there I drove straight to the car park of the charity house near to the hospital. One of the hospital staff had found us a room within the large house for the duration of Jack's stay in hospital. Clare, with great inner strength and to my heartfelt relief, elected to be the one to stay permanently with Jack on the ward, sleeping in the pull down bed directly next to the patient's bed.

"I'm his mother, John," she told me. "It's my place to be by his side." She gave me an affectionate look and ran her hand down my cheek. "And I think I'll deal with it much better than you."

There was no argument on my part.

Chloe and I travelled in every day from the charity house to the hospital. We brought fresh food and drink supplies, newspapers, magazines and treats to help while away the inactive hours between the tests and their results. On the first day of commuting with Chloe, Jack underwent an echocardiogram in the morning and a 12-lead ECG test in the afternoon. All results showed as normal. It was shortly after this test when we told Jack's consultant we wanted to go ahead with the ICD implant.

Jack's consultant nodded and made one single comment. "It's the right choice."

For much of the time, Jack was free to wander the ward and come and go as he pleased, albeit with the inconvenience of a 3-lead ECG and transmitter box to constantly monitor his heart and warn nurses of any arrhythmias. He and I spent much of the time chatting about football, reading about football and watching snippets of TV. We also discussed the possibilities of his new coaching career. Quite often during these discussions I would start to become very emotional, much to Jack's annoyance, and he would chastise me for doing so. In my mind this was a classic case of role reversal – I was supposed to be the adult and the strong one – and in deference to him I tried harder to control my displays. It was impossible and I found myself trying to hide my distress and fake my way through it on numerous occasions. At times I'm certain Jack knew what I was doing. I was only too pleased he had the grace to ignore my not-so-clandestine breakdowns and say nothing.

By this time I'd already contacted Ron and Nashie and they both expressed their relief at Jack's amazing recovery. Nashie was adamant he would visit Jack, a pledge he made good a week later by turning up to see Jack and presenting him with a shirt signed by all the first team players. Nashie's blunt rough and tumble rhetoric made for a welcome change and a breath of fresh air. I know Jack appreciated it greatly. My FD clique sent text messages of support and good wishes and a lot of the boys sent messages to Jack. This was something that both lifted and deflated him. He loved getting messages from them, hearing the latest dressing room banter, match details about who had a shocker and who played well. The problem was it reminded him of what he was missing and what he would always miss out on because his days as a player were over. When one of the boys asked if he would be able to play again, Jack answered back by saying it was unlikely. He couldn't bring himself to text a definitive negative and I could tell he still secretly hoped a massive get-out-of-jail free card would pop out of thin air. I kept my counsel, wisely as it turned out, thinking hope is never a bad thing to have in your locker.

In a way, Jack being in hospital seemed incongruous. Jack, my handsome super-fit son, appeared the least ill person on the whole ward and that included all the parents, doctors and nurses! We were surrounded by poorly children with varying grades of heart problems, many of who were bedbound by recent operations or their condition. Jack, on the other hand, looked a million dollars and roamed the ward with a restless energy and lithe athleticism unmatched by anyone. Paradoxically, hardly any of the poorly children had come as close to death as Jack. In vacuous moments I would wonder what the hell we were doing there. Then I would remember The Fear and get angry. With bottled rage I would look at my watch, convinced an hour had passed, only to see a mere fifteen minutes had elapsed. Frustrated and caged I fumed against the past, whipping myself up into a dark mood, one making me hate the present with equal intensity. My epiphany was still to come.

If the days were hard going at times, what with parents trying to help their sick young children pass the hours and ease their discomfort, then the nights were fraught. Sick young children wired to alarmed monitors prone to lead detachment, the inevitable ensuing warning noise and nurse intervention, coupled with snoring parents and the general commotion of many bodies in a confined space made sleep difficult. Equally, the suffocating feeling of being trapped on the ward wasn't pleasant. At least Chloe and I escaped for twelve hours, Clare and Jack were afforded no such luxury. The night the three-year-old girl in the adjacent bed died was the worse. The pain and sleep deprivation was etched on everyone's face the following morning.

"It was awful," a haggard Clare told me. "So awful. That poor little girl. Her poor parents. All the nurses were crying."

That could have been us, I thought. Despite being in hospital, despite being right there with everything to hand they still couldn't save her. She, or one of her parents, clearly never had a pact. To me, it was the only logical answer.

The next test Jack underwent was an MRI scan on his head and his heart. I sat in with him in the room housing the equipment, my headphones on to protect against the machine's noise, and watched uneasily as he slid into the machine's narrow claustrophobic tunnel. It was a long ordeal which Jack dealt with comfortably, performing the various repetitive breathing instructions without incident. After the scan he was subjected to a Flecainide challenge, the drug being introduced into his bloodstream to see if he suffered from an arrhythmia condition known as Brugada Syndrome. As the drug coursed around his body a 12-lead ECG monitored his heartbeat to see if it altered in any way. His heart never faltered and the subsequent MRI scan showed no imperfections whatsoever.

On the day Clare, Chloe and I were guinea pigs we had a 12-lead ECG test.

"I'm scared, Dad," Chloe admitted beforehand. "What if they find something wrong?"

"They won't, darling. You're fine, I promise you."

She was. So was Clare. I was the problem.

"Have you ever had any heart problems?" the young female nurse asked as she attached the ECG electrodes to my skin. "Any palpitations, breathlessness or fainting? Any pains?"

"No, nothing," I replied. "Obviously, I'm not as fit as I used to be when I played football because that was a long time ago. I guess the only thing I can add is I've always had a slow heartbeat. I can remember taking my pulse in bed when I was about ten or eleven.

It was always around forty-five beats per minute at rest and it's still like that now. That's a sign of reasonable fitness, isn't it? A low heart rate at rest?"

The young nurse nodded. "It can be."

It wasn't. It was something completely different from a sign of fitness. It was a sign of something wrong.

"There," she said, pointing to the incomprehensible squiggly lines on the ECG printout in her hand. "Definite complete heart block. You've a serious heart condition." It was the statement that made me snort in derisive laughter at the unbelievable ridiculousness of it all. "I've spoken to a colleague and we'd like to admit you now, bearing in mind what's happened to your son."

"I'm sorry," I replied, still shaking my head in a confounded state. "I can't do that. I don't want to sound ungrateful for you uncovering this and I'm not pooh-poohing your advice. It's just that my son has nearly died, my wife is sleeping next to him on the ward, my daughter is with me and we're coming in every day to visit. Jack's ICD implant is due to take place next week and I can't possibly dump all that on my wife and go into hospital. It's hard enough for her as it is. I've been like this," I waved a finger at the ECG printout, "since I was ten. Probably for all my life. I'll take the chance that I'll stay in shape, see Jack sorted and safely home, and worry about me then. I'm sorry. I'm not being rude. You can see my predicament, can't you? It has to be that way."

They could see my predicament and thankfully that was how it was resolved. The only preliminary investigation I agreed to was a 24-hour tape, one which I wore for a day and a night. When the doctors looked at it I was pleased to hear my heart was in the same stable rhythm throughout, albeit in complete heart block.

"How slow did it go at night?" I asked out of curiosity.

"Thirty-three beats a minute, Mr Dennett," came the reply.

I was slow. Almost one beat every two seconds. "What could happen to me?" I asked.

"As you get older the escape rhythm might deteriorate and your heart might go so slow as to stop at night."

"No waking up in the morning, then?"

The doctor smiled. "You must get this checked out after your son is discharged."

"I will. I promise."

I didn't feel scared. The Pact would look after me until then.

The final test Jack undertook before his ICD implant was the most strenuous.

"Well done, Jack," his consultant praised. "Very impressive. You're only the second patient I've seen run twenty-one minutes on the Bruce protocol. Heart rate up to two hundred, no arrhythmias and no sign of long QT syndrome. Excellent!"

"I'm blowing! That was as hard as pre-season training," Jack gasped, sitting on the small bed next to the treadmill, his upper body glistening with sweat.

"I didn't think exercise would show anything up," I commented, eyeing the portable defibrillator brought into the room for the worst case scenario. "He's been exercising hard for years. He's done something like this three times a week since he was eleven."

Something like it. During a Bruce protocol test the treadmill progressively speeds up and inclines to a steeper gradient at three minute intervals. The patient's one task, constantly monitored by an ECG machine and at given intervals a blood pressure monitor, is to keep going for as long as they can. During the test the heart is put under pressure, a more likely time to reveal any abnormalities than any other.

"None of our tests has shown anything up," Jack's consultant remarked. "You're all clear on every front. If you had come to see me before your cardiac arrest I would have classed you as an extremely fit and very healthy young man."

"Is that normal?" I asked.

"No. Jack is unusual. You're both unusual."

I grinned. "Does it change anything? Not finding anything wrong?" I asked, looking at Clare who was standing with her arm around Chloe.

"Not to the diagnosis. We must still fit the ICD."

"What about sport?" I continued. "Is it significant he can exercise without any problem?"

Jack's consultant nodded. "It is significant. We're entering a new age of technology and discovery in children with arrhythmias. The devices are getting smaller, better shaped, more rounded, and we're beginning to fit them to children with obvious dangerous electrical disorders of the heart. By way of prevention, if you like, before someone suffers something similar to what Jack experienced. The whole field of what is or isn't acceptable for an individual to do with an ICD in place is shifting." Jack's consultant walked over to a desk. He pulled a set of A4-sized papers from a folder. "I've got something for you to read. It's a paper on the current conflicts of sports participation for athletes with implantable cardioverter-defibrillators. It's very pertinent to Jack."

I took the papers from him and with increasing excitement silently read the bolded headline. 'Sports participation for athletes with ICDs should be an individualised risk-benefit decision.'

"What does it say, Dad?" Jack asked, his eyes burning bright.

"The last paragraph sums it up rather neatly," Jack's consultant prompted. "Read it out."

With trembling fingers I turned over to the final page, located the last paragraph and read it out loud. "'Although there are ample theoretical reasons to restrict athletes with ICDs from sports participation, in practice, data actually proving sports to be dangerous for all ICD patients are non-existent. A prospective registry, the ICD Sports Safety Registry is currently enrolling patients who have made the decision to participate in competitive sports and will follow those individuals for two years. This prospective study should shed considerable light on this controversial question. Although decisions regarding how we choose to view risk in our lives rarely are entirely rational, by quantifying the risks of sports for individuals with ICDs, we will give patients the information necessary to make an informed decision. Are sports entirely risk-free for individuals with ICDs? Probably not. But life is not risk-free, and ultimately an informed choice should lie with the individual athlete and his or her family.'" I looked up from my piece of paper to stare at Jack's consultant. "Do you agree with this? Are you saying he can go back to playing football?"

Incredibly, Jack's consultant nodded. "Given Jack's individual circumstances I'm quite happy for him to go back and try. He falls into a class of patient whose diagnosis would be described as having suffered idiopathic VF. That means there is no known cause," he explained. "He can go back to playing when he and his club feel he is fit enough. I'll write to them giving my full consent to his continued participation."

The look on Jack's face was a picture. Our spectacular day of joy.

"Shall I check on him one more time?" I ask Clare as we lie in the near darkness of our bedroom, sleep a concept beyond comprehension.

"Yes, please."

Her voice sounds tearful and strained. It's our first night home and the garish video replays going on in both our heads consume our souls. Being on our own has heightened the vividness of bad memories and pushed our fear levels way out of proportion to the actual risk. We know Jack has the device and we know it works, it was tested when Jack was under anaesthetic. It still doesn't help. Not yet. It's too soon. I get out of bed, grab the tiny torch resting on a chest of drawers and creep into Jack's bedroom through the door I made sure was never closed. He's asleep. I carefully walk over and shine the torch on the duvet over his chest. Transfixed, I stare at it checking for motion. The duvet rises and falls, rhythmically and evenly. I turn off the torch and slope out.

"He's fine," I tell Clare as I climb into bed.

"Are we going to be like this forever, John?" she asks. "Constantly checking our son to see if he's still alive?"

"Only until we die," I reply, trying to make a joke out of how I'm feeling.

"The way my heart's pounding that might not be so far away," she answers. Neither of us laugh.

"But he must never know," I say in all seriousness. "Our negativity will become his negativity. He's dealt with it so well and we mustn't sour it with our emotions. All we ever wanted when he was lying on the carpet was for him to be a normal boy again. As it's turned out, we couldn't have hoped for a better outcome. He has everything back. Even his football... Yes, there's a road to recovery and the future is unsure to an extent, but there's no denying we have been lucky." I reach out under the duvet and touch Clare. "We can't be the ones to stop him being normal. We have to be strong. We..."

"Mustn't be like your mother," she suggests, finishing off my sentence.

"Precisely. We mustn't be like my mother."

"When are you going to see your parents?"

"I'll take Chloe to school tomorrow and pop round then. I also promised Jack I'd phone Nashie to tell him he can carry on playing and that his consultant will be confirming it in writing... Clare?"

"What is it?"

"There's something else I have to tell you. I've been turning it over in my mind and I've come to the conclusion I can't face work yet. I can't face going back and having to start fretting over customers, ordering materials and organising jobs. I've no interest in it. I can't get my head around it. It'll be all too much."

"Don't worry about it, John," Clare reassures. "We've got some savings. We'll use those if we have to. We'll get by. You go back when you're ready. I'm sure my work will carry on giving me compassionate leave. Jack can't dress himself at the moment or wash properly. He needs me to look after him and I don't want to leave him on his own. I need to fill his time, take him out, do things with him. I don't want him left with nothing to do so he can start mulling over what's happened. He needs to be occupied. I've decided I'm going to ring the school and see if I can get some work for him to do at home. He'll be miles behind if I don't."

"He's going to love you," I remark, knowing my son's disposition towards anything academic. "But you're right. We need to fill his time. Six weeks of recuperation is a long time."

"And we mustn't forget about Chloe. It can't be all Jack, Jack, Jack." I nod in the gloom. Her silhouette, caused by the soft glow of the digital alarm clock, turns and faces me. "Are you worried about your heart?" she asks.

"Not really," I answer. "It all seems so strange. Fifty years plus without a single hint. Completely, what's the word they used? 'Asymptomatic'."

"As long as you're not blaming yourself. It's ridiculous to do that."

"I know it is."

"How about we try to get some sleep?" she offers.

"Yeah. We must try." I lean over and kiss her on the cheek. "It's early days, Clare. Our lives have changed. We've changed, or at least I know I have. But for Jack and Chloe the key is normality. Blissful bland normality. It's not going to be easy, but we have to believe we can do it... Goodnight, darling."

"Goodnight, John."

I close my eyes and see Jack take in a big gasp of air and stop breathing. I see blue lights, his body jolt and a paramedic pushing on his chest. I see a montage of horror. Then I try to dream, even though I'm still awake, of the day he plays football again. For some reason I think of Bill Shankly who once famously said that football was more important than life or death. Shankly was wrong, yet in his words there is a hint of something close to Jack's circumstance. Jack being able to play football again is symbolic of his amazing reclamation – one where my son has clawed back every facet of life after cheating death.

I'm now sufficiently calm to pull out of the parking spot I entered after dropping Chloe off at school. I'm on the way to visit my parents after an enforced break caused by my fifteen-year-old son suffering a cardiac arrest and nearly dying. The thought still has a surreal air to it, as if it can't be true because those sort of things only happen to other people in news reports and articles. Frederick was one, so was Alfred, Harold and Graham. They all ended up as news reports and they're all linked to Jack, the sole survivor.

As I near the end of the short journey I become massively apprehensive. In many respects I'm comfortable knowing I'm a changed man and think I can adjust to live with my shifted perspective. Being aware of this is one thing, how it will impact when seeing my parents again is another. The elephant in the room is having to try and explain to their non-functioning brains what has happened since I last saw them A task I have studiously avoided thus far. As I turn into their road I review the actions I took moments ago. The incident has surprised me. If I'm honest, it's caught me out and it doesn't augur well for interaction with my parents. In fact, it doesn't augur well for anything. It's evidence, if I needed reminding, of how very raw, how very wounded and how very combustible I am. It appears I'm likely to go off at any time, like a cheap imported firework. I'm not raging at the past, it's not anger, it's something different. It's what I presume to be a type of post traumatic stress disorder. It's what my mother suffered from for almost all of her life.

It started with the vindictive way I tore up Caroline's business card. There wasn't fury in my actions, more a desire to completely eradicate a course of action I once considered and now know to be wholly inappropriate and utterly wrong-headed. Ripping the card into ridiculously tiny pieces became an act of self-cleansing, a disassociation, a clean break from my past. True, the card only represented a notion, an idea I was toying with during a pathetic mid-life blip (at least I had recognised that), but even so, Clare never deserved it. Once it was done, although a tiny sliver of guilt felt as if it was shed, my head began to boil. And then came the wave.

If my epiphany not to rage at the past and to use the saved energy to shape the future seemed shadowed in the spontaneity of ripping up the card, then what followed showed it as completely lost. It was all very well realising a course of action when alone in a moment of lucidity; controlling my heaving restless emotions when confronted with life and carrying it out was another. As I flung the tiny pieces of card out of the van's window my head began to reel at the momentous happenings of the last month. The surreal air, the feeling of 'this can't be happening' I experienced during Jack's attack, swamped me. Images swam before me, decades' worth of dogma – The Fear and The Pact – my family's tragic history, my parents' dementia, Jack's cardiac arrest, the past, the present and the future all heaved themselves up into a giant wave of terror confusion and desperation. The giant roller broke with an almighty crash about my body, flinging me face down on to a hard unforgiving foreshore. As I lay prostrate and stranded, the wave receded towards the sea taking with it my optimism, my hope and my stability.

Shivering with panic I gripped the steering wheel of my stationary van as tight as I could, hanging on for what appeared to be dear life. I fought to focus on Jack's miraculous recovery, on his consultant's assurances, on the sad stories of the other parents I met and how they dealt with them. I homed in on how The Pact beat The Fear, on how I mustn't sink into depression, on how I must be strong and mustn't be my mother. I forced myself to remember my grandparents' wonderful nights of babysitting and my father letting me ride a motorbike. Finally, I centred on my dream for Jack. The one I've had from the moment the scan showed he was a boy.

"Still alive!" I cried, as if they were the words to an incantation designed to disperse evil spirits. "My memories and my dream are *still* with me!" I shouted through clenched teeth. Over and over again I thought positive thoughts and eventually the moment of panic passed. "There are going to be plenty more of those. You'd better get fucking used to it," I told myself.

Arriving at the house that Owen built with a strong sense of foreboding I find one of the carer's cars parked on the drive. I recognise it and know the owner. Cheryl has been a regular breakfast/midday call carer from the outset of her company's association with my parents. I meet her at the front door as she's stepping out of it.

"Hello, Cheryl."

"Hello, John. How's your son?" she gushes. "We all heard. How horrible."

"He's very well, thank you. As good as we could ever have hoped," I reply.

"Oh, thank God for that. A heart attack, wasn't it?" I nod, not wanting to be pedantic and correct her incorrect terminology. I also want the conversation over quickly. I could go off again at any time. "At fifteen! And he's really fit, isn't he? Doesn't he play a lot of football?"

"Yes he does."

"Will he have to stop playing?"

"No," I answer. "The consultant has indicated he can carry on. We're all hopeful he'll be able to. He's at home recovering from his operation at the moment, so it's early days."

"An operation? On his heart?" she asks, her hand covering her mouth in a display of shocked concern.

"No. Not on his heart," I reassure. For some strange reason I now feel compelled to tell her more, despite my earlier wishes. "He's had a special device put into his chest to monitor his heart. If it ever goes wrong it will give it an electric shock and make it start beating correctly." I can see Cheryl's grasp and knowledge of ICDs is exactly the same as mine once was and she compensates by nodding vigorously to mask her non-comprehension.

"Good. Let's hope he gets over it quickly. The poor love."

"Thanks, Cheryl. I'm sure he will. He's dealt with it magnificently so far... How have my mum and dad been?" I ask, moving the conversation on.

Cheryl wrinkles her nose. "Not *too* bad. Your dad did have a wander last week. We called the police when we arrived and found he wasn't home. Luckily, they tracked him down very quickly and he hadn't got far. We didn't tell you. We thought you had enough on your plate." I give Cheryl a weak smile of thanks. "We have started to find your dad wet in the mornings," she goes on, a slight grimace on her face. "We may have to start putting him in some kind of incontinence pad if it gets much worse. He still won't let me get anywhere near that beard of his," she adds, in a more light-hearted vein." I roll my eyes at this, tutting as I smile. "But, believe it or not, he has allowed us to put him in the shower a few times, which is a real step forward. Mum's pretty much the same, don't get an awful lot of sense out of her, bless her."

I'm surprised and pleased at my father's new regime of compliance. "That's good news about the showering, especially if he's starting to be wet."

Cheryl looks anxiously at her wristwatch. "Sorry, John," she apologises. "I've got to go. My next call is scheduled for nine fifteen."

"Of course. You crack on. Thanks very much for all you've done."

I find my parents sitting on the settee in front of the television eating the last remnants of breakfast. As I saw Clare anew during Jack's arrest so I see my parents' condition in a similar manner after my one-month sabbatical. The effect is depleting and saddening. Neither are aware it has been almost a month since I last visited them. My father looks up and greets me by my name whereas my mother only does so with a generic, 'Hello, dear.'

"I'm glad you're here, John," my father comments. "I was beginning to think you'd forgotten about that roof we've got to pitch. The bloke's been phoning me all morning asking when we're going to get there."

The looped cassette conversations and the various monologues from the past judder into my mind and I feel myself wilt. Where is the energy I was going to use to mould the future into a vista of positivity? Is there any future as far as my parents are concerned?

"Dad, you're retired. You don't work anymore," I wearily point out. "You retired years ago."

"No! He's been phoning me up all morning. I said we'd be there today."

"Well, we *won't* be there today," I snap. "Because the job doesn't exist."

My father's face turns into a frown. "We can't let him down, John. He's a good customer. A good payer. I've promised."

"You haven't promised because you haven't spoken to anyone," I say, my voice rising in agitation. "Besides, I have something important to tell you. *Much* more important."

The aggression in my voice stops my father dead in his tracks and my mother looks up in surprise from whatever she was staring at. With increasing emotion and an air bordering on martyrdom I start to tell them about Jack their only grandson. I tell them how he nearly died, how his heart stopped for seventeen minutes and what

228

my family has endured and contended with over the last month. It pours out of me, a torrent of words and emotions. I start to break down. My voice becomes uncontrollable, wavering in pitch and tone, my body shakes and wavers. Tears roll freely from my eyes as I vividly relive the words I'm speaking. I'm in meltdown again. The thin congealed layer serving as a lid on my emotions spectacularly ruptures and my red hot feelings spurt into the room like molten lava erupting from a volcano.

My mother eyes me as if I'm a madman. "Look at him crying," she remarks as an aside to my father when I'm in full flow. "Look at those tears."

"Don't you remember Jack?" I bluster, deviating from my tale as a response to her comment. "He's my son! Your grandson! You used to come and watch him play football, Dad."

"Yes... I remember Jack," my father says at last. These are his first words hinting at any real form of cognitive uptake to what I've been saying. "How's his football going? Is he playing today?"

Frustration engulfs me. This is why I avoided telling them. With hindsight maybe I should have done so forever. "He's been seriously ill. That's what I've been trying to tell you. He nearly died."

"Is he all right now?" my father asks.

"Well, yes he is. Much better now, but..."

"That's good," my father remarks, cutting me off. "Measles can be nasty. I remember when you had it. Covered in spots you were..."

"He hasn't had measles!" I exclaim, exasperated and in floods of tears. "When did I say he had measles? He had a cardiac arrest. His heart stopped. He nearly died."

My mother suddenly begins to cry, pulls herself off the settee, her handbag still over her arm as if it were glued there and she shuffles over to me. She puts her thin arms around me and gives me a hug.

"She isn't what up, dear," she garbles.

All of my vexation dissipates in an overwhelming surge of love for the woman who was once my mother. I return her hug, kissing her on the forehead and lead her back to the settee. We both sit down, me taking the middle seat between my two parents. My father is crying now, probably because both myself and my mother are. I put my arms around them both and pull them in tight. We all cry together. At last I get the emotional prop I was seeking. I know their empathy is only a fundamental human response to suffering, there's no comprehension in it, but it's enough to appease me. They're sharing my ordeal and that's enough. It's all I wanted. They don't understand and they never will understand the most frightening incident to have occurred in my life. In ten minutes' time they will have forgotten it completely whereas I will have to live with it all my life – unless I end up like them. I make the decision to never mention Jack's ordeal to them again.

I leave my parents' house after an hour in their company and arrive home to an empty house. Clare has obviously taken Jack out somewhere and I'm left to contemplate. What I'm thinking isn't pleasant. The full implications of my parents' disease are unmasked by my shifted perspective. The stark reality of what stretches ahead for them makes me start to think. Irrespective of their lack of understanding of Jack's attack seeing my father sitting on the settee, a wet patch over his groin hinting at the first signs of incontinence, my mother more incoherent than ever, looking through me as if I were a household fixture rather than her only son, I wonder, for the first time, if they'd be better off dead. What have they to look forward to? What reasons have they to stay alive? What good will all my efforts, the efforts and expense of the care company and the medical services actually achieve? The answer to all the questions, as far as I can see, is nothing.

The conclusion I come to is not pretty. I want my parents to die. I don't want them to live through this anymore. They've had their time – nearly eight decades of good health. Why blight it with a few horrid years? Better to quit now while they're marginally ahead. If they were to die, to drop down dead this instant, I could go away and celebrate their lives. At their funerals I could relate tales of my father on his motorbikes, of him playing football, loving his work and leading a full and satisfying life. Admittedly, with my mother it would be more difficult to be upbeat. She has lived the vast percentage of her life in the shadow of The Fear, right up until the moment dementia freed her from it and slyly took away all that remained. Having said that, she has loved and been loved. For all her difficulties she was always loved by my father, by me, by her sister and by her parents. For all her tragedy and anxiety she at least has benefitted from love reciprocated.

As a couple, the sun is setting on their lives and to my mind it can't get dark quickly enough. Their deaths would be acceptable, preferable even, to continued life. My earlier image of the pair of them riding a motorbike over a cliff, a manic grin on my father's face, in a spectacular 'Fuck you!' V sign to old age and deterioration, looks the perfect solution. I'm sure if they could look upon themselves, from a time of full mental functionality, they would be horrified at what they have become. The terrible thing is neither one of them has shown any true self-awareness of their deterioration. They would never have pulled the plug on themselves because they were insufficiently aware of their demise. Who else has the right?

My thoughts leave me feeling stained. Am I a terrible son to wish for their quick deaths? Am I cruel and uncaring? Does it mean I don't love them anymore? Am I wishing for them to die to make my life easier? To make me richer because I would inherit their house? Dazed by my inner conflict I struggle to come to terms with my home truths. In the end, the point convincing me I can be at peace with my thoughts is this; if Jack had died there could never be a celebration of a life terminated at fifteen. On the other hand, if my parents die tomorrow, I would genuinely be glad to see their

231

suffering end. It's a hugely complex moral conundrum and I'm left pondering the merits of euthanasia, dignity in death, quality of life appraisal and the labyrinthine legal issues of what is applicable, where it is applicable, and who, if anyone, can make the judgement call.

That night I tell Clare I'm going to buy her a gun and if I ever get like my parents she must shoot me.

"What if I get like it first?" she asks.

"Then I'll borrow it and shoot *you*!" I retort.

The black humour makes us both laugh and it's a strangely uplifting feeling given the grim nature of the subject matter. It's the first time we've laughed since Jack's attack. After the day I've suffered I hope it signifies a very tiny inching towards a better tomorrow.

Jack sits side saddle on the small bed. What looks like a large computer mouse, its lead draped over his shoulder, rests over his implanted ICD. The mouse has read his device – no episodes of any arrhythmias, continuous sinus rhythm throughout – and is now being used to alter his heart rate as part of his six-week pacing clinic check-up.

"I'm going to speed you up a bit," the technician tells Jack. "This might feel a bit funny." He presses the touch screen of the ICD's computer a few times. "Here we go. Can you feel it?"

"Err! Don't like that! That feels weird!" Jack answers.

"Nearly done." The technician taps another few buttons and the computer spews out reams of ECG printouts. He tears them off, places them on top of Jack's medical folder and removes the mouse hanging over Jack's shoulder. "Okay, that's it. Everything's fine," he tells Jack. "No issues with your heart, no shocks delivered and the device is working perfectly."

I breathe a sigh of relief and smile at Clare who smiles back. I wink at Jack and he gives me a thumbs up. It's been a day of worry, but the last six weeks have seen us all make steady headway. I've been back at work for two weeks, sleep comes a little more readily at night, the video replays of horror are waning and my panic attacks are reducing in number and intensity. Complementing this I now only flinch in worry, rather than jump out of my skin, when I get an incoming call from either Clare or Jack on my mobile. Better still, I'm more inclined to go into Jack's bedroom in the mornings with the expectation he'll be alive rather than the nagging fear he'll be dead. My hopes and aspirations of achieving bland normality are gradually coming to fruition. They're inextricably linked to Jack's good progress and today has nudged them on a little further.

Of all of us, Jack is the one who seems the least affected. It's a phenomenon I find as fascinating as I do pleasing. The fact he can shrug off such a momentous event leaves me in awe of my son's resilience. Clare and I discuss his bravery at length and inevitably, after the microscopic inspection process is over once again, we are left with the unsophisticated analysis that it simply is the way he is. Nothing other than an innate natural predisposition can explain his apparent lack of concern. I'm convinced Jack has no Pact because – ah, the simplicity of it – he has no Fear. The notion he may have another cardiac arrest doesn't seem to feature on his agenda. The long term implications of having an ICD are disregarded with apparent ease. He has no recollection of the attack and therefore suffers no consequences from it. 'It happened, I'm all right, let's get on with it,' seems his only philosophy. He is my father and my grandfather rolled into one and multiplied many times over. I'm so proud of him.

I, on the other hand, have more than enough baggage to make up for my son's ease of dismissing his attack. Some time back I dreamt up what now seems a slightly dodgy analogy involving playing cards to represent my parents' memory loss. Now I have another one for life, the universe and everything. It consists of everyone receiving a poker hand at birth. This hand evaluates their entire chances of winning a decent life, their 'pot', if you like, based on their genetic disposition towards health, their social status and their talents. Unlike real poker, the pot is constantly available to each player and it fluctuates in value as each plays their hand. If a hand improves as a player 'draws' their cards throughout their life, or has them changed for them, via clever play, good luck and fortunate circumstance, their pot gets bigger. If their hand weakens, via bad play, poor luck and dire circumstance, so their pot decreases.

I see this as fairly routine stuff, but in my game – and it's a big personal realisation – is the omnidealer of all cards to all players is the Grim Reaper. And he can take you out of the game at any time, at any age, when you least expect it. Living for decades with complete faith in The Pact, despite my family's association with The Fear, blinkered me to this most fundamental rule. I now see with a keen eye how each player has a considered choice, a balancing act to perform, when deciding how to use their cards. For example, who wants to end up with dementia and a million pounds in the bank after a life of chaste frugality? Who wants to blow the lot at thirty and be left with nothing? Who regrets not doing more with their suddenly deceased partner? Who wishes they'd done more with their kids when they were young? Who saved for retirement and never got there? Who squandered their hand inappropriately with no concern for the impact on others? These are tough choices to make without foresight, but at least now I know I need to make them to get the most from life – for me and my family.

The sad thing is, in reality, many have no choice, or very little, thanks to the hand they were dealt at birth. Some hands can never be made strong enough to offer significant choice, they only offer continued poverty, ill health and precious little opportunity to change. However, if you can make choices via the strength of your hand then that is a different matter. This is half the reason I was sufficiently motivated to go back to work. I do want to take all of us on a lovely holiday, but I also want to revisit some pleasant aspects of the past. I have gone back to work to earn money, but am determined to take more time off than I have in the past. Time I shall use to pursue leisure interests, some on my own and some with Clare and the children.

If these decisions were prompted by my new sense of perception to money, time, life and how to use them, then they were greatly invigorated by Jack's continuing good health. My determination to follow in my grandfather and father's footsteps is also a strong source of stimulus. I have acquired direction. I now know what I want. I recognise what's important and am motivated enough to do something about it, a situation far removed from my previous scenario.

My biggest hurdle appears to have been jumped, although I suspect this first hurdle is bound to be one of many, any one of which might trip me up in the future. Even so, my mother's choice of lifestyle is an anathema to me. It was when I was young – it was partly the reason why I devised The Pact – and it is now, despite my being constantly tested. As a family we have been lucky and that luck has given us an escape route to choices. The energy I vowed to use to mould the future is gradually, in tiny increments, coming back to me. The cards Clare and I had dealt to us were good. By our own efforts, by luck and by circumstance we have options and we intend to utilise them fully.

My pathetic mid-life crisis was built on not seeing my life as it was and by feeling trapped. I was blinkered and lacked the insight and willpower to make changes because I didn't know what I wanted. I couldn't see my cards for looking and I toyed with acts which ultimately could have ended in me throwing away a good hand. I was a fool. I only wish I could have known what I know now without needing The Fear to attack Jack to make me see it. I wish it and at the same time know it can never be. I try and force

235

myself not to think too deeply about it. The trouble is, it's so desirable and enticing it's hard not to.

Plea bargaining – a theological game of trade where I offer payment for Jack to have never been attacked by The Fear – is another difficult temptress to resist. I will myself to stop thinking of convoluted methods of bargaining him out of his plight, of using barter and brinksmanship to secure a deal where he escapes his trauma. It's a path leading back to the abyss, one heading back to raging against the past. So far, I've managed to keep myself in check. Despite temptation my epiphany stands strong. My anger remains locked away and I look forward, riding the wave of Jack's well being and my new understanding as I do.

As for the machinations of The Fear and the protection of The Pact? Well, my personally designed version of Satan fighting God is still with me, even if the absolutes are blurred. I still believe The Fear attacked Jack and The Pact saved him and will keep me safe until the doctors decide what to do with me. Other than that I'm unsure of either's influence. The whole concept has veered so wildly from its original premise, nothing seems clear cut. The intricacies of my condition and my possible link to Jack, via genetics, remain a mystery at this time, as do any future medical problems either of us might suffer. There is a new line of research indicating the possibility of a medical link from me back to my mother, which only serves to further muddy the water. This wholly different sphere of operation from The Fear's earlier work leaves me flummoxed. There appears little hope of clarity, however much I mull it over. In the end I'm left with one hope. That is to park The Fear and The Pact outside my mental peripheral vision and hope it rarely affects me on a day-to-day basis.

Jack's consultant enters into the room. He greets us all and asks the technician how Jack's pacing session has gone. The technician tells him all is well.

"Good. Jack, can you take your shirt off so I can take a look at your scar?" Jack obliges and shows him the neat white scar of less than three inches in length immediately below his collar bone. A slight bulge under Jack's skin gives away the tiny bulk of the ICD. "That's healed nicely," he tells Jack. "So, young man, back to school soon?"

"Next Monday," Jack answers, not sounding especially enamoured at the prospect.

"When have the club said you can go back to training?"

"I'm going back to training in December," Jack replies. "I'll do some stuff on my own before then."

"When you start playing there is a very tiny chance your device could be damaged by a boot or an elbow. It would be quite an unusual area to get kicked, but even so there is still a small possibility. It's highly unlikely, but your upper body isn't fully developed and your pectoral muscles lack bulk. I'm just wondering..."

"Some sort of pad?" I interject.

"Yes," Jack's consultant agrees, nodding at me. "Some form of extra protection."

"I could look on the internet and see what's available," I suggest.

"I would. Other than that I'll see you for your next appointment in February. Good luck, Jack."

"Thanks," Jack says, shaking his consultant's hand.

I want to shake it as well. "Thanks very much." I offer my hand. "Thanks very much for everything."

I'm already considering my task to find something to protect Jack's ICD. I'm also thinking about everything else Jack has to deal with. As if trying to become a professional football apprentice isn't hard enough on its own.

I'm being tested as I've never been tested before. Every inch of my being wants to leave the house, jump in my van and look for Jack. I get up from the settee and peek out through the curtains. It's

237

pitch black outside save for the street lights, a cold unwelcoming November night. In a state of angst I look at my watch and see he's been gone nearly three-quarters of an hour, the longest duration so far. A vivid image of Jack collapsed on a street corner formulates in my mind's eye. I walk out of the living room and into the dining room, our home 'office', where Clare is catching up on some work on our PC. She's back at work full-time now and the good ship SS Normality steams happily onwards despite this current setback.

"He's been gone three quarters of an hour. Do you think he's all right?"

"He did say he was going to run for longer tonight," Clare starts positively enough, "but he has been gone a long time."

"Well that clears that up, then."

Clare stops typing and spins round on the swivel chair to face me. She gives me a condescending look. "What was I *meant* to say, John?"

I breathe in deeply and open my mouth, only to expel the air out through puffed cheeks. "No idea," I admit.

"If you're looking for an excuse to go out and check on him, then go. Tell him I was worried."

"I can't do that." I'm frowning at the prospect. "Our negativity becomes his negativity. It's what we've always said."

"I know. And if that's the case you'll have to wait, won't you?"

"What, just wait? But what if...?"

"John," Clare starts sternly. "This isn't any easier for me, you know. He's my son, too. I might not have a family history of death and disaster littered through the generations, but that doesn't make it any different. It doesn't make me any less frightened or any less anxious. I lived through it as well. I saw exactly what you saw."

"Not *exactly*," I say childishly.

"You know what I mean," Clare says, putting me firmly back in my place. "And I know it's not my parents with dementia. But I treat them as if they were my own. I've helped wash both of them.

238

And *I* was the one who managed to trim your dad's beard off!" she points out, triumphantly nodding her head once at me as she bites her lower lip and raises both eyebrows.

I try to drag the skin on my cheekbones to a point below my jawbone with the palms of two hands. "Aarghh! I'm sorry. I hate it when I get like this. So stupid!"

"It's not stupid. You're not stupid. I feel exactly the same. You relate everything back to your mother, that's your trouble. You're so desperate not to be like her you don't cut yourself any slack. What other parent wouldn't be thinking what we're thinking now? Who in their right..."

Both of us hear the front door open and then close.

"All right, Jack?" I call out, trying to eradicate any note of concern from my voice.

"Yeah, fine," he replies.

Relief washes over me and I pull a face to indicate so to Clare. A few seconds later Jack's head pokes round the dining room door, his white iPod earphones in sharp contrast to his jet black hair. He walks into the room. He has picked up some mud on his trainers and it goes all over the carpet.

"What are you two up to?" he asks.

"Just chatting," Clare replies.

"Chatting shit, more like!" Jack admonishes.

Jack's cheek, and the mud he's deposited on the carpet, highlights another consequence of his attack. It's one I had never previously considered until a few days ago when he failed to shut the freezer door properly. Much of the freezer contents had to be thrown away because they had defrosted. It prompted a new post cardiac arrest question; what do I do about telling him off? If he does need reprimanding, what exactly do I do? If I do nothing, it implies he can do whatever he likes and surely that can't be right. Or is it? Are we so fortunate to still have him that it means he can never do wrong again? Do I turn a blind eye to every infringement

239

and transgression of parental rules? Do I tell myself if I'd suffered what he'd suffered would I be diverting one ounce of thought towards etiquette and petty rules? And what about Chloe? I can't run a double standard, that would be patently unfair. My monologues? Are they destined to remain unspoken, locked inside my head along with my card analogies for dementia, for life, the universe and everything and my fish analogy for young footballers? Must I never moan or talk of the generation gap again, narrow as it may be?

There's the rub and we're back to the big picture versus the nuts and bolts of life again. This time, however, there's no leeway involving the size of one's wallet. There's no get-out clause allowing wealth to sweep away the nuts and bolts with a deft waft of its opulent hand. This is a morality issue and my ideal of only ever wanting Jack to be a normal boy again must hold sway. The answer is to treat him the same as I always have. I am still his father and must act like it, whatever has happened.

"Don't swear indoors, Jack. It doesn't sound nice. And look at all the mud you've put on the carpet." It sounds as weak as I feel. I have no stomach to chastise him. I'm so lucky to still have him I don't want to waste any precious second of interaction disciplining him. Better for him to be a normal mouthy teenager than be hunched in a bedroom, paralysed with anxiety, agonising over the moment his heart might stop. "How'd your run go, anyway?" I enquire as Jack silently lifts his head up from looking at the dirty carpet.

"Yeah, good... I'll get the dust pan and brush and clean up the mud."

"That's all right, Jack," Clare tells him. "I'll do it. Just remember to take your shoes off in the porch next time."

I smile inwardly at this shift in her nature and know she feels the same as me.

"Do you think you're getting fitter?" I ask brightly.

"Well, yeah, obviously," Jack answers, as if it's a stupid question. "That's the furthest I've been and I'm upping the pace every time I go."

"How fit do you think you are compared to before... er... it happened?" I ask, tip toeing around The Fear's attack with all the subtlety of a hobnailed hippo.

"What? My arrest?" Jack asks without hesitation. "Don't know. Hard to say really. Not match fit, nowhere near." Jack shivers. It might be genuine or he might be fed up with my interrogation. "Brrr! I'm getting well cold, Dad. I'm going up to have a shower."

"Okay." Jack needs no second invitation and he disappears from the room. "Don't forget to take your trainers off before you go upstairs," I call out, trying to kid myself I'm maintaining some semblance of authority.

"Will do!"

I look at Clare and shrug in astonishment. "How does he do it?"

"You don't think he's bottling it all up, do you? Hiding it from us?" Clare asks.

"Not a chance," I say. "You don't really think that, do you?"

Clare shakes her head. "No, not really. It's just that sometimes it all appears so effortless for him to deal with what's happened I begin to wonder if it's too good to be true. Chloe tells me nobody's talking about it at school anymore, even though he's only been back a week. When she went back, it was *the* hot topic of conversation. She was bombarded with it. The pupils and staff were very shocked. Now Jack's had his official welcome back in assembly and everybody's seen him, seen he looks the same, he acts the same, plus he looks a picture of health, it's like they've all forgotten."

"Are you forgetting?" I ask. "For a few seconds at a time, here and there?"

"If you're asking, am I happier now than I was directly after it happened and am I learning how to deal with it? Then, yes."

241

"Me, too," I agree, thinking of my mother.

The mobile phone lying on top of the bedside cabinet rings in the dead of night. Wrenched from behind the wall of sleep into the world of the (barely) conscious I panic, groping blindly for the source of the unexpected alarm call. I pick it up at the third attempt. Blinking hard to focus on the phone's display, my eyes eventually make out a landline number I don't recognise. It's three in the morning. Something's happened and it's serious. My knee-jerk recently reprogrammed response was, 'Jack!' My more considered one is, 'My parents!'

"Hello?"

"Mr Dennett? It's Lucy here. I've got your father in my house again. He's just knocked on our front door."

My head tries to feverishly assemble the information it's received. "Are you the lady who phoned last time?"

"Yes," comes the brusque reply.

"Oh no! He hasn't has he?" I stumble. "Oh dear. I'm so sorry. I'll come and get him right away."

"If you could," Lucy responds.

"I'm on my way." I hang up, my head throbbing from the sudden arousal.

Clare's awake and has turned on her bedside lamp. She props herself up on her two elbows, squinting against the pain of the light.

"Your dad?"

I nod, exasperated. "He's only gone and walked to Joyce's old house again," I tell her in disbelief. "Look at the time! It's three in the morning! No wonder the poor woman sounded hacked off. Can you imagine someone knocking on our door at three in the morning?"

"Do you want me to come with you?" Clare asks, as always offering practical support.

"No, that's okay," I answer, swinging my legs out of bed. "You try and go back to sleep. I'll go and get him."

"Who was that?" It's Chloe speaking. She sounds frightened, standing outside our fully open bedroom door. I can see her shivering in her flimsy pyjamas.

"Pop-Pop's gone walkabout," I reply, making light of it. "I'm going to go and pick him up."

"I'm shaking. It reminded me of..." Chloe doesn't finish her sentence. She doesn't have to.

"I know. Come and get into bed with Mum. Have a nice snuggle with her. I can always go in your bed if you're asleep when I come back."

Chloe needs no second invitation and she climbs in alongside Clare, cuddling up to her mother for comfort.

I dress quickly in silence. I'm a hotchpotch of emotions; annoyed distressed and worried in similar measures. When I step outside and feel the temperature, amazement tops the list. What motivated my father to walk so far in the dead of night in sub-zero temperatures? What is going on inside his head? Whatever it is it's not pretty. I scrape the ice from the van's windscreen and, once inside, blow air into my cupped hands in an attempt to get some feeling back in them. I rub them together vigorously. It helps a little. I start the van and pull off down the road. I'm playing out my role as chauffeur again, only this time it's for my father rather than my son.

It takes me less than fifteen minutes to get to Lucy's house. I park the van directly outside and get out, closing the door as quietly as possible. I climb the few steps leading up to the terraced house and tap gently on the front door. A security light illuminates me and as I stand in its stark beam I can see the tiny billowing clouds of breath emerging from my mouth. 'Get in, get him out, get him home, send her some flowers the next day,' I think.

Lucy opens the door in her dressing gown and stands to one

243

side saying nothing. She looks how I felt when I was awoken by her call.

"Sorry," I say humbly, as I enter the house my father grew up in. I turn into the small front room and find Owen sitting on the settee with Lucy's husband. This time there's no tea. I greet Lucy's husband. I think she told me his name is Stanley, but I'm not inclined to take a punt on using it in case I'm wrong. I daren't upset them anymore. "I'm very sorry about all this."

Stanley gives me the most cursory of sharp nods whereas my father's head turns slowly towards the sound of my voice.

"Hello, John. Glad you could come," he says to me.

My father is wearing the same scruffy zip up fleece, trousers and moccasin slippers on his feet as last time. I have no idea what he has on underneath as a further barrier to the cold. He is also wearing a tartan cap similar to the ones worn by Scottish football supporters when they're trying to be ironic. I've seen it lying around his house for as long as I can remember, I simply never imagined he would ever consider wearing it.

"Come on, Dad," I say, ignoring his opening line. "It's time to leave these good people in peace."

Without further procrastination I attempt to pull him to his feet by one arm, an action more difficult than I first surmise. I switch to both arms and manage to haul him up.

"Oooh!" he groans. "Careful. My legs hurt."

I have little sympathy for his predicament. "Well, you shouldn't have walked so far, should you?" I reply, manipulating him out of the room, mindful of the two sets of agitated eyes staring at the undignified scene. "I'm very sorry," I say to Lucy and her husband. "Thank you very much for your help. I do apologise."

If I was keen to get my father out of their house the last time then I'm doubly so on this occasion.

"Come on, Dad," I tell him quietly, as I manoeuvre him over the threshold.

"He ought to be in a home," are Lucy's husband's first and only words as he shuts the front door sharply behind us.

"Christ, it's cold," my father tells me.

"I know it is, Dad. That's why you shouldn't be out in it."

I guide my father down the steps and into my van. I have to lift his legs and swing them into the passenger footwell because he can't do it himself. I don't know how the hell he's managed to get so far on his own. I put on his seatbelt for him and close the van's door.

"What on earth do you think you were doing walking to that woman's house in the middle of the night?" I ask him, pulling away from the parking space.

"It's my mum's house. I can go up and see my mum whenever I like," he tells me.

"It's not your... you do mean Joyce, don't you?" My father nods. "It's not Joyce's house, Dad. She's dead."

"No, I saw her yesterday," he insists.

"No you didn't! She's dead and you're a geriatric homing pigeon who's forty years too late!" I reprimand him. "It's half three in the bloody morning! It's the middle of the night!"

"No it's not," my father answers.

"It is. Look out the window. It's pitch black. The woman who lives in the house was in her dressing gown."

"No she wasn't," my father answers. "When I got there she was outside on her hands and knees scrubbing her front door step."

"Look outside," I implore him. "It's dark because it's the middle of the fucking night!"

My father doesn't respond. Instead he sits in silence. "I need a tom tit," he tells me ten seconds later.

I haven't heard him use this expression since I worked with him as an apprentice. "You can't do one now," I tell him. "You'll have to wait until we get home. It's only another five minutes."

"I can't wait," he says, shifting uncomfortably in his seat.

245

"You'll have to."

"Aw! It's no good."

To my disgust I hear the noise of my father defecating in his trousers. I look down and see a patch emanating from the right hip of his trousers, one spreading out on to the seat. A rank smell fills the van. I gag and quickly open the windows to clear it. The self-pity of old envelopes me and in this moment of defeat I wonder what I've done to deserve all this. What else can the world possibly throw at me?

"Have you got everything?" I ask Jack, fighting to keep control of my feelings. I don't want to let him down like I did so many times in hospital. He nods in such a way I can instinctively detect his underlying apprehension. "You've got your undershirt and the pad? Astro trainers? Kit? Drinks?" He nods once more. I'm not sure why I'm asking, we triple-checked everything before we left home. Maybe it's a protection issue. Maybe I want this moment to last forever, so I don't have to let him go into the ruthless world in which he hopes to make living.

"I'm nervous, Dad," Jack admits. I think it's his first truly negative comment since the attack.

"I am too. Anybody would be. It's only natural," I assure him. There are lots of reasons why I'm nervous, none of which I want to tell my son.

He shuffles across the middle seat in the front of my van, squashing my coat, hat and gloves against my left thigh and hugs me.

"I love you, Dad," he tells me.

My heart feels like breaking and I hug him back. What if I'd lost him? How could I have coped if I'd lost him? These two questions constantly pop up in my head, like unwanted internet advertising. The emotional recoil is like being strapped to a firing field gun. I ruffle his thick black hair with my hand, choking back tears. You didn't lose him, I remind myself. He's here and he's doing what he wants to do, what he's always wanted to do. How fantastic is that?

"I love you too, Jack," I respond, my voice thick with emotion.

"I'm going to be really rusty," he tells me over my shoulder.

I ease him back and look into his eyes, hoping he won't detect the moistness in mine. "Of course you are. Everyone knows you'll be rusty. It'll soon come back," I say, as positively as possible. "You go and enjoy it, eh? At one point we never thought you'd be doing this again. This is a massive bonus, one to be savoured rather than endured."

Jack nods his head. "I'd better go. I don't want to be late."

"Yeah, okay. Good luck."

Jack gets out and collects his gear from the back of the van. I give him an upbeat wave as he passes my window. Once he's out of sight I let myself go. I bury my head on arms resting on the steering wheel and experience a familiar mix of emotions. I'm frightened and elated in equal measures, happy and sad, positive yet haunted by negativity. As I see him disappear through the double doors for his first training session since his cardiac arrest I ask myself why it had to happen to him. What did my handsome son ever do to deserve such a monstrous assault? Why didn't The Fear go for me? Why pick on my son? What's it got to do with him?

"You know the rules," I mouth to myself, wiping a runny nose. "You can't go there. There's no point. It'll kill you."

If the conversations I've shared with my parents since their dementia are like a looped cassette, then so are the ones I have with myself since The Fear struck. I sit up straight and try to breathe deeply and slowly. The wobble on my inhalation reminds me of how I used to be after crying as a child. I tell myself to man up and consider the significance and enormity of achievement tonight brings. Kudos to Jack! He deserves it and so does everyone else contributing to his miraculous recovery.

These happier thoughts render me almost under control, but I remain dubious as to whether I can maintain this level of calm given the task ahead. Once I see the other FDs and they ask the questions I know they're going to I wonder whether I'm likely to crack. The answer, strangely enough, is I really don't know. My post traumatic stress disorder attacks continue to abate, as if they are in a mathematically proportional link to Jack's continued good health. The one random exception to this is how, at any given moment, I can suddenly be transported back to the attack. Talking about it, explaining it to other people, is an obvious catalyst for reliving the most awful experience of my life. Yet, at other times, I can speak freely with an element of detachment. The next second it can spring out of nowhere, catching me off-guard and by complete surprise.

Two days ago I was working, doing the partitioning for a small extension on a private property, and was right in the middle of fixing an upright stud when it hit me. I was back in the moment in a flash and it wasn't a pleasant feeling. Clare and Chloe have both experienced similar. One second you seem okay and aren't really thinking about it and the next you're up to your neck in it, immersed in the torture of the moment. Of all of us only Jack has remained impervious and tonight's blip, I'm sure, is motivated purely by football considerations rather than anything to do with his health. That and the fact he will have to get used to wearing his ICD protection pad.

From the earliest days, Jack was always a boy whose kit needed to feel right. Shirt, shorts, socks and boots had to be just so and any deviation from the norm, like putting on a less frequently worn away kit, receiving a different sized pair of shorts or socks, even a shirt made from a different material, left him making constant tweaks to them before he was happy. Sleeves were rolled up and pulled down, waistbands of shorts were turned over once, some-times twice, socks twisted and hitched upwards until everything felt right. Even boots were often removed, after having already been put on, in order to make minor lace adjustments. Due to this compulsion, bordering on obsessive, we both knew the addition of a brand new piece of kit, one completely alien to him, could upset the dynamic and cause him unwelcome distraction.

The pad itself is a modified version of one intended to protect recreational shooters from the recoil of a gun. (If only there was something similar for my addled state of emotions.) Sourced from the US, this particular ingenious pad cures to rock-hard in around ten minutes once opened from its airtight packaging. Before then it's soft and flexible, allowing it to be shaped during the process of curing. It was during this window of opportunity I cut and moulded the pad to the contours of Jack's body. Once this was achieved and we had a bespoke pad, we needed to consider what was the best method to hold it in place. Jack dismissed any thought of taping it directly to his skin on the grounds of comfort and the involvement of another person, something he wasn't keen on. I then struck on the idea of placing it within a correctly positioned pocket sewn on to a very tight fitting undershirt, one similar to the 'shooting shirt' the pad manufacturers sold.

This idea seemed a runner, especially as many top football pros consider wearing a tight body-hugging undershirt de rigueur. With Jack happy he wouldn't be subjected to odd looks in the dressing room, we pressed ahead. A friend of ours, a very talented seamstress, cut out material from one undershirt and sewed these pieces on to other pre-marked shirts to form the required pockets. Once we got the shirts back, Jack put one on, inserted the pad and went for a run. He reported the pad stayed in position by virtue of fitting snugly in the pocket and the whole shirt was tight enough to keep the pocket ideally located over his ICD, despite physical movement.

Both of us were very pleased with how it turned out and I was overjoyed to find something so suitable, particularly after scouring UK sports attire companies with no joy. (I'm actually rather looking forward to showing off the concept to Jack's consultant because I'm certain he won't have seen anything like it.) As well as the running test I've pinged balls at Jack for him to chest control in order to help him gain confidence in the pad's protective qualities. I've even gone to the lengths of knocking the pad with the sole of a pair of metal studded boots. Everything seems fine and a direct hit from ball or boot hasn't caused discomfort. All Jack has to do is forget he's wearing it and concentrate on his football. Tonight will be the first test, although I can't see the club allowing him to get involved in any physical contact at this early stage.

I glance at the time, brace myself, and make the decision to go and face the inevitable questions my FD clique will ask. I hope I can avoid embarrassing myself, and them, when answering. I grab my extra clothes, get out of the van and walk through the double doors into the lions' den. Before I get to my clique, as I traverse the busy bar area heading for where I suspect they're sitting, other FDs and their partners stop me and ask how Jack is. I thank them for their concern, keeping my replies brief and simplistic, avoiding the pitfall of detailed recollection for fear of getting dragged under. They're all glad to hear he's well and wish the pair of us the best, saying how good it is to see us again. They all express their utter disbelief at what's happened.

Caroline Briggs makes a special effort to seek me out as I edge through the crowd. Out of the corner of my eye I see her drift over and she intercepts me, laying her manicured hand on my arm, expressing her relief at Jack's recovery and how she couldn't imagine what it must have been like for Clare and I to have witnessed such a trauma. She tells me how 'things like that put everything into perspective,' and I nod, thinking she doesn't know the half of it.

"How are you coping?"

I shrug. "Some days better than others, but overall it is getting

250

more manageable. Time and Jack's continued good health are weaving their magic."

"Aren't you worried about him coming back into this circus?" she says, making a point of rolling her eyes.

I detect in her voice the slight tinge of resentment associated with an FM who, thanks to me, is convinced her son will receive the R word.

"This is more than football," I point out, "although I'm one hundred percent with you on what it is that really matters in life. It's more to do with living out opportunities. This could easily have been taken away from Jack. As fate would have it, it wasn't. He has all his life back. He hasn't been forced to give up any of it. He still wants to do this more than anything else and I fully support him."

Caroline squeezes my arm and I'm a little surprised to notice it's still resting there. "I'm so pleased for him," she replies. "He's a wonderfully brave young man. I hope he gets his heart's desire. Not everyone does." Her hand slides off my arm and she smiles warmly.

I nod graciously. "Thank you, Caroline. I hope he does, too."

I disengage from Caroline and head off, wondering if there's any hidden meaning in her words. I don't care if there are. Easing through the deeper throng close to the bar counter I reach my FDs' table. It's the same one they commandeered the last time I was at training. This time there's an extra chair and I'm puzzled to see an unfamiliar face sitting with Andy, Don and Ryan. I'm greeted warmly with handshakes all round and slaps on the back from my original clique trio. They gravely enquire what actually happened to Jack and I give them a sketchy résumé, a pen and ink outline of the facts, one with no colour, depth or shade. I try to remove myself from the story, making my tale as objective and factual as I can. I keep myself uninvolved and at arm's length, my foot and shoulder braced against the door leading to my emotions. With relief I gladly cross the finish line of my truncated version of The Fear's attack, the oscillating pint of lager Don bought me the only pointer to my perilous state.

The near slip twixt glass and lip serves as a warning. My clique cotton on and thankfully have enough nous to let ferocious sleeping dogs lie. I can't be bothered to tell them about my heart condition because it seems so ridiculous. It still sounds too improbable and it's an additional rigmarole to plough through.

"How are your mum and dad?" Andy enquires.

I'm pleased to move off the subject of Jack's attack, even if it's to one devoid of joy. I lift my eyes heavenwards and tell them of the night Owen went walkabout, his gross act in the van and the subsequent cleaning up process which left me to crawl back into bed at nearly six in the morning. Everyone pulls a face of revulsion.

"Christ! You're going through the mill at the moment, aren't you?" Don comments.

"Jack's okay. That's the main thing. I can take the rest as long as that stays a constant." I hope it doesn't come across as if I'm angling to be seen as some kind of heroic figure. If it does, then so be it. What I've told them is the fundamental truth.

"Too right, mate!" Ryan remarks, to vigorous agreement all round. He takes a pull on his pint. "So, Jack's completely clear to carry on playing?"

My head indicates the affirmative. "His consultant's given the okay. He knows his condition best, so I can't see a problem. Clearly, it's going to take time for him to get back fully to where he was, but no different than coming back from any other kind of injury." Even to my ears, this sounds suddenly fanciful. How many people come back to professional club level football after their heart has stopped for seventeen minutes?

Ryan's face clouds for a split second and he stalls fractionally before saying, "Good. That's great news." He shifts his gaze from my eyes to his drink.

I pick up on his demeanour and instinctively know he knows

something I don't. My heart thumps a little and I imagine a line of communication from Nashie, via his son, Sam, back to Ryan. Sam is always the one who gets hold of snippets of information. I can easily imagine a situation where the head of youth might let slip an unguarded comment concerning Jack's future. I say nothing else. No one else says a word and an awkward silence takes over the table. Eventually, the unfamiliar face takes a deep breath and decides to go for it.

"Hi, John," he opens, leaning over the table to shake my hand for a second time. "We haven't been properly introduced. I'm Duncan, Connor's dad. Connor got signed two weeks ago."

The one arm bandit in my head has had its handle pulled and the four reels of symbols spin viciously before stopping, Chunk! Chunk! Chunk! Chunk! on four downward facing thumbs. They tell my immediate impression of Jack's chances of getting his beloved apprenticeship. The club have written him off. They've signed the boy who played in Jack's position in the match he missed through having a cardiac arrest. And if they've signed Connor now, with around three months to go before they decide on scholarships, it means he's going to get one. There would be little point in doing so otherwise. I'm confounded. I already knew football was a ruthless meritocracy, now it appears it conducts its business wholly bereft of a single shred of compassion, no matter how deserving the cause.

"Congratulations," I say, trying not to sound as if it's coming through gritted teeth. "You must be over the moon."

The time soon comes – as a herd of migrating wildebeest we are duty bound to move – and we head outside to stand next to the barrier surrounding the training pitch. In the freezing cold I position myself on the periphery of my clique to watch the boys go through their technical drills under the guidance of Ron. I'm glad to see Jack fully involved in these contactless give and go routines, but my contentment ends there. I have no interest in any football chat and my truncated replies soon make it patently clear. I much prefer to stand in silence and fester, seething at the injustice of everything. What more could the club have asked from my son? He comes back from the dead, defies all medical convention, gets himself fit and despite all this, behind his back, they sign another boy to take his place. They sign someone else before Jack's had the chance to prove he can return to how good he was, if – and here's the crux of the matter – they thought he was good enough in the first place. Caroline was right, it is a circus and it's a crap one at that.

My head squirms and writhes with the new information. I try to calm down and rationally assimilate it into a clear precise train of thought. It's impossible thanks to the raging sense of unfairness coursing through my body. Underneath my dark cloud of injustice a secondary process keeps me on tenterhooks. One fretting over Jack's heart and whether it will ever suddenly go into an arrhythmia again. This thought has been a constant, a never-ending throbbing background hum since Jack was taken out of his induced coma. Tonight it seems even louder. A fact I can only explain by my thinking an arrhythmia happening now, at football, would be even more devastating. It's a preposterous concept, yet it has a credibility I cannot deny given football's place as a metaphor for his quality of life.

Watching my son like a hawk, in a state of bubbling anxiety, I wonder if Jack feels similar. Is a part of his mind, as he goes to control or pass the ball, thinking of how devastating it would be to have a cardiac arrest now, in front of all his teammates, their FDs and the coaches? Surely it must have crossed his mind, if only fleetingly? What a monkey to have on your back – King Kong's big brother – and there's the new pad and undershirt to get to grips with. Issues at either end of the spectrum, yet so intrinsically linked. The seemingly insignificant one only serving to remind of the frightening one, is only there because of the frightening one.

My respect for Jack heightens further, if that's possible. Is it supreme willpower or weapons grade insouciance which keeps all his problems at bay? Whatever the reason, it's hugely impressive and I'm convinced no other boy, given the same circumstances, would be able to handle it. They'd throw in the towel, hang out the white flag, call it a day and sit back, content to be alive. When Jack miscontrols a pass he receives I cannot categorically state whether it's caused by mental distraction or lack of practice, but I'd be happy to put a week's wages on it being the latter.

"Hello, Mr Dennett." I'm whisked out of my insular world by Nashie's voice. I've been so engrossed with my own thoughts I didn't notice him sneak up on me. I turn to face him. It's the first time I've seen him since he visited Jack in hospital. I shake the hand he offers, although given access to a machete I'd probably hack it off given the mood I'm in. "Great to see Jack out there," he begins, enthusiastically. "All the coaching staff are thrilled. Fantastic achievement. Shows a lot of character." I listen to his words and sarcastically wonder when the 'but' is coming. The one put in my head by Ryan's earlier behaviour and the signing of Connor. "Umm..." Nashie prevaricates, "what we need to do now he's back...er... is to make sure everything is all right from a medical point of view."

Inwardly, I sneer. I didn't have to wait long. It's obvious what's happened, however he tries to dress it up. He doesn't think Jack can get back to where he was – if that was good enough – or he thought he wasn't good enough in the first place. Either way, he's signed Connor to replace him. What a bastard!

"What do you mean?"

"The club has to be sure he's well enough to come back and play," Nashie answers.

"His consultant's written to the club giving his consent for him to carry on playing," I point out, acutely aware I'm airing my dirty laundry in public. "I presume you've had the letter. He's the expert and the one best placed to make the decision, isn't he." I make it a statement, not a question.

"Yes, we have had the letter..." Nashie dithers, unsure where to go next.

I realise he's struggling and out of his comfort zone. He's more used to bollocking young footballers and ordering coaches around. As an ex-pro still involved in the game on a daily basis, he revels in speaking the lingo of dressing room banter and football clichés, not discussing delicate medical matters.

"Well, I'm glad you've got it."

"The thing is, Mr Dennett," he starts off, now much more assertively. (Nashie might be out on a limb, but he's used to telling people bad news. He R words at least twice as many boys as he gives apprenticeships.) "The club doctor's in tonight and he's the one who wants to have a word with you and Jack to see where we go from here. This has come from him, *not* from me. I'm quite happy to let Jack play," Nashie points out, shifting the blame and getting more confident as he does. "I'm not in the business of stopping boys playing football, you know. Quite the opposite. He's the one who wants us to meet up and clarify the situation. I thought we could have a meeting in my office. Is that okay?"

"Yeah, fine," I answer, softening my opinion of Nashie and thinking I may have misjudged the situation.

"Good," Nashie says, giving me a hearty slap on my shoulder. "I'll catch you later."

Nashie ambles off to the white-lined rectangle where he belongs, his all-seeing football eye spreading consternation and the chance to impress in equal measures. He is the man who decides; the top dog, the head honcho, the career maker and the career breaker.

"Mattie! Get it under control, son!" he barks, as a first touch goes astray. "Left foot, Connor! Use your left foot!" he reprimands, his left leg mimicking a side foot pass. "Well done, you!" he shouts at Jack, after he accurately cushions down a simple header. I wonder if Nashie feels guilty.

During a break in drills, as Ron repositions the Frisbee-like cones with skilled flicks of his wrist, I watch Nashie sidle up to Jack and have a quiet word. Jack listens and nods, a lack of understanding written all over his face. Great, I think caustically, that's given him something else to brood over. He'll be lucky if he can trap a bag of cement at this rate.

"They're not going to stop me playing are they?" Jack asks, his eyes wide with alarm as he hands me his drinks bag.

I've already moved away from the barrier to catch up with him and get away from other ears. "Fucked if I know," I hiss.

It's not a helpful comment, but it captures my mood as we begin the walk to Nashie's office. I've spent an hour trying to weigh things up and am still none the wiser. The worst case scenario I can come up with is some kind of medical ban imposed by the FA or UEFA on players with ICDs. That or an insurmountable insurance issue.

As we walk on I'm aware the game after training is not the focus of attention for FD eyes. They've all turned to look at us with varying degrees of surreptitiousness, the FD grapevine having no doubt efficiently spread the news of my conversation with Nashie. Despite looking straight ahead – I'm unwilling to give the impression I'm remotely interested in what any of them think – I sense Jack's angst as we walk side by side. It arcs across the small gap between us, eking out of his body with very stride.

"The doctor can't stop me playing if my consultant reckons it's okay, can he?" Jack demands. "He's a top consultant. That's higher than a poxy doctor, isn't it?"

"Much higher," I concur.

"Dad, but what if he does stop me playing? After all I've done to get back," he whispers, his voice riddled with tension and disbelief.

"Let's see what he has to say before we start leaping to conclusions. It might not be as bad as we think," I add, mindful of my conversation with Nashie.

"Better not be," Jack snaps.

"We'll soon see."

"You know they've signed Connor, don't you?"

"Yes."

"It's well harsh."

His youth vernacular is spot on. Despite knowing it's childishly petty and unpleasant I can't stop myself disliking Connor.

The club's resident GP is even-mannered and has recently swallowed a whole bottle of respect pills. He sits behind Nashie's desk, hands humbly clasped, his face framed by a giant whiteboard on the wall behind him. One so densely covered in marker pen circles, crosses and arrows of varying length they look to detail the tactical teachings of a deranged madman. His calm logical reasoned approach creates an odd juxtaposition with the chaotic confusion of the tactics board. He tells me, Jack and Nashie, if he's listening – the expression on his face indicates otherwise – how he has already spoken at length with Jack's consultant. He praises Jack's fortitude and dedication, saying it's wonderful to see a young man so committed to a dream. There is, however, as Nashie indicated, a reason for us all being here.

"The problem we have as a club, Mr Dennett, is the duty of care we have to our boys. We have to ensure we do what is required of us, by the FA, to keep them safe and make sure their best interests remain the number one priority. This requirement supersedes any football considerations and in Jack's case is clearly to do with his health and his safety. Now, in a case like Jack's there is very little previous experience for us to go on. Let's be frank, there's *no* previous experience for us to go on. We've never had anything like this happen to any of our boys before. Therefore, we have to be guided by experts to make sure it's absolutely safe for Jack to go back to playing matches."

"But you have been guided by an expert," I retort. "Jack's consultant knows him better than anyone else. And as for keeping him safe I can assure you no one has a more vested interest than me and my wife in keeping our only son safe. If we thought there was the slightest danger of Jack's welfare being compromised by him playing football he wouldn't be doing it. He's had all manner of tests and there's nothing wrong with his heart that anyone can find. Jack's actually safer because he's got an ICD than someone who hasn't."

The club doctor nods. "I know, Jack's consultant's told me the very same. Nevertheless, because the youth scheme is run by the FA we need to have someone sanctioned by them to look at Jack. A second opinion, if you like." Both mine and Jack's reaction causes the club doctor to sit back in his chair. "Please don't think I'm trying to place obstacles in the way here," he pleads. "I want Jack back playing as much as you do, but there are obligations, legal obligations, the club must meet. The club will arrange an appointment with the FA's consultant cardiologist, he's based in Oxford, and once he has seen Jack and given him the all clear, then he can go back to playing full time."

"So what happens until then?" I ask. "There's only about three months left until the decisions on scholarships are made and the Christmas break's in that. That's not going to give Jack much of a chance, is it? You've got to be fair to him. What he's been through is nothing short of horrendous. He's done everything in his power to get back after making a miraculous recovery. The very least the club can do is give him a fair crack of the whip." I'm getting excited now and starting to sound aggressive.

"Don't worry, we'll arrange it as soon as possible," the club doctor insists. "It'll be a private consultation funded by the club. Jack won't have to wait in a queue."

"And what if he says no after Jack's consultant has said yes? What then?"

"We'll cross that bridge if and when we come to it. I'm sure there won't be a problem."

"Does that mean I can't play in any games until then?" Jack asks.

"It means you can't play a full game," the club doctor answers. "I'm quite happy for you to play for one twenty minute session per game, on the back of your consultant's recommendation, until we receive complete clearance from the FA cardiologist."

"What I've told Ron," Nashie interjects, coming into the conversation now it's turned to football matters. "Is that I want you to get involved in the game at the end of the training session from next week. Once you've got through a couple of those he can start to use you as a sub in proper matches. You'll still have plenty of time left to impress me," he finishes, winking at Jack.

As I leave Nashie's office alone, Jack has gone to the changing rooms to shower, I'm slightly less deflated than I was before. Despite this my overriding impression is still one of lost ground, of having to circle back and jump over a hurdle we thought we'd already safely negotiated. Jack and I discuss it on the way home.

"We need to find out if there's any reason why you can't play due to FA rules. See if there's a blanket ban on players with ICDs," I say to Jack.

"There won't be will there?"

"I wouldn't have thought so. I should have asked, but I got side-tracked by everything else. Mind you, if there was, what would be the point of going to see the FA cardiologist? The answer would be a negative irrespective of your personal circumstances. If there's no ban in place you must have a good chance."

"Good!" Jack clenches his fist.

I laugh, pleased he has once again managed to remain positive. "What do you think about Connor?"

Jack shrugs. "Fair play to him. Greg says he's played really well. I've got to make sure I do as good when I get my chance."

Taking your chance. 'One man's poison is another man's meat' should be the way round the saying goes for football. Injury and misfortune often opens up an opportunity for others. But how strange my son can be less emotive than I over Connor's achievement. That's the trouble with us FDs.

Once we're home I'm straight on the computer, updating Clare on everything that's happened as I sit in the black swivel chair. I Google 'ICDs in football' and to my utmost surprise and deep fascination I find a result leading to a YouTube clip of a Belgian footballer playing in their top division. I call out to Jack and the three of us huddle round the monitor. The minute long video shows a player collapsing, there's no one near him, on the far side of the pitch after the ball has gone out for a throw-in. He literally crumples and falls to the ground ending up on his back. The referee and several other players spot him and rush over, the referee blowing his whistle and frantically ushering on the trainer. By the time the trainer reaches the stricken player his knees jump and clamp together, the most demonstrative part of an entire body twitch. As this happens, the tag pointer overlaid on the video which has previously detailed other messages, reads, 'Shock!' Remarkably, the player sits up to the tags, 'Sinus rhythm restored' and 'Regains consciousness'. I look up from the screen, amazed by what I've seen.

"You're not alone, Jack," I tell my son. "And they didn't stop him playing."

"What's it saying?" Clare calls down the stairs.

I turn away from the BBC website weather report. "Light snow showers all over the south, nothing too disruptive," I shout back. Inwardly, I curse. The last thing I need today is stress coming at me from a fresh angle – due east by the looks of it.

"Do you think we ought to leave earlier than planned?"

"Definitely. You can never underestimate the bedlam half an inch of snow can cause!"

The cold weather of late has been a real pain, one where practical considerations have far negated the usual stirrings of excitement the white stuff brings. Like many British adults a child-like fascination with snow lies within me. Generally, as a nation, we have a deep-seated involvement with our topsy-turvy temperate climate, but nothing quite pushes our collective button like snow. Get an inch of it and it's the lead story on the news and on the front pages of the newspapers. Local news programmes demand images of it, schools shut because of it, adults take a day off work because of it and the three dovetail into a media frenzy of parents and offspring happily sledging, building snowmen and forming snow angels. Invariably, these images are preceded by ones of chaos; tumbling pedestrians, stranded motorists, delayed rail passengers and grounded aeroplanes.

My previous excitable attitude towards snow days – I was firmly in the camp where I used to embrace the thrill of the white blanket – is now no longer fit for purpose. I've moved over to the side of those who hate it, who detest the chaos and problems it brings. I now see how snow means care workers are unable to visit the elderly in their home. How football matches enabling my son to get valuable pitch time before his scholarship decision are cancelled. And finally I see how an appointment with an FA cardiologist in Oxford ceases to become a mundane two and a half hour drive and – in my mind anyway – approaches something akin to a Shackleton expedition. Snow and ice have become a pain, less an opportunity to gambol and frolic, more a reason to struggle and strive. Since Jack's return to training Christmas has come and gone and we're now into January. The weather has been consistently cold, exceptionally so, and on intermittent occasions atrocious.

A succession of cancelled games, due to frozen pitches, means

Jack has yet to kick a ball in a proper match. The more resistant AstroTurf pitch has allowed him to play in a number of end-of-training-session games, but that is all. In this same period of football inaction half-a-dozen snow days meant the care workers were unable to safely negotiate the treacherous road to my parents' house. The carers are all women driving on their own and not surprisingly many felt incapable of tackling the lethal network of icy untreated local roads. Clients with no immediate family were rightly given priority and carers walked to them if they could. As I was local and capable I was left to take up the banner and become the cavalry for my parents. Most of the time I managed to make the journey in my van, its front-wheel drive and heavy payload of tools affording reasonable grip, but on three mornings after overnight snow I was forced to resort to Shanks's pony. Luckily, I'd had the foresight to stock up on food – another very British trait, panic buying – and only needed to get there in order to prepare a meal.

Aside from reaching my parents, my initial biggest concern was the threat of my father going walkabout in the awful weather, falling over and being left at the mercy of the remorseless cold. Thankfully, this never happened – his continued physical deterioration probably made it an impossibility. However, my long-winded walks in the snow and cold gave me plenty of time to think. They were a physical reminder of how much weight the care company had lifted off my shoulders and how utterly reliant my parents were on others to keep them safe, snow or no snow. What I quickly came to appreciate was how the safety of many different types of vulnerable people was severely compromised by cold weather. It's no wonder so many dread it. My very personal snowy road to Damascus converted me from one side to the other there and then. I remember thinking here was one more window, one scraped clear of frost, I had learnt to peer through.

My father may be able to communicate better than my mother, but his physical attributes seem to be slipping at a quicker rate. Of late he appears quite unsteady on his feet and has to wear pull-up incontinence pants all the time, although he is not yet classed as doubly incontinent. These items have become worry threads in themselves and I unblocked the toilet twice after he took a pair off and tried to flush them away. It wasn't especially pleasant to be wiggling one of my ancient augers about in the toilet's bowl in an attempt to render the pad into a flushable mush, but compared to the night I had to peel off his soiled trousers it was a breeze. Every episode like this, every downgrade in quality of life, only seeks to underline my shifted perspective on wanting a quick end to it all. Sadly, the likelihood of this seems distant and all points towards a future of glacier-like retrogression – a slow and cruel path leading to an inevitable end.

The Christmas period itself was a sad affair. Clare and I made the deliberate decision not to take the children with us when we went to cook my parents' Christmas dinner. Their continuing demise was not something I particularly wanted Jack and Chloe to witness. The distress of seeing their grandparents in such a poor physical state, unable to communicate properly and, more to the point, most likely unable to recognise them, was a trauma we did not want them to endure. I much prefer my children to hold a memory of what was rather than sour it with what is. That said, there was no denying the possibility it might have been my parents' last Christmas meant we were tempted to spend it all together. In the end, Clare and I opted for the practical and ignored the sentimental.

We cooked my mother and father dinner on Christmas day, Boxing Day and New Year's Day and I watched my mother cling to her handbag and totally ignore her husband, a man reduced to the role of a stranger in the house that he built. A house neither of them recognised as their own. It was a sombre subdued affair, not even the people upstairs came down to wish us season's greetings as my parents seem to have forgotten about them. The only corner I turned was to end the farce of telling my parents the truth. Despite promising them I would always do so I reneged on my promise and never once tried to reset their brains. I retired my parental monologues there and then, conscripting them to a dusty corner of my memory. I fell in line with their fantasies, actually propped them up, and never contradicted them. What was the point?

As I spent a small section of the present with my parents I keenly felt the loss of past memories. Like an odourless and colourless gas they constantly seep from their failing brains, an insidious process of atrophy making them ever more hollow.

For my part, in my brain, Jack's continued good health allows me to park both The Fear and The Pact, for hours at a time, into my mental peripheral vision. A situation aided and abetted by Clare and Chloe's recent bill of clean health, after more testing, and the letter I received from London informing me my sodium channel gene defect results were negative. My mother's blood tests were also negative, leaving the reasons for my complete heart block, much like the reasons for Jack's cardiac arrest, without a known cause.

We allow four hours for the journey to Oxford and it takes a little over three. Despite snow flurries following us the entire way, none lingered on the roads and the traffic continued to flow at only a slightly slower pace than normal. I didn't get out and kiss the ground of the private health care establishment's car park once we parked in it, but I certainly feel like it. The entire drive did feel as if I was partaking in a perilous Antarctic odyssey. The weather and the frisson caused by the prospect of being late, plus the momentous decision awaiting, incessantly drained and agitated all three of us. Jack never once asked, 'Are we there yet?' probably because he was fixated on the satnav's ETA display. I'm sure he was attempting, by sheer willpower, to maintain the digital display's green colouration indicating time to spare.

Jack hates to be late and only once we arrived could he fully turn his attention to the decision that could, in one foul blow, fatally puncture the ball representing his football career.

"Do you think he'll let me carry on playing?" he enquires, as we dash across the car park towards the entrance, the snow scurrying around our faces in a gravity defying vortex, one formed by wind buffeting brickwork.

This is his true, 'Are we there yet?' question. It's the one he has asked me dozens of times since the club insisted on a second opinion.

"I'm sure he will," I lie.

Much like estimating his chances of gaining an apprenticeship I'm too close to be entirely rational. My love for my son is inhibiting all objectivity in these matters and clouds my judgement. I think the odds are with us, but who knows. Once inside, I nervously pass the time by beginning to deliberate on what I will say to the FA cardiologist. My role of chauffeur is over for now and I must turn my hand to another, that of chief representative of Jack's cause. I know what I want to say. I have it all planned and I've run through the speech many, many times in my head. I know it sounds eloquent and well thought out when safely trapped in my mind, but I know once I release it from my mouth all manner of things may go wrong.

As I ponder this disarming thought all my aspirations and confidence to make a difference, to passionately argue Jack's case, suddenly evaporate from me. 'You're delusional, John Dennett,' I tell myself – an affirmation in itself considering I'm referring to myself in the third person – 'It won't matter what you come out with. The medical facts will speak for themselves. Are you really that stupid to think you can counteract a medical condition with words and rhetoric?' My head slowly lowers to the floor in defeat and I shoe gaze. Best not to kid myself.

On time to the minute we are summoned. My sluggish heart startles somewhat and thumps heavily in my chest as we are led to the appropriate office by a receptionist. I spot Clare whispering something to Jack and he smiles apprehensively, catching my eye as he does. I smile back, oblivious to what his mother has told him. We enter to see the FA cardiologist casually attired in corduroy trousers and a comfortable baggy crew neck jumper sitting at a small desk. He rises to greet us, introduces himself and shakes all our hands in turn. He invites us to sit on three chairs to the side of his. The door closes behind us. We're trapped, there's no escaping the decision. Once he's happy we're comfortably embedded on our chairs, he sits back down and, after donning reading glasses, silently peruses the paperwork on his desk. I'm so nervous I feel my legs begin to shake and my knees actually start to knock. I pull my legs tight together before anyone notices.

"So, Jack," he begins, reading from his paperwork. "You suffered a cardiac arrest at home after you got up in the middle of the night to go to the toilet. It states here you were in a state of VF for seventeen minutes? Is that right?" Jack answers in the affirmative and I do too. I can't stop myself. There's so much adrenaline going round my body I feel hyper. Jack shoots me a dirty look telling me to shut up. "In response to this event I see you've undergone every applicable test, all negative, and have had an ICD implanted in September with no recorded arrhythmias since. Your club tell me you're back to full training, but have yet to play in any competitive matches due to the awful weather we've been having." The cardiologist turns through ninety degrees on his swivel chair and looks directly at me over the top of his glasses. "How was the journey? Not too bad?"

"Yes, not too bad, thanks. Just over three hours," I reply, thinking here's a man who knows a chauffeur when he sees one.

"Excellent," he remarks, apparently satisfied with my answer. He diverts his attention to Jack. "Well, I must say you look very well young man. Very well indeed. Good to hear you're back in training. Well done on a very impressive run on the treadmill, by the way. A completed Bruce protocol. Good stuff. Your consultant has told me all about you," he adds, smiling at Jack.

"Do you know him well?" I ask.

"We're acquainted. He's very good. Very well respected. You've got good people looking after Jack. Must have been a scary time for you two," he adds, eyeing Clare and myself.

"Very," we both respond in unison.

The cardiologist indicates his appreciation of how scary it must have been. "Let me explain a little about what I must decide today," he begins, leaning back in his chair. "My mission today, my job if you like, is to decide if it is safe enough to allow Jack to carry on playing football at professional club level. I have been asked by Jack's club, in my capacity as the FA's consultant cardiologist, to make a decision based upon my experience of similar issues within football, Jack's personal circumstances, his medical notes and his consultant's advice. What I decide today will be the end of the matter. I am employed by the FA to advise them and I am their expert in these matters. Effectively, I make their policy. The decision whether to allow Jack to play is mine and mine alone and whatever the outcome, either way, it's what the FA will accept."

"So, there's no blanket ban on ICDs within the FA?" I enquire. "We've managed to find one player with an ICD in Belgium playing in their top league. There was a video of him on YouTube. It showed his device going off during a game."

"Yes, I know exactly who you mean," the cardiologist replies. "Incredible footage. But in response to your original question, the answer's no. There is in Italy. If we were in that country we wouldn't be bothering to have this conversation. The Italians have made their decision, but no other country has followed suit. I can tell you, for instance, at this present moment in time there are several players within the world professional game who have ICDs." I nod enthusiastically. This all sounds very promising. "The problem with Jack is his age and the FA's responsibility to him. If a professional footballer decides to play with an ICD that is a direct contract between him and his club. With Jack, being on schoolboy forms, it's a different situation. He's assigned to a club, but his involvement is underwritten by the FA. It's an FA scheme, part funded, organised and run by the FA. Do you see the difference?" I do and now it doesn't sound so promising. "Jack is still a junior and the duty of care falls on the FA should anything happen to him. Not on you, not on Jack, but on the FA. That's why I have to be sure he's safe."

I hang on to the cardiologist's every word, every nuance, constantly adjusting my evaluation of how things are going. Truth be told, I'm none the wiser. He wants to look at Jack's device and I ask if I can show him what we've devised to help protect it. He's only too pleased to accommodate my request and I show him the tight fitting undershirt, which Jack puts on and models for him, and the two pads Jack inserts in the sewn-on pocket. Our latest modification is to have a thin layer of upholstery foam next to Jack's body and the special pad on top of that. It's a far more comfortable arrangement than just having the rock-hard rigid pad on its own. The cardiologist is impressed, especially with the shaped pad I sourced from the US. He asks me all the finer details, particularly how I set about moulding it, and writes down the company's web address, saying he will definitely mention it to his peers and other people who have had an ICD implant.

Finally, the cardiologist moves on to Jack's personal circumstances, commenting on how the arrest was clearly not induced by any form of exertion and how significant this is. He tells Jack how idiopathic VF, especially in the young, can be an isolated event. He sincerely hopes it will be for Jack's sake. He points out how all the trouble-free training Jack has done since the arrest is reassuring and how the tests would have picked up on any obvious issues. As a cautionary note, he also explains that this lack of a cause is not unique and clearly something extremely dangerous went wrong with Jack's heart. There must be a reason for it, albeit one outside the knowledge of today's medicine. At this juncture I mention the paper Jack's consultant gave us. I've brought it with me and show him. He says he's aware of the research and is pleased the subject matter is being addressed. I take the paper from him and seize my chance to say my party piece.

"As a parent, the only reason you want your son to lose his place with a professional football club is because he's not good enough," I tell him. It's the one line I use from my one-I-prepared-earlier speech.

The cardiologist nods in agreement. "Yes. Certainly not through circumstances like Jack's." He scans the three of us in turn. "Okay, I think we've covered all that needs to be said, don't you?" All of us indicate this is the case. "Good... If there are no further questions?" He pauses and checks us once again. "Right, it's time for me to make a decision on this." The cardiologist clasps his jaw with his right hand and contemplates in silence for several seconds. Sitting on his chair in this pose I'm reminded of Auguste Rodin's bronze statue named, The Thinker, and I'm ensnared in the moment of his deliberation, both mesmerised and paralysed by the significance of the moment. I can hardly breathe, the tension is unbearable – but brief. This isn't the X Factor. "I'm going to allow you to carry on playing, Jack," he states. "I'll recommend you be used as a test case for young footballers with an ICD. Congratulations, young man. You're the very first!"

My heart melts and for the first time in months I leak tears of joy, ones I desperately try to blink away. My spirits soar and I'm flooded with gratitude. I want to hug the cardiologist, I want to hug Jack's consultant, I want to hug his staff, I want to hug Maroon Scrubs and his nurse, I want to hug the ICU nurses in London and in Hastings, I want to hug the paramedics, I want to hug Clare, I want to hug Chloe, I want to hug Jack and I can, here and now in my head, thank The Pact. I also want to thank everyone involved. I want to shout out to every single one of them that their contribution has made a fifteen-year-old boy's world whole again. Back from the dead to a full life. How wonderful! How marvellous! What more of a reward could there be for anybody doing a job like theirs?

We say our goodbyes in a mood of euphoria – bottled euphoria. Social etiquette contains our feelings until we're on our own back in the car. Once there, it erupts like an uncorked champagne bottle that's ridden a paint mixing machine for ten minutes. Jack tells me he's 'buzzing' and Clare and I tearfully embrace and smother each other in kisses. Jack is no more well after this decision, it changes nothing in terms of what we have been through and it changes nothing in terms of his medical future. What it does is seal the deal on his miraculous recovery. He died for seventeen minutes and can now, officially, come back to everything he had before. That alone makes it a magical moment. My father and my grandfather would have been so proud of him. I'm so proud of him.

As we leave the car park, the snow falling heavier than before, I turn to Jack. "Everyone's done their bit, Jack," I tell him. "Now it's all up to you."

He arches an eyebrow and answers me, a smirk on his face. "So no pressure, then?"

The substitution Ron makes with twenty minutes left of the game is one Clare and I want to savour alone. For the previous seventy minutes we've deliberately kept ourselves to ourselves and we stand detached, as if we're social lepers, only ten yards from the corner flag, away from the bulk of the FDs and their partners gathered around the halfway line. As Jack runs on to the pitch I'm awash with emotion. Clare is too, and we press close together as we bear witness to a sight we wondered if we would ever see again. The magnitude of the moment is huge, yet the difficulty of what Jack is trying to achieve means today is not so much the end of a difficult road, more a rejoining of the journey. The journey to become a professional football apprentice. Whether Jack is feeling any pressure is hard to fathom, I'm not inside his head, but at this moment in time I want him to play well for this last twenty-five minutes more than anything else in the world.

The smattering of applause greeting Jack's introduction to the game shows at least some appreciation of what he's been through and the gutsiness required to reach this juncture. It's a reaction Clare and I appreciate even if we know it's one that will be short-lived. The generous reaction is merely a spike, a collective point of remembrance brought about by Jack's first competitive game, one likely to last about as long as the applause itself. I'm now genuinely of the opinion that Jack's ordeal has generally faded out of the minds of every FD and coach – like a pair of denim jeans stuck on a perpetual hot wash. Today is the exception that proves the rule. To outsiders his continued good health, the fact he looks exactly as he did before and acts exactly as he did before are all fantastic positives conspiring to degrade the trauma he's suffered and devalue the courage of his comeback. The parallels between what I've experienced at the club and what Chloe experienced at school are virtually identical. The golden rule to explain this is a simple one. Everyone not directly involved in a tragedy quickly moves on and forgets it. It's as simple as that. I know it's true because I've done it myself countless times before. Everyone has to. To live a life otherwise would be impossible. What person could hope to live a life of empathy for everybody else? Who hasn't read the grimmest of front page news for the effect to have dissipated by page four?

Jack's cardiac arrest, from the coaches' points of view, apparently changes nothing. For them there's one thing needing to be judged and it can only be judged on one level. They cannot, it seems, give Jack any leeway. Nevertheless, it does rankle deeply when they shout at him in training. It annoys me to the point I want to hit out. I want to tell them to shut the fuck up and I feel aggressively inclined towards them, violently so, in a manner I've never experienced in the past. It's actually been quite shocking to feel so strong a reaction in response to something so relatively minor. Equally, the whole FD grapevine, with its constant monitoring of the boys' progress, the endless tittle-tattle and the over-analysing of real or imagined plusses and minuses has also left me cold. As much as I still want my dream and Jack's dream to come true I now feel a sense of lost involvement. I have moments of wanting to scoff, to tell the whinging FDs to calm down and take a good look at themselves and their sons. 'Does any of this really matter?', I want to demand of them. 'In the grand scheme of things, is this so important compared to good health and still being able to spend time with your loved ones? You've lost no one. This is all secondary and of minor importance.' Honestly, who am I kidding?

To prove the point I audibly groan when Jack gets beaten in a one-v-one by the opposition's left winger. He goes on to cross accurately for his centre forward to score with a simple header.

"Should he have done a bit better there?" Clare wonders, her nose wrinkled.

I shrug knowing Jack should. "If he's going to learn to play right fullback prop..." I stop talking because I spot Jack being berated by one of his teammates before the restart. "Look at Greg moaning at him," I remark to Clare, my voice animated. "He's only been on five minutes and it's his first game in months. The last thing Jack needs is a teammate getting on his case. Doesn't he realise what Jack's been through?"

Clare rests her head against my shoulder. "At least he's playing, John. We must never lose sight of that."

"I know." I shake my head with frustration. "I'm getting pulled from pillar to post with this football lark," I confess. "I still want it for him as badly as I did before and then I think, hold on, what the hell am I thinking about? What does it matter? He's fit and well and just like he was before his arrest. What more could I want?"

Clare looks at me with a smile. "You want him to play well and fulfil his dream."

"And get his apprenticeship."

"And get his apprenticeship," she echoes. "Of course you do. Why wouldn't you want him to get it? John, in a way this is exactly the same issue as disciplining him, of worrying and fretting when he went out for a run, even of how you felt about going back to work. Life goes on exactly as it did before. Playing football at this level is still as hard as it was before. Nothing changes. The world still has the same faults, the same ethics, the same lack of ethics, the same problems and the same dilemmas. We're the ones who've changed. The only reason we forget we've changed and go back to how we were, if only for a short period of time, is because he's so well. If he wasn't, we couldn't possibly do it at all. I think the longer time goes on and if, pray to God, he continues to be perfectly healthy, then the more it will happen." Clare gives me an earnest look. "If we're fortunate, in the future, the trick might be to remind ourselves we ever changed at all. To never forget what's really important."

"That's very true," I admit to her.

"It's all to do with the right balance and the choices we make," Clare continues. "Don't beat yourself up if the scales swing wildly from time to time." I smile at this thinking how well she knows me. "It's natural for you to want to protect him after what's happened. What you have to remember is people will forget it happened and most won't even know in the first place. And that's how Jack would want it, isn't it? In essence, it's how we're trying to be with him." Clare rubs my arm affectionately. "Remember how far we've come. And remember you succeeded. You never turned into your mother."

I consider her point. "And nor did you."

I'm not sure what my mother has turned into.

"Tell him to get up and get my house out," she says, muddling her words. "Lying like all the place over." There is anger in her voice, malice almost, and it's far more telling than her disjointed words.

"Be quiet, Mum," I tell her gently. "Please go and sit down and watch the TV."

I crouch down beside my father and try to comfort him. He can't get up because he's fallen down the stairs he made all those years ago and is lying in a heap at the bottom of them. The ambulance is on its way. It's hard to know how long ago he fell. The worst case scenario is around two hours. The time from the carer's midday call until my fortuitous arrival with the shopping to find him sprawled on the floor. My father's complexion looks grey and sallow, his eyes won't focus and there's a carpet burn to his right temple, indicating he hit his head during the fall. Unusually, for him, he cannot communicate at all. Only a string of garbled sounds, emitted the first time I spoke to him, have come from what looks to me like a lopsided mouth. I'm convinced he's suffered a stroke.

"You'll be all right, Dad," I say, my voice quivering. "I've called the ambulance. They'll be here soon."

There was no feeling of déjà-vu when I saw a second closely related male collapsed on a carpet. I recognised the feeling of hopeless impotence from before, but The Fear is not with me this time. This is an altogether different affair, one of calm sadness rather than frenetic blind panic. As I kneel beside my motionless father, his shallow breathing the only sign of life in his otherwise inert body, I wonder if this is the end or if it will transpire to be the beginning of the end. If he survives then it must surely be the end of his time living in the house that he built. And if so, where does that leave my mother? What do I do with her? Do I keep them together or leave them apart?

I may scroll through my thoughts in relative calm, but I don't feel in control. I tell myself at least I've been proactive and that in itself is a huge stride forward from last time. Frustratingly, with the 999 call made there seems little more I can do. I'm loath to move my father, to try and sit him up, to give him a drink or revive him, in case he's broken something and I make matters worse. I rub his shoulder instead, feeling how scrawny it is due to his wasted muscles. My father reminds me of Olive on the night I received my first-hand experience of The Fear. He too looks like a marionette with every string severed – a thin dirty one made many years ago, one left to rot in a toy box until yanked out by a mischievous child and hurled heartlessly to the floor. I shake my head in disbelief that this body, and the brain stored within it, was once my energetic father.

"Don't worry, Dad. I'm here. I'm with you. I won't leave you."

I carry on stroking him like he's a dozing pet until the doorbell rings. I leave his side and rush to open it for the paramedics.

"He's over here." I lead them to my father. "I called in with my parents' shopping, both Mum and Dad have dementia, and I found him at the bottom of the stairs. He can normally talk reasonably well, but he's only spoken once and that was when I first got to him. What he said was pure gobbledygook. Just sounds, noises, no words... I think he might have had a stroke."

"Any idea how long he might have been there?" the younger paramedic asks as his partner kneels down beside my father.

"I reckon two hours at the most."

"What's his name?" enquires the kneeling paramedic.

"Owen," I tell him. "Owen Dennett."

"Owen! Can you hear me?" he asks in a slow exaggerated manner. "Can you hear what I'm saying?" He's holding my father's thin wrist. "Pulse is erratic," he tells his colleague. He feels the upper thigh of my father's right leg. "I think his femur might be broken, just below the hip. We need to stretcher him out."

"Hello, dear," my mother says, pottering in from the living room as if nothing untoward has happened. "Have you seen Mum and Dad? The babies. How do the babies?"

"Come on, Mum," I say, moving over to her and leading her back into the living room by the arm from which her handbag hangs. "We must let these men look after Dad."

"Dad's here?" she asks, trying to turn back round. "Cyril?"

"Come on," I cajole. "Would you like a cream cake? Sit down over there and I'll get you one." I'm buying her off, like you might a toddler, a treat as reward for good behaviour.

Within ten minutes, my father has been moved out of the house into the ambulance – never to come back. Of that I'm certain. The powers that be will never entertain his return and I'm in no position to argue given what's happened. The younger paramedic returns to take all my father's details and tells me to phone A & E in a few hours' time to confirm their diagnosis and the next course of action. Once they've departed and I've watched another ambulance containing a loved one disappear, with my mother safely devouring her second cream cake, I phone Clare and tell her what's happened. I tell her I'm going to stay with my mother until the carer arrives for the tea time call.

"Good idea. Are you all right? How do you feel?"

"That I want it to be over. That he won't suffer any more... When it happened to Jack," I confide in her, "I never thought I would see him back running about on a football pitch. When I saw Dad lying at the bottom of those stairs it was the other way around. I couldn't ever imagine that he used to run about on a football pitch. Funny, isn't it? How your brain works."

Spending a couple of hours in my mother's company makes my mind up on one decision. I decide she will stay in the house that Owen built until she is no longer capable. My father's time in the house has run out – hers hasn't. Why consign her to a nursing home simply because my father is in one? My mother is so removed from real life it's clear she has no idea where he is or what's happened to him. She doesn't miss him. In fact, his presence

277

was often a source of unease for her as she took my father to be a stranger. The people she truly misses are her mum and dad and nothing can bring them back.

"Do you remember your little Johnny?" I ask out of curiosity, as we sit together on the settee. "The little boy who was your only son?"

"Did I one?"

"Oh, yes," I answer. "You used to say he was the apple of your eye."

"There," my mother says, pointing to Jamie IV who's suddenly appeared from nowhere and is padding into the living room with his tail aloft.

I stroke the purring cat under the chin as it nuzzles around my legs. It's only too pleased to have the attention.

"That's right," I agree, leaving the cat alone and giving my mother a hug. "That's him."

Her face crinkles into a smile and I become lost in the cruelty of her disease, not only for her sake, but for the havoc it wreaks on those closest.

I leave my mother in the safe hands of the carer and walk to face something I'm scared of. The time has finally come, like I always knew it would. It was as inevitable as the sun rising in the east. I open the door of the super massive black hole of a garage and stare in with wide-eyed fright on the lawless anarchy to which I will have to give order. The scale of the bedlam causes me to take a half step backwards, but I muster myself and push on, entering its domain. I cross the event horizon without suffering spaghettification to turn on the light. A fluorescent tube splutters into life causing a myriad of hanging objects to cast undefined shadows across my view. Ducking here and there I shuffle slowly into the centre of the garage to stand directly under the light. Like a child in Santa's grotto I rotate in wonder, soaking up the overwhelmingly cluttered panorama before my eyes. I stop when I get to my father's motorbike. I sidle over to it and run my fingers gently across the Bonneville's black seat. I reach up to the handlebars and blip the throttle with my right hand and pull in the clutch with my left. Furtively, with a quick backward glance, I throw my right leg over the bike and I kick away the side stand with my left. I sit astride the bike, both hands on the handlebar grips, and push with my legs to the left and to the right, assessing the machine's weight and centre of gravity. I hear petrol slop in the tank. An ancient feeling from long ago works its way up from my buttocks and ends up on my face as a melancholic grin. I make another decision. Dad would like it I tell myself. Given the circumstances, his former self would definitely approve. In his memory I tell myself. I'll ride it in his memory and for the memories of all the bikes we rode together in the past.

Chloe runs out to me before I get to my front door. Her face is blotchy from crying. She hugs me tightly and I hug her back.

"Is Pop-Pop going to die?"

"I don't know, darling. He is very old. Come on, let's go indoors."

I shepherd my daughter inside. Jack is sitting at the bottom of the stairs, elbows propped on knees, his head resting in his hands. His face is etched with sorrow. Clare stands a few yards from him, as upset by seeing her children so unhappy as her father-in-law's fall.

"Is Pop-Pop okay?" he asks. "What happened? Did he fall down the stairs right from the top?"

"I'm not sure how far he fell, Jack."

Inside I feel myself start to unglue. Clare and I have deliberately kept our children at arm's length from my parents' dementia and I suddenly feel very remorseful at how their illness has robbed my children of their influence. My father revelled in watching Jack play football and Chloe was always his special flower, a young female, a rare orchid he'd never experienced as a parent. My mother always feared the worst for them and found it hard to relax when given the

279

responsibility of care, but her love for them was never in doubt. And all of this has been taken away. My parents might as well have been dead given the amount of interaction between them and my children over the last couple of years. However, 'might as well have been' and 'are', are still mightily different concepts when dealing with death.

In one way mine and Clare's plan has worked. Our children know their grandparents are poorly, but coupled with the fact they are still alive and having not witnessed their demise, they get by well enough on memory. On remembering how my parents were with them in a time of full capacity. Today has seen the reality of them losing a grandparent come closer. Jack and Chloe don't want their grandfather to die. I, on the other hand, who have been at the coalface for the entire duration of his illness, do. As painlessly and as quickly as possible.

"One step or all of them, when you're as old and fragile as Pop-Pop, any fall can be very dangerous. He could have fallen over anywhere. Even in a nursing home he wouldn't necessarily have been any safer."

"Do you know what?" Jacks declares, as if he's suddenly made up his mind about something. "If I get my apprenticeship I want to tell Pop-Pop myself."

I look at my son and I'm profoundly moved by his laudable intentions.

"He won't understand, Jack," I warn him. "He probably won't even know who you are."

"I don't care," Jack replies. "I'll know. I'll know that I was the first one to tell him."

Jack's decision to want to tell his grandfather about his apprenticeship, should he get it, is still a possibility. My father's femur was broken, he had suffered a stroke, and although the doctor told me the operation to plate and pin it might kill him, it didn't. My father opted out of the easy option to pass away painlessly and without suffering under a general anaesthetic. The Do Not Attempt To Resuscitate form the doctor and I both agreed was appropriate never came into play. Whatever life force remained within him was enough to see him through the operation and back into the cold light of day. One coming through a hospital window on to a bedbound, doubly incontinent, non-cognisant skeletal man.

When I saw my father after the operation I couldn't believe what he had done. It was my first question to him. It went unanswered, like all the others.

"Dad, what have you done?" I pleaded, shocked at how ravaged he looked. How could he possibly look so much worse than he did at the bottom of the stairs? "Why did you hang on?" I asked, resting my hand on his. "Why didn't you just let go?"

The fall was the beginning of the end of my father's life. Sitting alongside his bed I saw he was close to the end of his days and wondered whether Jack would have the chance to carry out his wishes. So appalling was his state I hoped he wouldn't. I now had two reasons for wanting my father to die – to spare him and his grandson.

As I put on my shoes, my father, remarkably, is still keeping up his end of the bargain. He lives on, if you can call it living, and the meeting with Jack remains pencilled into his diary for tomorrow. Tonight we will find out if Jack still needs to keep the appointment. Today is Judgement Day. Seventeen fledgling football careers will be marked, handed back during an allotted fifteen-minute slot and decreed as either a 'Pass' or a 'Fail'. Dreams will be crushed, lives will lose focus, confidence will be shattered and aspiration will be dashed for the majority. A mirror image will see the minority float on clouds of ecstasy to the giddy height of the first couple of rungs on the ladder to becoming a professional football player.

Once the date of Judgement Day became set in stone, all the FDs slipped into a frenzy of speculation, one not even a raved amphetamine-addled shoal of sharks could hope to emulate. Their sons, however, suffered huge bouts of introspection in dread of the ruling taking all meaning from their young lives.

Entering into the FD spirit, despite kidding myself I was somewhat above it all, I made a false list of the boys who I thought would pass and those who I thought would fail. Only my clique were shown my list, although they don't know, or at least daren't admit even if they do suspect, that there are white lies contained within it. In line with tradition I didn't fail any of their sons or pass judgement on my own. The real list tells otherwise – I suspect both Sam and Tom won't make the grade. Greg definitely will – he is NO – and so will Connor. From outside my clique I think Scott, Mattie Smith and George will also get the nod. I think there's probably room for one more and that's where Jack fits into the equation – or where he doesn't.

"Are you ready, Jack? Time we made a move."

"Coming!"

My son's voice makes me try to evaluate his chances one more time. Like the last 'one more time' and the one before that.

I think Jack has acquitted himself fairly well in the last few games and has begun to understand his role of fullback much better than during his initial twenty-minute debut disaster. His natural speed has stood him in good stead when facing speedy wide players and his positional sense is much improved. Going forward when attacking takes him to an area of the pitch with which he is more familiar and consequently his overlapping and crossing have been quite good. The problem is, he's far from the finished product. His lack of pitch time in general and specifically in playing the new position – to accommodate Connor who the club clearly think is better – 's evident in the inconsistency in his play. I can see how this new position might suit him provided he can learn to defend better. He could, given time, develop into a decent fullback. Could, but he's not there yet. Will Nashie give him the benefit of the doubt and afford him two more years of development? And if he does, will the Grim Reaper allow Jack the time to tell his grandfather. I call both chances fifty-fifty given how close my father is to death. Five years of football development and an entire lifetime reduced to two flips of a coin. What else can I say? Only that in moments of mawkish sentimentality I envisage Owen hanging on to what life he has left for the sole purpose of meeting his grandson and hearing good news.

By the time we arrive at the training ground, forty minutes early, we already know the fate of many others. Jack has the penultimate slot at ten forty-five in the evening; the first one started the process at seven. The so called 'play list' of boys, the order in which they were to be seen, was exposed to much inspection for hidden meaning. Some FDs were convinced there was a secret code in the order which could unlock the key to those who would pass and those who would fail. Utterly absurd. Knowing Nashie, he probably just picked the names out of an old cut-in-half football or stabbed them out with a sharpened corner flag.

"Connor, George, Mattie Smith and Greg have all got one," Jack hisses, looking up from his phone, the social media grapevine coming up with the goods. "Four out of twelve. Five more to go!" he adds, as we pull into the car park.

I nod, fighting back any form of smugness for being spot on so far. Tonight is definitely not the time for smugness. If you and your son end up personally elated there is too much heartbreak around to dare to be extrovert. Bottled euphoria's the answer. Jack and I know the trick. We've done it before. I hope we have to do it again.

"Everything going as expected. No surprises yet," is all I offer. Jack has seen my list and knows my worthless fifty-fifty call regards his chances. Once he swore to secrecy I also told him of the white lies contained within it.

We've made our way to the closed-off-for-the-night bar area and are waiting for our turn. There with us and Jim, the U14s' coach, are Caroline and Billy, and Don and Tom. Ryan and Sam, the next ones in, are seated in the corridor outside Nashie's office. Scott and his father are already ensconced in the room of judgement with Nashie and Ron. Don and Tom obviously couldn't face hanging around at home for any longer and decided to make a break for it. They're the last ones in after us and our turn comes after Caroline and Billy. I briefly consider how embarrassing it'll be if I'm wrong about Billy. There'll be no place for me to hide from his mother's elegant withering look if that scenario turns out to be the case.

No one – boys, FDs and the solitary FM – has an inclination to mingle and brief initial acknowledgement is as far as any interaction goes. The tension is far too oppressive for idle chit-chat and a nauseous anxiety hangs in the air. This grotesque ambience has gradually filled every cubic inch of the bar area's considerable volume. Not even a scramble to the top of a ladder to suck in air from the remotest meeting point of ceiling and wall would avoid it. I briefly speculate – again – if this is how my mother felt on a permanent basis when she was under the spell of The Fear. My stomach grinds in apprehension of the upcoming decision and I feel a little ashamed that my first reaction to my mother's curse was always to try and escape it. It must have been like living in purgatory for her.

Standing in silence alongside Jack I soon become lost in my own world. I run through all he's been through, all his efforts, the efforts of everyone else in securing his miraculous recovery and the bravery he's shown just to be able to get to where we are tonight. Before I can stop myself I postulate, for the umpteenth time, on whether it will have any bearing on the decision he will receive today, on whether it will afford him a little leeway and give him any benefit of the doubt. Deep down I know it won't. As callous as it might seem, Jack's cardiac arrest isn't on anyone's radar tonight, certainly not in the sense of it gaining him any advantage.

Unfortunately, I can see it more likely to be a reason to lean towards R-wording him, like any physical weakness, whether be it an ankle, hamstring or knee.

I already know the deal. It's a mindset formed through observation over the five years Jack has been with a professional club. Football is a ruthless meritocracy concerned with only one thing – playing ability. Morality plays no part in it, adherence to social code and convention has no place and any ethos of justice simply does not exist. From a schoolboy player's point of view it's simple in its structure and the way it works. Are you good enough? Are you still of some use to the club? If you are then your dream can live on. For now. Woe betide if you falter or someone better comes along. And yet, conversely, this lopsided dynamic can change if the player himself becomes better to the point of being one of the best. Then the football world turns turtle and power changes hands. The player becomes the God, rather than the club, and the clubs are forced to beat a path to his door (more likely his agent's) offering gifts and riches beyond comprehension in payment for his services. It's no wonder these players take all they can and act the way they do; they've seen the other side of the arrangement from the moment they were signed as boys.

I snap out of it as Scott and his father enter back into the bar area. Caroline and Billy, guided by Jim, take their turn to leave. The look on the faces of the emerging pair tell it all. Scott's home and dry as predicted and relates the positive verdict to Jack by signalling with an upturned thumb and a mile-wide grin.

"Nice one!" Jack remarks.

"Well done, Scott," I say, winking at the young man. I smile at his dad, "Fantastic stuff!" Whether I will get to share their feeling of elation this evening awaits to be seen.

As the two of us respectively consider what it must feel like to be in Scott and his father's shoes, Jim saunters up to us and tells us we're next as soon as Ryan and Sam return. With his duty done, Jim engages me in a chatty conversation concerning Premiership players' wages. It's one I'd rather not have to get involved in and I find myself distractedly nodding and answering in flat monosyllables. Eventually, it dawns on Jim that I'm not up for talking and he leaves me alone. I shuffle in small circles, intermittently looking up to smile supportively at Jack's drained face. I wonder what his heart rate is. Mine's flying compared to normal.

Time crawls. An eternity passes. Mountains get eroded to sea level and rivers cut mighty canyons. Twelve minutes later – as I'm checking the time – Ryan and Sam emerge. Their faces tell a different outcome to the one we saw earlier. My white lie is revealed as the truth. We offer the most rudimentary of condolences to one of our clique, partly because we have to go and partly because Ryan and Sam want to get the hell out of it as quickly as possible. Sam is in tears and no sixteen-year-old boy wants anyone to witness that. Jack and I walk off, both of us now considering what it must feel like to be in Sam and his father's shoes.

On our own in the narrow corridor outside Nashie's office I tell Jack the only thing I have left in my locker. "Whatever happens in that room in a minute, Jack, I want to tell you how proud we are of you. We know how tough it's been. You're a star. Mum and I love you lots." I lean over and kiss his thick black hair. I hold out my hand. "Good luck, Jack."

A bit unsure of my formal gesture, Jack awkwardly shakes my hand. His palm is sticky with sweat. "Thanks, Dad. Thanks for taking me everywhere and coming to watch."

"It's all on my timesheet," I tell him. "Fifteen quid an hour. You owe me thousands."

We wait on in silence. I sit and stare at the opposite wall, my ears primed for the first noise of the door handle to Nashie's office being turned. Again it takes forever.

When it comes I nearly jump out of my skin. My head snaps round and I see Caroline and Billy emerge. The almost subliminal shake of her head means there's no withering look coming my way tonight. I catch a whiff of perfume, but no mordacious attitude. My relief is short-lived as Jack and I go into the room to find Nashie sitting behind a desk and Ron, Jack's team manager, standing behind him. I close the door behind us. We'll get out alive all right, but will our dreams?

"Good evening, Jack. Mr Dennett. Have a seat."

"Hello there," I reply, sounding like an ancient radio presenter.

"All right?" Jack blurts.

Nashie smiles and pulls a face. "You know, doing this job isn't easy at times. Sometimes it's hard when you get a boy like yourself, Jack..." It's like I'm punched in the face by a professional heavy-weight boxer. The bell's rung. I've met my opponent in the middle of the ring, expecting at least a few seconds of sparring to allow both of us to settle into the ordeal in hand, and he's thrown an instant haymaker that's caught me flush on the temple. My ears ring so loud it drowns out the sound of Nashie's words. Jack's not getting it! They're not offering my son an apprenticeship and it's over by a knockout in the first few seconds. Our dreams are dead in the water. I look at my son to see if he's picked up on the words Nashie used and realises their significance. If he has then he's controlling himself very well. Disorientated and groggy from the blow I fight to pull myself back into the moment." ... missed a lot of football and that hasn't helped. Unfortunately, I've got to make a decision now and on those grounds I'm afraid the club won't be offering you an apprenticeship. You've shown a lot of character to fight back, Jack. I want you to use that character and prove me wrong. Go to the exit trials and shove my words back down my throat. Think to yourself, 'I'll prove that bastard Nash wrong!'"

I sit on my chair like a cold granite statue. Inside I'm seething, disbelieving and gutted for my son. I want to get out as quickly as I can before I say or do something ridiculous. I'm hardly a novelty act – the disgruntled FD who thinks his son is better than he is – but

Jack is a unique player in the literal sense of the word. If I thought, 'Why him?' at the time of his cardiac arrest, then I'm thinking it again now. Hasn't he been through enough? To get all this way back and then be dismissed in seconds. Don't five years commitment and surviving a cardiac arrest warrant more than that? Apparently not.

In the heat of the moment my big picture mentality spectacularly crashes and burns. I despise Ian Nash, him and his tired cliché, the one he trots out to every boy he releases, about 'proving him wrong'. I hate Ron. I hate the club. I hate football. At this most raw of moments I think I hate pretty much everything.

We stride past Don and Tom and I mimic Caroline's earlier head movement to the pair of them. Jack just about holds himself together until we get back into the van. Then the floodgates open and he cries openly. I cry for him as well as with him. We have both suffered a loss tonight. I always envisaged this moment would be difficult for any FD and his son. What I couldn't foresee is how Jack's brush with death has magnified it into an issue so bloated and ripe with emotion it has the power to sweep all else away before it.

Driving home, much to my surprise, perspective shifts and my big picture mentality rises Phoenix-like from the ashes I feel are lodged in my mouth. I'm still gutted for Jack, but as my wife has warned me, the trick is never to forget we've changed. With an air of something approaching magnanimity I also feel marginally more kindly disposed towards Nashie. I decide to give him the benefit of the doubt over his football decision on Jack and accept his brusque delivery was due to his considerable discomfort at having to deny such a deserving cause. He might have become accustomed to releasing the majority of the boys under his stewardship, but how many has he come across like Jack? I know the answer. None. There has never been another Jack. There may be in the future and if there is my son will have played his part, a huge part, in setting the precedent to allow others a second chance. If he achieves nothing else in football he has still made an indelible mark.

I doubt Jack shares my first steps in coming to terms with what has happened. I would wager the last thought going through his head is one consoling himself that it doesn't really matter because he's alive and healthy. He remains locked in silence throughout the journey and I don't feel inclined to press him on how he feels at this early stage, as much as I want to. The tears stopped pretty quickly, but all energy and vitality appear to have been sucked from his body. He has the vacant stare of a fully paid up, union-card-holding member of the lost generation and I hate to see it. I picture football as a cruel mistress, one so beautiful, so beguiling, so intoxicating and yet so demanding, few can tame or satisfy her. She takes you, she uses you and then, when she desires you no more, she drops you. The fall is long, but it's the sudden stop that hurts.

As we near home I can bite my tongue no longer and have to ask him how he feels.

"Pissed off," he answers. "Really, really disappointed. What am I going to do now? All that time and effort for nothing. All your time and effort."

I smile at him and take my hand off the steering wheel to rub his leg. "And do you know what, Jack? I loved every minute of it," I tell him earnestly. "What football dad wouldn't love watching his son play for a professional club. Thanks for the ride. You must have enjoyed it too?"

Jack gives me a joyless smile. "I guess. But it's over. What am I going to do now?"

At this moment I don't think either of us have a clue as to the answer.

Clare and Chloe have both waited up for us and they console Jack by fussing over him like only they can. Chloe hugs him constantly and snuggles up to him while Clare brings him a hot chocolate and some biscuits. All the love and attention helps and gradually Jack stands up from the battering he's received and looks to the future with some positivity.

"I'll do the exit trials," he tells all three of us. "Give it a crack. What have I got to lose?" He runs his hand through his black hair. "Still really upset I didn't make it and won't be able to tell Pop-Pop I'd got my apprenticeship, though."

Later that night, in a turn of events I decide are serendipitous, my father dies. Perhaps Owen somehow found out there was no good news coming his way and finally let go.

We sit in an unfamiliar room along with other parents and their offspring. The man making the current presentation is stressing the need for every young person to take the education they will receive over the next two years very seriously indeed. To be honest, I'm barely listening. The educational part of Jack's life has always been Clare's domain. She's far better qualified to advise than I. Instead of listening I'm finally facing up to the ramifications caused by the squiggly lines on the ECG printout that made me snort in derisive laughter at the unbelievable ridiculousness of it all. In two weeks I shall return to London to have my pacemaker fitted under a local anaesthetic and I can't see me laughing, ironically or not, at any stage of the process. Although still asymptomatic I can't ignore the warning of there being something amiss, especially one flagged up as a by-product of my son's suffering. What would he think of me if I dismissed medical opinion after all he went through to bring it to light? In this matter I'm chained to Jack; our link isn't broken and love and memory remain. Like Jack, modern medicine and a technological device will protect our hearts rather than a concept concocted by a thirteen-year-old boy.

Once my period of recuperation is over I intend to carry on riding my father's motorbike. The old rush of being a biker is back and I love being out on the road again. I've been out on the

Bonneville many times, the most significant being when I rode behind the hearse carrying my father's body to the crematorium on the day of his funeral. I rode his bike in memory of the times we bought bikes together, rode them off to nowhere in particular together and then swapped over and rode each other's back. To represent his other passion, a wreath of flowers fashioned to look like a giant football was placed on the coffin lid. Despite suffering moments of agonising doubt over the suitability of both these celebrations of my father's life I never once questioned the decision to not take my mother. To have taken her to something she couldn't possibly understand, to have bewildered her and placed all attending in such an awkward position seemed wholly inappropriate. Instead, I left her safely at home with the carers, pottering around with her handbag and continuing not to miss him at all.

Nothing, it seems, is beyond the scope of dementia. It sweeps all logic before it and eases it out of the way like a glacier moves rock – slowly, sometimes imperceptibly, but always with pitiless power. Nothing can push it back – I tried everything I could think of to reset their brains in the early stages – but eventually the point comes where there is no point in trying at all. To go with the flow of the glacier is the only route possible and with hindsight to have fought it, to have pushed back, was folly on my part. Trying to reset a demented brain does nobody any favours at all. Perhaps the problem lies in feeling the need to do 'something', to not give in, to 'fight back'. All I know is given the time again I wouldn't try to do so. My efforts changed little and helped even less. My parental monologues are retired, the ones for my children equally so. They seem irrelevant in my new world.

As with my father I hope my mother's time in this world will fade as quickly and painlessly as possible. I don't want to see any more because I know what's left is odious for her and for me. She's lost The Fear, she's lost her husband and she's lost nearly everything that made her 'her'. There is no solution to her illness and there is no Disneyesque happy ending. Death can be as welcome as it can disturbing. Grateful for it to release my father, wanting it to take my mother; unthinkable and unacceptable beyond measure had it taken my son.

At my father's funeral many of the footballers he once played with came to pay their last respects. I remembered younger versions of them scurrying energetically around the pitch and it was a genuine delight to talk to them about old times, matches and seasons they spent playing with my father. I know Jack really enjoyed hearing first-hand football stories concerning his grandfather as much as I did. I already knew some of them because Owen had once told them to me or I had witnessed them myself, but others, especially the dressing room banter and training session antics and dust-ups, were fresh to my ears. Of course, Jack had his own football story to tell and several of the older players encouraged him and told him to go again and never give up on his dream. Some told stories of how they, in their own way, overcame adversity such as injury, rejection and fall outs with managers and coaching staff. Several of them were at professional clubs when these incidents occurred, long before they slipped into the Southern League to play out the tail end of their careers with my father. This fact alone added much gravitas to their counsel.

Whether their words did galvanise Jack I don't know. I suspect it's quixotic on my part to think they did however much I would like it to be true. I suspect the truth is far less poetic. Jack went to the exit trials and with nothing to lose and with no real level of expectation he went and played with no fear. Relaxed and not under pressure he played in his preferred position and he played well. I told him so afterwards, but we both agreed the chaotic nature of so many players playing at one time on three different pitches meant the likelihood of being spotted was slim. In my mind, the only way a player would get noticed was by doing something very striking to stand out or by playing exceptionally well in a position which a specific club needed to fill. Whatever the truth, there was huge elation and much surprise when a professional club contacted Jack a few days later and offered him an end of season trial.

The new club's youth team play at the same level as Jack's old one and, with just over a month left of the season, I gladly dusted down my chauffeur's outfit, slipped into my FD alter ego and took him to training twice a week for the duration and to the last four matches. It was a very strange feeling going somewhere different after five years of familiarity. A different training venue, different match day venue, different boys, different coaches and a different set of FDs. From Jack's point of view the pressure to perform reared its ugly head again and I tried to downplay any notions of last-chance-saloon syndrome. I told him to take with him, if he could, the same attitude he enjoyed at the exit trials. For my part, through-out the training sessions and the matches, I deliberately stood on the touchline alone. An FD without a clique, I dared to hope Jack could pull it off. When the season was over and the last match was finished I wondered if he'd done enough. When Jack emerged from the changing rooms and told me we had to go and see the club's director of youth football I knew I was about to find out.

"Here we go again," I said to him as he led the way.

"Tell me about it," he answered.

All the presentations are over and our time has come to take part in the final and most important part of today's itinerary. It's the point of no return. We already know the decision and yet, until this part is completed, I'm firmly in line with my ex-clique FD, Andy. For all the times I ribbed him over the same mentality I refuse to celebrate prematurely. Ridiculous as it is, even now at this late stage, I still consider the possibility of something going wrong; that some unforeseen last minute medical setback will bring the walls crashing down. Seated at a table with Clare and Jack I hold my breath and watch in fascination as the man who was speaking earlier about Jack's education slides a document over to him.

"If you can sign there, please, Jack. Next to the pencil cross."

Another man to his side looks on and smiles encouragingly. His face is tanned and weathered. This man has already signed his name above the space left for Jack's signature. In what seems like slow motion I watch Jack pick up the pen. He writes his name and I think how terrible his handwriting is. I wonder what he'll 'do' if his dream of becoming a professional football player doesn't come to fruition.

"Congratulations on your scholarship, Jack," says the tanned ex-pro, who is director of youth football at Jack's new club.

"Stick with the education course. Don't neglect it!" the FA's representative reminds Jack. "It's your plan B."

All three of us smile and stand up, expressing our appreciation to a backdrop of noise caused by the synchronised pushing back of plastic chairs. It's done, it's legal, the document is signed and I feel myself coming to the boil. Slightly self-consciously, we move out of the way to enable the one other end of season trialist to sign up to his dream and for his parents to witness the wonderful moment. We walk towards the exit of the building, nodding our goodbyes to all the other signed boys in the youth squad, and to the parents, who have attended today's League Football Education presentation. Underneath the veneer of normality I fight to control my expanding jubilation until we get outside. Once there I let rip, a torrent of pleasure rushing through my soul. In my over-enthusiasm I pick Jack up, his feet clearing the ground as I hug him. Two more years of a new marriage! He's on the lofty first and second rung of the ten tread ladder to becoming a professional footballer. Things get harder and more difficult from here, but at this stage, who cares? It's only football, but in Jack's case it represents so much more.

"Well done, Jack! Fantastic! You made it! After all you've been through, you made it!" I tell him once I've lowered him on to terra firma. I grab his head with both hands and plant a kiss firmly on the top of his thick black hair. He's the first one. The first boy ever to be a professional football apprentice with an ICD.

"Congratulations, Jack. We're *so* proud of you," Clare says, wiping away a tear and kissing his cheek.

Heroically, Jack ignores the recent onslaught of parental petting by merely wiping away his mother's kiss with the back of a hand.

"Thanks, Mum. Thanks, Dad. That was something special. I feel great!" Jack remarks, his face the epitome of pure joy.

He's right. It is special. Very special. It hardly seems possible, after all he's endured, that he's managed to claw his way back to where he so desperately wants to be. Now, for a while, we have the luxury of time as there are two whole years ahead for our dream to run. Our new dream, not to become a mere apprentice – tick that box – but to become a professional footballer. I'm so excited at the prospect of what's in store I'm hoping it will push The Fear and The Pact into my mental peripheral vision for good. At this precise moment everything points to the future; one where Jack's continued good health permits me the energy to mould it with positivity. A brighter future, one in which I never forget that I've changed; one forever taking me further away from the darkness of the past.

Author's note

The novel you have just read is a work of fiction based on true events. The four manifestations of The Fear resulting in the deaths of my relatives, as depicted in this book, actually took place. Both my parents suffered from dementia simultaneously and many of the conversations detailed in The Fear *are adapted from notes and recordings I made at the time. My son suffered a cardiac arrest, shortly after waking up to go to the toilet, when aged thirteen and his heart stopped for seventeen minutes. Surviving this event, he was given an ICD to help protect him against any further dangerous arrhythmias. At the time of the arrest he was nearing the end of a two-year schoolboy contract with a professional football club. This was extended for another two years, but when it ended he was released. Only after further trials with a different professional club did he managed to obtain his two-year football apprenticeship. During this process my son became the first player with an ICD to play under the FA youth apprenticeship scheme. During family screening performed shortly after his arrest it was discovered that I, despite being asymptomatic for over fifty years, suffered from congenital complete heart block. I was seen as an outpatient and eventually had a pacemaker fitted.*

Mark Cunnington – January 2014

Acknowledgements

Lyrics from *That Sunday, That Summer* written by George David Weiss and Joe Sherman. A Comet Music Corporation Recording first published 1963.

Extracts taken from *Sports participation for athletes with implantable cardioverter-defibrillators should be an individualised risk-benefit decision* by Rachel Lampert, MD, David Cannom, MD, FHRS.